Miss Harper
Can Do It

Miss Harper
Can Do It

Jane Berentson

VIKING

VIKING
Published by the Penguin Group
Penguin Group (USA) Inc., 375 Hudson Street,
New York, New York 10014, U.S.A.
Penguin Group (Canada), 90 Eglinton Avenue East, Suite 700,
Toronto, Ontario, Canada M4P 2Y3 (a division of Pearson Penguin Canada Inc.)
Penguin Books Ltd, 80 Strand, London WC2R 0RL, England
Penguin Ireland, 25 St. Stephen's Green, Dublin 2, Ireland (a division of Penguin Books Ltd)
Penguin Books Australia Ltd, 250 Camberwell Road, Camberwell,
Victoria 3124, Australia (a division of Pearson Australia Group Pty Ltd)
Penguin Books India Pvt Ltd, 11 Community Centre,
Panchsheel Park, New Delhi–110 017, India
Penguin Group (NZ), 67 Apollo Drive, Rosedale, North Shore 0632,
New Zealand (a division of Pearson New Zealand Ltd)
Penguin Books (South Africa) (Pty) Ltd, 24 Sturdee Avenue,
Rosebank, Johannesburg 2196, South Africa

Penguin Books Ltd, Registered Offices: 80 Strand, London WC2R 0RL, England

First published in 2009 by Viking Penguin, a member of Penguin Group (USA) Inc.

1 3 5 7 9 10 8 6 4 2

Publisher's Note: This is a work of fiction. Names, characters, places, and incidents either are the product of the author's imagination or are used fictitiously, and any resemblance to actual persons, living or dead, business establishments, events, or locales is entirely coincidental.

LIBRARY OF CONGRESS CATALOGING IN PUBLICATION DATA
Berentson, Jane.
Miss Harper can do it: a novel / by Jane Berentson.
p. cm.
ISBN 978-0-670-02077-5
1. Young women—Fiction. 2. Diaries—Authorship—Fiction. 3. Long-distance
relationships—Fiction. 4. Soldiers—Fiction. 5. Self-realization—Fiction. I. Title.
PS3602.E7515M57   2009
813'.6—dc22   2008041836

Printed in the United States of America
Set in Adobe Garamond   Designed by Francesca Belanger

For all teachers and all soldiers, but mostly for my parents, Dan and Susan Berentson, who are each technically neither, but in many ways, both.

Miss Harper
Can Do It

1

*T*oday I'm calling my book *Wartime Alone Time: When Abstinence Fights for Freedom.* Technically, presently, it's still called *raindropswhattheflipamIgoingtosay.doc*, and it's a Microsoft Word document I created on my computer three days ago. To celebrate the commencement of my writing career, I had purchased a bottle of moderately priced scotch and settled down to my laptop with a loosely knit wool scarf draped dramatically around my shoulders. I don't particularly enjoy scotch, but drinking it seemed to be the right kind of tortured artist thing to do. It was raining a good, thick curtain of Washington rain outside, and I watched drips of water scoot and slide down my kitchen window. I thought: *Now am I supposed to describe these raindrops and then draw together some sort of complicated metaphor where they're, like, representing my life?* Then I turned to my blank screen and typed:

raindropswhattheflipamIgoingtosay

I saved the file and closed the computer. I took my glass of scotch to the sink and tossed it down the drain. It just didn't feel right. I was going about this all wrong. So now, with a whopping three days of perspective under my belt, I'm ready to really bust out the words. My memoir: my rules. (My memoir rules!) 1. There must be a title. 2. I must abandon my inhibitions; abstain from analyzing my intentions; and simply GO GO GO. 3. I can always fix it later; scrub out the shocking indignities and shine up any shards of integrity, intelligence, or humor.

I think *Wartime Alone Time* has a certain snap to it. I can imagine Tom Ashbrook or Katie Couric pronouncing it nice and slow—crisp and clear on the *t* sounds. Media professionals can make any title sound sophisticated and weighty.

Today we're talking to Annie Harper, a courageous young woman who will discuss her new book, Wartime Alone Time: When Abstinence Fights for Freedom, *a poignant, fresh memoir recounting the year she and her boyfriend, a U.S. Army soldier, spent apart while he was serving in Iraq. Thank you for joining us, Annie . . .*

Oh, it is my great pleasure to be here, Katie.

Like Ms. Couric would endorse a book that is anything less than poignant. The president will read it too. He'll have to. Even though I plan on making fun of him about a million times. Even though I'm going to rip apart all of his decisions and all of his speech patterns and all of his everything that just might lead to the man I love being killed whilst driving a truckload of toilet paper across Baghdad—old W. will still read it. And then he'll invite me over for dinner at the White House to have some sort of civil, intelligent conversation. I'll wear something very nice and chat it up with the first family. *What a fetching necklace, Laura. Jenna, don't you just love this wine?* They will all certainly adore me. W. will stand, raise his glass, and toast Annie Harper, peace, and the American Soldier. And by the time I leave, I'll have convinced his sorry ass to reimburse me for the hefty therapy bill I will accrue this year while David is gone.[1]

And as for the *When Abstinence Fights for Freedom* part of the title, it's an aspect of wartime coping that's recently fascinated me. David will

---

[1] Presently, I do not have a therapist. Naturally, I have nothing against acquiring one in the future should it become necessary. Honestly, I have no idea what the signs of that necessity will be. Compulsive flossing? Crying in public restrooms? Joint pain?

be gone for at least 392 days on a mission that is supposed to be saving people and helping them. Something that is supposed to be working toward big abstractions like freedom and peace and progress. A
considerable laundry list for 392 days, that's for sure. Not that I'm a
big counter or anything, but he did tell me and I did remember. Three
hundred ninety-two days equals thirteen menstrual cycles, but only
two times paying my car insurance. It all depends on how you look at
it. But right now, in the early stages, I'm a little hung up on nature. I
keep thinking about the grandly arrogant act of taking two happily
mating creatures and ripping them apart for a significant length of
time. David and I have been living blissfully for over two years in the
great barking zoo that is Tacoma, Washington. We've been galloping
back and forth to one another's respective dwellings (mine a tiny
one-bedroom rambler; his a dank, unadorned officer's apartment on
base), picking mites from each other's hair and swapping bushy pieces
of bamboo: peaceful inhabitants under a shared dome of safety.
Thriving in our contained, functioning ecosystem! And now someone has stepped in, and for reasons I don't entirely understand (because I am such a simple animal), shipped him across the world to
another, more volatile, cage. So because I keep thinking about this
zoo creature business, I keep thinking about this: Aside from 392
days of worrying and missing and taming my imagination and counting my lucky stars, it will be 392 days of no sexual intercourse (*When
Abstinence Fights for Freedom*). Commence the repression of all mating urges now! So now when I watch or read something about Lonesome George—that poor, poor mateless creature[2]—I can raise my

---

[2] For the uninformed: Lonesome George is the rarest living creature on
the planet. He's the only remaining specimen of his certain subspecies of
Galapagos tortoise. I think scientists discovered him back in the seventies
when he was still a young spry thing. Now George is pushing seventy or
eighty or so, and though they've scoured the lush Galapagos islands high

drink (not scotch) in a toast of solidarity. To our celibacy, Georgie!
To our thick, thick skin!

In wondering about historical patterns of female wartime alone-
ness, my mind conjures up this image of the loyal woman at home as
a diligent provider or worker bee or tireless organizer. Ration-coupon
stashers. Child-rearing nurturers. Enthusiastic sign toters. And there's
this vague memory of a Greek (or Roman?) lady whose husband was
gone for something like fifty years and she just kept knitting and knitting[3] some ginormous blanket until he got back. It was one of those
epic battles that lasts for decades, to the point where no one really remembers why it started in the first place. It's always something about
border disputes or crowns or rights or beautiful women. Or oil. All
this to say, if there is a woman at home, she is doing *something*.

> whattheflipamIgoingtodo???
> raindrops . . .
> whattheflipamIgoingtosay???
> fucking sliding scooting raindrops!

Two weeks before David left, we took a road trip. Packed a tent and an
inflatable mattress into his car. Drove down the Oregon coast, stop-
ping at small towns to buy saltwater taffy at shops with wind socks out
front and picnic tables out back. Gas prices were ridiculous, but we

---

and low, zoologists still haven't found another tortoise of his kind. George is
doomed to plod along in solitude. No friends. No family. No lovers. I think
the scientists may have tried to mate him with other closely related subspecies females, but Georgie just won't have it. He's holding out for his true
partner; one who very well may not exist. Talk about patience! 392 days or
forever.

[3] Note to self: Check on this when you actually write the book. It could
have been quilting. Or some type of ancient weaving thing. I seem to remember a loom.

didn't care. The whole trip held this weird pressure to be absolutely marvelous, but at the same time to be just normal old David/Annie fun. Like each meal had to be irrefutably tasty, but no different from a meal under any other circumstances. Our final cheeseburgers together had to be juicy-thick with bacon. Steaming curly fries on the side. But we could not say anything about it out loud. We could not name them *The Special Before-You-Leave-For-War Cheeseburgers;* we just had to enjoy their drippy meatiness and know that they were. And that's kind of how I feel about attempting to write a memoir. Am I allowed to label the cheeseburgers here? How much sentimental smarminess will the U.S. military ration out to a gal like me? How much, Georgie?

No, not you, my dear lonesome tortoise comrade. The other Georgie.

So as I conclude this first (but on the second attempt) writing session, let me slap down a thesis statement that I aim to keep flashing in the front of my brain throughout the duration of this year and this project.

> *Dear Annie,*
>
> *You must write to provoke, elicit, and understand your deepest emotions. To coax them out and paint them plain and ugly. Sweet and/or bitter. In documenting how you pass this year, you will hopefully come to understand something more profound about yourself, David Peterson, Lonesome George, George W. Bush, and maybe (if you're lucky), the ENTIRE UNIVERSE.*
>
> *Fondest regards,*
> *Annie Harper*

Nine days after David leaves, school starts. I'm not as prepared this year. Last year I spent hours coloring in the SpongeBob name tags for my kids' desks. Making sure all the colors matched the actual hues of the show. I had six weeks of lessons planned. There was a field trip arranged and this very elaborate calendar to count down the days until the end of the year. This year we're not counting.

"So that's a little bit of information about me, boys and girls. I'm very excited to have you all here this year. You will see soon enough that third grade is a blast. Does anyone have any questions?" A girl in the second row uncrosses her ankles and lifts her little tush off the seat as if her flailing arm has caused her to levitate. I did a real half-ass job making name tags for the desks this year. They're rocket ships. The proportions are all wrong and they are really, *really* ugly. Squinting for the child's name, I notice for the first time (even though I should have noticed shortly after making twenty-eight of them) that the rocket ship name tags are blatantly phallic.

"Yes, Caitlin?"

"Miss Harper, do you have a boyfriend?"

"Why, yes. I do."

"Does he live in your bed with you?" The kids giggle at their peer's gumption. Except they don't know that it's gumption because they don't use words like that since they are eight. *I* almost giggle at her clumsy, childish rhetoric. But then it's exactly her clumsy, childish rhetoric that evokes an image of a horizontal David with a comatose stare and swollen ankles: an invalid *living in my bed with me.*

"No dear, he lives really far away."

"How far?"

"Like, really, really far," I say.

"That's not a very exact answer," says Caitlin.

"Well, I'm fucking sorry, but that's all you're going to get."

Okay, so I probably shouldn't write fake moments of dialogue where I cuss out my students. Thankfully (and perhaps luckily), I have never cursed at a child. Now that I'm nine pages into this whole narrative experiment, I'm finding myself tempted to fictionalize. Not because I want to change the way I'm represented on the page—Annie

Harper will do what Annie Harper will do—but more because mixing it up, imagining what could have happened instead of what already did, is simply more interesting. I never considered the boring repetition of documenting one's own life. Something happens. Then you watch it happen again in your imagination as you write it down. If things don't fire up, this project is in danger of becoming exceptionally tedious. I guess the second time—the writing time—is when I'm supposed to add the pretty words and the laugh tracks and the complex analytical questions. Don't just make shit up, Miss Harper! You will fail the assignment with no chance at extra credit.

If I had dropped the *f*-bomb like that, I'd have been out of a teaching job in minutes. Thank goodness my fuse is not so short. When Caitlin spat that sass at me, I simply sighed and said something like, "Well, let's talk about VIP days!" or "Let me tell you about the hall pass!" My teacher persona isn't easily rattled to the point that awful things escape. They brew, they fester, they tickle the insides of my lips, but they always stay inside. I rarely lose my cool.[4] I rarely get hysterical.

What's weird about these first David-free weeks is that I seem to have a free pass for hysteria. People are genuinely expecting me to be all weepy and frazzled. The teachers in my school with whom I am relatively close have all commented on how "put together" I seem to them. Like it's some incredible feat that I've managed to button my blouse the proper way and keep my bottom lip from dropping sadly to the floor. And then there is my dear, sweet mother. The morning David left, I drove to my parents' house. My father was at work, of course, but my mother really insisted that I come by. She had it all oddly

---

[4] Okay. I lost my cool last year when Derek Metticus fed chewed-up Skittles to Churchill, our class beta fish. Churchill went completely cuckoo bananas and banged his head against his hard plastic bowl until he died. *RIP Churchill. Unknown–February 23, 2003.*

planned out. There was the special quiche she knows I love. Fresh melons all cut up. Kleenex strategically placed throughout the house in places I'd never seen it while growing up. On the bookcase. Near the kitchen sink. Had Kleenex always been there, and I merely too snot-free and happy to notice? My mom was just inside the door when I entered. Surely she had started brewing the coffee just as she heard my tires on the driveway gravel. She's always been great at having coffee ready.

"Oh, Annie," she said. And she lifted her eyebrows with her arms as if they were both waiting to cradle my sobs or something.

"Hey, mom." It was supposed to be one of those big emotional moments. One of those times when you know exactly why you have a mother. I was supposed to collapse into the soft of her postmenopausal abdomen and transfer to her half of my grief and half of my worry and half of my depression. And we would share it.[5] Instead, I complimented the new paint in the entryway, "Blue is so clean-looking," and we went inside.

That morning there had been this big flag-waving, yellow-ribbon, send-off hoopla. I hated it. I hated the other women waving yellow ribbons and white handkerchiefs. Actual cloth handkerchiefs! Who even uses those anymore? I know it's supposed to be helpful. Remind us all that we're not alone. It's supposed to remind me that the mission is for something that someone somewhere thinks is a good idea. It's supposed to make soldiers feel that we'll be here smiling and waving and waiting—wearing the same low-cut tops—the whole damn time they're gone.

This was our last conversation in the flesh:

"Annie, I love you. I'm going to miss you so much."

"I know. This totally sucks."

"I'll call as soon as I can."

---

[5] What's to share so far? I'd barely had an hour to start collecting it.

"Okay."

"I love you, babe."

"I love you too. Keep track of your limbs!"

Keep track of your limbs!!! Who says that? They should have handed me a goddamn handkerchief, and then maybe the blinding white cotton would have induced some tears. Some reasonable reaction. He smiled anyway, but in a sad way. Not sad "my-girlfriend-is-a-heartless-spaz sad," but more "I-can't-believe-this-moment-is-really-here sad." And of course I really was sad. And of course I'm not really a heartless spaz all of the time. I'm still sad. And we're keeping track of our limbs.

I crossed my legs and folded my arms once my mother and I sat down to quiche.

"You're not hungry?" she asked.

"Meh. Not really." I picked up the copy of *Us Weekly* on the table. An Olsen twin was dangerously thin. "An Olsen twin is dangerously thin, Mom."

"And you'll be too, if you don't eat," she said, pointing to my quiche with her fork as if I'd forgotten where it was. I stabbed a chunk of melon, gave it a spin, and ate it. I knew my mother was thinking that my lack of appetite was directly related to some heinous Boyfriend-at-War anxiety, but really, I had eaten two very ripe bananas on the drive over. And a muffin. The mature twenty-four-year-old would have simply owned up to the untimely binge and assuaged her poor mother's worries. But I didn't do it. I pushed my food (so lovingly prepared!) around my plate and acted like a pouty, despondent, can't-be-comforted brat. "Don't you want to talk about it, Annie? Tell me how you're feeling or something?" She did the eyebrow thing again when she said this.

"I don't know, Mom. I feel like shit. I'm sad."

"You don't really seem sad."

"Well, I am. Sad people can still care about the Olsen twins."

"Oh, Annie." She said it again, this time with wisps of exasperation. She asked me more questions about the send-off. And I answered
them, trying to make it sound nice.

"It will go so much faster than you think."

"Ugh, Mom. That's what everyone keeps saying. But a year is a year
is a year." Then I told her that time only seems to slow down or speed
up when you're not paying attention. Like when you've been drinking
too much in college or when you haven't read the newspaper in weeks.
I'm going to be paying attention. It's going to be a year. She said she
didn't quite understand what I meant. She poured us both more coffee,
and I could tell that she was pleased that I had begun to open up—albeit
with goofball speculations about the perception of time.

"I mean that's it. It's long. It's going to be exactly as long as it's going to be."

"Well, I guess that's sort of a realistic viewpoint." My mom looked
confused and I think a little surprised. Did she expect me to be announcing how proud I was of David? (Of course, amid the frustrating
situation, there is still much room for pride.) Did she want me to make
political forecasts? Or maybe just weep weep weep? I knew I was failing to meet some behavioral expectation she had for me, and although
I knew her intentions were the kindest, I didn't have the energy to play
a role I couldn't even define. So I steered the conversation to a place
where I could safely exit. I think we ended up talking about gardening. I mentioned the need to clip my sweet peas.

"I need to go, Mom. Thanks for the food and everything," I said. I
meant it too. I did appreciate the foods. I would appreciate them more
when I ate the leftovers (quickly ushered into foil packets and Tupperware) the next day for breakfast. And I appreciated that my mom was
so set on being there in case the weep weep weep actually happened.
Maybe we were both equally perplexed that it had not.

"Of course, sweetie. Now don't ever hesitate to come over. I know
you'll be busy with school soon, but call me." She hugged me again,

and though I do love being hugged by my mother, I was annoyed by the way it lasted longer than usual. It had to be a special your-boyfriend-left-for-war hug. Wrapped in my mother's arms, I could almost see myself reaching into my pocket for a white handkerchief, pulling it out, and flailing it around. Let me go! I surrender! Let me out! Instead, I stayed there and returned the hug as best I could until she let go and kissed my cheek.

And then I left. I stopped at the gourmet supermarket on the way home. I purchased a Swiss Gruyère, a Spanish manchego, a small log of herbed goat cheese, and a smoked Dutch Gouda. Three types of crackers. And a baguette!

Lactase is this stuff your small intestine produces to break down the two sugars that form lactose, the main sugar in milk. At eight P.M., I ate the Swiss Gruyère. If for some reason you don't have enough lactase in your small intestine, the lactose gets down to your large intestine still intact. Around quarter to nine I ate the Spanish manchego.[6] There it ferments with some bacteria that are just hanging out being otherwise quite healthy. I ate the herbed goat cheese and licked my fingers clean. And this fermentation, this rumbling in the colon, produces some nasty, treacherous effects. Your guts basically freak out. I ate the smoked Dutch Gouda, savoring its hearty, woody finish. Excess gas, cramping, and loose, painful stools. Most humans on earth are lactose intolerant. But not most humans in North America.

The crackers disappeared. The baguette was blasted into a storm of crumbs. The coffee table in my living room became the front line of an epic battle: dairy versus carbohydrate. Both sides suffered severe losses. I basically destroyed everything. You might even call it *hysterical*. I asked David once if the lactose intolerant were allowed to join the army.

[6] It wasn't really a manchego, but a boring Vermont cheddar. Manchego = $13.99 a pound!

"Sure they are," he said. "The army takes anyone."

"But then does the army supply you with Lactaid[7] or soy substitutes when you're out on secret missions?"

"I don't know. Probably not."

"So you have to waste space that could be used packing books or photographs by toting your own little packets of Lactaid or dehydrated soy milk?!?"

"Just don't eat dairy."

Just don't eat dairy.

I didn't sleep well that night. Maybe I did it on purpose—the cheese binge. Just so I wouldn't sleep. Fed my lactase-lacking intestine all sorts of yummies I knew that it couldn't break down. So my feet would wear paths to and from the toilet. So my body would physically protest that first evening spent alone. So I would feel as miserable as I suspected I should have before my lips even hit the salty Swiss Gruyère. Yeah, it was pretty bad. I almost called my mother from the toilet to say, "See, Mom?! See! I *am* freaking out. I *am* crazy upset about my boyfriend's risk of injury and death and that he might have to shoot guns at innocent people! Mom, I am so upset that I ate pound upon pound of fancy cheese!"

This is Wartime Alone Time. There is no rain on my windows at the moment, and I have no idea what to expect.

---

[7] Lactaid is a registered trademark of McNeil Nutritionals, LCC. Go McNeil!

2

Today I'm calling my book *Spoon the Air* because that totally relates to both of us. David spends about a hundred hours a week with this software satellite million-dollar computer stuff that scans the air for enemy business. I can only speak about it vaguely because he can only speak about it vaguely. Not because he's inarticulate, but because the army often makes you sign a vagueness pact[8] when it comes to speaking to your family and friends about certain types of work. (So he scoops at the air to find stuff.)

And me, I'm getting used to spooning it too. The curve at my hips that grew accustomed to the pressure and warmth of his body is now cupped by the small patch of air under the blanket. I bought a new comforter that weighs about fifty pounds, and it actually feels great. Like that lead blanket at the dentist. Funny thing is, now sometimes I wake up with my mouth feeling all full. Like those cardboard X-ray things are choking me in my sleep.

It's been thirty-three days since he left now. I've received fourteen e-mails and seven phone calls. Not really so bad. The time difference makes it tough to talk on the phone. He's something like nine hours ahead and working this insane night shift for the first six weeks. And I'm at school all day, and I can't really answer my phone during reading groups or Mega Math Olympics.[9] The first time we spoke was

---

[8] Not really called a "vagueness pact," but some substantially less negative-sounding phrase. It might even include the term "top secret."

[9] A totally awesome game I made up last year.

so great. He told me about the long-ass plane rides and the mess hall and the soldiers his company is replacing. They got ribs their very first night! David surely would not be eating ribs if he were still here with me.

A conversation I remember:

"You cook too much chicken, Annie," David said.

"Well, I really like chicken. And it's cheaper than beef or pork," I said.

"You should really get your own chickens or something."

"Yeah, David, you're right. I should. You know, that's a great idea."[10]

During a phone call last week, David told me this story about Beanie Babies. I wouldn't be surprised if I hear it again three weeks from now as an e-mail forward from my mother. Goes like this:

This guy who works with David is called Flores. He's already been in Iraq for several months and has been teaching David to use some secret equipment. Anyway, several weeks ago Flores received a package from his grandmother's church somewhere in Texas. Among the things that people usually send soldiers (toothpaste, beef jerky, car magazines) were a dozen or so Beanie Babies. The ladies of St. Charles Catholic Church included a note for Flores to hand out the toys to Iraqi children who might want them. And Flores, because he really did appreciate the toothpaste and the beef jerky and the car magazines, did as told. He gave those legume-stuffed bears and kitties and lizards right out to Iraqi children he ran into. The son of the barber in their camp. Some girls playing in a field just outside the compound. A kid selling illegally burned copies of *The Sopranos* on DVD. Flores didn't really think much of it.

A few days later, while he's leading a convoy for something pro-

---

[10] Note: Consider a chicken. Ask landlord about building a henhouse.

tected by the vagueness pact, his vehicle is forced to stop in the middle of the gravel road. A small girl of about five or six is standing right out in the middle of the convoy's path. Once Flores and his men get closer, they can see the fuzzy head of a stuffed Beanie peeking out from under the girl's bare arm. She's pointing to the road. To the earth. To an irregular patch of dirt just meters in front of the vehicle's tires.

Pointing to a land mine.[11]

I had asked David for Flores's first name. He didn't know it.

"But you work with this guy a ton. Didn't you ever see it somewhere or think to ask?"

"No. He's just Flores."

So for my purposes I'm going to call him Ray. Ray Flores, saved by a Beanie Baby!

"And what kind of Beanie Baby was it?"

"I don't know, Annie. Flores never said. It was just a Beanie Baby."

So for my purposes, it's a polar bear. Ray Flores, saved by a polar bear!

Yesterday I went to Wal-Mart, which is something I typically try not to do, but I figured just this once wouldn't taint my soul completely. I purchased nine small plush puppies, six cans of Play-Doh, and six boxes of twenty-four-pack crayons. I seriously considered the forty-eight-pack crayons because they include my favorite color, Jungle Green, but if Iraqi children don't already have crayons (and they obviously don't have jungles), then I guess they really won't know what they're missing.

This morning I sent the toys, along with three sticks of deodorant,

---

[11] Actually, it was a trigger point for an IED, which means "improvised explosive device." An IED can be numerous types of patched-together bombs. They can be detonated by motion sensors, magnets, tripwires. Tons of shit.

a batch of brownies vacuum-packed with this machine my neighbor the commercial fisherman has, a copy of the latest *Best American Science and Nature Writing* collection (that I just read and that I know David won't read, but maybe someone in his company might enjoy), a basketball magazine, and two pounds of beef jerky. Oh, and a pink low-rise V-string that I don't wear anymore because it chafes in all the wrong places. I sent that too. But I'm not telling anyone.

When you send packages overseas you have fill out this customs form, listing the entire contents of the parcel. So I wrote "TOYS, DE-ODORANT, TREATS, PERIODICALS, BEEF JERKY, UNDER-GARMENTS." The woman[12] at the post office asked me to be a little more specific about TREATS, so I crossed it out and wrote "HOME-MADE CHOCOLATE CHIP FUDGE BROWNIES WITH A SWEETENED CREAM CHEESE SWIRL AND COCONUT SPRINKLES," which was really quite ridiculous of me because they were actually just plain brownies made from a Betty Crocker mix. I didn't think until after I wrote it and it was in a big bin across the counter that David would probably read the customs slip and think he was getting some extravagant, homemade creation. I was just annoyed at the lady. But I already wrote David an e-mail about it, and I'm sure he'll understand because he knows I'm just a strange bird sometimes.

After the post office, I met my friend Gus at the bowling alley. Neither of us really bowls, but Gus will sometimes refuse to meet at conventional places like coffee shops or bookstores. I often accuse him of being that guy who always has to be different just for the sake of being different. And he usually takes the criticism well. Gus is basically the smartest person I know. He studied philosophy and math at Yale and

---

[12] She was wearing a Seattle Mariners hat, a Seattle Mariners sweatshirt, and, honest to god, Seattle Mariners earrings. I just can't trust people who are that shamelessly passionate about anything.

loves to joke about how the meaning of life is probably just embedded in an algorithm we haven't found yet, and that when someone does find it and owns the rights to it, only the wealthy will be able to buy it and only the really smart wealthy people will be able to understand it and those people will just keel over and die when they find out the truth and then humanity will be left with common folk, thick-skulled heirs and heiresses, and brilliant poor people to get things going right again. Wow, I totally just botched his theory trying to write it here. I promise it makes more sense when he explains it.

"Annie Sue Harper, glad to see you," he said when I walked in. He was playing with the joystick on that impossible toy-grabbing crane game. I could tell that he wasn't actually playing the game, but imagining it or calculating something about the mechanics of it all. And Sue is not my middle name. Gus just says things like this. And Gus is not even his real name. It's Michael. But his father, Rex,[13] started calling

---

[13] His mom left (disappeared without a trace!) before Gus could walk. His dad never ever talks about it, so naturally, over the years, Gus has LOVED to discuss his missing mother with me. It's interesting to think about how his theories regarding the absent parent have really evolved over the years. They've darkened and changed as adult life taught him to reserve a portion of his heart for dry cynicism. Back in middle school when Gus and I first became great friends—back when he was this goofy, happy kid who built model rockets and was charmed by the way his home rock tumbler could turn regular sidewalk gravel into smooth, lustrous stones—back then he had these cheery, optimistic ideas about his mother. He fancied that her departure was due to some heavily demanding, altruistic career path. She had to leave to fight some evil virus from killing entire states of third-world countries. She was a top member of a super secret international crime-fighting force. But by high school, his fantasies started to sour a bit. She was brainwashed into joining a religious cult. She couldn't help it; it was hypnosis. Or she had left Gus and Rex just after finding out that she was terminally ill. Maybe she thought a fast departure would be less devastating than a long, brutal one. I think Gus liked this theory best because it allowed him to

him Gus around age four when a young couple named Miriam and
Michael moved in next door. Miriam would always yell for Michael
(her husband) from all parts of her house and her yard. Her voice wasn't
shrill and annoying, but rather pleasant and beckoning. So four-year-old
Michael would often wander over. Miriam never picked up on why,
but didn't mind at all having Gus/Michael around. And sometimes
she'd give him Popsicles and tell him about when she used to live on a
houseboat, which Gus/Michael absolutely loved.

But Rex got sick of Gus/Michael being at the neighbors' all the time,
so he bought a bag of Popsicles and made a plan. He was reading
Lonesome Dove at the time, so he chose to call little Michael Gus after
Gus McCrae. "Hey Mikey, I'm reading this book about a really cool
cowboy named Gus. How would you like to be called Gus?" Apparently, Michael accepted the name change with little hesitation. This
was before the 1989 miniseries, of course, but whenever people hear
the story, they always point out, which is in fact very odd, that Gus

---

simultaneously mourn her loss and forgive her for going away. How can you
blame a dead woman? And then it wasn't until two summers ago, right after
we graduated from college, when Gus and I were helping my mom set up for
a garage sale, that I realized that his mom-hope had fizzled out completely.
We were carrying card tables out to the lawn and the topic of his mother
came up. "It doesn't matter if she was an alcoholic, a drug dealer, a tightrope
walker, a schizophrenic, a con artist, a flat-out bitch, or any combination of
any of those, I really just don't care anymore." He had started to flip through
a box of old disco records my parents were giving up. "If there was really
something positive about her that would make me feel better about who I
am and where I come from, my dad would have told me by now. I know
that." And something about this made me very sad for Gus. Obviously there
was *something* positive about his mother somewhere. She couldn't be an entirely loathsome creature. It was like he finally swallowed this sweet nugget
of hope he'd been carrying in the back of his throat for so long. But I guess
it is a rather silly hope when logically you know there will never be something real to bite down on.

does look strikingly like a young Robert Duvall. In ninth grade when we read *To Kill a Mockingbird* and watched the film in class, Gus was stoked to learn that Duvall also played Boo Radley. "I feel so much better about my name now," he had said. He was also fond of saying, "Imagine how different my life would be if my father had chosen to call me Woodrow."

"Annie Sue Harper, glad to see you." He did tilt his baseball cap as he said this. It was very Gus McCrae-esque.

"Hey Gus, how are you?"

"Meh. Reasonably well. And you?"

"Just okay." I hoisted my handbag on my shoulder as I said this, and we walked toward the counter to check out shoes. I was wearing flip-flops and forgot to bring socks because I'm a moron, so I suggested we just have a beer and some deep-fried ravioli in the lounge. Gus insisted I wear his socks.

"I'm immune to most foot fungi," he said.

We bowled two games.

Game one: Annie 68, Gus 149

We talked a lot about our friends from high school. The couples that married and divorced in between presidential elections. The Mormon guy who made heaps of money with Amazon. I told him about how I ran into Charlene Wilson—this girl he once dated, smoked weed with, and wrote stupid poetry with—at the bank. I told him how she was remarkably overweight and that she pretended not to see me.[14] I could see Gus suppress a smile at my mention of Charlene's corpulence

---

[14] She did not pretend not to see me. She came up and said something like, "Oh, Annie Harper. I didn't know you lived down in Tacoma now?" And then we chatted quite pleasantly. She works for a small independent publisher of parenting books downtown and has no children of her own. We're only twenty-four. But she was remarkably overweight. That part was true.

because he pretends not to be superficial and evil like we both sometimes are.

Just two months ago Gus returned from a two-year stint as a Peace Corps volunteer on the Caribbean island of Dominica. It's one of the tinier, poorer West Indies, and Gus split his time there teaching high school sex ed and doing bookkeeping and accounting projects for small farmers. He's always quoting Mr. Lionel Spence, one of the farmers he worked for. "As Lionel Spence would say, 'If it's growin' righ'now, it will still be growin' tomorrow.'" According to Gus, Mr. Spence was very wise. Gus also enjoyed describing how the two jobs complimented each other. Mr. Peter Benoit's farm produced both bananas and cucumbers, so there was never a shortage of props for condom demonstrations.

As we reached the middle of our first bowling game, he confessed how hard it's been for him to acclimate back to the USA lifestyle. "So many cars," he said. "Everyone is in a hurry." He stayed with his dad for the first several weeks and just recently moved into his own place. I asked him if he considered going back to New Haven, and he said he'd had enough East Coast for a while. He was standing over the machine that shoots the balls back up, waving his fingers over that sweat-blowing hand fan when he said, "I'm just glad you're around, Annie." He smiled. "It feels like I don't know too many people in Tacoma anymore." And after he turned to chuck his ball down the lane, I shouted to his back, "I'm glad you're here too."

Game two: Annie 97! Gus 109

Gus switched to bowling left-handed, and I filed my thumbnail down to the skin. I told him a bunch about David leaving and how I felt like a real asshole for not acting as sad as my mother thought I should have. David and Gus have met only a few times. Most recently, we all hung out last month when Gus's dad hosted a little welcome-home-Gus barbecue at his house. I could tell that Gus liked David alright after the soldier held his own in a Nietzsche conversation and said that cricket is a completely underrated sport. Cricket is something Gus pretends he picked up in the Caribbean.

"So you sent him Beanie Babies and Play-Doh?"

"Yes, I did."

"Oh, Annie. Sweet, sweet Annie." Gus shook his head slowly back and forth.

"What? I think it's a good idea."

"Iraqi kids don't need Play-Doh. Their backyard is a sandbox."

"But, but Play-Doh is gooey and fun. All my students like it."

"Yeah, and it also looks and smells like magic bread batter."

"So?"

"So. Those Iraqi kids might try and eat it."

It was a stupid argument. There's no way of proving whether or not, if introduced to Play-Doh,[15] Iraqi children are going to consume it. But it is nontoxic. Kids eat it all the time. Eating Play-Doh is just a universal impulse of children. But for my whole drive home I couldn't stop thinking about fretting Iraqi parents rocking their children to sleep, concerned about bombs, raids, money for shoes, and a strange bout of neon pink vomit.

I still haven't told my class where David is. Caitlin hasn't asked any more questions, and everyone is all wrapped up in making new friends and playing on the new plastic playground unit that was installed over the summer. We're starting a science unit about space next week, which I love. I love the giggles when I say "burning balls of gas." I love flipping the light switch on and off and on and off while trying to explain the speed of light and the concept of a light-year. I love discussing infinity and teaching the kids to draw the symbol for it. Someone always wants to talk about aliens. And I always ask if anyone has ever

[15] If they haven't been already.

encountered one before. And some little liar or show-off always has a story. I let him tell it for as long as he can manage, before everything just gets too absurd to be remotely believable. The alien eats the kid's younger sister and spits her back out as a boy. A whole swarm of aliens zap away the house and ask for maple syrup. How old are we when our imaginations sour? I say this like I'm some old hag teacher who's been at it for aeons. But really, it simply doesn't take long to notice patterns in children. Or grown-up humans, for that matter.

On Tuesdays I drive one of my students, Max Schaffer, to his violin lesson after school. It's just a few miles away, but his parents work and can't do it. We had to sign all these official school district papers to make it legal, and the Schaffers have decided to pay me (bimonthly) in gift certificates to upscale restaurants. This is only the second week, but I'm taking my parents out to some oyster bar this evening. The Schaffers said that teachers probably can't afford fine dining. Naturally, they are correct. I only wish David was around to be my date, because he's really good at faking knowledge of expensive wines.

This Tuesday as we drove to his lesson Max asked me if I had any books on teleportation.

"Teleportation?" I said.

"Yeah. You know, Miss Harper—the process of moving stuff from one place to another by taking it apart and making it into a code, then using that code to put it back together somewhere else." He adjusted the shoulder strap of his seat belt from rubbing him in the face.

"No, Max. I don't think I have any. But I could probably help you find some, or at least some articles on the Internet."

"Really? Because that would be totally awesome, Miss Harper."

"Okay then. We'll do that sometime."

Max started banging his knees excitedly against the violin case

between his legs. "You know, Miss Harper, they've already successfully teleported particles of some atoms."

"Wow, Max. You seem to know a lot about science."

"Yeah. It's pretty much my favorite subject. You know, if teleportation worked for humans, they could bring your boyfriend back every
night then teleport him back to Iraq in the morning." I almost ran a red
light whipping my head over to face Max and then leaving it there for
too long. The violin still bouncing back and forth between his knees.

"What? How did you . . . ?"

"My mom told me."

"I barely know your mom. How did she . . . ?"

"I don't know. Maybe she teleported into the future and found out
somehow?" Max smiled, picked his shoulders up to touch his ears. I
sighed.

"Then maybe you should ask your mom for books on teleportation."

"Nah. I was just kidding. She just always knows things. And gives
me lame books for like, music stuff and *The Canterbury Tales for Kids*."

I dropped Max off at his lesson and went home. I purchased *The
Canterbury Tales for Kids* online and *Teleportation: The Impossible Leap*.
I read Chaucer years ago in high school. I remember hating it because
Gus loved it so much and took to speaking in Middle English for
weeks. I can't have my students knowing more than me!

Subject: Who put the bag in Baghdad?
Date: Monday, October 15, 2003 21:23:06
From: david.peterson13@us.army.mil
To: missharpercandoit@yahoo.com

hey there A-star. how are things back in T-town? i must say, the
baghdad air actually beats the tacoma aroma. even on a hot

day, a deep breath isn't as rank as that nasty pulp mill scent.
I can't believe I've been here a month already. the guys we're
replacing are leaving in a few days and then I guess all the real
work starts. how are the booger-pickers? giving their hottie
teacher any trouble yet? oh, before I forget, you know that
digital camera I bought before I left, well, I forgot to get a flash
card for it and I can only hold like thirty pictures at a time, and
it's sometimes days before I can get to a computer and
download pics. could you maybe buy me one and send it? it's a
Cannon PowerShot 8.0. just tell that to someone at Best Buy
and they can show you the right card to get. I think I might want
at least 64MB. I'd buy it myself online, but I'm not sure exactly
what I need, so if you could do it that would be awesome. and
I'll pay you back with four hundred sexual favors and a trip to
Mexico when I get back. so yeah, things here are pretty good.
I'm just now getting used to everything being loud all the time.
the first few days we were all pretty jumpy, but now a big boom
in the night hardly phases [sic] me. you just get used to it. like
how I used to freak out at first when you'd twitch in your sleep
like a puppy. now I never even wake up when it happens. Ahhhh,
I miss your puppy twitches and faces. maybe I could adopt a
puppy here to remind me of you! ha! there are plenty of mangy
mutts wandering around. how is your mom doing? my parents
have been writing me like every day. my mom tells me that
everyone back home is always asking about me and praying for
me and stuff. she'll say, "yes, David. Gwen Robinson says she
keeps you in her prayers." I don't even know who Gwen
Robinson is!?! I can't help but feel kind of bad given that she's
praying for me and all. she might be my sister's old ballet
teacher or something. Or maybe someone from church. oh and
also, I wanted to tell you. this guy I work with Henderson, his
wife and some of the other wives in our company have started

this group thing where they get together and knit and talk about
how their [sic] coping with us being gone. I know you don't knit,
babe, but maybe it'd be a good way to make friends and deal
with it all. you know what I mean? Henderson's wife is named
Angela and her email is angiespice456@yahoo.com. you should
totally write her and hook up with them. I'll tell Henderson to
tell her you will. ah shit, I've been on this computer for too long
and I need to write my parents and confirm my status as not
dead before I let the next guy use the computer. I miss you,
Annie! I'll try to call in the next few days. I love you!

Later,
David (that hot guy from your dreams)

I just read this e-mail, and now I feel pretty lousy. I haven't prayed
for David once. Prayer doesn't exactly align with my quiet atheism,
but in these circumstances maybe it's worth a shot? Fucking Gwen
Robinson has prayed for him. Probably more times than I manage to
cuss daily outside school hours. AND I don't want to join any knitting group either. Doesn't David know I already have friends? Gus is
back now. And there are a few friends from college who live in the area
that I could hang out with more. What would I do with them? Sit
around and talk about the State of the Union? How cheap a gallon of
milk is at the on-base commissary? Our lovers can't even benefit from
snuggly warm knitted goods. They are in a desert! I guess I better
e-mail her; David seems to think it's a swell idea. Maybe it will make
him feel better about leaving me here all alone. Perhaps it's a way I can
help him. I'll e-mail Angie Spice tomorrow.

I just got back from the bathroom. Since David lived in a jail cell,
mini-apartment before he left, he spent most nights over here. He'd
wake up long before Teacher Annie, and I'd barely lift out of

consciousness as he stealthily left for his five-thirty PT[16] exercises on base. Sometimes I'd murmur at the sound of his dog tags clinking back around his neck. The jingling reminder that he first belongs to Someone Else. It's worse than any alarm. But anyway, he'd always leave the bathroom so tidy for me. The seat never up. No splashes of water, licks of shaving cream, nor the coffee grinds of his beard. He'd place a hand towel gently by the sink, and best of all, he'd fold the corners of the toilet paper's edge into a perfect little point. Just like they do in fancy hotels. And of course he did this the day he left, and even though I don't like to admit it, I am a sort of a schmaltz-face. So I left it just that way.[17] The neatly folded ass-wipe. Almost pointing to the toilet seat like a message from its careful creator. "I'm coming back here."

So in honor of Gwen Robinson and her prayer chains, I'm going to try something prayerlike in bed tonight. Just for the fucking sake of it.

"Please keep First Lieutenant David Peterson safe tonight. Amen."

Or

"I hereby send all the positive energy from my chakras to David Peterson's heart so he can sleep soundly and wake with a clear mind."

Or

"Think again, suicide bombers! Think of your children! Think of your mother!"

Or

"Bad health to George W.! Worse health to Dick Cheney!"

Or

"Be kind, sweet fate. Be fleeting, bad luck. Don't be absurd, you nasty bitch circumstance."

Or

---

[16] Physical training

[17] I keep the toilet paper I actually use on the back on the tank now. Those dispensers are sort of superfluous anyway.

"David, I wish you morning wood, and the privacy and time to tend to it."

Or

"All we can do is spoon the air. Spoon the air. Big fat dripping spoons of air!"

3

*I*f I exclude the following story, perhaps I can call my book *Grace in His Absence.*[18]

It was lunch time. I was simultaneously correcting spelling tests and eating leftover spaghetti. Just multitasking with my bad self. I do it all the time. Max Schaffer got 100 percent. Caitlin Robinson missed seven out of ten. I laughed out loud at her attempt at delicious. *Dili-shus.* Phonetically, I guess that's not too bad. I can fly through these tests pretty quickly. Some schools don't use traditional spelling curriculum anymore, and I worry about that a little. Creative, touchy-feely spelling should not be encouraged. I cringe every time I drive by the Kwik N Kleen car wash. Caitlin Robinson just might pencil that down some day.

I don't even remember what I was doing when it happened. I had my red pen and my fork in the same hand. Each resting in a different finger slot, traveling back and forth from mouth to paper to plate. I thought I was pretty deft at it. Like how hairstylists twirl scissors and combs in the same hand. I must have been flipping the pen over to the eraser side or trying to catch a defiant noodle from falling on a test. And I don't even know if it was the fork or the pencil, but it gets me straight in the eye. I shout some crass profanity and I yelp. I yelp

---

[18] Except I would surely not capitalize "his," because I definitely don't want people to think I'm talking about God or Jesus or somebody. This title would be doubly cool if my name were actually Grace. Oprah would eat that shit up.

pretty darn loud. Like I'm a puppy with my tail smashed in a sliding glass door. It doesn't bleed, but it hurts like you wouldn't believe. My contact lens quickly assumes some advanced yoga pose and I pluck it out, bringing my napkin straight to my eye. Carrie, the teacher next door, comes busting in. She must have heard my cries.

"Annie, what the . . . ?"

"Shit, Carrie. I stabbed myself in the eye."

"Oh, ick. That looks bad."

"Fucking hurts," I whimper.

"Watch your mouth, Annie. The warning bell just rang. I'll call for a sub. You should really go home." Carrie leaves. I start crying. It's not a sob, but a modest, contained weep. I'm still weeping when the first kids start to trickle in, glistening from freeze tag and fall sunshine. *Miss Harper, what's wrong? Miss Harper, what happened? Look, Miss Harper's crying.* It's hot. My eye is hot hot hott! The room is blurry, and the kids blend together in clumps of twos and threes as they shuffle chaotically to their seats. *What happened? Why is she . . .* I drop my head to my desk and close the wounded eye. The good eye focuses and unfocuses on Caitlin Robinson's test below me. *Dilishus. Dilishus.* Pain swirls like noodles on a fork. I groan, but I don't even know if it's audible. Carrie's back and I hear her announcing to the class that Mrs. Blake will be in for the rest of the day. I hear, *Awww, Mrs. Blake. Miss Harper, are you okay? I think she's going to puke. Why is she crying?* And somewhere in all the noise—Carrie trying to hush my kids, noisy nylon jackets being yanked off, a pencil being sharpened, someone humming a Jay-Z song—I hear a small but pestilent voice, *I bet her boyfriend was shot.*

I stand up and go, leaving the tests, the fork, the pen, my dignity, and the remaining hunks of my spaghetti. Looking oh so *dilishus.*

From the teacher's lounge, I call Gus to pick me up. All nine of the admin staff are fussing over me, bringing cooling creams in paper packets and those blue fake-ice pouches. Each of them has offered to drive me home. "Oh, Annie, even with one good eye, your peripheral vision will be all sorts of crazy." But I don't think I can handle it. Gus works for a linen service, swapping bags of bleached, pressed aprons and towels for soiled, nasty ones from restaurants and bars. Because he's so charming and scrawny he gets free food everywhere he goes, and I'm pretty sure that's why he took the job as his first employment back in the diverse USA. He's eating sushi one minute and Ethiopian food the next. He drives a sweet van and maintains a flexible schedule conducive to philosophizing and taking power naps. He agrees to pick me up. With the blue ice to my eye, I wonder what David will say. I wonder if this is a story worthy of precious phone-call time or if I should simply type it out in an e-mail. If I should even tell him at all. Will it seem completely absurd compared to his stories of shrapnel in skulls and lower-body lacerations?[19] But I don't care. I just want him to be home when I get there. Maybe dumping fruit in the blender for smoothies. Or finding a nice animal program on On Demand cable for me to watch with one eye. He'd say, "Oh, Annie," but not in the way my mom says it. He'd say it in a way that tells me that whether I stab myself with a fork or a pen or a gold-plated letter opener, it doesn't really matter.

"Well now, matey. Hop in." Gus's van smells like bleach and Chinese food.

"Thanks for coming, Gus."

"No problem, kiddo. I was around this area anyway. Mind if I make a stop at Pete's Kitchen before I take you home?"

"No. But can you score me some gravy fries?" I ask, half meaning it. Defeated, I slump over to the window and press the closed lid of my busted eye against the cool glass.

---

[19] He actually hasn't told me anything like this yet, but I read the news. I know a time will come when his phone voice will sink into more morose tones and he'll relate to me the tragic injury of some dear friend.

"I'll try." We pull into the parking lot of the diner and Gus jumps out with a sack of laundry over his shoulder like some sort of sanitation Santa Claus. He turns around and motions for me to roll my window down. I moan and do it anyway. "Hey, look in the glove box, Annie. I think there might be something in there you could use." He turns and runs into the building.

I rummage through papers, a spilling bag of sunflower seeds, Ovid's *Metamorphosis*, a box of condoms (gross!), and then I find it. A black felt eye patch, the cheap, costumey kind with the elastic stapled on. I laugh for a moment and put it right on. I tilt my head to see my reflection in the rear view mirror. The good eye even looks awful. Smeared makeup. Streaks of red like lines from my teacher's pen. I make a tough, grimacing face that starts as forced but becomes real as the weeping resurrects in my lungs. A voice in my head says, *Arrr. Poor wench! Her man be shot in a nasty skirmish!* I just want to go home.

So I told David a Reader's Digest Condensed Version of this story tonight. He called on a "chow break" (I hate it when he talks that way) and I gave him the quick, embarrassing facts. Scratched cornea. At least one week of a beige medical eye patch. I could tell that he felt really bad for me. Sympathy dripped from his voice that usually sounds so scratchy from what I imagine is sand or damage from shouting. "I'm sorry, babe. You taking any time off school to rest?"

"No, I'm fine. It's really not that bad. I can still see and everything. Not like I have glaucoma or anything."

"What's glaucoma?"

"You don't know what glaucoma is? Never mind, I'll tell you later," I said. "How are things with you and the U.S. Army?"

"The same. We might be getting some more phones in soon. And then I can call more. I think my great-aunt had glaucoma. Wait, maybe it was her cocker spaniel."

"Don't worry about it, hon. Just tell me a story or something. Did you get my package?"

"No, not yet. The super-duper-fancy, ultra-delicious brownies have yet to arrive." He chuckles a bit. "Hey, did you write to Henderson's wife about the knitting group?"

"Oh, yeah. I did. I'm going on Thursday."

"Well, you don't sound very excited." I was trying to. I'm a terrible actress.

"I don't knit, David. What am I supposed to do, bring a crossword puzzle or a pile of math quizzes to grade?" I'm trying to sound reasonable, but I know I just sound whiny.

"No. You socialize. Tell stories and laugh and bond and stuff. They seem like cool ladies." I agree, and then I say something about how it might help me feel less alone to be around people who are also alone in the same way. I don't really believe this, but I could tell it's what David wanted me to think. He shouldn't even be worrying one tiny worry about me anyway. He needs to be looking both ways before crossing the convoy path and double knotting the laces of his boots. He's barely been gone at all; I'm really doing fine. I don't need knitting strangers at this point. And as I write this, I can't help but think about how before he left he really emphasized that the ARMY was his JOB and that he was going away to do some WORK. Now, here he is trying to foist a bit of his JOB onto my LIFE. I've never asked him to sit in on parent/TEACHER conferences. Am I being a bad understander? Do I not want to meet the knitters because I'd rather wallow in my own loneliness than feel like I'm just one in a kabillion women who are doing the same?

I could feel the exasperation swelling on both sides of our conversation, so I steered us away from the knitters, hoping that by the time I reported back to David regarding Mrs. Angie Spice Henderson and Co., I'd have something more positive to say. We spoke for a few more minutes about normal things—life, lust, when I should change the oil in my car. It was really pretty nice. And as I was hanging up the phone I knocked the bed lamp over onto the floor. It broke with a loud snapping sound and a flash. Not fazed by my complete clumsiness, I left it on the floor and rolled into sleep position—just happy that the boom of the crash sounded nothing like a gunshot.

4

*T*oday my book is called *Dear John,* but it's not a book anymore. It's a reality television show on Fox. I just got off the phone with my friend Monica from college, who works for them in development. You see, she was helping me write this proposal for a new series that documents the lives of wives and girlfriends of soldiers at war. And it was accepted to film a pilot episode! Angie Spice Henderson and I are flying to L.A. tomorrow to talk to the producers and sign the contract. Aside from The 301st Company Stitch Bitches, we're going to find three or four other women (and maybe one man) in similar situations. Some will have children. Maybe one will be the wife of a private contractor. One will have to be pregnant, maybe even due in the next few months. Camera crews will follow us around while we cry and change diapers and obsessively flip through news channels. They'll zoom in on the photographs of uniformed men on our refrigerators. They'll pan the still-masculine areas of our closets and the vacant men's softball cleats in our garages.

And there will be funny moments too. Annie Harper composing letters to the White House about her therapy reimbursements. Little kids discovering pretend weapons of mass destruction in their tree forts and saying things like *No, I'm Saddam this time. It's my turn.* Hopefully, they'll abstain from a gross patriotic soundtrack and anything too political.

I'm pretty sure America will love it. We can sell ad time to companies like Ford and Oscar Mayer and Coca-Cola. My students will get to be on TV, and they'll love that. They'll love me even more than they already love me. And maybe that could spawn a whole spin-off series:

Miss Harper's Class: A Reality Show for Kids.[20] People will start to send me mail and presents. A kind billionaire may even offer to fly me in his private jet out to Qatar to meet David when he's on his five-day leave. That episode can be an hour-long special. Commercial breaks just after the cameras watch us giggle and close our hotel room door. So I guess you could say things are looking up.

That was all obviously a lie. Tonight, after a thrilling two hours with the knitting group, I passed up karaoke with Gus and his new girl-friend to sit at home waiting for David to maybe call. All the knit-ting wives were really very nice and really very cool and only spoke in army-abbreviation-speak for about half the time. They are mostly a few years older than myself, except for this raging goth chick, Dan-ielle, who got married when she was eighteen and is now a whop-ping nineteen. She's from Texas and said she was so ready "to get the hell out of there" last year when she married her high school sweetheart and moved to Tacoma where he was stationed. Now she's going to beauty school, loves the Tacoma music scene, and misses her husband, Chuck, desperately.

"At least I have our two pit bulls," she said at one point.

"Dogs are great," I responded. It was my first contribution to the conversation in several minutes. DOGS ARE GREAT. Wow, David. This is so rich and stimulating.

Angela Henderson has a beautiful home and made these delicious biscuit-wrapped baby cocktail sausages with four (4!) different dipping sauces. And although varieties of mustards do impress me very much, and although it was *kind of* a release to rant about the scratchy sound quality of our phone calls from Iraq and sadly shake our heads about

---

[20] "Next week on *Miss Harper's Class* watch as Steven threatens to sabo-tage Max's science project and blackmails him for fifty Yu-Gi-Oh cards! Does Max even have fifty Yu-Gi-Oh cards?"

a recent helicopter crash, in the end, the women were still strangers and Miss Harper did not have fun. The night would have been better spent with Gus. Or even my own sweet mother. Maybe if I'd known the women before and we were already invested in each other's lives somehow, I would feel better; trying to muster up a connection with them now just feels contrived and artificial. Angie baby, your honey dill sauce blew my mind, but I don't think I'm quite ready to start that cabled scarf.[21]

So I came home instead of joining the knitters for a drink downtown. I ended up watching the season finale of *The Bachelor* on TV, where the dude totally made it seem like he was going to pick Rachel but ended up giving Sharon the final rose. What a load of shit! Sharon is a vapid slut whose boobs will probably drop with that rose's first petal. What was he thinking? I was so mad I batted an empty yogurt cup with my spoon at the television. And I actually hit it! I started thinking about how fake all those people seem. How everything they say seems so scripted and generic. They talk about "deep connections" and "sharing genuine moments," but then the camera just shows them saying things like, *Yeah, I love spending time with family*, and *Communication is sooo important to me*. Then they giggle and do something gross like put food in each other's mouths. Then they make out. Maybe I'm just jealous because I haven't made out in a while. But mostly I'm mad because I know my life (and probably Angie Spice's and Danielle's lives too) is crispier, heartier, more amusing, and more real. Just

[21] One more thing about Angie. SHE DOESN'T HAVE A JOB. A few months before her husband left for deployment, she quit her post as an office manager of a real estate firm to spend more "quality time" with Mr. Henderson, or Captain Henderson, or whoever. She claims to be sending out résumés, but there was something about the vacuum streaks in her carpet and the spotless grout of her kitchen tile that saddened me. How can full-time fretting be good for the psyche? Well, fretting and knitting.

two seconds of me slapping my own sleepy hand as it accidentally reaches for the triangle of David's perfect toilet paper would show people. I'm real. This is life.

I'm real.

This is life.

I'm real.

This is life.

Wipe carefully.

Dip carefully.

Eat carefully.

Give roses carefully.

Do everything carefully.[22]

---

[22] So a few days have passed since I wrote this, and I just came back and reread that last bit about *The Bachelor*. Jeez, I am such a big-stage dramatical. Sure, I miss David, and deep in this quivering lobe of my brain I worry about his safety nonstop, but how much does my missing have to do with the W.A.R.? And how much of my missing has to do with the fact that I'm simply A.L.O.N.E.? (And how much of it actually has do with him?) ? ? ? Alright. I'm going to flip to the back of this book now and have a peek at the answer key.

Ugh. If only.

5

*T*oday I'm calling my book *Don't You Call Me a Hero.*

My mother took me to a quilt show. She likes to plan little mother/
daughter outings for us. Many of these events are rife with girliness—
things that she cannot drag my father to. There are some outings that
I enjoy (opening nights of Jane Austen movies) and others (scrapbook-
ing workshops) during which I work very hard to conceal my distaste.
We often go to lunch at cafés where they ask you, "Would you like to
sit in our tea garden?" To which I usually say something like, "Oh, you
grow tea out there?" and the waitress, who is surely told to perform
with unfaltering cuteness, says something like, "Oh no, dear, the garden is for drinking tea." Then I order black coffee. Then my mother
gives me a look.

So yesterday at the quilt show, while we were walking through
aisles of colorful, detailed patchwork in a private high school's gymnasium, my mother said, "You know, Annie, I've gotten a few e-mails
from David recently."

"You what?"

"Don't act so surprised. You gave me his e-mail address before he
left. I like to know how he's doing. He's such a sweetheart."

"I know. I just didn't expect you guys to be e-mail buddies. How
much does he write you?"

"I don't know. I think I've gotten three e-mails from him. But I
wrote him first." My mother rubbed her fingertips along the border of
a small square quilt. "Tight stitching."

"What do you guys talk about?"

"He tells me about his company. How he misses you." She nudged me with her elbow as she said this, and somehow, for some reason, I wanted to vomit. Puke all over a blue and white masterpiece called "Paisleys on Parade." David hadn't told me he was writing my mother, or that she was writing him. It's stupid, but I can't help but feel a little betrayed. He should spend that time writing more to me. Telling me more than the temperature and the condition of his boots. Saying 'miss you, I love you' in a different way for once. Painting me a picture of his life because from his news and *the* news, I still can't really tell what it's like.

"Oh, and he told me how you joined the knitting group with some of the other wives. That's so great, Annie. I bet the support—"

"What? I did *not* join. I went once. And I'm *not* going back." I hate it when I talk to my mother this way. It's plain awful. Hearing my words screech so loud and so snotty and so insensitive makes me feel I'm not qualified to be a teacher. Before my mother's cheeks totally dropped, I tried to backpedal. "I'm sorry, Mom. I didn't mean to erupt like that. It's just that I don't think the group is for me. I don't knit. I don't know them. I'd rather just spend the time with the friends I already have . . . and you and Dad, of course." She smiled.

"David did sound kind of excited about you joining, but I'm sure he'll understand why it's not quite your cup of tea."

We neared the end of the quilt show. It was set up like a maze. Quilts hanging from portable, wheeling chalkboards and volleyball nets. The PA system was playing the kind of country-string-quartet-type music that sounds like everything is right in the world. The harvest is good. The cattle are healthy. The town well hasn't dished out cholera in decades. There were women at the end of the maze selling fresh fudge and small cuts of fabric. And of course they were smiling at each other like everything really was right in the world. A quilt on every bed! A bed for every human! And I couldn't help but think about Greek/ Roman lady and her endless wartime tapestry. I looked at all the elaborate blankets draped around me—barely swaying in a breeze that had snuck in. And for a moment I did think they were beautiful. And for a moment I did think that maybe Greek/Roman lady knew what she was doing. And for a moment I even considered picking up some fabric and a beginner's quilting book. Fuck, maybe even some god-damn yarn. But then I saw a kid nuzzling his face up to a quilt in a very normal, playful way. He had those sneakers with the lights on the heels and a very faint Kool-Aid mustache. His mother turned around and squawked at him, "Timothy. Timothy, stop that. I told you not to touch the quilts." Not to touch the quilts! How ridiculous! Blankets are for nuzzling and having sex under and getting crumbs on and puk-ing on if you have to. I started to think about how many normal-sized quilts Greek/Roman lady could have made in the time she wove that ginormous one. How many families could she have helped? Families whose equally lonely mothers didn't have the time or the servants to waste all day crying over a loom and making blankets. What a fuck-ing bitch, I thought.[23] Right there at the end of the quilt maze, my mother could see the scowl on my face. And Timothy's mom is a bitch too, I continued with my hate-fest. Go ahead and touch the quilts, I say! My mother would never snap at me like that. She may be a sneaky boyfriend e-mailer, but she is not a stern, wrist-slapping barker. My mother is warm and soft and touchable. "Annie, what are you frown-ing about?" she said.

"Oh, nothing. I'm just hungry. Sorry." I tried to smile.

"Well, come on then. Let's go vote for our favorite quilt and I'll take you to lunch. I know this place with a great terrace. In the fall, they

---

[23] At the time. Now that I'm writing this and trying to think critically and stuff, I'm a little more sympathetic to Greek/Roman Lady. It's so hard to think rationally when you're bathed in the warm, viscous mess of self-pity.

have . . ." I followed my mother to a sickly cute painted mailbox with a slot on the top. We were to vote for our favorite quilt and the winner got some fat ribbon, a gift certificate to *A Stitch in Time,* and a place of honor at next year's show. My mother held the mini number-two pencil to her lips for a second, pulled her eyes up to the top of her head like she was thinking real hard. She looked just like one of my students pausing in a history test. Grasping and searching for some element of truth that could garner at least partial credit. She quickly scribbled something down.

"Come on, Annie. Vote. People really rely on this for feedback." I grabbed a slip of paper and a pencil and wrote "Puke on Parade" really fast. Before she could see, I slipped it into the mailbox, and we left.

That was Saturday. Sunday, my friend Hillary called and asked me to go Rollerblading on the water.

"What? They make water Rollerblades now? How does that work?" I had asked. I don't know how I got so obnoxious. Maybe because I hang out so much with third graders.

"You know what I mean, Annie. We used to do it all the time in college. Go Rollerblading on the water*front.*" I told her yes, even though I didn't really want to go. But I haven't been exercising much lately, and I hadn't seen Hillary since last spring. So we went.

Strapping my skates on, I noticed they felt tighter around the ankles than I'd remembered. Hillary's skates fit perfectly. I watched the white tips of her shiny fingernails carefully buckle the straps. It's hard to talk while Rollerblading, but we managed a decent, half-shouting conversation. Hillary didn't know about David's deployment, though she should have. Our web of friends from college had its kinks and tangents, but the lines usually went through. I knew that Josh Bowers and Maria Rodriguez were getting married. And that James Carver, that slimeball from the crew team, had lost his job selling insurance because of some scam. But Hillary didn't know that David was gone.

After the first few minutes of skating, she snagged my attention from a nearby ice cream vendor with her question. "So how's David doing? You guys still together?" Hillary and I were never great friends.

"Yeah, but he's been deployed." The wind rattled my voice, muffling it in velocity, like it too wanted to obscure the truth.

"He's unemployed? I thought he was still in the army?"

"No, he's been *deployed*. He's in Iraq now." Hillary stopped adjusting the waistband of her gym shorts and gave me the look that everyone gives me. Like I caught pinkeye from helping orphans. Or like I adopted a two-legged kitten and engineered prosthetic legs to help it walk, but then it died. Or like I just shaved my head (even though I have an unsightly birthmark) and donated the hair to one of those leukemia-patient wig-making charities. Like I'm doing something so brave or making some amazing sacrifice. But when really I did nothing. I fell in love with a nice man who just happens to have a job that has taken him away from me. Who just happens to work for an entity that has a shitload of guns and an odd sense of what constitutes "helping out."

"Wow, Annie. That's got to be tough."

"Yes. Yes, it is tough. But it's just a dumb situation. Dumb circumstance." I looked out to the bay. The tame waters of the Puget Sound were only slightly glistening in the afternoon sun. A few small boats puttered around, and a gray castle of industrial something pumped out steam on the other side of the shore. It was only kind of pretty, but fine to look at while skating.

"Have you guys been able to talk much? When is he coming back? Is he in a dangerous place?" Hillary spat out the usual repertoire of questions, and I forced the exhausted lump of neurons in my brain to pull up the tattered file that contains my usual answers. But I'd rolled to a stop.

My left skate had just run over something soft and lumpy. I wanted it to be ice cream, but it was not. It was dog poo, and I was barely surprised. If anything, I was relieved. The ten gross minutes it took to wheel my skate back and forth on the grass, to fill a littered coffee cup with sea water and flush it through the bearings—those were ten minutes I had to not tell Hillary about my life. The mundane but genuinely sad details of a girl whose boyfriend is at war.

Funny thing, shit, how it can distract you from its other forms!

Recently, on the telephone . . .

> *David:* So you're really not going back? Won't they be offended?
> [pause]
> *Annie:* Why would they be offended? We just met. I wrote Angie and told her that I already have too much going on and that I also have a book club that meets once a week.
> *D:* You're in a book club?
> *A:* No. But I'm sure I will be someday. And I do read a lot. That's kind of like having my own private book club. I didn't want Angie to think that I was quitting the knitters because I didn't enjoy their company.
> *D:* But you didn't enjoy their company. That's why you quit.
> *A:* So?
> *D:* So you could have given them more of a chance. There are guys here that I couldn't stand when I started working full time. But people can grow on you. Eventually you'll find out you *do* have stuff in common and that you *can* have fun together.
> *A:* I don't want to have fun with them. I have fun at school.
> *D:* Jeez, Annie.
> *A:* What?
> *D:* I thought you were a hard worker. Building new relationships sometimes takes a little work, you know.
> *A:* I don't want new relationships.

D: Right.
A: Right.
D: Anyway.

Later, on my computer:

November 1, 2003

Dear President Bush,

When I met David, I lied to him. I told him I was seventeen
and visiting a sister at the university over my spring break.
We were at a house party hosted by the soccer team, and he
approached me with some lame comment about how the
music totally sucked. I hadn't even been paying attention to
the music, but was instead counting girls with matching
peasant-style tops and making fun of them in my head.

I first noticed David's clean haircut, and after he told me
his name, I asked if he was in the military. He explained the
whole ROTC scholarship thing to me briefly, and I nodded
along the way. Maybe that's why I felt okay lying. Why when
he asked for my number, I denied him, subtracting years from
my age and inventing some story. Maybe because at that first
conversation he seemed to think that this whole free-school/
serve-the-country get-up was a good idea. At that point,
maybe I thought he was easily deceived.

It was early in our senior year of college, and soon after the
encounter at the party when I ran into him at the library.

"I thought you weren't a student here." That's all he said.
Not even "hi" first. I was squatting to a low shelf, reshelving
nineteenth-century Russian literature, and I was suddenly
aware that my pants were low and that maybe he could see my

butt crack. That's right, Mr. Bush, I said butt crack. I worked at the library to pay the bills. Lots of students do this sort of thing.

"Err, um. I don't. I work here." I didn't know what else to say.

"Are you sure?" he said.

"Yes, I'm sure. Do you think I'd organize old Russian poems for fun?" I stood up and tugged the back of my pants, making sure all was decent.

"No, are you *sure* you don't go to school here?" All I could do was sigh. I put a crusty maroon volume back on the shelving cart and tried to formulate some socially normal response.

"Yes. I mean, no, I'm not sure. I mean, yes I do go to school here."

"And you're not seventeen?"

"Yes. I'm not seventeen. You figured it out."

You see, George. That lying to David about my age thing was stupid and impulsive. It accomplished nothing. I could have easily used an honest form of phone number rejection. All it really did was make things more awkward in the future. And well, yeah, things did work out pretty well. I learned he was more than his haircut, and somehow, amazingly, he learned to trust me. We grew to love each other and have remarkably good premarital sex nearly every day. So what I'm getting at here is quite simple. We all do silly things at strange moments. We make fast decisions based on finding quick fixes and on what we think will be most safe at the time.

So.

If you could please yank on your powerful strings and

bring these soldiers back home in the next seven to ten business days, I'd be very much obliged.

Best wishes,
Annie T. Harper, PhD

P.S. Please send my regards to your family. Please tell Jenna and Barb how lucky they are that they are not spending twenty hours a week in college shelving books. Though from what I understand, it was remarkably more difficult for them to obtain a decent fake ID.

Gus called me in the fucking middle of the night. He said he needed my help with something. Gus has never called me in the middle of the night. Even when his dad told him more about his mom leaving and even when he lost his virginity and even when he got into Yale. He never rushed to tell me these things. He always waited until the next time we saw each other. He's not really the sort of guy who is pestered by urgency.

"Right now, Gus? You want me to get up right now and go to the Dairy DeLite?"[24]

"Yes. I need help scratching off the pumpkins."

"What? I don't get it."

"Just come, Annie. I'm turning the soft-serve machine on right now. It'll be ready when you get here."

"I don't eat ice cream."

And he hung up. And maybe because I wasn't sleeping well anyway, and maybe because I just wanted to see what this pumpkin-scratching business was all about, and maybe because I still kind of owed Gus for picking me up after the eye-stabbing thing and for sacrificing his socks at the bowling alley, I went.

[24] Oh, the spelling! My community is plagued.

Pulling into the empty parking lot of the drive-in, I noticed a few lights on and Gus's slim figure shadowed against a half-painted window. Oh. Pumpkins. He was scratching off that dusty, flaky window paint with a tool, and as I walked through the door I noticed he was whistling "Jingle Bells."

"What are you doing?"

"Scratching off paint. Here." He reached into his pocket and pulled out an identical tool and tossed it to me. I stood there waiting for an explanation and knowing that he was waiting for me to start whining out questions before he revealed any speck of his absurdity. I just gave in.

"Gus, why are you doing this in the middle of the night?"

"When else would I do it, Annie? This place is open eleven to eleven. I'm busy in the morning. And plus, they don't want me scraping flakes of paint into people's onion rings and milk shakes and stuff. Could you please begin over there next to that confused-looking witch? I can't believe I painted her with those dimples." I wandered over to the far edge of the window. With neither of us speaking, the scrapers on the windows sounded like some odd mix between someone crying and someone smashing croutons. I asked Gus how long he's been doing window art. "Well, this was my first mural here, and I've done the public library just once since I've been back in Tacoma. They're giving me a hundred bucks each time I paint here, and I'll be doing the library for free, but not really free because I've negotiated an understanding about them clearing any future fines I might incur. And those can get pretty bad."

"Well, it is pretty nice of you." I squatted down to the lower vines of the pumpkin patch. I noticed his work was detailed enough to have included prickles along the twisting vines of the pumpkins. I cautiously lifted a finger to the glass and the fine black brushstroke of a prickle. I touched it tentatively like it was actually going to poke me. It reminded me of something I'd see one of my students do when he or she didn't know I was watching.

"Art is art is art, you know. I'll do what I can," Gus said, jumping down from a bar stool and grabbing a rag to wipe the glass. "Could you hand me that Windex behind you?" I grabbed the bottle and handed it to him with the handle first, like it was a pair of scissors. "Thank you, Miss Harper," he said, "I really wish we didn't have to do turkeys and pilgrims. You know how much I fucking hate that ridiculous pilgrim image? Those industrious hats and devious smiles. 'Share your corn with us and we'll exploit you forever!'"

"I kind of agree. But did you say *we*? Because I'm not painting anything, Gus. As soon as these little goblins are gone, I'm off to bed. It's a school night, you know." I turned back to the glass and scraped ferociously, trying to pretend that the sound didn't hurt my ears. Gus began to whistle the theme from *Indiana Jones,* and I did my best to ignore him while we both worked diligently at the scraping. It took maybe thirty minutes. The whole scenario reminded me of projects Gus and I would do together in high school. There was once this assignment for Advanced Geometry where we had to construct a polyhedron with more than twenty sides out of paper and glue. Then we were supposed to make a poster explaining how to find the volume and surface area of the polyhedron. Gus spoke to the teacher and cleared permission for us to make our sixty-four-side-agon not out of paper, but out of aluminum soda cans. It turned out to be an outrageous undertaking where we stayed up all night in Gus's garage. Around three A.M., while attempting to score and fold a particularly rigid Mr. Pibb can, I sliced my thumb rather severely. Without waking our parents, Gus drove me to the ER, and by the time I had seven waxy-looking stiches sewn into my skin, he'd completed the entire poster in the waiting room and even had time to fetch me a slice of pie from the hospital cafeteria. He'd acquired several fans among the waiting and the ailing, and they were gathered around to stare at the poster: math equations in perfect Gothic-style calligraphy. As he helped me put on my coat and we turned for the door, I noticed a small child with his chubby hand wrapped around one of Gus's silver-tipped pens, drawing loops and circles across the cover of *Time* magazine. Even though we weren't even halfway done with the construction of the polyhedron, Gus insisted that I go home to bed—the aluminum was his idea, after all—and when he picked me up just hours later for school, there was the sixty-four-side-agon, shiny and perfect and finished, buckled with obvious care into the back seat of his Volvo.

I broke the screechy silence of our paint scratching to say "Hey, Gus. Remember the sixty-four-side-agon?"

"Of course. That thing was awesome. My dad still has it in his study."

"And I still have the scar on my thumb."

Once all the paint was gone, I helped myself to some Diet Coke from the fountain while Gus squeegeed the whole thing. When he finished, he just stood there in front of the glass, the squeegee dripping a small puddle on the floor. I joined him with my soda, making slurping noises because I filled the cup nearly all the way with ice. The window was so clean and so clear; we just stood there staring through it at my car and his van and the dank ugliness of the parking lot.

"That is some clean-ass glass," Gus said.

"Yep," I said. "Doesn't get much cleaner than that." I slurped at my soda again.

"You know, Annie, I don't think I've done a better, more thorough job of anything in my entire life. This glass is perfect." He said this with awe. Gus has always been prone to hyperbole.

"You're probably right. This glass is definitely your best work." And I have always been prone to encouraging him.

"Looks like you could just run right through it. Like it's not even there." We stood in silence for another minute or so. It wasn't really one

of those meaningful, contemplative moments for me. I was just looking at my car, thinking about how tired I was. Just bullshitting with
Gus like I have for years. Then he turned and said to me, "So, Annie,
how are you?" And I didn't quite know how to take it. I didn't know if
he was asking me the same way that Hillary asked me and the women
at my school ask me and my mom asks me and everyone fucking asks
me. "Annie, how are you?" they say. And it's usually at a moment
where I'm not thinking about David at all. When I'm not thinking
about all the chances my boyfriend is having to die. It's usually a moment when I'm just being a normal, functioning human, talking
about the weather or thinking about how many eggs are in the fridge
or when I need to pay for cable. And when they say it, it's usually accompanied by some degree of head tilting or eye narrowing, or if I'm
really lucky, a tender hand to the shoulder.

At this moment, when Gus put his squeegee down on the table and
reached in his bag for jars of powdered paint, I couldn't even tell if he
meant it the same way. For years I've been shooting the shit with this
kid, discussing everything from world peace to free-range beef to
whether our alter-ego superheroes would prefer nylon or lycra. I can tell
when his heart is mopey or when he's recently gotten laid. I can tell
when he's been fighting with his father or drinking too much or watching lots of the History Channel because he's been spitting out stupid
facts. But after I sucked down the last drops of my Diet Coke, as I stood
there biting and chewing my straw, I just didn't get it. I couldn't really
tell what Gus meant. I walked over to the trash and tossed the paper cup
inside, being careful not to get my hand whapped by the germy swinging door. Pulling it out, I stared at my fingernails and the chunks of
paint beneath them. Remnants of a white ghost and a black cat. Orange
from the pumpkins and a lot of green from those gnarly vines.

"How am I?" I paused and switched to examining the fingers of
my other hand. "Well, Gus, I'm fine. A little tired, but pretty good.

And I need to trim my fingernails." I kind of wanted to tell him about the knitters.

"Well, if you're not too tired, I was still going to let you paint." I wondered if he even wanted to know my answer to the question. If he wanted to know about my fingernails or my sleep deprivation. My students or my addiction to CNN. Or if it was just Gus transitioning the awkward silence into the next act of his show.

6

*T*oday I'm calling my book *Nine Times Forever Equals Way Too Long,* and I told my kids about David. I pretty much had to. Jessica Marquez brought in this whole gimongous photo album from her cousin's wedding. Jessica, the proudest flower girl in America, wouldn't shut up about the dresses and the veils and her slow dancing with the best man. Obviously, the boys didn't give a rat's ass, and when Jacob Ware pointed out that you could see one of the bridesmaids' fat rolls under her turquoise satin dress and that it was "raunchy," I wanted to kiss the top of his awful head.

I am sitting at my desk in the front of the class, and Jessica is standing right in front of me pulling 4×6 prints from their plastic pouches and passing them around the aisles. I'm considering outlawing photographs (especially twenty-page albums of photographs) from show-and-tell. Where the fuck is the creativity?

"Miss Harper?" Caitlin Robinson pipes up from the back row.

"Yes, Caitlin?" I peek around Jessica to see the class.

"When are *you* getting married?"

"Um. Well, Caitlin. Probably not for a while. I'm still pretty young." And then it's one of those moments. Those explosions of twenty-eight eight-year-olds spouting and blabbing and word vomiting all over my tidy, orderly classroom. Each grabbing bits of each other's speech and commenting with pure, unbridled reactions. No one phrase belongs to any one child. It's just high-pitched verbs and pokey question marks bouncing off my forehead and back onto their grimy desks. *How old are you? My cousin is twenty-two. My mom got married when she was thirty-three. I'm getting married when I'm. Your*

mom is a grandma. You're a. Miss Harper. When can we. I have to. Miss
Harper. Miss . . .

And I guess I usually let it carry on for too long. It isn't until I hear
the loud kids (Katie Wells or Ben Morris) start to dominate the roar
that I remember it's my job to stop this sort of thing. I have this bell
on my desk. One of those silver push-button domes you ring at the
dry cleaner when the clerk is in the back watching TV or working.
Yeah, it's hokey—we call it the *shush bell*—but it works most of the
time. Katie Wells is *Miss Harper*ing me like it's her sole purpose in life,
and one of the boys is dangling a photo above his head while Jessica
cries for some female comrade to *Get it, get it back. Miss Harper?*

Okay. I bang it. Rap my hand on the bell one, two, three times. By
the time the reverberation calms, one last hastily whispered *No, you're*
stupid settles amongst the squeaks of the desk chairs.

"Alright. Thank you, Jessica for sharing your photos. They are very
nice. Looks like you had a great time at the wedding. Now please take
your seat." Jessica carefully closes the pink volume, clutches it to her
chest, and struts back toward her desk. Before she sits, she turns back
to me.

"Do you think your boyfriend will propose to you soon, Miss
Harper?" I sigh, too tired to feel awkward or annoyed in front of the
kids.

"No, Jessica. My boyfriend is in the army. He lives in Iraq right
now. And he's not coming back for a while." And the air in the class
does not change. No one gasps and no one starts spitting off questions. They know already. And really, I knew that they know that I
knew they know. I just hadn't said it. I just hadn't made it real. Max
Schaffer raises his hand. Bless his heart; he always raises his hand.

"Yes, Max?"

"Perhaps, Miss Harper, he will propose to you by mail. Or by
DVD." I laugh out loud. It's a comfortable laugh. It's a laugh you would
use drinking beers with close friends in a noisy bar.

"Yeah, maybe, Max. That would be pretty funny."

The conversation is over. There are no pictures of me shoving cake in my lover's mouth. No one is doing the macarena. There are no bubbles blowing. No limousines. No mustachioed caterers carving flanks of meat. What a relief. I am a third-grade teacher, and I am wearing a navy blue cardigan that perfectly matches the ugly shell beneath it that has a bleach stain on the back the shape of a lima bean. I'm not even wearing earrings. The realization is smooth and gentle, and I feel a comfort with my students that hasn't happened yet this year. I am only an educator. I am not a show. I tell them to take out their math workbooks. That we are going to do some speed tests with our times tables. I can hear the whiners whine and the nerdy ones eagerly fumble in their desks for pencils. Someone asks if we can do the quiz without the nines.

"Of course not," I tell everyone. "What is the universe without nines?"

A transcript of the letter I get when I get home:

Hola babe,

It feels weird writing you on paper. I'm the soldier and you're the girl and I'm supposed to do this, right? I'm supposed to curl up on some cot or some corner of my tent and tell you (in cursive) how much I love you and how we'll get such a nice house when I get back. I'll take you to the soda shoppe and we'll go to the movies. Just like old times, Annie! It will be swell. Ha! Not the case. Mostly because you fall asleep in movies and don't eat ice cream. I don't sleep in a cot either. My bed is actually better than the ones in the dorms back in college. And you know I can't write in cursive. The thing about this paper, Annie, the thing is, that it's waterproof, fireproof, vomitproof, bulletproof, deathproof, spaceproof, semenproof paper. I think the army pays something

*like $4.50 a sheet for the stuff. They issue us a bunch, but I'm not
really sure what we're supposed to use it for. So I'm writing you
with it. Maybe you can use it for a science experiment with your
kids or something? See if you can burn it in an airtight jar. I don't
really know what to write since I'll probably talk to you and
e-mail you six times before this actually reaches you, so what's the
point in giving you all the scoop? It will be old scoop in no time.
So, SO ANNIE, what I'm going to do is imbed a secret code
word. No, a secret code phrase. And when you get this and you
read it, the next time we talk on the phone, you have to use the
secret code phrase. But don't just say it, you have to weave it into
the conversation all smooth like. And that's how I'll know you got
the letter. You ready? The secret code phrase is . . . "Below the
Mason-Dixon line!" I don't know where that came from. A bunch
of the guys were fighting the other day about whether or not
Maryland is considered The South. But that's it. That's the secret
code phrase. Use it well, my pretty one.*

    *I guess I should be going now. My turn to drive laps around
the compound and listen to AC/DC with this douche bag
Robertson. I just don't think AC/DC suits the desert night. I love
you and miss you, my Annie. This will all be done soon enough.
It's already been almost two months. Can you believe it? Of course
you believe it. I said so. Ahhhh.*

    Love and kisses and hugs for you. XOXO. Yours,
    David

Secret code phrases? Secret fucking code phrases!??! Yeah, that's
cute and all, but when I take my boy back from the army, I do hope I
can chisel the army out of my boy. Below the Mason-Dixon line.
We've both never even been.

7

*T*oday I'm calling my book *Time Out for Karma*, because I've realized that with David gone I finally have more time to pursue semialtruistic[25] deeds. Back in college I was really into helping out for all the different awareness weeks, and I even spent every Thursday night of my junior year playing dodgeball with about twenty Mexican-American children in a school gymnasium while their parents took free NGO-sponsored English classes.[26] But since I started teaching full time and since I started snuggling David Peterson full time, my life has managed to squeeze out any aspect of service. And what's scarier is that until very recently, I hadn't even noticed.

I was standing in the kitchen section of Home Depot looking at different patterns of shelf paper. You know, the kind where you peel that back off and stick the top layer inside your cupboards so they look pretty and are easy to clean. It was between a classic red gingham and this floral print that reminded me of a favorite dress I had in elementary school. I had never used shelf paper before. It wasn't a poor college student necessity, but that morning as I moved my cereal boxes into ABC order, the thought of a lovely patterned floor on the shelf struck me as nice. Nice and organized. Put together. With it. A twenty-four-year-old with shelf paper is a twenty-four-year-old with her ducks in a row. If there had been a shelf paper at Home Depot with ducks on it, particularly ducklings, I surely would have chosen it.

---

[25] 100% true altruism?! Does that even exist? Does the word itself leave space for a sliver of selfish intentions? I certainly do hope so.

[26] Christ, those dodgeball games were fun.

But as I stood there, debating the aesthetic future of the DARK IN-SIDES OF MY FUCKING PANTRY, I suddenly changed my mind. Who was I kidding? Shelf paper? What an indulgent waste. What a load of crap.

So I decided that I need to throw positive energy back into the universe—not behind closed doors. I have shamefully chosen not to spend time with the First Wives Knitting Club. I even lied about be-longing to a book club. There is something in me (hopefully warm; hopefully patient; hopefully kind) that can affect change or provide assistance to other humans who might need it. And though it's only about 59 percent altruistic of me, I figure giving something back might just line my luck up right. David, I am helping the community to preserve your precious limbs!

I knew I couldn't handle any more children. It wouldn't be fair to my students to over-saturate my life with kiddies and risk burning out my patience and my mysteriously abundant cheer. I also knew that helping animals would make me cry. And really, it was a human con-nection that I craved. So fund-raising—though donations save sooo much—didn't seem right either.

I thought this out as I wandered through the lumber aisles of Home Depot, enjoying the wafting scents of cedar and pine, occasionally stop-ping to rub my fingers along the prickly grain. And then I saw this cou-ple. They were old. So very very old. The man was pushing a cart with just three tiny things in it. And the woman was saying something about how they didn't really need a tool shed. She said, "Frank, you're not even supposed to use a hacksaw anymore." I could tell she had one of those hairstyles that must get "set" once a week at the salon. I imagined her name to be Dorothy or Wilma. I hoped very much that it was Wilma. And that's when I figured it out. Helping old people! A nursing home! An old folks' home! A sterile assisted-living complex! Surely therein lies a poor old soul who needs a hand with letter writing or reading out loud or maybe just talking about *The Golden Girls* or something.

I left Home Depot without a single purchase, and I thought about old folks the entire way home. An old woman (or man, whatever) will want to talk about herself. She'll have one hundred years of stories rattling around in a brain that no one really pays attention to. Except I'll be paying attention, and I'll ask questions, and we'll never ever talk about boring little me. Maybe we'll watch old films together and she'll tell me about how her dead husband looked just like Clark Gable when he was young. And that on their honeymoon cruise they pretended he actually was Clark Gable and he signed autographs for all the other guests. Oh, those were the days. She'll laugh. I'll laugh. It will be so awesome.

When I got home I searched for nursing homes online. There are three within ten miles of my house, and I decided that Violet Meadows sounded like a promising name. Gentle violets swaying in a breeze. Clean, crisp sheets and giggling exercise sessions in wheelchairs. I gave them a call.

"Hi, my name is Annie Harper. I teach third grade at Franklin Elementary, and I'm looking for a volunteer job." The woman on the phone sighed. It was one of those super exasperated sighs, and I wondered what I had done wrong.

"Sorry, sweetheart, no kids here. The little ones are just too germy. We don't allow groups of children on premises for the safety and health of our residents."

"No, no. That's not what I mean. *I* just want to volunteer. By myself. Alone."

"Oh, well, in that case, you will need to come by between ten and five on a weekday and fill out an application with our volunteer coordinator."

"Okay. Great. Thank you. I'll be by tomorrow. Thanks." I hung up the phone and made myself some popcorn. I know it's supposed to give you cancer, but I stood right in front of the microwave staring into the semitranslucent door and watching the bag spin and swell. Just like my heart, I thought. Add some new force and heat to it. Watch it grow grow grow. Taste good. Feel better. Share. *This* is how the universe functions.

The Violet Meadows Retirement Center is completely gray inside. I guess I shouldn't be too surprised. I know these kinds of homes are expensive and that extra funds are probably not spent on snazzy interior design. Maybe I can propose a paint day? I imagine paint rollers with super long handles so any wheelchaired octogenarian with enough arm strength can help out. Maybe we'd play big band music while we work. But as soon as I see the first little clump of residents, half of them snoozing and drooling in front of a fuzzy television screen of MacGyver scaling a wall, I realize that painting isn't too likely at all.

The volunteer coordinator is also the activities coordinator, and she has three of these creepy kitty bobblehead dolls affixed to the top of her computer monitor. They're made of felt-covered plastic, and the way they bobble is nothing like the way a real cat would actually move. Her office is just a little more pleasant than what else I've seen of Violet Meadows, and I see that her calendar has *X*s marked over each passed day.

Promise promise promise. I promise on every healthy, vital organ I have NEVER to do this.

"So, Annie, what are you interested in helping out with? We can get you a conversation partner. We have plenty of residents who are sick of each other and eager to converse with a new face."

She says this without a flicker of enthusiasm and with a distance and disgust that freaks me out. Like the residents are rabid dogs that need someone to calmly make hushing noises while slipping trays of food through a cage door.

"Yeah. Perfect. Exactly. Sounds just right. Sign me up." I fill out this questionnaire about myself that the woman (her name is Jean) pulls from a faded red folder that looks older than me. It asks questions about my employment history, my interests, what kind of books I read and what kind of movies I like. It reminds me of e-mail forwards that would get passed around in college. Except no Bud Light vs. Coors Light or top vs. bottom type provocative stuff.

When I finish, Jean asks me a few questions about my availability, how much time I can commit to, and whether I've ever been convicted of a felony. She says she'll give me a call. As I'm trying to shuffle quietly down the corridor toward the exit, I hear a *pssst* behind me. It's the kind of noise my ears pick up all the time when eight-year-olds try to pass notes during silent reading. It's a noise meant to grab someone's attention in a gentle, sneaky way. It is just so strange turning cautiously around to find the noise maker a white-haired, robe-wearing, curvy-backed old woman. I say hi.

"Well now, Francine," she says to me, slowly and like she's said it four thousand times before, "it's about time you got your ass out of that whorehouse and in here to see me. It's about time." I do that classic head check behind me thing to see if some Francine has appeared behind me in the hall. It's empty, and I start to say something like *no, no, I'm sorry, I'm not.* And then I stop. The woman sighs and asks me if I'm going to come on into her parlor or not. I'm frozen. Just then Jean comes shuffling out of her office. She tells me she's sorry and that Mrs. Jameson is just confused.

"Let me walk you to the door," she says. And we're not even that far away. Mrs. Jameson is still leaning against the door jam of her "parlor," and unless the batteries in her hearing aids are dead, of course she can hear us. Of course she can hear fat Jean and her loose, uncensored mouth say to me with a harsh, grating tone, "Don't worry, Annie. I won't pair you up with anyone delusional."

Jesus Fucking Christ. I figure this whole deal might be a bit depressing. Once I get back home I eat a bowl of cornflakes for dinner. I slather them in honey and lactose-free milk and think about Mrs. Jameson in her parlor. Hoping that Francine will actually pay a visit someday.

"Old folks, Annie? Damn, you are such a sap. But in a good way. Like a cute sap." There is a long, staticky pause. The heavy breathing of the miles between us. "Sounds like an okay idea, but if you were too busy for Angela Henderson, how do you have time to do this?" I re-explain to him that I wasn't too busy for Angela Henderson, I think she makes great pigs in blankets and is a totally sweet lady, but I just wasn't into sitting around and griping about this stupid ride we're all on. I think I succeeded at least a tiny bit in showing him my side of the story, but I could still sense a bit of hurt in his voice because I had chosen strange old ladies over the wives of the men he was surely growing closer to. Can't say I blame him too much.

"So how's everything? You guys getting along? Anything awful happen lately?"

"Aww. No not really. Same old tra.[27] There was some rumor floating around about Jessica Simpson coming to our base to give a concert. But it didn't take long for us to figure out it was bullshit. The XO even had to make an official announcement.

"XO? Kisses? Hugs?"

"What?"

"What does XO mean?"

"Commanding officer. Jeez, Annie. I feel like I've told you that a hundred times."

"Sorry. But anyway, that's too bad."

---

[27] "Tra" is a word I made up in college that means "stuff." Mostly boring stuff. Or even annoying stuff.

"What's too bad?"

"About no Jessica Simpson."

"Whatever. She's a ditz. She'd probably call us the navy or some-thing."

"Yeah."

So basically I'm the worst phone talker ever. And whenever David and I have a conversation like this, after it's over, I end up sprawling on my bed and inventing fourteen different things I could have said to make it better. Or else I write myself some notes of what we should talk about next time. Maybe when I get my oldie conversation part-ner, I'll have all sorts of amusing anecdotes to spout off. I could even pick up some charming 1940s vernacular. *What the dickens have you been up to, David? Good heavens, I miss you so, darling.* I also resolve to make a cheat sheet (The teacher must always stress the cheat sheet!) with all of David's abbreviations. And then I won't waste precious phone time asking for the same old silly definitions.

On my first day as an official Violet Meadows volunteer, I wake up early and eat Cream of Wheat for breakfast. I think about what hav-ing dentures must feel like and if one has ghost memories of the ex-teeth. When I arrive at the home, Jean leads me to the room of my new conversation partner, Mrs. Loretta Schumacher, rattling off facts about the resident like she's trying to sell me a used car. "She's (a) ninety-three. Been here (on the lot) for six years now. One of our sharper ones in her nineties (solid engine). Doesn't stress much (good tires). Keeps her room clean (leather interior). Has moderate arthritis (a shimmy). Diabetes (slow oil leak). I think that's it. Nice lady. You two should have fun. Here we are." Jean has that jiggly tricep arm fat (known as the dreaded "chalkboard flab" in my profession), and it quivers as she knocks on the door. Its trembling reminds me that I'm kind of trembling. I don't even have a moment to consider why I'm nervous because before Jean has a chance to lower her reverberating arm, Mrs. Loretta Schumacher has opened the door and is standing right in front of us like she's been waiting in this exact place all afternoon.

"Good afternoon, Mrs. Schumacher. This is Annie Harper. She's a volunteer. Here to chat with you for a bit."

"How do you do, Miss Harper?" Mrs. Schumacher extends a weathered hand to me and I take it, surprised that it feels soft and robust at the same time.

"Very well, thank you. Pleased to meet you."

"We'll see about that in an hour or so, sweetheart. Right? Don't be pleased to meet me until you've met me and until you've sat here in my lousy room for a bit of time. Huh?" I laugh nervously and steal a look at Jean, who is blank, not amused, probably planning her next four years of vacation days.

"Okay. Um. Sure." That is what I actually say. Brilliant, I know. An amazing representation of my oh-so-articulate generation. Jean backs out the door and shuts it with a gentleness that I didn't expect from her.

"I have two chairs, you know. Please do take a seat."

"Oh. Thank you. Thanks." I pull a folding chair away from the wall, and it makes this loud sticky sound like it hasn't moved for years. I imagine a mop being swabbed around it once a week for a decade. There's this dirty muck crusted around the base: the buildup of solitude. Loretta slowly lowers herself into a wooden rocker by the window. It's exactly the kind of thing you see in nursing homes in movies. I'm stunned that Hollywood didn't make up the detail and that Loretta is actually afforded the luxury of a chair that can bring motion into what is probably a nearly stagnant existence.

"Well," I say, "Nice day out. Supposed to snow tomorrow."

"Do you like poker?" Loretta fires this out all sharp tongue. Like an accusation.

"Poker?"

"Yeah, you know. Texas Hold 'Em. Five-Card Stud. Tramps 'n' Floozies."

"Tramps 'n' Floozies?" I imagine Loretta wavering on the edge of sanity, mixing her card games with the titles of pulpy Western novels she once read. I'm picturing her, all ninety-three years and raisiny, vamped up in some ruffly Western gown with an ace slid seductively down her bodice. She's asking for another whiskey and I'm smiling. And Loretta sees me smiling, and she's taking my smile for a yes. Yes, I love poker. She reaches down to her left into a satchel that's hanging from the armrest of her rocker. I figure she's pulling up a deck of cards. Tattered, sticky cards that I'll watch her rigid, unyielding fingers attempt to shuffle properly before dealing them out. And what will we bet? Cough drops? First dibs on the style section of Sunday's paper?

Loretta hands me a small piece of black plastic, and as I realize that it's not a deck of cards at all, she says, "I'll give you the easy one." I turn the portable video poker device over in my hands and read its name. *Power Pocket Poker.* Loretta has pulled a pair of reading glasses from her rocker's satchel and has already fired up her machine. "Oooh. Pair of queens," she says.

And I don't know what to think about it. We're not talking. We're not talking about the old days when she'd make lemonade on Sundays and walk her toddling grandchildren in the park. We're not flipping through vitamin catalogs and discussing the positive effects of riboflavin on the kidneys. She isn't smiling a toothy, denture smile and I'm not breaking age boundaries and transcending generational gaps and laughing recklessly as my youth absorbs into the dull, gray walls. We're playing video poker.

"Hey, Loretta," I say after a minute, "I just got a full house."

"I told you that was the easy one. Last month I hit it big. Royal straight flush. Hearts!" We play for another thirty minutes or so, announcing our more daring bets and triumphant hands. And though the beepy-beep-beepness of the games grates on my ears, sounding like the erratic chirp of a faltering heartbeat monitor on some dramatic medical TV show, the way that Loretta says, "Let's go. Let's go now, darlin'," while she presses the deal button is actually kind of nice.

8

*T*oday I'm calling my book *Without an Artifact*, because this is a war that will produce no yellowed envelopes with patriotic stamps and no tiny ration coupons for butter. David and I speak over garbled satellite phone lines and exchange electronic messages that I will probably delete by accident with the latest promotional announcements from Victoria's Secret.[28]

David calls late late late at night. It's after midnight, and I'm still up because of a certain pint of a certain lactose-stuffed frozen dessert.

"My Annie Woman!"

"My David Man!"

"How are you, babe? Did I wake you?"

"No, I've been up. Not feeling too well."

(Delay, delay, delay)

"I'm sorry. You got a cold or something?"

"No, I had ice cream. So things are a bit rumbly down there. You know, below the Mason-Dixon line." I snort at myself. Pleased with the way I slipped it in. Finally. It's a crapshoot how long the mail takes anyway.

"You got my letter! You used the code!" David is nearly giddy about it. And I smile too. Despite the lousy connections, it's rare for

---

[28] Perhaps I'll start printing out all my antiwar/anti–George W. forwards that old friends from college send on classy parchment paper and stash them in some fancy chest at the foot of my bed. Now that sounds like an artifact!

his voice to sparkle like this—for it to inflect the kinds of tones that cause pictures of his smile to pop up in my mind.

I tell David about Loretta and the video poker and how she's already called me "honey" twice. I wait until I've painted a clear picture of Loretta and her rocking chair saddlebag and the way her eyes nearly close when she smiles. And then I tell him that Loretta's dead husband, Ron, was in the navy.

"He served in World War II and Loretta didn't see him for eighteen months!" I'm almost oddly jubilant. Like if she can do it, I can do it. And if he knows she did it, there's no way he'll ever think that we might fail. If anything, knowing Loretta's story will make things easier.

"Yikes."

"Yeah, and the whole time he was gone, she never spoke to him on the phone once."

"Jesus. I guess that really puts it in perspective." (Delay, delay, delay) "Annie?"

"Yeah, I'm here. I'm just really glad we have the phone. But at the same time, we'll have fewer artifacts."

"Artifacts?"

(Delay, delay, sniff, delay) And then I explain to David what I mean about the artifacts. He promises to send me even more letters on the fancy paper and some sand from the Iraqi desert in one of those mini room-service ketchup bottles they give out in his MREs.[29] He says it's almost like a vial.

"Not souvenirs, David. Artifacts. Things we don't create on purpose,

---

[29] Meal Ready to Eat. It's a foil packet of food kind of like you get on airplanes. Except the nutritional content is designed to make your poop really dry so you don't have to wipe much and can go days without having to wash your crusty bum. Ick! Definitely take this part out of the real book, Annie.

but objects that simply exist and tell us something about an event or time."

"Whoa, Annie. What, were you like, secretly an anthropology major? Why don't you keep a journal or something? Aren't you keeping a journal?[30] I tell David that it's late and I'm sorry for being so odd and that I must have been having that dream about the dinosaur bones again or something. He tells me he loves me anyway and wishes he were sleeping in my bed with me so he could calm me down when I start digging through the sheets in a wild search for petrified femur bones. I swear to god, I'm such a numskull.

I'm hoping Loretta will help, though. She's most certainly my number-one role model now. Back when there was no e-mail and no satellite phones, she was strong, committed—a full house of nonstop love. And she made it. Captain Ron came back, and they picked up their life together where they'd left off. I guess this would be a good time to mention something about my own commitment. David and I never actually discussed the option of putting our relationship on hold while he was away. For me, I resented the situation so intensely that I wasn't going to let WAR win and put an end to all my giant love fun. It can't take us too, I thought. After college, we knew deployment was inevitable. David was lucky enough that he got to stay in Washington and wasn't shipped out to an ugly brown base in Bellybutton, Kansas, or something. He found out he'd be staying at Fort Lewis rather close to graduation, and just weeks later, I got my teaching job at Franklin Elementary here in Tacoma. It was perfect. Easy

---

[30] I have not told David about this journal. My pre-memoirs. My womanly memoirs. My femoirs. My fem Wars! It'll be more touching when I hand over the publisher's bound proofs for his approval. Sometimes I feel deceptive for not sharing my authorial aspirations, but doesn't everyone secretly kind of want to be a writer/rocker/movie star/artist? I'll tell him someday. I promise.

cheesy, right? We had a good three-month warning before he left. And it was about a month before the stupid flag-waving departure, while on the road trip/camping excursion, when I learned that David was a little scared of the commitment himself. It was one of the nights we'd splurged for a motel room and I had woken up alone just after dawn—tiny slivers of light peeking through the heavy, floor-length window drapes. He had left two notes on his pillow. One said that he'd gone to get coffee and doughnuts. The other was vastly more serious, and even after he gave it to me, we never talked about it. I tucked it into the jeans I wore for the entire vacation, and it's been sitting in this basket by my washing machine for months now. I regret that I accidentally washed the note at least once, rendering it nearly illegible. But I'm proud to say that I remember its contents verbatim.

Dear Annie: I can't get out of what I'm doing. The federal government would have my balls. But if you ever want out of what we're doing, the laws of your heart are yours and yours alone. Love, David.

I imagine this is one of the most sentimental artifacts that David Peterson has ever produced. I feel like he should get some medal for his uniform because he wrote such an awesome note. I actually chuckled when I first read it, thinking that David was being melodramatic. I know myself. I know my heart and that I govern it and that I love you. Duh. Thanks for the reminder, Lieutenant Peterson, sir.

But now that I'm in the thick of this whole thing, I kind of get what he's saying. NOT THAT I WANT TO QUIT, GENTLE READER. But if I need to bow out at some point, if I can't take another moment of the Super (lame) Army Girlfriend Show, it's a sort of a comfort to know that he's already given me that option. Declared permanence is rather scary. Shouldn't we always be free to change our minds?

So I'm becoming one of those slacker teachers. It's only my third year and I'm already floundering into pathetic stock art projects. I nearly cried in the supply closet when I pulled out a full pack of brown construction paper knowing the skeptical and disappointed looks I'd get when I told my class to trace their hands and attempt to render the silhouettes into reasonable likenesses of turkeys. They've passed kindergarten; they'll call me on my bullshit creativity.

I'm out for a drink with Gus and I'm telling him this. We're at this bar under South Tacoma Way that's shaped like a teapot. The actual building, a teapot. Like a construction paper cutout, but concrete. Bob's Java Jive has a jungle motif inside, and rumor has it that back in the seventies Bob kept real live monkeys in the bar. Gus takes a sip of his beer and says, "Damn, Annie. That is low. Hand turkeys?" He's going through one of his sketchpad phases again, and I'm trying not to look to see if he's drawing me.[31] Gus likes to come to this bar on weeknights for the people watching. I don't tell him it was a regular hangout for David and his army friends and that sometimes I'd get dragged onto the stage for karaoke renditions of Queen songs. Despite his burly physique and the way he can occasionally bark like a hockey coach, David has a lovely falsetto.

"I'm sure you can think of something else. Why don't you just steal ideas off the Internet? Art doesn't matter much anyway. As long as you keep the booger pickers up on their three *R*s." Gus half looks up from

---

[31] When we first went away to college Gus would mail me sketches of all the new friends he'd made. It was always quite amusing when I finally met the people in person or saw them in actual photographs. After having the sketches for so long, it was hard not to notice their cartoony features—droopy earlobes; catlike eyes; this one poor guy with a birthmark the shape of Ohio.

his sketch pad and half smiles with the far side of his face so all I can really see is a tiny sliver of a smirk.

"I can't believe you just said that, asshole."

"I know," he laughs. "Neither can I."

I order us another round of two-dollar beers and Gus asks about my old lady. He's been very excited about the whole thing. He said some of his best friends back in Dominica were senior citizens. "They were the first people there to actually trust me," he once said.

"You mean Mrs. Schumacher?" He nods. "She's pretty awesome, I guess." I tell Gus about the video poker and that it was in fact quite impersonal and boring, but that later, on my second visit, she told me about her husband being in the navy. He says I can't expect to be all bosom buddies with her right away and that fostering a genuine friendship takes time. I say that maybe she doesn't have much time—she is ninety-three.

"Try and speed things up then." Gus looks up from his sketch pad and turns it around to face me. It is me. The eyes, the nose, the dark, spastic hair. Except I am old. Gus has sketched an alarmingly detailed age progression of my face. It's actually quite elegant, but I don't tell him that. Instead, I say that it's a bit haunting and thanks for the obvious Botox job around my smile.

"How do I speed things up then?" I ask. "How do we get to bosom buddies faster?" Gus has returned to the sketch, accessorizing my portrait with a tiny, formal hat and a lace collar.

"First, you have to ditch the video poker," he says. "Pick up something more clever and interactive." Interesting. David told me earlier that day that we should watch Humphrey Bogart movies. Lots of interaction there when Miss Harper is falling asleep.

"Like what sort of interactive?" I ask, plucking the tab off my beer can and staring off toward a huge jar of pickled eggs.[32]

---

[32] Yes, this bar sells pickled hard-boiled eggs. I've seen David and his friends actually eat them.

"Like backgammon." Gus says this like it's the most obvious an-swer in the world.

We each drink a few more beers, and Gus tells me about how his Dad is pissed because Gus is spending Thanksgiving with his girl-friend's family. I say that I'd probably be irked too, considering they've only been dating for a couple months.

"Months schmonths," Gus says. "Gina's mom owns a fancy restau-rant with three-hundred-thread-count linens. I know, I deliver them. How could I pass up such fine dining? I invited my dad to join us. He's just never been one for holiday mingling unless his fellow Rotarians are involved."

"Well, Gus. You must be serious about this girl. When do I get to meet her?"

"I am serious. Serious about good food." He takes a handful of beer nuts and sloppily shoves them into his mouth. Gus has always been reluctant to discuss his relationships with anyone. He's the kind of person who avoids looking vulnerable at all costs. I only remember his heart being broken once, after our sophomore year of college. He spent the summer working for one of those college student painter organizations, and I don't think he ever changed his clothes. I'd come over in the evenings to hang out or go walk around or something, and he'd be lounging around in his splattered, stinky coveralls blasting the Who in his bedroom and reading Neruda poems. And he wouldn't talk about it with me, which angered me at the time. I wanted to help and he was all brooding and clamming up. A few years later, just after I started seeing David, Gus finally started asking me for a bit of rela-tionship counsel. Valentine's Day was coming up, and he wanted to make this girl a mosaic of heart patterns out of chewed-up gum. They'd only been dating for a few weeks, and she was one of those cynical, alternative chicks who loved *The Vagina Monologues* and hated all the traditional flowers and fluff of a commercialized Valentine's Day. This girl, I think her name was Echo or Hope or something, also had this very strong aversion to gum. Like it absolutely disgusted her. She even had to leave rooms when people were smacking it with their mouths open. So Gus decided that if he could take two things that she so vehemently loathed (already-been-chewed gum and V-Day hearts) and combine them into a genuine expression of adoration and beauty, then that would be the ultimate act of kindness. He knew it was a risky move, so he called me up to consult. And me, having no problem with casual gum chewing or red and pink M&Ms, told Gus to go for it. So he did. He left it on her doorstep with a single red rose. She never called him back. Not even to say "thanks, but no thanks." I assured Gus that it had nothing to do with the gum mosaic, that the gum mosaic was a truly sweet gesture. There must have been other issues, I told him. Or someone else. He wasn't completely smitten with her, so he recovered quickly. He still talks about the glory of the mosaic and how he wishes he could get it back somehow.

When we leave the bar, Gus hands me the sketch of my ancient self.

"Keep this," he says, "as a reminder of the future. Or as a souvenir of today."

It's the Wednesday before Thanksgiving, and I'm stoked because we have early release. The school lets out a whole hour early so kids can go help their parents peel potatoes or something. As a teacher you're not supposed to act stoked about these things. You're supposed to say things like "utilize our time" and "make the most of our shortened math period" and not be secretly thinking about the four glorious days you won't be making shushing noises or listening to stupid kids mispronouncing "winning" as "whining" and then actually whining when you tell them they're wrong.

The final bell just rang, and I'm in the middle of calling the roll.

"Damian Matthews?" I say. I like to use full names for all of my students during roll call. It just feels more adultlike. And that way, Thomas Peterson and Thomas Espinoza don't have to be the only two-named kids in the class. Damn, I am so fair. Despite the pile of future brown turkeys waiting on my desk, I like to think I'm still kind of a good teacher. Damian chirps his usual timid response as someone knocks on my classroom door. No one knocks on classroom doors here. The principal, the admin staff, even Carrie simply barges in during the middle of class to borrow books or check if I'm going out for lunch or not. And I'm such a space case that I don't say anything. I don't even *do* anything. The knock again. Finally, all the way from the fourth row, Max Schaffer takes initiative and shouts a very polite "Come in!"

It takes a moment for the visitor to manage the doorknob because his arms are full with a brimming and seemingly heavy cardboard box. At first, all I can see are the hands—crusty and thick-knuckled— and for a moment they're alarming. Who is this gnarly, box-toting oaf stumbling into my roll call? Before I can muse any further or generate any actual fear, he drops the box in front of the whiteboard and stands up. Gangly and slightly panting, cheeks flushed, he straightens his tie (a tie?!?!!!). "Good morning, boys and girls. My name is Gus."

"Good morning, Gus." My class rings with sweet obedience. My darling, precious robots.

"Now everybody hold up one hand like this." Gus holds up his right hand in front of his face, palm out. My robots obey. "Now what does it look like to you?"

"A hand," five robots say.

"A turkey!" shouts another with a sharp memory from last year.

"Right," says Gus, shooting a mischievous glance toward me. "But this is a lame, two-dimensional turkey. Now turn your hands like this." He twists his wrist so his thumb stares him in the eye. "Today, my friends, we're going beyond the restricting world of two-dimensional turkeys. Who wants to eat a flat wimp of a turkey? Nobody, right?"

"Right!" shout the robots. How easily a stranger can rile them up!

"Today, fellow artists of Miss Harper's kick-ass class,[33] we are going to make plump, feisty, 3-D turkeys!" Suddenly Gus sounds like he's advertising a monster truck rally, and all my kids are hooting and whipping their mullets around in approval.

Gus unloads his box of supplies: buckets, mysterious bags of chemicals that he assures me are nontoxic, paints and brushes, and three ancient-looking hair driers. The kids giggle as he guides their hands into the vat of peppermint-scented casting goop. He gently holds their waists as they stand on a stool and dump the plaster into the molds of their personalized turkeys. Carrie comes over when she hears the ruckus of the hair driers, and by the time the one-thirty early-release bell shrilly cuts through the air, my class has twenty-eight fully formed, brightly painted, kick-ass, 3-D turkeys. I equip them each with plastic turkey bags in case anything is still wet. I prompt them in an enthusiastic "Thank you, Gus!" where all their robot voices are tuned to the most genuine tones. Gus stands at the door as kids file out and says things like "Gimme some turkey skin" to prompt the last couple stragglers in spirited high fives.

The last kid is gone, and I'm sitting on top of my desk, where I'd spent nearly the whole day perched and peacefully observing. I had even stolen a few minutes during the painting phase to go check my e-mail, write David, and even look up pumpkin pie recipes online. "Thanks, Gus," I say as he walks toward my desk. "You've got plaster in your hair."

"You mean turkey guts. And I'll get it later."

"No really, thanks. The kids had a great time. That was great. You're great. Thanks a million. I really mean it."

"It was my pleasure. Those mugwumps[34] aren't half bad. Don't

---

[33] I cringe when Gus says "kick-ass," knowing the damage control I'll have to perform later.

[34] Gus uses some strange words that I think he steals from obscure fantasy novels.

know what you're always griping about." Gus smiles and starts to reassemble his supplies in the box. "I'm your friend, Annie. I'm supposed to help you during this rough time. And here." He pulls a rectangular leather case out of the box. Something he hadn't used for the art project. "This is for you and Mrs. Schumacher. Let me know if you need me to explain the rules."

I tell him that it's actually not so rough thus far as I flick open the metal latch on the slender case and open it like a book. The smooth stone circles cascade down my lap and plink and roll across the floor. Gus laughs without even trying to stifle it and says he'll help me pick up the black ones. He says he has to get going to meet Gina and I'm on my own to find all the elusive white pieces that are already blending into the floor. I thank him again as he drops a handful of pieces into the felt-lined box. It makes such a cozy, comforting noise.

"Talk to you later, Annie. And happy Turkey Day!"

Then he leaves.

9

*T*oday I'm calling my book *Almost Too Ripe for Squeezing*, because I'm getting sick of people hugging me all the time. Acquaintances whom I've never ever hugged before somehow instantly feel the need to drape their arms around me the moment they find out David is in Iraq. I even bumped into my high school volleyball coach the other day at the drugstore, and he'd somehow heard about David and dammit, Coach Tskuda—who'd always opted for a high five over a congratulatory shoulder pat—dove right in for the full-out embrace. And while I was wrapped in it, forced to pierce the toxic sphere of his aftershave bubble, all I could think about was whether he was assessing the atrophied state of my arm muscles.

A SMALL LIST OF OTHER AWKWARD HUGS

Don, the school janitor, as I was supervising the lunch line.

Max Schaffer's father (but not his mother) during a parent/teacher conference.

My Uncle Richard during a commercial break in a Thanksgiving Day football game.

And I'm sure there are others I've already forced myself to forget. Sure, I understand that it's supposed to be nice and all—people expressing their sympathy or empathy[35] and letting me know that they're sorry I'm in such a shitty position. But really, all those sap-infused hugs and saggy eye corners and *It must be tough*s and *keeping you in*

---

[35] Fuck. I can never get those two straight.

*our prayers*es are really just over the top. It's making me feel like David is already dead. Like I should be worrying more than I am actually worrying and that I'm not crying enough while I toil away at the hoop of my gimongous love-and-loneliness quilt. I mean, tapestry. Whatever.

I spend Thanksgiving at my Aunt Carol's house, and she is the Hug-Master2003. Carol and her partner Rebecca,[36] who are both usually so cool—standing beside me in fiery political debates, keeping me from flinging gravy across the table in response to Uncle Richard's über-Christian, pro-life tirades—were out-of-character, out-of-control schmaltzy.

"I know a really good therapist, Annie. Are you seeing someone?"

"No. I'm not, but I don't think . . ." Carol reaches across the coffee table to place her hand on my hand, which is not looking for affectionate touch, but really just trying to pick up my coffee.

"Rebecca's sister's husband spent six months in Afghanistan with the National Guard, and she saw this doctor who specializes in this kind of thing.[37] She loved him. Helped her a ton. She was spacing out at work. Her whole herb garden died because she just wasn't herself. And she counts on that basil each year to make her famous Christmas pesto." I don't grow herbs. I want to tell Aunt Carol that, but I don't. I keep listening. "And Dr. Grinstead, he even directed Janice toward this organic farm out in Puyallup where she was able to buy basil in bulk and make the pesto after all. We have half a dozen jars or so from last year. Rebecca, go grab Annie some of Janice's pesto."

I think about Janice, my aunt's girlfriend's sister whom I've never met, all chipper and optimistic, tearing leaves of basil off impressively

---

[36] Even after eight years, a shared queen-sized bed, and a very openly loving relationship, my mother still calls Rebecca Aunt Carol's *friend*.

[37] Specialize? So what is he during peacetime? A florist? A mailman?

green plants and tossing them cheerfully into a food processor. Dr. Grinstead has mellowed her neurosis, pepped up her melancholy loneliness, and replaced her worry with all-natural, pesticide-free produce.

"We can give you his number, Annie." Rebecca has returned, hands proffered forth with the pesto. There's a perfect bow of red ribbon tied around the lid.

"Sure," I say. "What the hell. Why not?"

The Saturday after Thanksgiving I visit Mrs. Schumacher. I have to schedule all my visits in advance, and that kind of bothers me. Jean—arm-flab Jean—says it has always been the policy. They just can't have people dropping by unexpectedly at all hours. She gives me no reason as to why it's impossible. *Policy* is apparently reason enough. I reckon it's because there are certain times when the staffers tranquilize the residents or tube feed them for days on end so they can dominate the televisions and read *Soap Opera Digest* undisturbed.

I rap lightly on Mrs. Schumacher's door, and she says, "Come on in, Annie." It pleases me enormously that she knows it's me and that she says my name like I belong to her. My dad's mother died when I was young, and my mother's mother has always lived in Arizona, never able to leave the sun for more than a few days at once. As Grandma Ardelle gets older, her condos keep moving closer and closer to the first tee. Presently she claims she can call my grandfather, Bruce, home from the clubhouse by barely raising her voice. *He's usually drinking at the bar and he can hear me. Honestly, we're that close.* None of us grandkids took up golf. They've always been disappointed.

"Good afternoon, Mrs. Schumacher. How are you?"

"It's Loretta, please. And I'm fine. Fit fine shape, actually. Suzanne and I walked three miles yesterday after lunch." I don't know who Suzanne is, and something makes me doubt that Loretta left her room all week. But I smile.

"Wowza. That's quite the trek."

"Yes. Very good for my heart. I used to walk eight miles to high school as a girl. Eight miles!" Oh my goodness gracious. Loretta has pursed her lips in this way that is simultaneously smug and challenging. I'm waiting for her to add "in the snow" or "barefoot" or "leading a cow on a prickly rope." It's eerie when people say exactly what you're expecting them to. Like they're doing it on purpose to freak you out. I wonder if I ever seem so scripted or if I ever say such pat, predictable things on purpose, nudged forward by some easily amused side of my subconscious. What does Loretta expect of me? What does she want me to do? Or bring? Oh shit, I think. I should I have brought something. A potted poinsettia. A copy of *Vogue*. A plate of Thanksgiving leftovers wrapped in foil, the roll prebuttered. Something makes me think that the Violet Meadows Retirement Center doesn't even use real butter. They slather frozen peas in margarine. White toast with margarine. Squeaky wheelchairs lubed with margarine! I realize I'm thinking too long and not talking and completely failing as a conversation partner. More time. Another moment. She's looking at me, smiling at me in this *I know what you've been up to* sort of way. Like this is exactly what she expected me to do: clam the fuck up. "Any hot hands of poker lately?" I say this after about fifty years of staring, smiling, staggering silence. It's a miracle she's still alive.

"Well, I did win a two-hundred-and-fifty-dollar bet yesterday. That nurse Martha was here when it happened. You can ask her if you don't believe me."

"I believe you," I say.

Silence. Silence. Silence.

Silence!

And then I think about my family at Thanksgiving. My loose-lipped mother, the hugging aunt and her lover, my father piping up at inappropriately high volumes every now and then. Uncle Richard talking through bites of stuffing, parsley pieces dangling off his yellow teeth.

Christ, how they can talk! Talk. Talk. Talk. Question. Question. Question. And oh, the things they asked me![38] And with all my demanded

---

[38] Annie, does David write often? Have you two talked about marriage? Have you seen his living will? Does he have siblings? Where do his parents live? Are you going to take time off when he returns? Can he send you videos via the Internet? What kind of care packages do you send him? Does he need any books or magazines? Have you sent him shaving cream? Don't they always need shaving cream? How often does he call? Are the connections usually good? Have there been any injuries in his unit? Does he carry a gun all the time? What kind of gun is it? Do they have a chaplain in their camp? Do you know the denominational affiliation of the chaplain? Does he sleep well? Do you sleep well? Does he tell you about his dreams? Are you having bad dreams? How are his love letters? Are you saving all the letters? When does he come back? How much longer will he be in the army? Do you think he'll stay in? Have you talked about it? Are you going to eat that drumstick? Are you in some sort of support group? Do you have a flag in your classroom? Do your students say the pledge of allegiance? Do your students know he's gone? Do you watch Fox News? Do you get Fox News? Do you think it's going to be weird when he gets back? Does he complain about the heat? Do you know if he smokes? Do you smoke? Have you been going out much lately? Who are you hanging out with? Are your friends supportive? Would you want to adopt one of our neighbor's kittens? Do you want me to send David my issues of *Reader's Digest*? Can I have his address? Do you want whipped cream on your pie? Have you been losing weight? Are you stressed? Are you miserable? Do you get the *Times* or the *P.I.*? What's the difference in time zones? Can't you just wait until he's back? Wouldn't it be fun to have a welcome-home party? Do you want me to start planning? Is David religious? Did you two ever go to church? Can I send him an annotated Bible? Can he call you much, Annie? How often does David call? What do you talk about? What does he tell you about? Can he e-mail? Can he tell you what he's doing? What is he doing? What's his rank? What does that stand for? Do you think he'll want a government job someday? Would you mind moving to D.C.? Have you ever been to the Holocaust Museum? Do you like museums? Does David like museums? Does he get to watch sports over there? Is he a Seahawks fan? Are you a Seahawks fan? Is the game

answering, it was the first Thanksgiving I didn't fall victim to the agony of severe gluttony. Didn't end up moaning on the floor of the dining room dreaming of elastic waistbands and religious fasting.

"So Mrs. Schu—I mean, Loretta—did your husband write often when he was away?"

"Away?" She looks confused.

"Away at war. Did he have time to write you?"

"Oh, sweetheart, all the time." She smiles and motions for me to take a seat on her bed, and I feel so privileged. Like she's letting me into her front room with the plastic slipcovers and the lamps that are dusted more times than they are ever lit. Her bed is mushier than I expected and better smelling. A bizarre mix of Aqua Net hair spray and chamomile—both chemical and comforting.

Loretta launches into a monologue of love stories. Ron wrote her daily, but the letters usually came in groups of five or six. To save money during the war, she moved back in with her parents in rural Kansas, and they only had a post office box three miles away in town. She rode her bike in every day to check the mail. Rain or shine. And when it was snowy, she hoofed it. She kept the key for the box around her neck on a sturdy gold chain, a first anniversary gift from Ron. Real gold, she said. She still has it. She'd still have the key too, if the post office hadn't made her give it back when she moved.

"And what did he write about?"

He'd tell her he missed her and draw pictures of the two of them together. Cartoons of their wedding day and their future babies. He'd

---

on? Is there any more wine? Annie, can you check the pantry for more wine? Have you sent him a Christmas gift? How long does the mail take to get there? Do you want to go to Arizona for Christmas? Did you know it's eighty degrees there? How hot is it in Iraq, Annie? Do you know how hot? How hot? How hot? Hot hot? Hot? Annie? Annie, do you know? Hot, Annie? Are you hot?

tell her every move his company made and what he had for dinner and where the latest, safest place was to store her precious photograph. In his first aid kit. The lining of his combat helmet. In between double layers of socks. Tucked in the pages of a mini Bible. Right over his heart.

"Do you still have all the letters?"

Of course she kept all the letters! Until they were lost by a shady group of movers when Ron was back and they left Kansas for Washington and a logging job. Loretta is quiet for a few minutes, and I wonder what else the shady movers might have shadily misplaced. Her childhood diary? Some special dried-up flowers?

She's staring out the window, and I take this moment to really look at her. I've been told that I'm not very observant. I always compliment haircuts a week too late. I don't notice when stoplights are erected in places I've never stopped before or when a Tupperware dish of moldy leftovers is festering right at eye level in my refrigerator. So I purposefully try to really take a good, long look at Loretta. The gray frizz of her hair. The tips of bobby pins pointing out of her bun that I imagine are her original bobby pins. The only ones she's ever owned. I can see her pulling them out at night and gently sliding them on to a tattered piece of cardboard with a faded 1930s-style logo. The edges worn round and soft. Or maybe she keeps them in a small aluminum tin that was once the home to the throat lozenges that chased away a 1941 cold. Loretta Schumacher, a woman who has never lost a bobby pin.

Her shoulders are still rather angular, and the smooth curve of her upper back is ever so slight—a tall blade of grass yielding to a very gentle breeze. She's wearing slippers and the kind of wool socks I would guess are unbearably itchy. But then maybe she knit them herself years ago and made sure to choose a soft, nonabrasive yarn. While her husband schlepped missiles around on a submarine, Loretta sat in front of her mother's stately wooden radio, knitting socks and scarves and the optimistic plans for an entire life together.

She breaks the silence by asking me about my Thanksgiving. I divulge a few small details about my family, the kinds of conversations we had. Then we trade horror stories about Jell-O salads and tasty recipes involving canned yams. I tell her that marshmallows and gelatin are both made from the by-products of cooked horse hooves.

"Nonsense," she says. "And I'm made out of cloves and motor oil." I honk out one of those uncontrollable bursts of a laugh and zip my hand up to my mouth to cover the smile. I love Loretta Schumacher. I let her hug me on the way out.

9.5

*C*hapter 9.5 is to be printed in that cool disappearing ink that lasts for a few days but then magically dissolves into reputation-saving blankness. This part will be cut out for sure for sure for sure. Nobody should have to read this shit. Not even a prisoner in a very stringent prison where reading is banned. Even if *he* gets his hands on this chapter because some demented cafeteria worker has rolled a piece of paper up inside his chicken potpie. Even if that prisoner hasn't read a single word in fifteen years and is so starved for print that even just staring blankly at the shape of the letters feels kind of good. Even if he's murdered fourteen babies and raped the entire female population of Alaska. Even if he's stolen every dime from his sick mother and dumped shipload upon shipload of toxic sludge into the ocean on purpose. If he stares at the letters long enough they will start to make sense. But still, even he shouldn't have to read it.

Please kill me now. Or at least lock me up with that prisoner guy and let him have at me with his plastic spork. One last surge of gory joy before he gets caught for reading contraband materials and sent to the chair.

Subject: notes and notes and notes
Date: November 26, 2003 06:22PST
From: missharpercandoit@yahoo.com
To: david.peterson13@us.army.mil

Good Morning, Sunshine of the US ARMY!

You know I'm such a horrible secret keeper, but I'm getting anxious and I have to ask. Did you get the package from my class yet? Huh? Huh!!!? We sent you a totally awesome package. Did you give the notes to your co-workers? Please let me know when you have a chance. Marco Antolini keeps asking if the "big tough soldiers liked our haikus."

Fondly,

Miss H.

Subject: RE: notes and notes and notes
Date: November 28, 2003 03:03PST
From: david.peterson13@us.army.mil
To: missharpercandoit@yahoo.com

Sorry, Annie. I did get the cards and the candy, but I haven't had a chance to look through them or pass them out. You know how it goes. So many people are sending us stuff and we don't really have time to sit around gushing over it all. Love, D.

Subject: RE: RE: notes and notes and notes
Date: November 28, 2003 06:58PST
From: missharpercandoit@yahoo.com
To: david.peterson13@us.army.mil

how long can it take
just seventeen syllables
to read one or two

kind words from afar
of kids who actually care
sad to hear you don't

Subject: RE: RE: RE: notes and notes and notes
Date: November 30, 2003 02:43PST
From: david.peterson13@us.army.mil
To: missharpercandoit@yahoo.com

Annie, Didn't mean to hurt your feelings. Just so much going on
here. I'm sure you can make up something cute to tell the class.
Tell them we loved the poems. We've hung them up in our bunks.
Whatever. Please don't be mad at me. I love you.

Subject: RE: RE: RE: RE: notes and notes and notes
Date: November 30, 2003 06:42PST
From: missharpercandoit@yahoo.com
To: david.peterson13@us.army.mil

Why *don't* you hang one in your bunk?

p.s. I *am* mad.

Subject: RE: RE: RE: RE: RE: notes and notes and notes
Date: November 30, 2003 22:00PST
From: david.peterson13@us.army.mil
To: missharpercandoit@yahoo.com

Because that's where I hang *your* picture.

p.s. You *are* crazy.

So what do you think, Mr. Prisoner? Do you want to claw your eyeballs out? Do you wish your tubesocks were just a little bit longer so
you could fashion them into an effective noose? Don't you think I'm a
melodramatic, overreacting, unsympathetic, selfish prat of a woman?

Is it people like me who remind you why you defied society in the first place?

little by little
the teacher on the home front
her brain turns to mush

10

*T*oday I'm calling my book *So Very Alone*, because I'm having a huge-ass pity party.

Winter break! Winter break! Winter break! Of all the perks of being an educator in America, the glorious chunks of vacation time are certainly up there.[39] Any teacher who claims that three months of luxurious holiday wasn't a factor in choosing a career path is full of crap. Those few weeks between Thanksgiving and winter break pass in a whirl of chaos and cookie crumbs.[40] The kids can't concentrate with the hope of new PlayStations and skateboards glimmering in their eyes, so I usually slack a bit and give in to several long, uninspired sessions of cutting paper snowflakes.

. . . . . .

[39] That and the 15 to 20 percent discount at Barnes and Noble.

[40] Add to that chaos one solid week of reading and watching about Saddam's spidey-hole capture. I didn't write. I didn't cook much. I just stared at that scraggly image of him, searching for some insight or glimmer of what he's really about. I'm a huge fool, I know. But it was somehow particularly captivating without being exciting. I didn't feel like capturing Saddam was going to bring David home any sooner or make him any safer. I can't even figure out if it's making anyone any safer. Happier? Maybe. Some people. Lots, maybe. Now what? Now what? Now what? I almost wanted to dig my own spider hole in my back yard. I'd take a bottle of water, a flashlight, and the latest issue of *Time* magazine. I'd fold myself into the cool, dark space and wait. Maybe that would help things make sense. Who knows?

Last week when I was driving Max to his violin lesson, he asked me about Gus.

"Your friend Gus is pretty cool, Miss Harper. Is he an art teacher?"

"Nope. He's an artist." I told Max about the windows at the Dairy DeLite and how Gus had recently created a winter wonderland where the reindeer have actual fuzz on their antlers.

"That must be so fun," Max said. "Can we paint our classroom windows?"

"Probably not, unfortunately, but I can ask Gus if he needs a helper when he does the Valentine's Day display next month."

"You mean like hearts and kisses and stuff? No, thank you."

"I'm sure you two could make more of it," I said.

"Maybe dinosaurs?" Max asked, and I immediately pictured a T. rex in a slinky red negligee and long, exaggerated eyelashes. It was really a stupid image, but one Gus would probably be willing to try.

"Yeah, maybe."

Later, Max invited me to his holiday violin recital. He told me there would be cookies, punch, and wine for the grown-ups. I asked him if he'd be performing Han Solo, and he actually got my *Star Wars* reference and laughed. "Yes, I do have a Han Solo part," he said. I told him I'd love to go and that I hoped the force would be with him.

Max's concert is Saturday the twenty-third, the day after the last day of school. I drag Gus along because I know Max will be happy to see him. I pick him up at his apartment and we argue in the car whether it's appropriate to bring Max flowers. Gus tells me that eight-year-old boys don't want flowers, don't like flowers, will not know what to do with flowers. I argue that Max is remarkably sophisticated and will both understand and appreciate the traditional gesture. I pull into the florist anyway, we bring the battle inside, and exit shortly after with the compromise of a small potted cactus. Gus was shocked that the florist didn't carry Venus flytraps.

The concert is quite lovely. I was expecting shrill, window-cracking tones and the discomfort of watching young, chubby fingers struggle to emulate the athleticism of movements that were invented by wiry old men who possessed the kind of genius that disregards both pain and hunger. But Max and his small ensemble (a flautist, a pianist, and another violinist) are pretty fucking good. Gus even looks over at me a few times and does that pretentious music-snob nod of approval. Every now and then I look down at the flecks of dried paint on his khaki pants. White and beige and taupe that nearly blend into the fabric. He catches me staring a few times and bounces his legs to the music in response. We exchange smiles. The venue is warm and comfortably lit, and the folding chairs are padded; I could have sat through at least another dozen concertos.

After the performance we drink wine in the lobby with the Schaffers and other miscellaneous family and friends, and though I hardly know anyone and they hardly know me, it all feels so welcoming. "I'm Max's teacher" is all I have to say and it is enough. The mother of the flautist, who is trendy and pretty and seems to be about my age, gives me a weird flirty look and whisper-asks if Gus is my boyfriend. I snort a little bit and drop a big chunk of my sugar cookie. After bending to pick it up I say, "Oh, no. We're just old pals." The woman gives me an odd look, and it's a moment before I realize I've placed the cookie piece from the floor carelessly into my mouth. Her face goes flirty again and she says "Well, he's really cute. Do you know if he's seeing anyone?"

"He is, actually," I say and try to smile back. Who is this woman? Since when do the mothers of Max Schaffer's peers get the hots for goofball Gus Warren? Did she see the paint stains on his pants? Does she know they do not match her designer handbag? I always feel a little guilty for the shock that I feel when women express romantic interest in Gus, but it is perplexing to me. It's not the interest itself, but more

the types of women it comes from. *Really?* I want to say. *Are you sure?*
Are you sure pistachio ice cream is your favorite flavor? Are you sure
you want to watch the *Dune* movie on a Saturday night?

Max loves the cactus and thanks Gus and me in his adorably
proper fashion. We tell him that he was awesome and that we are really glad we came. On the way home we stop by a strip mall so Gus
can pick up a half gallon of eggnog and some whiskey. I drop him off
at Gina's because they have plans to build a gingerbread Taj Majal. It
was Gina's idea—she loves Eastern cultures—and I can tell Gus thinks
it's totally cool. And I agree. I thank him for coming to the recital
with me and warn him not to eat too much frosting.

At home I am bored. And I hate to say I'm bored, because whenever my kids say it, I chide them with "Only boring people get
bored," and I like to think that I actually believe that. It's uncomfortable to admit that I am a boring creature, quietly shuffling through
the world with my heavy, lolling head chock-full of lackluster thoughts
and ideas. I check my e-mail and go to the post office Web site to track
the Christmas package I sent David[41] three weeks ago. The site offers
little information, and I find myself staring blankly at the screen,
twisting my hands in my lap and imagining the package toppling out
of the back of some large truck and getting run over by a tank. Sand
grinding into the soft cotton of the black size-large boxer-briefs. The
shattered screen of the mini DVD player. The shitlike smudge of my
homemade fudge destroying the flawless white of the brand new, tag-
less undershirts. I also included a small chapbook I made with cutout

[41] We have reasonably recovered from that haiku showdown that may or
may not be removed from the real book. Once I talked to him on the phone
about it all, I realized that he did appreciate the work and thoughtfulness of
my students more than his terse and emotionally sloppy e-mails let on. We
made a truce not to e-mail fight, and if something is bugging us to wait until
the phone lines allow us to detangle it. Fair enough.

pictures of food products from grocery flyers, scenery images from travel magazines, and clippings from high-quality linen catalogs: a promise to David of all the caring and nurturing I'll do when he gets back. I told him to circle all his favorite items. I even pasted in several pages photocopied from an encyclopedia of dog breeds. Pick a puppy, I told him. And I'll time everything right so it's potty-trained but still perfectly perky by the time he gets back. We'll name it Georgie, G.I. Puppyface, Tony Fucking Blair, whatever he wants.

All this package disaster fantasizing isn't helping me at all. The anxiety of his smashed gift evolves into the anxiety of his smashed body and then dips into a series of guilty waves because I'm worrying about a stupid package and not the future of a tumultuous country. Or all countries. Or innocent slaughtering. Or the future of democracy. Or all the women in the world who will lose their lovers tonight. But isn't there still such a chance it could be me?

Oh, how the holidays stink of self-absorption! So I decide to give in. I pour myself a glass of wine and light a pine-scented candle. I'm sitting here at my desk with a box of fine chocolates gifted to me by Max Schaffer's parents, and I'm going to fucking indulge by recounting the lovely holidays that I, Annie Harper, have shared with my darling lover, David Peterson. And it's going to make me feel so lavishly consoled. I just know it.

Our First Christmas, Senior Year of College

David and I had only been dating for a few months. All my girlfriends warned me that my gift idea was a little too much for a first holiday together. They had said it was more of a second- or third-year gift and that it'd be better if I just gave him some CDs or a sweater or something. But I was set on it. One of the reference librarians had made one for her high-school-aged son, and I saw her working on it in the basement lunchroom.

"Yeah," she said, "I got all the gym shorts for under ten dollars at the thrift store, and fleece is always on sale in the fabric store this time of year." I ran my fingers across the cool smoothness of the mesh fabric, and it instantly reminded me of how David liked to come to my apartment after his morning ROTC workouts and slide into bed with me. The briskness of his cold skin and slinky mesh workout wear was always invigorating and delightful. I wanted him to know how nice it was. So I made the blanket. It was a simple pattern of squares cut from the gym shorts. A few with the logos of local teams and the cheap plastic lettering of recreational leagues made things a little more interesting visually. The back was all a snuggly red fleece, and the librarian showed me how to simply tie the quilt with yarn rather than actually quilting it.

He loved it. Right away he commented on the contrast of textures and how the bold colors made it seem enticingly capelike. I was so pleased and even more pleased that he too opted not for a safe CD bundle or a lame scarf/hat/mitten set from Banana Republic, but instead surprised me with a shiny chrome blender and a bottle of expensive tequila. "You mentioned once that you wanted to have a Cinco de Mayo party," he said. "I thought you could use this to mass-produce margaritas." We exchanged enthusiastic gracias in the form of giggly hugs and kisses. I didn't gloat to my girlfriends about how the gym shorts blanket[42] was received fantastically. I knew that being in love was vindication enough.

Second Christmas, Mountaineering

David surprised me with a weekend trip to Whistler, this fancy ski village in British Columbia. He made reservations for Martin Luther King, Jr. Day weekend and arranged to have a few days away from the

---

[42] No wonder my blanket-making instincts are now stifled. I've already done it!

base. It was my first year of teaching, and he told me that I'd needed a getaway after the winter break withdrawal. Neither of us had ever skied, and that made it so awesome. It was like discovering a foreign land together, tightening the straps of our rented goggles and fumbling our gloved hands to affix the funny clasps of our lift tickets to our parkas.

David was a natural, slicing graceful lines down the beginners' slope on his first run, while I managed to biff it three times in fifty meters. The third time wasn't my fault, because a bunny—an actual fluffy bunny whose tush was lifting in adorable ways as it hopped along the tree line—had distracted me from heeding my attention to all four pieces of ski equipment at once. David is wonderful because he always takes this kind of thing as legitimate and logical. Like it could have easily been him tumbling from the effects of a serious bunny leer.

The skiing lasted just a few hours before I succeeded in breaking my wrist. He was so concerned and so kind as he carried[43] me to the edge of the slope, where he waved down the medic who later snowmobiled me to the village's small clinic. While I was getting my wrist set, David returned all of our rental equipment and upgraded our suite to one with a more striking view and a real Jacuzzi. Even though I was on heavy painkillers, that night we drank beer and ordered room service nachos while watching crappy movies on the TV and recounting the hilarity of all my various wipeouts. David even invented a way to cradle my wounded wing in a hammock of towels he rigged around the faucet of the Jacuzzi so we could both comfortably bask in its luxury and engage in some pleasant underwater snuggling. "I don't think you can get out of this tub without my help," David said. "I could boil you in here like a lobster." I pulled my good hand above the bubbles and flicked away the pools of water that had gathered in the dips of his collarbones. "This claw still works," I said, and stuck my index finger playfully into one of his nostrils. It's something I do because it's supposed to be gross and shocking,

---

[43] Though I fervently tried to insist I walk.

but if you ever really look inside a nose, or better, feel around a bit inside, it's no less revolting than your average bodily orifice. It took David a while to understand this, but eventually he got it and didn't shriek like a baby when I chose to sneak attack his nose with my pinky.

Third Year, Into Adulthood

David was bound to spending a whole week in his hometown of Portland, Oregon, so we celebrated the holidays together in mid-December. I remember thinking it all felt so grown up and because of that, borderline lame. But really, it was a fantastic day. We drove up to Seattle and spent the morning in the aquarium[44] and the afternoon touring his favorite microbrewery. We were already tipsy when we settled down for a steak dinner, a meal hearty enough to induce the sort of food coma where sitting for two hours during the Pacific Northwest Ballet's *The Nutcracker* was both welcome and almost necessary. Our seats were close enough that I could see the sinewy lines in the arms of the lithe dancers as they flapped and waved with a grace not unlike that of my new octopus idol. Retrospectively, though this outing was pleasant, it was kind of a boring thing to do. See the f-ing *Nutcracker?* I probably won't be due for another session of waltzing gumdrops for a good decade at least.

---

[44] Which was surprisingly lively for a winter morning. I stood in front of the giant octopus's tank for a good half hour watching the fluid movements of the creature playing with this floaty ball toy that would sink—but not all the way—to the bottom of the tank if she stopped whapping it with one of her legs. David stood behind me with his arms around my waist while I kept stammering out stupid phrases like *And it has no bones* and *Can you imagine having that many appendages?* and *What a magnificent organism* and *It's so happy just to play . . . alone.* Later I read about octopuses online and found that they are the only invertebrates known to play. They're that smart.

This Year, With Mountains and Oceans and Deserts Between

Annie: Will fix her hair to suit the tastes of her sweet mother and convince her parents that smothered enchiladas is a traditional Christmas Eve dish in Mexico and a great idea for their own holiday feast. Did Annie mention she's an only child?[45] Her parents will warmly and

---

[45] Sadly, it was probably obvious. You would think a sister or brother would have come up by now, right? I should probably get this out sooner when I write the real book. Ah, the sad, lonely, only child. A fact about myself I've tried my whole life to ignore. I know it sounds strange: trying to hide something that is in fact a lack of something. I don't know when I became aware of the stigmas and stereotypes attached to only children—the selfish personalities due to coddled rearings—or how I decided that ignoring the topic would prevent me from ever being labeled such. And putting my energy into not being a certain way was definitely a distraction from the fact that as a child, I was regularly lonely.

When I get to know people, I don't ask about siblings until the other person asks about siblings. Books, movies, television, everything, all cultures, all stories—most people have siblings. A sister or a brother is an automatic friend and the closest thing in the whole universe to being you. With shared DNA, shared meals, the shared backseats of cars and bathroom sinks and overbites, I've always yearned for that closeness. I've resolved that I long/ have longed/will long for siblings for the rest of my life. Something happened during my birth that rendered my mother's womb unsuitable for further childbearing. In junior high she told me the specifics, and it was so sad and awkward that I never asked again and have since let the details fog up. Ovaries something something. We were driving in her car up to Seattle for a shopping trip. I think I needed a dress for the eighth-grade dance or maybe a swimsuit for an end-of-the-year pool party. I had just received the menstruation/uterus talk about six months before, and I still couldn't wrap my mind around what it meant to be sterile and what—as a woman who had already successfully produced offspring—it must feel like to know that you no longer can. I remember feeling this kind of pressure to be awesome. To please and support and amuse my parents more than I ever had. Because

eagerly go for the plan o' enchiladas, and they will eat at their kitchen table. It still has four chairs.

. . . . . .

I was all they had. The only combination of themselves and the only shot they had at raising a perfect piece of progeny. And so I tried really hard in high school. And for a while I stopped feeling so bad for myself for being the only one. I was fairly certain my parents would have welcomed another Harper into the universe. And later I learned that they definitely would have. Because they did!

When I was in eleventh grade, digging through the attic, rifling through my mom's boxes of old clothes in search of anything fantastically retro, I found a box of photos. The first pages of a simple, black vinyl album showed my parents with a baby. My dad had a mustache then, and my mother's hair was feathered in that Farrah Fawcett way that can make anyone look care-free. The baby was a red, swollen infant bound in flannel blankets, snuggled against my mother's face. There was this one photo of the baby in a pale blue onesie touching its chubby hand to a brighter blue sock with that almost alarming baby flexibility. What's with all the blue? I thought. Instantly I figured my garb to be the result of some friend's or relative's generous hand-me-downs. My parents being either too poor or too cheap or too in love with their baby to give a fuck about gender-appropriate attire. And then I turned the page.

In the next set of pictures my parents are slouched low in the sofa. It's a pose I know means the camera is resting on the television and the photo is being taken using the timer feature. My mom is holding the baby, cradling its head in the cozy nook that signals the end of her lean upper arm. My father's arm is draped over her shoulders. His legs are crossed in that special dad fashion with the ankle resting square on the knee in a way that forms a triangle-shaped hole between the legs. And sprouting out of the triangle—like a scouting gopher or a jack-in-the-box or a cheery sunflower greeting the morning light—is me. I know it's me because I'm wearing this kelly green sweatshirt with a daisy stenciled on the chest in fabric paint. My mother had made herself a matching one that I eventually wore on camping trips in college. Later, I learned that I am two in this photograph. And later, I hated

David: will spend as much time as possible on the telephone spouting well-wishings to his parents, his grandparents, and six brothers and sisters. And hopefully his girlfriend!

I wonder what Gus and Rex (his dad) and I guess, maybe Gina are doing.

---

myself—despite the neurological impossibility—because I can't remember this day. Or the three months after it. The three months of my life where I actually had a brother.

The confrontation with my parents was expectedly emotional. One of those moments teenagers have where your head spins from the feeling of being stuck inside an after-school special. Something that while it's happening you can already feel a stiffness in your back that will result from staying up all night thinking and brushing your hair and calling your best friends.

When I was two years old, my parents adopted a baby boy. It was one of those things where an agency sets you up before the baby is even born and they practically hand it off to you once the cord is cut and the birth mother's shaky hand signs some form. The birth mother wanted to name the baby Alden after her grandfather, and my parents agreed to keep the name, finding it both crunchy and classic. My mom said he was a happy baby, slept a lot, and that she'd find me emerging from his room with two vertical red lines running down my cheeks: the result of pressing my face to the bars of his crib and watching him sleep for periods of time that are typically considered too long for your average two-year-old to stay still, let alone quiet. When my mother told me this, I cried. I was sixteen and prone to fits of melodrama anyway, but I flat-out sobbed. The three of us were sitting at the kitchen table (of course we were sitting at the kitchen table!), and like most kitchen tables, it has four sides. So at this point, it probably seems like baby Alden is dead. Thankfully, no! Baby Alden is now twenty-two-year-old Alden, and we haven't had an update since he graduated from some high school in the LA suburbs. After those first three months, Alden's first mommy changed her mind. It's a classic move, a legal loophole that rips hearts and brings the toughest judges to tears. It's like temporary insanity, but more like temporary emotional instability where mothers give their babies away and then realize they need them back. I figure biology has a lot to do with it, the body carrying the fetus for so long and twisting a mother's hormones and neurons around to generate the capabilities for many years of nurture. Alden's mother (I only know her first name: Julia) didn't think she could handle a family—didn't think the father would be there to help out. But I guess the couple reconciled and decided that raising their baby was vital to maintaining that reconciliation. My parents lost and Alden left us.

But why didn't you tell me? Why couldn't I know? All the usual questions. We knew it'd upset you. It was a terrible time. We couldn't handle it. All the usual answers. My parents realized they'd erred on the side of overdue secret keeping and made up for it by answering every single obnoxious question I could think of about my once-upon-a-time sibling. My whole senior year of high school I was practically obsessed. I wrote weird short stories about Alden and me making tree forts and performing short plays for our parents. I talked Gus's ear off about it. As an only child himself, he was almost equally fascinated by the situation. We practically launched a campaign to find Alden. We knew he lived in California with his mother and maybe his father. Gus even started writing a screenplay about the two of us driving down the Pacific coast searching for brother Alden. *Where Is Brother Alden?* was to star unknown teen indie actors, and Gus himself would hand-select the soundtrack. My parents kept telling me they were legally restricted from attempting to contact Alden. They knew his last name and wouldn't even tell me, an issue I took years to get over.

Every fall, Alden's grandmother, this woman my mother referred to as *Bless Her Heart Barbara*, would mail us his school photograph. He wasn't a particularly attractive kid (I was so pleased to see he got braces in eighth grade), but there was something about his bony shoulders and curly dark hair that made me confident he could easily pass as my kin. I could see us posed next to a snowman, sharing a quilt and playing Super Mario, fighting over remote controls and insulting each other's blotchy teen skin; I knew, I believed, I would bet my bottom dollar that we were soooooooo, so very alike.

And then in college, I kind of got over it. I was living in a massive dorm with hundreds of kids my age and was suddenly flooded with companionship. At the university I joined a Spanish club and had weekly potlucks with other education majors. My junior year I moved out of the dorm and into a scruffy apartment with three female friends. We'd make breakfast together on weekends and eat it snuggled up to a showing of the PBS miniseries of *Anne of Green Gables*. I cherished the close relationships I had and slowly stopped mourning one that never was. And then I met David. He occasionally teases me in brotherly ways and would shield me from flying glass in a bar fight. He sometimes calls me *dude*. Of course I still think about Alden, but like my parents, I'm relatively healed. It's just things like the holidays that occasionally make our family feel so small.

11

*T*oday I'm calling my book *Pins and Fucking Needles* for reasons that are very obvious.

Talk about tumultuous. The first day back from winter break is always messy. The kids are nonstop bragging and sharing and practically buzzing inside their new oversized sweaters. There are always fresh haircuts and a couple of boys who seem to have grown several inches over the holiday. Like all the ham and candy canes stimulated the production of growth hormones. But this year when I stumble into the teacher's lounge, the secretary immediately tells me to stop by Gene's office. She says it in a way that reveals nothing as to why the principal needs to see me first thing. So of course I get nervous, rolling through any potentially questionable words or actions I've committed that could merit a talk from the school's top dog. The kids call him Mr. Barkley, or Mr. Barfley when they think I can't hear. Barfley has an air about him that makes one suspect he was once hip and attractive—nice clothes, good hair—but like anyone, age has betrayed him, and he just can't wear the paunch belly and falling jowls with the kind of frat-boy confidence it seems he used to possess. He's always saying one-word sentences like *Absolutely!* and *Awesome!* with more enthusiasm than anyone can believe. He coaches JV girls' basketball at one of the high schools in our district, and I swear every time I visit his office, he's poring over catalogs for uniforms and snazzy warm-up gear. It's a bit disturbing.

"Harper," he says this morning. "You've got a new kid today."

My natural reaction is pure glee. A newbie! Another story, another personality, another potential friend for the few seemingly friendless shy kids. My brood of twenty-eight bumped up to twenty-nine, which sucks for partner assignments, but is a prime number and somehow that makes it feel like a more cohesive bunch. An indivisible group! I've had new kids before, but usually a few weeks into the school year. Never halfway.

"Lacey Atkins. Here's the file from her last school. Looks like a bright and easy-going kid. Let me know if you need anything." Barfley doesn't give me a chance to talk and really, there's no need to. I head for my classroom and prepare myself for an even bubblier first day back.

"Class, this is Lacey Atkins. She just moved to Tacoma from California and she'll be with us for the rest of the year." I give the standard *Let's all help Lacey feel at home here* speech, which basically means *No crap or I'll kill you*. Lacey is a doll. Is she a doll, Principal Barfley? Absolutely! Long, skinny braids pulled up into a thick ponytail. Real stylish clothes and dangly gold hoop earrings that have a delicate scrawling cutout of her name cradled in the bottom curve. She's wearing a belt encrusted with plastic gems, and I can almost smell the cherry ChapStick–scented envy from the eight or nine prissy girls in my class. As Lacey walks to her desk, I almost feel intimidated myself. The sort of ridiculous inferiority I felt as a college sophomore at parties, surrounded by sorority girls and their perfect, shiny everything. It's silly how an eight-year-old can remind me that I'm inarguably a huge dork, but Lacey just radiates coolness.

The day goes well. By lunch recess, Lacey seems to have attached to the trio of girls led by Lizzie McDonnell, and I'm relieved to hear them talking about tetherball rather than hip-huggers as they shuffle out of the room. A few minutes after the final release bell rings and the troops[46] have all departed, I hear the sound of sneakers slapping

---

[46] Ugh. David would pee his pants with delight if he saw me type that word. I don't know if it's interesting or scary that his lexicon is finally penetrating my own.

and heels clacking in the hall. Lacey bursts through the door panting, followed by a woman a little older than myself with the same gold name earrings (though I can't read them from a distance), the same long braids, and the same big, dark eyes.

"Mom! And this is my teacher, Miss Harper." Lacey yanks her mother's arm so that she flies forward a few steps and is standing so close to my desk that she could be turning in a math test. I stand up and come around. I'm about to open my mouth when she beats me.

"Hi, Miss Harper. Lacey wanted me to come in and say hello. I'm Charese, Lacey's mommy. Looks like a really great classroom you have here." Charese sounds very sincere. Not patronizing and skeptical like many of the other moms.

"Oh. Thanks. I like it." I don't know how to gracefully receive the compliment. It's not like it's a sweater and I can say, *Oh, it was on sale* or *Just a hand-me-down from my old roommate.* The classroom, with all the wild animal posters, the beanbag chairs by the Book Nook, the fourteen spider plants and six cacti along the windows, and the giant butcher paper collage of the water cycle,[47] it actually is genuinely mine. And theirs, of course. But theirs under my guidance. Tutelage. Leadership. Mentorship. Awesomeship. I notice I've been taking too long sweeping my glance around the classroom, but when I look back Charese is smoothing Lacey's hair and smiling. Her casual compliment is the nicest thing anyone has said to me in a very long time. I say thanks again and that I hope Lacey will like it here.

"Sure, she will," Charese says. "We weren't too hot on leaving San Diego, but Lacey's daddy was a bit too hot on his buddy's little sister. So we had to get out." I can start to feel my shoulders curl forward because that's what I do when I'm socially uncomfortable. In my three years teaching, the personal lives of my students have stayed conveniently out of the classroom. Yeah, there are always the ones who wear

[47] I love love love teaching the water cycle.

stinky clothes and who complain about weekends at their dads' houses, but I've never had such a fresh family dysfunction spewed in my face.

"Well, if you have any questions about the Tacoma area, I've lived here most my life." Yes. I can show you the grimy diners of my youth and shortcuts along South Tacoma Way.

"Yeah, me too. Met Lacey's daddy while he was stationed at Fort Lewis. We moved down south four years ago." Charese's directness is killing me. I suddenly feel like one of my eight-year-old slackers stuttering to give an oral book report on something he didn't read.

"Oh. Well. I bet it's kind of nice to be home." I'm trying so hard to remove the goofiness from my smile and replace it with compassion. I mean, I think I'm feeling compassion. It should look authentic.

"Right. My mother's house really beats a day at the beach. Anyway, nice to meet you, Miss Harper. We better hit the road." Charese reaches down to Lacey and fixes a twisted shoulder strap on her daughter's backpack. Turning it over causes the purple pack to shift and align in the middle of Lacey's back, distributing the weight of her first day at a new school into a uniform, manageable burden. And there's something about the way Charese does it that's so natural and mature. Like she wasn't even thinking about it but subconsciously knows that the simple act will save her daughter from any risk of scoliosis. I am in awe of Charese. It's obvious that she'd been with Lacey's father for years—probably since she was a teenager herself—and here she is back in her hometown, wounded and probably tired. But her makeup is perfect, her demeanor pleasant, and her child obviously adoring. This woman has got her shit together.[48]

[48] Later I told this story to Carrie. You know, teacher-next-door Carrie. And she said (this is an exact quote): "Yeah, infidelity is a big problem in the military, but you have nothing to worry about. David's sooo in love with you." Like she thought I was telling her to express some anxiety I have about being burned. I didn't even think about that. In all honestly, I didn't even

· · · · · ·

So I know that it's kind of lame, but I spend Friday night with Loretta. Gus had invited me to the opening gala of some art exhibit, and even though it promised nude photography and free wine, I passed. By Friday night I'm usually so tuckered out, and I knew I just didn't have the wit to clink glasses with Gus's hip friends. If I'm not super aware of myself at those kind of events, I end up spitting wine down my shirt when one of them says, *It's like totally neo-cubist fundamentals under the auspices of bourgeois sentiments.* Or something like that.

I've brought three surprises for my evening with Loretta: an AM/FM clock radio,[49] the backgammon set Gus gave me, and a plastic tub of sugar-free spice drops I bought at the drugstore. I figured old people love spice drops; they're classic, like Ovaltine and Preparation H. I even called Jean to ask if Loretta could eat the candy, and she answered me with her typical exhausted/exasperated tone. Like I'd asked the most obvious thing in the world.

LORETTA'S ENTHUSIASM ABOUT THE SURPRISES
IN DESCENDING ORDER

Backgammon: "Hot dog! Have we got a night ahead of us! My son once won two hundred dollars playing this game."

---

think about The Military or David. It was just a sad story about a woman having to uproot her life. Cheaters span all professions. Infidelity is as old and as universal as love itself. Carrie and I were in the photocopy room, and she was sitting on the counter swinging her legs. I didn't really want to continue the discussion, so I mashed a bunch of the buttons on the Xerox machine I was using so it made this beeping noise and I could pretend to be distracted by a paper jam. This was a really good move, I thought. I will use it again.

[49] The woman has no source of music in her room.

Sugar-free spice drops: "Delightful. Except the green ones taste like fermented toothpaste."[50]

Clock radio: "I wake up with the sun, Annie Harper. And I *don't* listen to the radio."

I guess two out of three isn't bad. Turns out Loretta avoids the news on all fronts. She says it's all just depressing and reminds her either of what she is missing ("trapped in this hellhole") or of how the world is falling apart ("that terrorism gobbeldygook"). I ask her if she likes music, and she says that she does and that there's a stereo in the common room where the residents play jazz records and compact discs. She's glad the holiday season is over because "there's only so much Neil Diamond a woman can handle." We laugh, and I hope I'll be so funny at her age.

We resolve to give the radio a try. I tell her that KPLU, the local NPR station, only plays jazz, and by this time of night all the news shows have already broadcast. The game is fun. The music is smooth and gentle. We end up talking about the contraceptive methods of each generation, and I learn more about the diaphragm than I thought I'd ever like to know. Apparently, they were as commonplace as egg creams in the 1950s. I tell Loretta about the birth control patch that I was on before David left and how my boobs increased a whole cup size when I first got on it. She says she should try it.

Around ten P.M., halfway through our third game (Loretta is kicking my ass), the languid tones of a sax solo are interrupted by breaking news. Loretta says, "Ah, shit. Breaking news," and I laugh until the reporter's snappy words start to take form in my ears.

Major bombing.

U.S. army base.

---

[50] I did not know that toothpaste could ferment.

Just outside of Baghdad.

No confirmed fatalities.

Dining hall tent.

Feeds hundreds of soldiers.

Suicide.

Bomber.

Fire.

Chaos.

Instantly, my body lurches into a mess of strange sensations. It's like I'm standing on the edge of a slippery bridge with no railing. It's like the delayed heartburn of carnival food. It's like the dread of a hefty credit card bill. It's both the swirl of being wasted and the emptiness of a hangover. It's like every bone is a funny bone and I've hit all of them on the cold edge of a concrete wall. Something is stinging, pulsating, jolting through my body. It's like I crashed a car that doesn't belong to me. It's like I served undercooked cupcakes to my entire class and every student is bedridden with salmonella in the same dreary hospital wing. It's like being pressed under a pile of rocks, choked by a lumpy rice pudding, stung by a queen bee in the eyeball. It's almost debilitating.[51]

I'm clearing the rice pudding from my throat when the reporter confirms what I already know: Camp Warhorse. David's camp. Yeah, there are like twelve thousand something soldiers there, a Burger King, and a spa,[52] and the odds of David being in that particular

---

[51] At the time, "debilitating" was really the only thing my brain could recognize. Okay, maybe "fucked up." It's just now (after three cups of coffee) that I've sat down to write about it that my brain is frantically grasping for the right description. Maybe I should take out all that slop that I just wrote. Maybe I'm coloring myself an absurd shade of melodramatic. Not sure. But for now, while things are still fresh, the rice pudding feels right.

[52] I might have made the spa thing up.

dining tent at that particular moment probably aren't too dismal, but I can't help it. I am totally freaking out.

Somehow, amazingly, despite the blinding bee stings and the funnel-cake heartburn and the credit card debt and the wicked hangover, I manage to pull myself together and leave Violet Meadows. I don't know how long I listen to the broadcast—motionless, probably drooling—but at some point Loretta has put the game away and waddled over to the bed to fetch my coat. "Go to your mother, sweetheart," she says as she hands me my jacket. She's pulled my car keys from the pocket and is reaching up, dangling them in front of my eyes. Oddly enough, they don't seem to be making any noise.

As I drive home, everything is still weirdly silent. I don't turn the radio on, as a safety precaution, and I concentrate on keeping my hands at ten and two and making slow, deliberate stops and turns. And I don't go to my parents' house. Listening to my mother (though her intentions are always the best) *and* the thick, hyped-up tones of TV reporters seems like a recipe for extreme drama. I know I'll be able to kick up enough on my own.

When I get in the house I jump right into worst-case scenarios. *David is dead, so I'll be hearing from his mom soon.* I go into my room and change into sweatpants and a hooded sweatshirt. I pull the hood up and the long sleeves down over my hands. I fetch a glass of water. *David is dead, so I'm taking two weeks off of work to mourn.* I walk to the laundry room and find this pair of thick red socks with rubber tread on the bottom.[53] I put them on and slowly pad into the living room. I find the remote, settle myself in my regular television viewing position, and sit very still for many minutes. *David is dead, so I'm calling the White House tomorrow.*

I pull my feet up under my body and finger the rubbery *V*s of the

---

[53] A birthday gift from David one year because I'm always slipping in my socks.

tread marks. I try to think about something mundane like how the invention of rubber and plastics has changed the world, but it doesn't last long and I know I'm not fooling myself. *David is dead, so is a long-term girlfriend considered a widow?* I get up and find the cordless phone and my cell phone. I line them up on the coffee table next to the remote: the little ranks of my own fragile army. All I have between a bright future and a miserable one.

I turn on the TV. And it's weird because I've never watched it like this: with urgency and a desperate need to extract information. Yeah, I've taken notes about insects from programs on the National Geographic Channel, and I spent weeks after 9/11 glued to the set—stunned and crying. But the pace of the television was fine then. I couldn't handle more facts on the reproduction of fig wasps, and the fewer stories of devastated New Yorkers, the better. I didn't necessarily ache for a higher pace of information. But this is killing me.

I flip back and forth between CNN, MSNBC, CBS, NBC, ABC, and even Fox News. It's the eleven o'clock news hour, and everyone is just saying the same thing over and over, but with slight changes every ten minutes or so. Eight deaths turns into twelve deaths turns into twenty-one. The largest incident of soldier fatalities in a U.S. camp since the beginning of the occupation. No one knows how the bomber entered the camp. Twenty-two U.S. soldiers, two U.S. contractors, and three Iraqi cafeteria workers. That's where the numbers level out, and they stay put past midnight. Once the reporters run out of hard, vital facts, they begin adding more sentimental details to their broadcasts.

"Hundreds of army soldiers shaken from their peaceful meal of chicken fingers and macaroni—allegedly a dining hall favorite at Camp Warhorse—by a substantial bomb detonated near the serving line."

Chicken fingers! I know this sounds silly, but these are the two words that finally flip the switch on my tear ducts. Up until this point,

I've been solid, in control of my limbs and bodily fluids, moving gracefully around my house, courageously dragging my heart behind me on a rope made of my large intestine. I've been doing okay. But I know David Peterson. I arguably know him better than anyone in the entire galaxy knows him. I know his favorite spot to floss his teeth and about his fear of moths. I know that when he's been drinking he tends to sleep with his eyes partially open. I know that he stirs his coffee counterclockwise with his right hand, which is highly unusual. And I know that David Peterson *does not* skip out on chicken fingers.

One of the first meals we shared was at one of the university cafeterias. I'd taken a bit longer to compose my feast at the salad bar, and I sat down to find David with one of those disgusting baskets from the deep-fry line. The grease was settling into the paper lining, rendering it transparent and disgusting. Now don't get me wrong, I'll never turn down a hot onion ring at the proper occasion, but a meal composed solely of foods that rely on large quantities of oil for their preparation—there's just something wrong with that. Petty as it may seem, I almost wrote him off right there, sure that he'd be lifting those crusty chicken fingers and dunking them oafishly into a brimming ramekin of ranch dressing. I despise ranch dressing. People typically blame the "freshman fifteen" that often afflicts young coeds on the overconsumption of high-calorie beers, but for those who dine at the University of Washington cafeteria system, there's an entirely different culprit. It's ranch dressing. Girls splash it on tacos and pizza. It's a dipping sauce for not just vegetables, but also breadsticks and sushi rolls. I swear to God, I've seen a guy swirl it into marinara sauce. Chicken fingers, with their carby/protein balance, provide a natural venue for the white, globby fat. And when I looked over to see that David had positioned another plate to his side, and that it contained a small pile of carrot sticks, a modest sea of applesauce, and two ramekins of honey (his chicken-finger dip of choice), I decided to give him a chance. He doesn't eat like a gluttonous, unrefined teenager. He eats like a five-year-old kid. And an extremely polite one who observes appropriate condiment ratios and never chews with his mouth open. His love for childish foods (pigs in blankets, celery with peanut butter) has actually become quite endearing.

So when I hear this, when I hear the sleek, sophisticated news lady say the goofy words "chicken fingers," I know instantly that David is dead. I can see his square jaw behind the counter, smiling as he lifts his tray for the cafeteria worker to drop the breaded (rhymes with dreaded) poultry onto his plate. Yes, please, he says. And then the plate shatters. And then his head shatters. And then my whole life shatters. I know it. Well, I don't know it. But I feel like I know it. I really really feel it. I really really feel like shit.

I run to the bathroom and vomit four times because I am a horrible, fucked-up person. I return to the television, and I'm tempted to throw it out the window, because I have been thinking the worst possible things. Really, they're awful. I nearly hate myself because of them. As I'm sitting there sobbing, wiping my snot on this throw blanket that I know is dry-clean only, I think about my book. This stupid whine-fest book. Well, what a better book this will be, right? The boyfriend dies. The girl is faced with a timeless, brutal sort of mourning. Will I be able to pace everything out to form a satisfying plot arc? How much of the post-David-death story should I include? Will it sell better because he dies? Will I have to wear black for all my TV interviews and book signings? All very sick sick things. Who fantasizes about how they will capitalize on their lover's death? I do. I did it! I am a horribly evil person. And I knew this. I knew it before I even started thinking it. Did I really want to throw the television out the window? Or did I want to do it because it makes my story better for the book? Can I even lift a television?

I cry and cry about that, and then I cry harder because I'm crying about my own evilness more than I am about my boyfriend's death.

Then the phone rings. It's the landline, and I snap out of my fetal cry-ing position like a popped kernel of corn. I look at the caller ID. It's my mom. I know I'm in no condition to speak to her, but something about seeing her number on the screen zaps a little sense into me. I brush my hair back and sit back down. Let the machine pick up. "Hey, Annie. It's Mom. I've been watching the news. Hope you're not too worried. I imagine everything's probably fine. Let me know when you hear from David. Love you. Bye." Everything's probably fine! She imagines! My mother's voice is so cool, so sensible, like she hasn't fret-ted one baby fret of fret. And she's probably right. I mean twelve thou-sand people, twenty-two dead. That's not horrible odds. I decide to perform some statistical experiments.

I turn the TV back on. It's CNN on commercial break. I tell my-self that if the next advertisement uses the word "the," then David is alive. I figure that out of every twelve thousand commercials there are probably only twenty-two that completely avoid the use of the English language's most popular article. And those are commercials with no words at all. I squeak when the first one opens with "At the Mattress Warehouse, you'll find exactly the night's sleep you're look-ing for!" Two "thes"! The phrasing of the sentence makes me think of people sleeping in the Mattress Warehouse, and I resolve that I'd sleep in a Warehouse for the rest of my life if it meant David not be-ing dead.

I realize that I'm losing it and that waiting and sleeping is the best I can do. He will call. Or he won't call. Sooner or later, I will know the truth. I take a double dose of sleep aid, and as I fall into that hazy, drug-enhanced sleep, I manage to round up three more completely miserable thoughts.

1. By hoping my brains out that David is not one of the unfortunate twenty-two, I am wishing death on other people.

2. I ended our last phone call with the words, "Peace in the Middle East, my brother."
3. If David is dead, will I have to wait several years before it's appropriate to have sex again?

See you in hell! Look for the flaming cave with my name on it!

I wake up to the sound of my cell phone chirping from the living room. It's my mother, and I feel guilty for ignoring it again. I flip on the television, and nothing much has changed. They suspect that the bomber was one of the camp's contracted Iraqi barbers who had managed to hide his allegiances and involvement with the Ansar al-Sunnah Army. I wonder if he had ever buzzed the hair of any of the now-slain soldiers. I try to plan out my day. I need to do laundry. Pay some bills. Go grocery shopping. Should one do these things whilst her boyfriend's life is in the air? I really don't feel like doing much of anything. Lying on the couch, staring at the walls for minute after wretched minute, seems like all I can manage.

After several hours of wall staring and disgusting thought thinking, I get up to brush my teeth, realizing that I haven't done so since the morning before. Then the phone rings again. I run to the living room, toothbrush in my mouth. The screen says 012345678 and my heart soars. The corn dogs settle down, the swelling around my bee-stung eyes instantly disappears, and my kids come running, ruby-faced and healthy, from the front doors of the hospital. The salmonella is gone because I know that 012345678 is some weird shit that shows up on the screen when David calls from the satellite phones on base. He's alive! "You're alive!" I say as I pick up the call, except that my mouth is full of toothpaste spit foam and it comes out as "You lie!"

"What? Annie, is that you?" I spit my toothpaste into the water glass on the coffee table.

"Yes! It's me! And it's you! You're okay! I've been eating my chicken fingers off worrying." And then I ramble off a dozen other questions, and David, though noticeably shaken and somber, seems to benefit from my barrage of joy. His tone lightens, and I tell him like a million times how worried I was. He wasn't even in the dining hall. Ironically, he was getting his hair cut.

"Plus, Annie, I work days now. Only the night shift guys eat chicken fingers at nine A.M." I didn't even think of that. That the fated meal was happening midmorning. But I didn't care. I felt amazing. You could have thrown me in a vat of moldy ranch dressing and dunked my head under for minutes at a time—and I'd have been fine with that.

12

*T*oday I'm calling my book *While Fleeing the Coop of Terror.*

After I spoke with David I drove straight to Violet Meadows. I called my mother on the way and explained to her in this really calm, grown-up way that David is fine and that it's really quite a miracle that he was able to call me so soon. You see, Mother, (I'm such an expert on all things army) they must notify the family of the deceased before they can let anyone else call or e-mail home. It prevents information or *mis*information from reaching people in the wrong ways. I think the military should use that exact language in their official literature. I actually just learned all this from David ten minutes before, but I told my mom like I knew all along. Like I've always been this super-informed army girlfriend. I think my maturity impressed her. She was very nice about it all too. She said if something like this happens again that I should come over to their house and let her and my father distract me somehow. I tell her that that's probably a good idea.

As soon as I saw Loretta I raised both of my fists to ear level and said "Wahoo" in a quiet but triumphant voice. Yeah, it kind of felt inappropriate, but I didn't much care. She told me that she knew he'd be fine. She could feel it in her joints.

"Oooh, so you have the clairvoyant type of arthritis," I said. She laughed at my joke. Loretta sat down in her rocker, and I plopped carelessly on her bed like a teenager. And then I kind of told Loretta everything. It was as if my brief tango with extreme pain had left my tongue fast and floppy. Like when people get put under anesthesia and wake up in midsentence, talking to the doctor about their most intimate ideas. I told her about all the sick fantasies I had and the way I was almost sure that he was dead. I really, really believed it for a while.

"Do you think that because I believed it so seriously that I wanted it to be true? Am I really that demented?"

"Sweet Jesus, no, Annie. A woman's instincts can't always be right. And under such unusual stress, there's no telling what our assumptions are feeding on. It's likely you were just preparing yourself for the worst. Don't mistake your defense mechanisms for darkness, dear."

Sweet Jesus, Loretta is so wise.

She went on to tell me about how when Ron was away, she used to fantasize that if he died, she'd hook up with this guy Lars Svenson. "He had a crush on me all through school, and I knew he'd be trying to court me the instant Ron arrived home in a casket." Loretta said she liked to imagine being with Lars because it meant that if Ron was gone, she wouldn't always be alone and wounded. Even if the worst happened, she'd find a way to get by. For a moment I thought that Loretta was even more fucked up than me—planning her next romance while the present one was still intact. But when you think about it, it kind of does make sense. Creatures reproduce because we are replaceable. Human connections fire up again and again and again. Soul mates, schmole mates. I've never bought into that crap.

"You know what you need after all this?" Loretta said, smoothing the skirt of her housedress. "You need a pet. Something to care for and nurture. Take your mind off all your worries."

"I don't know, Loretta. I've been thinking about growing more plants outside, and I want to get a puppy for when David gets back, but I don't know if I'm ready for that kind of responsibility."

"Responsibility? Aren't you in charge of a whole gaggle of schoolchildren?"

"Yeah, but just for a few hours on weekdays. A pet requires around-the-clock consideration. You always have to know where it is and when it last ate and when it might need to shit again." Loretta didn't even flinch at my profanity.

"Well, you could get a fairly self-reliant pet?"

"Like a hamster? I don't like pets in cages. Too depressing."

"My goodness, Annie Harper, I've got it. I know just what you need." Loretta folded her hands neatly in her lap and smiled at me in such a pleasant, self-satisfied way that if she'd have said "Komodo dragon," I'd have ordered one that day.

"What? What do I need?"

"Do you have a backyard?" Her eyes narrowed.

"I do. Yes! I do!" Six hundred bucks a month will get you a lot in South Tacoma.

"Does this yard have a fence?" Eyebrows lifted, forehead so wrinkly.

"It does! I have a fence!" I don't know why I was so giddy, but Loretta seemed so sure of herself. It was thrilling.

"Well then, it's quite clear. You need a chicken."[54]

POTENTIAL NAMES FOR MY CHICKEN
Tiger
Spice Drop
Janice, the Reference Librarian
Danielle Steel
Fingers of Victory
Mrs. Feather Face McGee
Gloria
Desiree
The Official Mascot of Oprah's Book Club
Rainbow
Selena

[54] Interesting, because I've actually whimsically considered this before. Loretta saying it cements it as an entirely fabulous idea.

Subject: cluck cluck cluck
Date: January 25, 2004 17:22PST
From: missharpercandoit@yahoo.com
To: david.peterson13@us.army.mil

OMG, David! I am getting a chicken! It's official. Loretta talked
me into it. She had them for years and says they're totally
pleasant and don't live long so it's not like it's this big
commitment. I'm going to build a coop in my backyard and eat
fresh eggs every day. Do you have any suggestions for names?
It's going to be a girl, obviously. Do you think I'll get high
cholesterol? Woop! I wish you were here to enjoy omelets with
me on the weekends, but all in good time, my love. All in good
time!

So how's everything going in the desert? Have things settled
down after the bombing? Have they increased security measures?
Are you having any bad dreams? Are you having any hott hott
hott dreams??

I miss you tremendously and hope you can call sooooon!
Love love love,
Miss Harper, future chicken owner of America.

Subject: Re: cluck cluck cluck
Date: January 27, 2004 03:34PST
From: david.peterson13@us.army.mil
To: missharpercandoit@yahoo.com

Things are going alright. They're having us each do an extra two
hours of patrol every day b/c of the stepped-up security. I'm
working with this dude Erikson, who used to be a bouncer in
Vegas, so his stories keep the night pretty lively. He says Paris

Hilton once hit him with her handbag. I said he should sue
because if you have over $500,000 they can kick you out of the
military. Damn, I gotta run, babe. Talk to you soon.
David.

I couldn't help but be a little annoyed because he didn't mention
the chicken. I mean, maybe he was going to address it, but was pulled
away from the computer before he got to it. I shouldn't be hurt because Paris Hilton upstaged my future chicken. She's doing that to
people all the time. I resolved that next time he called we would definitely talk about it. And in the scope of things—wars and love and
Vegas nightclubs—chickens are bound to stumble far behind.

A few days later, David did call. I was making spaghetti, and the
phone rang at the exact moment I threw a noodle at the fridge to
check its level of al dente. I jumped, and the noodle inched a few steps
down the fridge and froze. I turned off the burner.

"How's it hanging, sweetheart?" he said. His voice was so warm
and friendly that for a moment I forgot that he's in a war zone. He
could have been driving along I-5 after a normal day's work, calling to
casually ask me what kind of Chinese food I want him to pick up for
dinner. General Tso's Chicken, please!

"I'm great," I said. "How are you doing, Lieutenant Peterson, sir?"

"Not too shabby. Not too shabby. We had tacos today."

"Was there ground beef involved?"

"There was."

"Oh, David. You do love the ground beef."

"Yep." And here is where I paused and waited for him to ask about
my chicken plan. The pause ended and he told me how he's excited
about this new equipment they're getting in soon and that he'll get to
go to Mosul for a few days for some training. And it's always so nice to
hear these sorts of things, it really is, but then he reaches this point in
the sharing where our wrists are slapped by the Vagueness Pact and

the conversation abruptly ends. No *What kind of equipment?* No *What will you be using it for?* No *Where is it coming from?* He probably wasn't even supposed to tell me about the training in Mosul. I say things like *That's great. Glad you have something to look forward to. Hope it makes your job easier.* And I care. I do care care care. I just hate hate hate only knowing a few concrete nuggets of detail about his job. It's not enough of a taste to generate a serious interest. Back when David was working here in Tacoma, I could at least see him and smell him at the end of the workday. I could physically assess whether or not his secret-keeping-secret-government-biz-with-secret-guns stuff was tearing him apart.

A few minutes later: "So I'm getting my chicken on Sunday." I said it nearly yawning. Like I wasn't totally bothered that he didn't remember to ask.

"Oh yeah. You were serious about that?" David can't help but sound condescending when he's actually just incredulous.

"Um, yes." Then I told him how I was going to buy the materials and build my chicken coop the very next day.[55]

"Jeez, Annie. A chicken? Are you sure you're okay? You don't want a kitten or something?"

"No. I don't. Loretta says chickens are the perfect level of companionship. They require little maintenance and they give back."

"You really like eggs that much?" He sounded tired.

"Yes."

I really like eggs that much.

Later, after we hung up, I slumped down against my fridge to pout over David's lack of chicken understanding and wonder if he was feeling the same frustration over my lack of new-secret-army-machines understanding. I felt the spaghetti noodle flop into my hair, and I reached up to pull it out. Without even checking for hairs or dirt or anything, I stuffed the noodle in my mouth. It was a little dry, but the

[55] Saturday.

act of picking it from my hair and eating it made me feel so warmly animal. Like I was surely going to survive somehow due to my base but utilitarian instincts. And regardless of how stoked my boyfriend was about chickens.

Earlier this morning in my class:

"Kids, I have something to share today." I fold my hands in front of my chest, a classic move of gentle authority. Show-and-tell has just wrapped up, and half the class is yawning in preparation for math class.

"You can't share, Miss Harper. You're the teacher."

"Yeah, teachers can't share." Stupid, stupid kids.

"Well, then if you want to jump straight into math, let's go ahead. . . ."

"Noooooooooooooooo." Thank you, losers. I sit on top of my desk and cross my ankles. As fun and natural a pose as it is, I try to save the desk sitting to emphasize moments of extreme hipness. Teaching is a performance in several aspects, and the kids can sometimes tell when certain moves are overused.

"So I know that many of you have pets." The shouts: *Yeah. Me. I do. Snuffles. Three kittens.* "And I very recently have decided that I am going to acquire a pet of my own." *A puppy? A guinea pig for the class. Get a dinosaur!* "This weekend, I am going to get my very own chicken." Self-satisfied, hip-teacher smirk.

Silence. Silence. Silence.

A chicken? What? Why? Chickens smell like poop. Can you teach it to talk? Gross. Why a chicken? Lame. I honestly thought they'd think it awesome.

"But you see, kids, chickens lay eggs, and I will have fresh eggs every day for breakfast." *Can you bring it inside? Will it have babies?* Max Schaffer's distinctly adorable voice: "Won't you need a rooster for your chicken to produce eggs?"

Shit. A motherfucking rooster. Embarrassingly, I'm not sure. But at the moment, it kind of makes sense. A girl chicken needing a boy chicken to nudge her hormones along, to administer some chicken loving, to coax those eggs out. It's probably just because I honestly believe Max Schaffer is brilliant, but I falter.

"Um, well, Max, no. I'm pretty sure I don't need a rooster." Loretta would have mentioned this, right? First rule of teaching: Stick to your guns![56]

So maybe it's not just David's opinion on the chicken that's getting me down. Maybe I'm not so annoyed at the fact that he seems uninterested in my daily life. It's not just him; no one else seems to be into it either. In order to avoid total frustration, I'm not telling my parents until that chicken has settled her feathers on my land. Or maybe I'll just have them over for brunch one day. "Like the eggs? Oh, they're from my chicken. More coffee?"

---

[56] First thing when the boogerfaces go out to recess, I look this up on the Internet. No, I will not need a rooster. A rooster's presence is only necessary if you want your chicken's eggs to hatch. Duh. Annie, please remember to omit this mortifyingly ignorant moment from the real book. Christ.

13

*T*oday I'm calling my book *Inside the Yolk of the Sun*, because I think it sounds calm and Zen-like. And I'm obviously really into this chicken business.

I'm building my chicken coop when Gus calls to tell me about his new job.

"But what about the linens, Gus? You love that gig."

"And I will still have it. Part time. The new job is also part time." Gus is now a graphic designer for a Budweiser distributor. He gets to make those huge vinyl banners that swing outside of dive bars and convenience stores advertising deals on half racks and six-packs.

"But you hate domestic beers."

"So. I'll have access to some premium equipment. Design software. Laser printers. I can make whatever I want." I almost drop a sheet of plywood on my foot, and I yelp. "Are you in the middle of something, Annie? I can call back."

"Yeah. Actually, I'm building a chicken coop."

"Sweet. Talk to you soon." Gus always knows the right time to prod and the right time to leave me alone. He knows that if it's important enough, I will certainly tell him later.

My chicken coop is glorious. I have one blister from digging, two splinters from forgetting to wear gloves, and three scratches from unrolling that pokey chicken wire. I called my dad twice to ask basic questions about caulk versus wood glue, and he's so amazing that when I tell him the project is a surprise he doesn't pry in the slightest. It took pretty much the entire day,[57] but it felt amazing. I can't remember the last time I built something so elaborate that wasn't a seven-layer dip or a craft project for eight-year-olds.

I downloaded the building plans from this Web site about having pet chickens and then tweaked the plan a bit to suit my tastes. Future Unnamed Chicken of Mine will reside in a stately A-frame dwelling complete with a sunroom (the front section is just wire) and a more private bedroom suite (ideal for discreetly entertaining guests and sleeping late into the weekend mornings). The sunroom has a flapping, doggie-style door that can be latched shut by Chicken's landlady (me!) if need be. The bedroom suite has a floor that pulls out like a drawer so Chicken's housekeeper (me!) can easily remove waste, change the sheets, fluff the pillows. Now all my chicken coop needs is some decorative flair, which I will wait on until I'm familiar with Chicken's personal style and coloring.[58]

Despite his skepticism or maybe because of it, I wrote David this super long e-mail about the glamour-coop. I'd paste it here but it's basically everything I just said. After I described the coop, I started talking about what to do when my chicken dies, and then that spun into more senseless blab about death in general and how I shouldn't be worried about Chicken's death right now. Then I ruined the e-mail by spitting out a series of really wack questions like this. I'm going to try really hard not to number them.

[57] Loretta excused me from our regular Saturday visit.

[58] I'm thinking about lining the eaves with this hot pink feather boa left over from a random night in college that ended at a strip club, but I'm not sure if Chicken will appreciate the use of feathers, however faux they may be.

Has anyone in your group[59] of soldiers died yet?
Do you read the *New York Times* Names of the Dead list?
Do you know I look for your name there every day?
Do you know anyone who has been seriously injured?
Do you know why the army kicks you out if you have $500,000?
Do you think I could make $500,000 raising prize chickens?

The Names of the Dead list creeps me out. It somehow feels anti-
quated and otherwordly at the same time. It's in between a simple,
wooden announcement board in a sixteenth-century town and the
harsh, news-dispensing method of some futuristic alien community in
a Vonnegut novel. We get the *New York Times* at school, and I read it
every morning in the teachers' lounge before class. If there are
names—lately there have been a couple every few days—I wait until
school's over and plug them into Google. Usually I end up reading the
slain soldier's hometown newspaper. He was a state champion wres-
tler. Third-generation marine. Those sorts of details are expected—sons
of marines and wrestlers become soldiers all the time—so they don't
really trip me up. But every now and then one of The Dead will surprise me: an origami enthusiast or a ballroom dancer who volunteered
at his local animal shelter. And then I weep. And if there are any photographs at all (even for the wrestlers) of the family, miscellaneous
babies, a mother broken and slumped onto her companion's shoulder
as a flag-draped coffin passes, cradling the remains of her blown-apart

---

[59] I know there is some word like "company," "platoon," "fleet," or "unit"
that refers exactly to the group of three hundred men who left Tacoma for
Iraq with David. And I know they all work together on the same stuff, but I
never remember what word it is, and it's embarrassing that I don't. The military has this very precise Kingdom, Phylum, Class, Order, Family, Genus,
Species type of organization, but there is no snazzy mnemonic device for it,
so I always forget. King Philip Conquered Over France, Germany, (and)
Spain. Go Philip.

babe, then I definitely weep. It's never horrible. Never a lurching sob or a dam-breaking flood. I like to think it's more dignified than that. I imagine myself as a graceful, painted movie star; sad and stoic, not scrunching my face and wailing in unflattering ways. Tears don't fall on my keyboard. My mascara smears just a little. And what's weird is that I'm usually comforted by these moments. Like I'm fulfilling this role as I'm supposed to. (It's hard to explain the satisfaction being tied to the sadness.) I'm waving my white handkerchief into the breeze. My hand is resting gently on my chest while my heart labors courageously to keep on beating.

Later we talk about the NOTD list on the phone, and David tells me there's no need to look for his name in the newspaper. He says that if he's killed, I'll find out before a pressroom in New York. He also says that he's certainly not the only David Peterson in the army and most likely not the only one presently deployed to Iraq.

"What if my doppelganger dies and you freak out?" he says.

"I don't think I could reasonably not freak out in that situation."

"Well, just don't worry so much."

"I'm not. I mean, I've got it under control." David sighs. I say, "But maybe you should consider changing your name?" The sigh swings up into a laugh, and I'm pleased. "You can keep the Peterson because it's your family and all, but how about something really unique for your first name, like "Sputnik" or "Jebadiah"?"

"Jebadiah Peterson? Isn't Bush's brother named Jeb?"

"Oh, so what. It's still got this exotic, romance-novel feel. Like the son of an ambassador who abandons his diplomat family to become a woodworker."

"Hmm. I don't see it, but I'll take your word for it." And then David has to go. The requisite parental phone calls are overdue, and it's almost time for one of his shifts.

"Check you later, Jeb," I say after we hang up. Our conversations often end like this. He is hurrying away, and I puke out one last dose of goofy word vomit in a ridiculous attempt to lighten the mood. I'm not sure why I do it. We never talk to our hearts' content, so maybe it's my last desperate stab to fit more into what was already a meatless conversation. Like when you pack a box to move—just books or shoes or something—then before you tape it up you throw fifteen pieces of miscellany on the top. A flashlight. A deck of cards. Two tampons. That way when you're looking for a flashlight or a tampon days later, you'll remember where you put it. Its image will stick out sharp in your mind's eye. That freaky tube shape on top of all the rectangles. It's like if David dies tonight, it will not be a generic "I love you I love you" that I will remember from our last conversation, it will be this crisp, original moment where we pretended his name was Jeb.

Yeah, right. That was all such bullroar. I wonder if any of the Stitch Bitches are so recklessly inappropriate.

I borrow one of those kitty carriers from Carrie to use for the official chicken transportation. It takes several phone calls to find a farmer who will agree to sell me just one chicken. They either say: *We don't sell chickens. We sell eggs.* Or they say: *We don't sell chickens. We sell poultry.* I gather that "poultry" is the word one uses for dead chickens. Edward Harrington, owner of Harrington Egg Farm in Puyallup, didn't even flinch when I said, "Hi. My name is Annie Harper. I've built a chicken coop in the backyard of my Tacoma house and I'd like to purchase one chicken to raise for my own personal egg harvest."

"Sure," says Edward Harrington. "Stop by anytime there's daylight."

"Really? Great. How about this Sunday?" I am thrilled. Practically wiggling to my wishbone with delight.

"See you Sunday, Annie Harper." Edward Harrington is my hero. I wonder if he's too young for me to hook up with Loretta. Or if he's married. I imagine Loretta escaping from Violet Meadows into the fluffy, feathery solace of some beautiful country home. Edward Harrington probably has a live-in cook/maid, and Loretta can spend her days knitting and laughing and stroking the four hairs of Edward Harrington's comb-over as they watch *Wheel of Fortune* side by side on a floral-patterned sofa.

Gus offers his van and his company for Chicken pickup day. I can tell he's kind of envious of my idea and its actual execution.[60] He lives in an apartment the size of a toaster oven that could barely accommodate a guinea pig. When he calls me back Saturday to ask why I'm building the chicken coop,[61] he immediately asks to come along.

When he picks me up, Gina is perched in the passenger seat. I see her hair all sloppy and beautiful, tied up in an exotic-looking scarf. It's the kind of style sorority girls attempted to affect in college when they were wearing cutesy, low-rise sweatpants to their morning lectures. The casual look. But I've seen the sorority girls agonize over these hairstyles in the bathroom mirrors between classes, twisting and puffing the tucked-under ponytail poof to achieve the perfect semblance of carefree grooming. But Gina, you can tell she has just tossed it up there with her eyes closed and probably while walking or talking to Gus about eco-friendly microchips. I've met her once before back around Christmas—very briefly—and she managed to compliment my earrings, make a reference to pogo sticks, and say nothing about my boyfriend being in Iraq. Four hundred fifty-five points for Gina.

---

[60] Earlier this winter I made elaborate plans to purchase a sewing machine and make sheets for all my friends and relatives for Christmas. This did not happen. Obviously, I would have mentioned it. Gus gave me crap and still reminds me that he wanted lumberjack plaid flannel for his. Not every idea is a good one worth follow-through. George W. Bush and I have already gone over this. I would have ended up throwing a three-hundred-dollar sewing machine into my television and ruining two perfectly good grown-up appliances.

[61] Seriously. I thought Gus was smarter than this.

As I'm locking my front door, Gus rolls down his window. He shouts, "Come along, little lady. We're going down to the farm!" And then he whoops. I toss the kitty carrier in the back and fold myself into the van's only bench seat. In between my directions to the farm, Gina politely asks me about what I did the night before. I tell her I made pudding and watched the first three hours of the *Pride and Prejudice* miniseries that I own on DVD. And after I say it, I realize how lame it sounds, so I specify, "tapioca pudding," like the clarification will prove that I'm actually interesting. Gina politely comments that pudding is definitely one of the things she misses most since she turned vegan over the holidays.

Gus and Gina are both very excited about my chicken (which convinces me that David would be too if he were here. It's his present living/working situation that's making pet chickens seem so absurd by contrast. Right?). Even though she doesn't eat animal products of any type, Gina totally supports me harvesting my own quasi-organic, semi-free-range eggs. And this makes me feel great. To have people understand me like that. To have their spirits lifted at the same time for the same reason. Gus turns the radio up when "Don't Stop Believin'" comes on, and we all sing along. We really belt it. *People. Streetlights.* Everything. It's amazing. That song just makes me feel so good. I won't stop believing. Ever.

The gravel driveway that leads to Harrington Egg Farm is marked by a plywood sign with faded lettering hanging from a post by chains. And dangling from the sign by ropes are three rubber chickens. The classic jokester kind.[62] I love the place already. We park alongside a

---

[62] Note to self: Research the guy who invented the rubber chicken. What was he thinking? How did rubber chickens make their way into mainstream culture? Why are they so sleek and aerodynamic? Why do they look nothing like actual chickens but are then absolutely recognizable as chickens? So much.

long, narrow barn with a paint job that looks straight out of a dusty old movie. A sign on the barn says OFFICE and points toward the house just across the way.

Before we're halfway there, a man (Edward Harrington himself, I'm instantly sure) comes busting out the screen door. "Good afternoon, folks. How can I help you?" I pipe up.

"Hi. I'm Annie Harper. I called earlier about buying a chicken." I shift my weight and start to question my footwear decision of rubber rain boots. Edward Harrington is wearing loafers. No socks.

"So you are. Right this way, Annie Harper. I've got someone in mind." He leads us into the long barn, and I hear Gina muffle her gasp at the rows and rows of caged chickens. Chickens stacked on chickens beside chickens. It's like four dimensions of chickens. What's weird about it is the noise. A high-pitched jumble of cluckings. It reminds me of the sound a group of one thousand old women might make before the curtain rises at a burlesque show: nervous, fidgety, but somehow ready for a blush-inducing shock.

Edward Harrington doesn't take us in very far. Gus and Gina actually step back outside for air. "Right here," he says, unlatches a cage, and reaches his hands inside. He asks me to hold my carrier up as he removes the fluttering bird with a gentleness that takes my breath away.[63] His hands are thick and creased like tree bark, and I can tell that he knows the perfect way to hold the animal so that it calms and quiets just so. I wish Gus and Gina were here to see it. To see that this is a man who respects the creatures who earn his living. He murmurs things like *easy does it* and *in you go, love* as he guides my chicken into the kitty carrier.

Once we're outside, he explains to us that my chicken (yes, he says *your chicken* already) spent her first week as a chick in the petting zoo of the Puyallup State Fair. So she's great with humans, he says. Over

[63] Very few things take my breath away.

five thousand people go through that petting zoo each day of the fair, he tells us. Immediately, I want to nuzzle my face into my chicken and see if her feathers smell like caramel apples and feel like cotton candy. It's nice to know her beginnings and that she's already received the affections of thousands of snuggling children. Edward Harrington explains that his wife—"God rest her sweet soul"—was heavily involved in the fair committee and that they started using their chicks in the petting zoo years ago. I can't wait to tell my students this.

When I ask Edward Harrington how much I owe him for my chicken, he laughs at me. "One chicken?" he says. "Well, I've got a pickup truck full of alfalfa that needs unloading. How about your gentleman friend have a go at it while you two ladies join me for some coffee?" I look at Gus. He's smiling and nodding, and I can tell he's thinking that his labor will qualify him for partial chicken ownership and regular egg rations.

"Sounds like a deal," he says, and Edward Harrington directs him toward the truck and a smaller barn with a tired-looking horse milling around behind a fence.

Gina and I follow Edward Harrington to his front porch, and as he holds open the screen door I notice a wooden sign nailed to the side of the house. WELCOME TO OUR HOME, it says, and scrawling along the top (in a script that reminds me of the way my grandmother signs her checks) are the names EDWARD AND HELEN HARRINGTON. We sit down, and as the coffee brews, I'm instructed on the proper care techniques for my new hen. Temperatures. Heat lamps. Waste disposal. Feed. When to be alarmed by excess molting. How many eggs to expect when. Edward Harrington even imitates the cluck of a sick hen, a worried hen, a happy hen. Gina and I are both beaming the whole time, wishing Edward Harrington into our own families. I can tell Gina has forgiven him for his cruel, prisonlike ways. He gives me his business card and one for a local feed store where I can purchase the perfect meals for my new friend. He says, "Tell them Ed Harrington sent you. They'll give you a discount."

When Gus returns from his barn chores, he's sweaty and smiley and seemingly very pleased with himself. I'm certain he's never tossed bales of alfalfa around before, and I know he's the kind of person who loves to diversify his life experiences by adding such things to his list. I thank Edward Harrington over and over again for the chicken, the coffee, his kindness. "You better get that happy hen home, Annie Harper. Let her settle into her first night in the big city."

In the van my chicken is kind of jumpy. I try to whisper soothing things to her while she clucks, but it doesn't seem to make a difference. When she finally settles down a bit, Gina asks me what I'm going to name her. And though I do think "Janice the Reference Librarian" and "Spice Drop" are very wonderful chicken names, I make a quick, easy decision about the identity of my chicken.

"My chicken," I say, and I pause dramatically. "Her name is Helen."

As we drive home, the sun sinks into the horizon, gushing its last light into a partially cloudy sky. It's that dusky glare that begs for sunglasses and can illuminate one thing (a mini golf course on our left) and drape another (an abandoned gas station on our right) in complete shadows. I have no sunglasses, so I close my eyes and let my weight melt into the vinyl seat of the van. I think about how pleasant the day was. How there was no explaining and no insecurities and this huge sense of accomplishment. I had woken early to mend a few holes in my backyard fence and sprinkle the fresh sawdust into the bottom of Helen's coop. I had driven to a feed store[64] for chicken food and this insulating blanket for the coop, graded a

---

[64] Not the one Edward Harrington recommended, but the staff was still quite helpful.

stack of math quizzes, and made a pasta salad. My mother would say that pasta salad is a summer food and not for February consumption, but I like making huge batches of things on the weekends and eating them all week long. I know that's rather boring, but feeling organized makes me feel safe. I hope that makes sense. So I'm very tired in the car.

I realize now that I'm writing this down that once I stepped my booted feet onto Edward Harrington's land, I didn't think about David for the rest of the day. I thought about me and Gus and Gina and Edward and Helen Harrington and my new Helen Harrington and horses and chicken food and the smell of alfalfa and the noise that a barn door makes when it slams shut. I'd be lying if I said the distraction wasn't lovely.

We pull into the driveway and I invite Gus and Gina in for some pasta salad and a beer. "It might be vegan!" I say, hoping the bow-tie pasta I used doesn't include eggs. Gina doesn't seem too concerned. First we head around to the backyard, where I set Helen's carrier down in the middle of the yard and I open its door. We shuffle inside—to give her space and peace—and watch from the kitchen window as nothing happens. I turn on the porch light and start saying things like "Come on, girl. Let's go, Helen. I promise you'll love it here." Gus moves to the fridge and returns with three bottles of Heineken. I don't tell him it's left over from David and this summer. And I don't really mind that we're drinking it. The three of us stand there silently for a few minutes, sipping, staring, mentally coaxing Helen into her new world.

About halfway through the beers, we see a beak. There's a simultaneous intake of breath. We hold it. It's a timid little beak followed by a head and brown feathers coated in glistening trepidation. And then she does it. Helen—oh, she is so brave and I so proud—steps into the moonlight/porchlight/limelight of our evening. We all cheer. We clink our beers together and settle down to the kitchen table, pasta salad, baby carrots and hummus, a full bag of Fig Newtons. Later, as Gus clears the dishes and moves them into the sink, he says, "Wow, Annie. You have a garbage disposal, a dishwasher, *and* a chicken." He turns and looks at me as I'm shoving another Fig Newton into my face. "You've made it," he says. I smile. Crumbs fall everywhere.

14

*T*oday I'm calling my book *Reactivating the Fumes* (You will see why in five to ten minutes, depending on how fast you read), and it's going to have a collage of small scratch 'n' sniff stickers on the dust jacket. Everything from french fries to strawberries to a little mini chicken coop. Glue sticks. Roses. Dishsoap. Chocolate. Maybe one of David's secret weapons that smells like sulfurous gunpowder. I understand that this will probably cost the publisher an ass-load of money, but they will certainly sell tons more copies with this sort of gimmick. Scratch 'n' sniff is sooooo my generation.

Having a chicken has really improved my productivity and relaxed my mind. I wake up in the morning and see Helen scratching around in the patio outside her coop, poking her beak in and out of my dewy grass, sending her shiny feathers into waves of ripples with brisk, good-morning shimmies. And I go outside and greet her with a disgusting baby-talky, chirpy sweetness. I never knew I was capable of speaking in such diminutives.[65]

Anyway, almost every day I find an egg and shower her in praise, thanks, and congratulations. I think it helps. I think it really makes

---

[65] "Good morning, little pretty feather lady."

"How's my precious baby omega-3 producer?"

"Let's eat some of this yummy-yum-yum grainy grain."

"Look at you, feather princess. What a good girl—what a pretty beak."

"Come along, hen of mine."

"Helen of Tacoma, the world is waiting for you. Time to conquer breakfast!"

her feel good. And there's something about the way she fills her role so perfectly. She keeps to herself, clucks a bit, stays relatively tidy, lays eggs, sleeps, eats—success! A perfectly functioning creature! And thank goodness and Edward Harrington, she's a perfectly functioning *content* creature. She's really become quite the role model.

So in less than ten days, I've planned a Valentine's Day field trip. Annie Harper, perfectly functioning teacher. I knew it was going to be tough—in ten tiny days—to jump through the school district's flaming administrative hoops, to remind my children to get their permission slips signed, to coax five parents with minivans (and a day off) to chaperone, and most of all, to convince Jean and her dubious, undulating arm fat (whose grip on Violet Meadows policy is surprisingly taut) to allow my brood of babies in for a visit.

But I did it.

There was resistance from Barfley, who's known for vetoing field trips that aren't to the local trout hatchery or the lame children's museum downtown. But I quoted some bullshit line from the school's mission statement and then commented on the new girls' basketball trophy in Barfley's office. Done.

Jean was slightly more difficult to sway. It was primarily a health issue.

"I'm sorry. We absolutely cannot have children on the premises. The germs they carry are a substantial hazard to our residents." I swear Jean was reading out of a manual.

"Come on, Jean. Just this once?"

"Absolutely not." And then I hung up on her.

I knew instantly that some damage control and stupendous effort was required at this point—that pouting and quitting so soon was no way to get what I wanted. What would a chicken do? What would the industrious, courteous Helen do?

So I called right back before Jean had a chance to leave the office.

And in a flash of negotiating genius, I suggested that the students all sport paper surgical masks and that we slather their little hands in liquid sanitizer as they walk through the door. And maybe it wasn't those brilliant closing terms, but more Jean's desire to punch out and get home, but she said yes. Yes! I do a little dance in my kitchen and bang on the window to inform Helen of the victory.

I wake up on Valentine's Day humming. I select a bright red cardigan and black skirt, tights with a thick ribbing, and the trendiest of my low-heeled teacher shoes. Blow-dried hair replaces my usual limp, damp ponytail, and I apply four different makeup products to my face.

We spend the hour before we leave practicing our songs and rehearsing our skit one last time. It's a story the class wrote as a group about a gorilla and a piranha who become friends when the gorilla saves the piranha by throwing bananas at a group of ninja/pirate[66] fishermen along the Pokemon River on planet Neptune. The piranha then teaches the gorilla how to swim. Meanwhile, the gorilla's family abandons him because he's fraternizing with fish—"those ick-nasty gill breathers!" Eventually the two friends swim down the Pokemon River to a different village, where they open up a very successful comic book store. The skit is complete nonsense, but I still think it's outstanding. A whimsical tale of friendship and tolerance. It took everything in me to gracefully veto a super awesome decapitation scene. The two-years-ago Teacher Annie wouldn't have blinked twice and let the ninja/pirate heads roll, but then some lame parent would make a phone call and then Annie's head would roll. I now know better.

I told David about this skit the night before. It took far too long to explain it (I've never been good at summarizing), and David was obviously confused by the blatant nonsense. "So how can they be ninjas

[66] There was a split vote on having them be ninjas or pirates. So we decided *Why not both?* Multitalented criminals.

and pirates?" he had asked. Then he said, "You really let those kids go wild—they must love you." And then I said (perhaps more defensively than I intended to), "It's not wildness, David. It's called creativity, and it's good for the brain." I certainly don't question him about the numerous nonsensical elements about his job. But anyway, there are more important anecdotes for me to be typing here: the ones involving hand claps, tambourines, and big huge helpings of joy.

As we're waiting for the chaperones to arrive (amongst them are Lacey Atkins's mom, Charese [applause], and Caitlin Robinson's mom, Denise [boooooo]), I go over some behavioral rules with the kids.

"We need to be extra polite and remember not to touch anything."

"Will they give us candy like my grandpa does?" says Ben Morris.

"No, but I will give you candy if you act like angels."

I think we're fairly well prepared. *Miss Harper's Class Presents V-Day at V-Meadows 2004* is going to rock the house slippers off that oldie gang. I am so sure of it.

We all gather in the scarcely populated parking lot to position our surgical masks and roll our sleeves up in preparation for the hand sanitizer. On my drive home from school last night I was struck with the idea to decorate the surgical masks respective to each student's role in the skit: *Mambo and Spike Conquer the Universe*. If David was going to call me on my nonsense tolerance, I was going to go all-out nutso. NONSENSE RULES! So I pulled over at a drugstore to stock up on construction paper and Magic Markers. Sharp, angular teeth for the piranhas. Fat, dark lips for the gorilla family. Gold[67] and blacked-out teeth for the ninja/pirates. The rest of the cast—dancing trees, a sunshine, the narrator, myself, and the chaperones—have Valentiney hearts and kissy faces on our masks. The project became so

[67] I used glitter!

elaborate, I went through five episodes of a shark program marathon on the Discovery Channel and had to tiptoe over the thirty-five masks sprawled on my living room floor to dry. They looked like bulbous alien creatures growing on the surface of Neptune, I thought as I teetered through. They looked fantastic.

So I get out the masks, and the way my students shout *Cool!* and *Awesome!* and *You made these, Miss Harper!?* makes my insides gurgle like a brimming root beer float: fizzy and sweet and perfect. After the crew is perfectly costumed and after their hand germs have been viciously slaughtered by chemicals,[68] Miss Harper's class heads inside. And Loretta doesn't know we're coming. (!!!!!!!!)

We gather in the recreation room and Jean makes an announcement over the PA system that there will be a special Valentine's Day performance by surprise guests in the rec room. I'm so pleased with the way she inflects the words "surprise guests" with what sounds like genuine enthusiasm. After the announcement, we wait. It's quiet. Seconds pass and I start to think that no one is coming. Denise Robinson looks at me, raises her eyebrows, and smacks her gum. I'm nervous. "Where is everyone?" some twerp says. And just like that we hear it. The gritty murmurings of ancient vocal chords. The slow swish of plastic-soled loafers on linoleum. The high-pitched creaks of wheelchair bearings. The three hallways that lead to residents' rooms sprout off the recreation room, and the students follow my gaze from one corridor to the next as our pale, cottony audience approaches. I try to read the faces of the seniors. Most are blank, some carry the standard crumpled brow, and a few—a gorgeous few—are already smiling.

"Annie Harper, what have you brought us?" Loretta scurries up to me and rests her hands on top of Max Schaffer's and Steven Wright's

---

[68] Marco Antolini (such a yay-hoo) starts a slimy high-five movement that really catches on. The slappy sounds of the small, moist palms is particularly satisfying as it thu-wacks above the giggling voices.

little heads. "A pack of baboons?" She looks around at all the masks. A few students giggle quietly.

"Well, Loretta and all residents of Violet Meadows, please welcome my third-grade class from Franklin Elementary." Two people clap softly. It sounds like a fat dog lazily thumping his tail on the ground just a few times to snag his owner's attention and ask for food. I explain to our audience as they begin to seat themselves on the three sofas and various chairs of the rec room what kind of show we have in store for them and that we hope this will be a pleasant Valentine's Day for everyone.

We kick things off with a bumpy[69] but adorable rendition of Nat King Cole's "L.O.V.E." While rehearsing, the kids got in the habit of overemphasizing the first syllable of "extraordinary," and I see a woman with a fancy hat hop in her seat at the shock of the volume.

Despite its absurdist-style humor and multiple references to twenty-first-century pop culture, *Mambo and Spike Conquer the Universe* is received swimmingly. Spike, played by David Taylor, steals the show with an indistinguishable European accent, and one old man actually slaps his knee when Mambo (Lizzie McDonnell) goes ape-crazy throwing real bananas at the pirate/ninjas. It's a huge success. I can tell my kids are pulsing with pride.

We sing a few more songs, accompanied by tambourines and maracas, and then Max Schaffer takes front stage for the final act. He's brought out his violin, and I can almost hear the crowd sigh at the first few bars of one of Beethoven's sonatas. Max's face is serene and angelic while he plays. The rest of the class stands motionless and attentive, like they've been honing their ears for this exact moment since the first of September. I can't tell if it's the music or the tender tilt of Loretta's head or the obedient stillness of my perfect class, but a tear buds up in my right eye. The bridge of my nose can't support its weight for

---

[69] You try singing in a surgical mask!

long, and it cuts a quick, clean path and disappears into the fibers of my surgical mask. And that's when I hear the scream.

My head snaps to the source of the shrill noise. It's one of the wheelchaired women, and she's pointing a knotted finger at Garrett Wagner, who has toppled over, a crumbled wad of red sweatpants on the gray linoleum floor. "Shit, Garrett!" I shout and rush to his side. Max is still playing, reaching the climax of the piece, unaffected, seemingly unaware of the ruckus that has erupted around him. And it's all the same feelings I had when I thought David was blown into crumbs eating chicken fingers. But worse. I'm wearing a bodysuit of bee stings. My every organ is chili-dog nauseated. My head is a spinning clothes drier filled with steel-toed boots. I wave to Max to cut the music. I roll Garrett over onto his back and rip his surgical mask off his head. The pirate/ninja teeth go skidding across the floor, and I say his name a bunch of times. A few kids start crying. Almost immediately I feel that Garrett is breathing, and after a few miserable moments, his little eyes flutter open and he says, "Uhhmpha" or something very close to that.

"Garrett, sweetie. Are you okay? What happened?"

"I don't know." I silently curse myself for asking too many questions too fast, but then I can't help it.

"Are you hurt? Did you hurt anything falling down?" Garrett sits up, pushes his floppy blond hair from his eyes, and looks toward his pirate mask across the floor.

"No, I don't think so. I just got dizzy. My mask smelled funny." Smelled funny? I don't get it. A friend from college worked as a masked Minnie Mouse in Disneyland over the summers, and I remember her saying that Chinese food or hot dogs for lunch could ruin your entire shift. The air in the mask being so recycled and everything. Then I hear the smack of Denise Robinson's gum and she butts in.

"Yeah. I was worried about that. The moisture of the child's breath must have reactivated the fumes in the Magic Marker ink or the glue holding the glitter on. Inhaling all those toxins likely caused him to pass out." What was she? A fucking chemist! Magic Markers are non-toxic, and I always use Elmer's glue sticks that are impossible to get a buzz from huffing. That's outrageous. I hate Denise Robinson. The kid simply fainted. Probably exhausted from all the hefty pirate noises he had made, the shanty singing, and the maraca shaking.

As soon as Denise makes this proclamation, I can see the chests of my students rising and falling with exaggeration. I guess I can't blame the little shits for testing to see if their masks will also give them the spins. "Everyone, take off your masks." I order. Charese Atkins takes over tending to Garrett. She pulls a bottle of water from her purse and helps him to his feet. The kid seems fine, really. He's probably just a fainter. All teachers get one every few years or so. Mine was overdue.

I get to my feet and awkwardly thank everyone for their participation in the program. I thank the V-Meadows residents for being a great audience. And I apologize for the startling interruption of the violin finale. Loretta flashes me a look that says not to worry, but of course I am worrying my fucking brains off. Kicking myself over and over and over for endangering my students, terrifying a group of weak-hearted seniors, and mortifying myself in front of the chaperones. Jean is actually quite cool about it. She grabs my elbow on the way out the door. "Don't worry, Annie. Everyone had fun. Looks like that boy will be just fine. The residents will be talking about this for weeks. Don't worry. Fumes, schmumes, that woman doesn't know what she's talking about." And if I didn't have to chase down Marco Antolini as he bounded through the parking lot belting "Very very ¡EX!traordinary," I would have wrapped my arms around her smooshy shoulders and hugged the living crap out of her.

15

*T*oday I'm calling my book *101 Ways to Go Nuts While Your Lover Is at War*. Self help is always popular. While I was busy orchestrating dangerous field trips and poisoning my students, Helen was busy laying two beautiful eggs. Two! So I'm making myself a special treat for V-Day dinner: deviled eggs.

Garrett Wagner's mother agreed to come pick him up instead of letting him ride the bus home. I really think he would have been fine, but the possibilities for taunting are predictably high after such an incident, and I didn't want to subject the poor wimp to even further humiliation. After the class scurried out to the bus line, I bought Garrett and myself cans of Coke and Snickers bars from the staff lounge vending machine. While waiting for his mother, we enjoyed the snack by one of the computers,[70] looking up different breeds of dogs on the Internet. I asked Garrett if he'd ever passed out like that before.

"Oh yeah," he said. "Once at soccer practice and a couple times at my grandma's house." I spoke to him candidly because other than letting kids occasionally break the rules, frankness is the best way to show them respect.

"Do you think it was the scent of your pirate/ninja mask that made you dizzy?"

"Nah. I don't think so." And then he leaned in close to me and whispered, "Honestly, I think it was the smell of the old people."

---

[70] Eating by the computers is usually strictly prohibited. I made Garrett pinkie swear to never ever tell.

When Garrett's mother arrived (I'd only ever met his father at a parent/teacher conference), I was relieved to discover that she was one of those tough-skinned, no-fuss type of parents. The kind that trusts her kid to peel the stickers off his own apples, choose his own clothes, and read grown-up books whenever he's ready.

"Nothing to worry about, Miss Harper. Garrett has a history of wiping out. He looks fine to me already." She turned toward her son. "How was the skit, dude? Is that your Coke? Can I have a drink?" Garrett handed her the soda like he didn't expect or even want it back. Like he'd give his mother anything. I thanked her for coming to pick him up, and she was so calm and genuine in assuring me that she totally understood (her words). As the pair shuffled down the hallway, I heard Mrs. Wagner telling Garrett that his dad was picking up a pizza for dinner. The door slapped on Garrett's tiny "wahoo."

It's just so great when the right kind of people have the right kind of kids, when parent and child so perfectly match. It's seeing these sweet, symbiotic unions—*kid needs ride, mom needs caffeine*—that make me think of Baby Alden and what made his mother think she couldn't make their baby/momma partnership work. And then what changed to make her think she could. Did she find a stash of diaper coupons one day and think *Oh, 2-for-1 Pampers! This might not be so bad*? Or was it more biological than that? Perhaps her breasts ached when she took off her bra. Or maybe she woke up cradling her pillow and dreaming of her baby's soft, soft skin.

A few years after I found out about Baby Alden and his brief time as a Harper, my mother told me about how in the weeks following his departure my father—a lifelong sleepwalker—would get up in the night, walk to the nursery, and return with his arms cupped around a ghost of a baby. He would pace the room, rocking the dream baby to sleep and humming. Eventually his arms would just drop and he'd float, zombielike, back to my mother's side. I think enough years had passed so that my mother was able to smile and laugh at how cute and goofy it was. "He did it when you were a baby too, Annie."

"Sleep walked/rocked me?" I asked.

"Yes, but he wouldn't actually hold you. You'd be happily asleep in your crib, and he'd be wasting energy and startling me. But it was so sweet, of course." I didn't tell my mom that dreaming about a baby you still have isn't as sappily tragic as fake nurturing one you've recently lost. It was still a tender image to her. I really do have the sweetest parents. Too bad I so briefly got the chance to share them.

I think about this again back at home as I plop the creamy yolk mixture into the dips of the cleanly sliced boiled egg whites. Deviled eggs have always reminded me of little bassinets. Well, bassinets and funerals. They're such a typical wake food. Perhaps paprika and mayonnaise naturally lift moods and soothe tired eyes.

David just sent me an e-mail to thank me for the V-Day gift that he actually received a whole week early. He says the cookies were still fresh and delicious and that he's already worn the high-tech cooling socks three days in a row. He also asks if I got his package yet. A package! For me?! I have not! Instantly I realize that it's probably been days since I've entered my house through the front porch, where the postman leaves anything that doesn't fit through the mail slot in the door. My urgency to check on/dote on Helen has had me busting around to the backyard and entering the house through the rear door.

I open my front door to find a small parcel the size of a watch box. Inside there's a typewritten gift card—a square piece of pink card stock—and I can't help but imagine some package-processing stranger typing and printing out David's personal sentiments.

> TO: ANNIE, THE GIRLFRIEND WORTH ONE
> MILLION POINTS. HAPPY V-DAY.
> LOVE: DAVID

Points? What the dickens is he talking about? Some "Hot or Not" Army Dude game where they rate the aesthetic value of each other's lady friends back home? Possibly. But I doubt it. One million points can't be an easy score to achieve. I also wonder about the message's lack of exclamation points. Our last six months of electronic communication have taught me a lot about the man's textual communication style. With his proper manners, immaculate personal hygiene, and superior household cleanliness, I wouldn't have pegged him as the type to throw out "☺ ☺ !!!!!!!!!!!" as liberally as he does. But it is endearing. I figure he likely forgot to tell the customer service phone rep or the online order form to add the extra enthusiasm.

The box inside the box is the small velvety kind that announces "precious jewelry" in a smooth, classy voice. David has never bought me jewelry before, and the sophisticated texture of the box causes my guts to tense up in a way that makes me glad he isn't here to witness the reception of the gift. Jewels mean it's serious. A diamond pendant he'll see you wear for anniversaries to come. Dangly tennis bracelets that symbolize an unending love. Pearl earrings to show that you're precious and that you're worth it. It's all a bunch of crap to me. And I thought David knew that. Did he forget about the note he left on the motel room pillow promising my freedom if I want it? Isn't this whole mess about obtaining "freedom" anyway? Did David send me a diamond-bedazzled set of handcuffs? A four-million-pound engagement ring? The only other tiny velvet box I own belonged to my mother and contains the entire set of my baby teeth. Could David be sending me *his* baby teeth? Is that creepier than sapphire studs? Should I make the teeth into a necklace? Should I bleach them first?

I turn the box over in my hands one more time before I open it. It snaps open with a loud crack, causing the contents to hop off their plush resting place. It rattles and settles. It's a necklace. I force out an exaggerated sigh and laugh at myself. At David. Along a delicate sterling silver chain and resting in an equally shiny silver bearing is a

Scrabble tile. An *A* for "Annie" worth a measly one (million!!!!!! ☺ ☺
☺) point(s). It is cute. As long as I don't equate it to those gross sweaters that teachers wear with appliquéd pencils and school buses on the
pockets, I like it. It's a very thoughtful gift. A reminder of how many
times I've kicked his business-major ass.

16

*B*ig fat sigh.[71]

The rest of February and the first weeks of March were unremarkable. In the movie version of my story, they would be depicted through a musical montage of the following scenes:

Driving in the snow.
Demonstrating long division to my class on the chalkboard.[72]
Flipping through news channels on my television.
Diving for the phone when it rings.
Looking at a picture of David.
Scattering grain for Helen.
Cracking an egg in a skillet.
Cracking an egg in a skillet.
Cracking an egg in a skillet.
Diving for the phone when it rings.
Eating Indian food with Gus.
Learning to play pinochle with Loretta and two of her friends.
Cracking an egg in a skillet.

---

[71] Today I'm calling my book *Caution: This Book Has a Surprise Middle Part,* and the cover is traffic-sign yellow with a drawing of me baring my teeth. Maybe I'll even have fangs.

[72] Actually, like most modern classrooms, mine has a dry-erase whiteboard. The fake classrooms they use for the filming of the movie aren't quite up to date. The dull green chalkboard doesn't glare in the lights like the whiteboard does. This is total bullshit. Annie, you're losing it.

Driving in the rain.
Driving Max Schaffer to his violin lesson in the rain.
Looking at a picture of David.
Combing Loretta's hair.
Eating pizza with Gus.
Trying to pet Helen.
Helen running away.
Trying to pet Helen.
Helen trying to fly.
Scattering grain for Helen really close to my feet.
Trying to pet Helen.
Walking casually to the phone when it rings.
Cracking an egg in a skillet.
Demonstrating the cursive *Q* to my class on the chalkboard.
Trying to pet Helen.
Cracking an egg in a skillet.
Eating clams with Gus.
Letting the phone ring and ring.
Laughing with Loretta.
Flipping through the news channels on my television.

Even that was a bit long for a rather dull month. But the editors will know how to pare it down. So it's probably a wise editorial choice to glaze over it and get straight to my spring break camping trip. I took a break from writing because I was starting to feel too self-indulgent and repetitive and generally lame about it. One night I went online and read all these blogs[73] of wives whose husbands are deployed in Iraq. The blogs are called things like "On the Homefront" and "While My Love Is Gone." All the ones I read belong to young women with babies. Two

[73] Perhaps I should call them *blahgs*.

babies, three babies, a woman in Nebraska with four babies—ages six months to six years. And reading these blogs depressed the hell out of me on many levels. Please allow me to explain.

Level 1: The Risk of Fatherless Babies

This is quite obvious. All those cute, chubby offspring with stewed carrots dripping down their ARMY BABY bibs have no idea that Papa might be blown to smithereens. They probably just know that he's gone and that his certain variation of peek-a-boo has been discontinued. The older children—Stevie, Junior, Mary Rose, Freedom[74]—they understand that Daddy's away working and that he's fighting in a WAR. I know twenty-nine third graders. They're amazingly, disturbingly, well acquainted with the subject.

Level 2: Lack of Surprises and Encouraging Sentiments

When I stumbled upon the first blog and started to search for others, I thought I'd busted into some new resource: a backstage tour to the women who were similarly coping. I thought that I'd cluck my tongue at clever survival tips and snort at amusing anecdotes. I thought these women—army and marine wives of years—would say things to encourage this Woman at Home and teach me more about the fucked-up situation we all share. I thought it would be like the boiled-down version of the Knitwhit Wife Ladies. I'd get the helpful scoop without all the shit-talking and social pressure. It'd be this authentic, insightful dialogue . . . but organized! Miss Harper Loves Organized! But my expectations fell far outside of what actually

[74] I'm not lying. Freedom is a precious three-year-old in Maryland with dark, curly hair and a severe peanut allergy.

exists on the World Wide Web. It was all wholesome, obvious, and a big fat waste of time. It was kind of like reading the directions on the back of a shampoo bottle, but with all the lovely adjectives missing. Or maybe the instructions on a can of soup. Or the ingredients label for a jar of applesauce. Wash. Rinse. Repeat. Heat. Stir. Apples. Sugar. Yawn.

> Roger called today. Mary Rose was so excited to tell him about losing her first tooth.
>
> Five months down! Three to go!
>
> Thank you to everyone for all your prayers!!!!
>
> Their [sic] are times when I don't think I can do it, but I just turn to his picture and remember the commitment he made to our country and the commitment we made to each other and then I know that I have to be brave.

Am I the only psycho who fantasizes about my lover's death and gets pissy when he writes short, boring, no-meat e-mails? Well, I guess I can't blame a woman for not posting that kind of confession on the Internet. But still. Nothing to learn really. Generic, weepy crap.

Level 3: Guilt for Severely Passing Judgment on Bloggers for Properties Listed in Level 2

Generic, weepy crap is a horrible thing to call someone's real life. Especially someone with whom I share a common risk and situation. Our hearts are all cast across the same fat ocean and dangling from the same wimpy fishing line with the same incompetent Texan holding the reel.[75] I shouldn't scoff at their woes. And I shouldn't feel superior because I think I'm approaching this in a different, more creative, more analytical way. Because I'm not really. They're raising humans. I'm raising a chicken and learning to play pinochle. Big whoop.

Level 4: Eighty Pounds in Eight Months

So pretty much all of the blogs have wedding pictures. The husband decked out in his dress blues, the now-blogging wife radiant in a sweeping white gown. Her arms are sleek, tapering down to a modest bouquet of lilies that nearly covers the span of her feminine waistline. And then there's the *now* photos of Mrs. Blogger standing behind her twin three-year-olds on the swing set. The kids are smiling for Daddy. She's smiling for Daddy. But there's a whole lot more of Mommy behind those swings. A stomach bulging out of an elastic waistband. Mounds of flesh draped over her cheekbones. Thick arms and thunder thighs. She's too busy wiping off drool and washing peed-on bedsheets to get to the gym. She's eating the Tater Tot and taco casseroles, rich with creamy condensed soups and kindly delivered by a member of the church ladies' guild each week. A few of the bloggers even discuss their deployment weight gain on their sites. They are all good-natured about it, owning up to stress-eating and whatnot. Dare I ponder if it's from lack of S.E.X.? P.S. None of the blahgers mention anything about S.E.X. on their blogs, which I guess I get, because their mothers probably read them.

So that's why I quit writing for a bit. David and I don't have any children. I'm not praying or thanking anyone else for praying. Everything I say is probably Generic Weepy Crap. And thank Jesus and

---

[75] Can you tell I recently went fishing? Teacher Gone Wild: Spring Break Camping Trip. Tonight on *The Annie Harper Show*!!!

Helen that my protein-rich, poverty diet has kept me fit as a fiddle. What do I have to complain about?[76] slkdfjf slkdjhfskldj fskldjfh sdkjnv,xmnseduiskjhsd. !!!!!!!!!!!!!! fuck.

But first, the fishing trip.

Gus invited me to join Gina; himself; and his college buddy, Stephen, on a five-day fishing/camping trip at the Potholes State Park in eastern Washington. The Potholes are this smattering of tiny lakes (some are natural volcanic leftovers; others are manmade reservoirs used for crop irrigation) nestled at the eastern side of the Cascade Mountains and the Columbia River. Their plans coincided with my spring break, and I couldn't think of a more lovely way to spend it.

The weather was perfect. And in Washington State, perfect weather permits incessant commentary. It's not considered lame or master-of-the-obvious to say things like *Oh, it's so gorgeous* or *What an amazing night* several times an hour. So we did. We packed up Gus's van on a Saturday morning that was crisp and clear enough to necessitate sunglasses. I rolled my dorky cargo pants up to midcalf and we listened to a cassette tape of Aesop's fables that Gus brought along in the van. We cracked our windows and slipped our fingers outside to curl over the lip of the cool glass. Stephen turned out to be a great guy. Not that I expect Gus to have lame friends, but I was skeptical when he told me of Stephen's prep-academy upbringing and present enrollment in dental school. Yes, he was a bit soft and

---

[76] See, that's what I thought then, when I quit writing after V-Day. But my my my how things have changed, boys and girls. This is one fucked-up world. Something happened that I would never have guessed. It was flying low and sad, below the radar, below the range of my classroom, my telephone, my chicken coop. Even in my disgusting self-absorption, I couldn't have made this up to amplify the interestingness of my story. It just happened. So here I am. Back at the keyboard.

delicate-looking, but he jabbed that first earthworm on his first fishing hook with a fearless, devious smile that both impressed me and scared me a bit for his future patients. Stephen was big into making up songs about fishing[77] and looking for animal tracks. The way nature can set city folk[78] reeling in raw wonder is beautiful. It's like when I show my students a simple crystal of salt under a microscope or this one video about deep-sea creatures that look so much like aliens. He had that same stunned appreciation for things. Stephen is fantastic.

The four of us had long talks around the campfire. Gus and I told embarrassing stories about one another from our teen years. Once he went off about how I got my eyebrow pierced junior year and that it got so infected that my eye swelled shut and he had to build a dam out of a playing card and masking tape to prevent the pus from leaking down and seeping into my eye socket.

"Yeah, I drove her to the emergency room, where all the doctors wanted to take pictures for their medical textbooks. It was that gross. Do you remember the names of the books that published the photos, Annie? Didn't they give you free copies?" The fire had dwindled down to a few glowing embers, and it was too dark for Stephen or Gina to see my hand wrapped across my face holding in the laugh.

"No way!" Stephen said. "I bet we have those books in the Harvard Medical Library!"

---

[77] It's this danglin' line of mine
and some good ol' concentration
a danglin' lure,
the fishies' cure
for overpopulation!

[78] Stephen lives in Boston. He does not know my friend Michelle, a nurse, who also lives there. I'm considering setting them up.

But then Gina asked, "Did you ever get any other piercings?" and Gus and I both lost it.

"Sorry to disappoint, guys," I spit out after finally allowing a laugh to escape my lips. "None of that never happened. Gus is full of shit." Stephen threw a beer cap in Gus's direction and Gina cursed him playfully.

"Full of macaroni and delicious lake trout, to be precise," Gus said. But now that I'm in analyzing/writing mode, the story about my pus-filled eyebrow could have happened. Gus told it so well I nearly believed it myself. I've known Gus for so long, and we have so many dumb stories about one another, that we can fictionalize small bits of our past without it feeling artificial. I very well could have pierced my eyebrow. (I did dye my hair black twice junior year.) And if I had pierced it, Gus and I both know that I wouldn't have been too great at remembering to swab the healing hole with alcohol and keep it sterile. And when the pus started to brim and swell, Gus would certainly have put his perfect-SAT-math-score brilliance to work and constructed the described apparatus. So as humorous as the fireside fable may have been, it just as easily could have been fact. When you know someone well enough to properly portray their character, what's the harm inserting that personality into an alternate reality? Not factually true, but pretty much *actually* true. Annie, you need to home in on this theory a bit before you attempt to present it to the critical reader. Yikes.[79]

---

[79] Gus and I have always been big on lying to each other. In college we had this weird game where we made up fake news about our former classmates to see how crazy a detail we could get the other to believe. I hear Jennifer Rendell is acting in a toothpaste commercial. Oh yeah, Mark Picha lost a finger in a construction accident. The lie had to strike a balance between absurd and mundane in order to be reasonably received. A story worth telling, but not one that's obviously contrived.

. . . . . .

I shared a tent with Stephen, and he slept still and silent like a corpse. We stayed up late each night talking about worthless things like the prices of certain magazine subscriptions and the social patterns of kids at sleepaway camp. And it felt so rich and siblinglike. Stephen has four brothers and two sisters and endless tales of their hair pulling and high jinks. I always thought that Gus was so brotherly, but now that I think about it, that idea makes very little sense. He's as much nobody's brother as I am nobody's sister. How could he possibly fit the bill? But Brother Stephen, he teased in a way that was so totally avuncular; without a hint of flirtation and with this underlying wisdom that I completely trusted. Occasionally, we could hear Gus and Gina giggling from their tent (and nothing more than that, thankfully), but every time my hearing picked up the deep tones of Gus's unique laugh, I honestly couldn't help but innocently wonder who was spooning whom.

The last morning of the trip, I woke up super early. I swear there was a bird perched right outside the tent, brushing his beak up to poke the nylon wall and coo straight into my ear. I looked over to find Stephen stiff as stone, smiling peacefully and probably dreaming of rugby or tight, clean gums. I heard someone walking around outside, so I slipped on my sneakers and zipped myself out of the tent. Gus had just sat down on a stump and was doing something with his hands. I assumed he was fussing with a lure.

"Going fishing?" I whispered. Our campsite was the most remote corner of the Potholes State Park. No outhouse. No running water. A three-mile hike from the last human. The reward for schlepping in all our stuff was our own mini, but glorious, lake—flat and round like a shiny tin plate. We'd christened it Hobo Lake because it reminded Gus of something a hobo would eat beans off. I thought hobos didn't bother with flatware, but the name stuck. Whispering was in order because the water made everything so darn loud. Gus simply shook his head, and I walked over to see what he was doing.

"I woke up this morning and remembered that I brought these. We have to use them before we head out." Gus was snapping together little pieces of balsa wood: the wings and rudders of mini planes. Gliders. Gus has always been into aviation. I think I may have mentioned the rocket-building phase before. "Let's go to the clearing up there." We'd set up camp about fifty feet from the lake's edge, at the foot of a gentle hill of volcanic gravel and pale green shrubbery. At the top of the hill was a fairly level patch of land the size of a baseball diamond, where the vegetation was substantially thinner. When we found it on the first day, Gus said we could play cricket there. Gina said we could dance. Stephen said we could perform ritual sacrifices to the gods.

There was no need to talk as Gus and I launched our planes, watching them loop and swirl and lift with the morning breeze. At first we stood side by side, throwing and chasing the toys in tandem. Keeping silent track of whose plane was floating further and whose was making the more dramatic dives. Then, without either one of us giving instructions or announcing the idea, we took to different sides of the clearing and threw our planes in each other's directions. Awkward enemies with clunky missiles. First, we'd simply chase them until they landed, scoop them up, throw them back. But then Gus got all fancy and starting trying to snatch the planes from the air midflight. He was actually quite good at it—obviously the Ultimate Frisbee type. I'd never seen him so graceful and athletic. Leaping over plants, boosting off a rock to gently snag the plane by its nose, his body seemed so comfortable and harmonious. Balanced, clean lines, his flannel shirt never pulling too tight. Everything was so quiet except for the occasional bird, my heavy breathing, the red gravel crunching under our feet.

So then I tried to catch the planes too. The first couple times I'd outrun them and they'd be bumping along the earth behind me as I turned to nab them at eye level. But I got better at judging the distance and I finally managed to snag one out of the air. "Yessssssss!" I shouted as I felt my fingers latch around the light, almost cardboard-like wood. The momentum of my leap pulled me down to the ground, and when I stopped hearing my "yesssss" echo across the hills and glide along Hobo Lake, I noticed that I'd completely crushed the main axis of the plane. And these were my thoughts, in chronological order:

1. Gus is going to be so pissed I broke his plane.
2. David flies in planes[80] all the time and could easily be crushed like this.
3. I should have thought 2, then 1.
4. Why am I thinking 3? What does this mean?

And then Gus noticed that I wasn't getting up and came over.

"You alright, Harper?" He put a hand on my shoulder. Its warmth surprised me.

"I busted it. I'm sorry." I must have looked so ridiculous, looking up at him like I was delivering the news of a loved one's death.

"No worries, Annie. I got these for ninety-nine cents. Besides, we should probably head back to camp and make breakfast. Gina doesn't know that I brought blueberries for pancakes. Her favorite." Gus smiled and wiped his hands on his pants before helping me up. As we sidestepped down the incline I almost lost my footing because the clear sky kept luring my vision away from the earth. "It's so nice out," I said. Twice.

I slept almost the entire drive home. I woke up because my cell phone was vibrating in the pocket of my jacket. I had turned it on as we were

---

[80] Well. Helicopters, technically.

leaving, knowing that we'd roll into a service area at some point and maybe I'd have a message from David. (Un?)surprisingly, it was kind of the first time I'd thought about David since I'd laid eyes on the gloss of Hobo Lake. Having the phone off and the Internet and the newspaper and the rest of the universe on the other side of the Cascade Mountains, the camping trip was both a breath and a release. I didn't worry about David. I didn't have to get mad at myself for getting mad at him and not being accepting enough of our standby excuse: "It's the War zone." I left no breadcrumbs for anxiety to follow and gobble the fun out of my perfect, sunny campsite. Once I noticed the phone shaking, it took too long for me to lift my head off the fogged-up window, wipe the drool from my chin, and fumble with the zipper of my pocket; I missed the call. I saw that it was my parents' house and that they didn't leave a message. So I called back. They knew I was going out into the sticks, and I figured they simply wanted to know I wasn't returning with only seven and a half frostbitten toes. My dad picked up.

"Hey, Annie. Where are you?" There was that exact pitch in his voice that said *Something is wrong but I'm trying to manipulate my voice to sound like Nothing is wrong.* Very few people can fool someone they love with deftly hidden concern. Even on cell phones. I told him that we were heading back from camping. About fifteen minutes outside Tacoma. He asked if I could stop by the house.

The environs of Tacoma are not pretty. Strip malls, strip clubs, strips of freeway speckled with soggy trash. If you're already scared or depressed or pissed off, the suburban scenery will do little to assuage your mood. If you're lucky, you'll pass a cheery billboard about winning the lottery. I tried not to stress out too much on the way home. To distract myself I started asking Gina a bunch of questions about vegan living. She did an amazing job of describing the process of making soy yogurt. And I never knew that spelt was such a versatile food.

American flags kept popping out at me from the gutters of car dealers and the side windows of 18-wheelers. It can't be David, I thought, trying to be the kind of positive that would prevent me from vomiting in Gus's van. Nothing wrong with David Peterson! As we rolled into city limits, I asked Gus if he could drop me off at my parents' house. "They said they have some sort of news," I said. "Sounds dire." And then the four of us exhaled at once. Almost a scripted sigh.

"No problem. I need to pay my old man a visit anyway." My parents and Gus's dad have lived in the same West Tacoma neighborhood since the late eighties. Our two split-level houses are near replicas of one another, but mirror images. They each have an attic window that makes for easy access to the gentle incline of the shingled roof over the garage. Gus's roof gets sunrises, which was great during his old yoga days.[81] And I had the sunsets. His dad paints his place a new, interesting color every few years. There was the Pepto-pink of late elementary school, the blue bubble gum ice cream of junior high. I remember this past summer when Rex just finished the topcoat of a striking, almost metallic light gray. "Chromey and homey," Gus had said at his coming home from the Peace Corps party. My house has always been a very dull beige. Typical Taupe. Ordinary Oatmeal or Banal Baby Puke.[82]

As Gus pulled the van into the driveway, I leaned across the bench seat to hug Stephen and then up to the front of the van to offer a teetering half embrace to Gina, then Gus. "What a trip," I said, but it didn't sound right. Because I was freaking out inside, I couldn't infuse

---

[81] Freshman year of high school. Before the big yoga comeback.

[82] I was really into those contests Crayola had in the midnineties where you could make up the names of the new color crayons. I still can't believe that "Macaroni & Cheese" beat out my obviously superior "Speckle of the Poison Dart Frog" for the new bright orange. I suspect a sizeable chunk of $$$ from Kraft Foods had something to do with it.

my voice with the zeal and earnest gratitude that our adventure deserved. It *was* a great trip. I promised Stephen to visit Boston over the summer, and he made a joke about remembering to keep my mouth shut.[83] As I heaved my pack over my shoulder and slammed the sliding door of the van, Gus snaked his head around to where I could see it through the window. He made the universal hand sign for "call me if you need to."

I busted through the front door and threw my pack at the foot of this gnarly coat tree we inherited from a dead aunt. It's something I did every day with my gym bag in high school: the kind of thing that drives every mother nutso. "Just take it five more steps to your room." That's what she would always say. This time when my parents came shuffling out of the kitchen to greet me midfling, my mother said nothing.

"So, what?" I asked. "Is David dead?" And I said it in this weird tough-guy voice. This grisly shield I'd never heard myself use before. Like I was pulling a sleek gun from my shoulder holster, telling my darling parents not to fuck with me. But my mom was too quick. Before I had a chance to widen my stance and lift that gun to eye level, Mom-dawg was rolling.

"Oh goodness, Annie. No. We knew you'd be thinking that. David's fine—he actually e-mailed me this morning. Sit down. This is a lot and I hope that we—" I flopped onto the sofa and burrowed into the smooshy back cushions: the unaffected, apathetic slouch of a teenager. I rolled through possibilities in my head. All my grandparents were reasonably healthy. My father's a veteran union worker on the path to retirement—couldn't be laid off. My mother was just boasting about her perfect mammogram last month. I thought that if David was fine, then there was nothing else they could get me with. Perhaps

---

[83] A reference to an incident where I accidentally ate a mysteriously crunchy bug and earned the nickname "Bullfrog."

Helen was killed by a pack of wolves? My dad interrupted my mother.

"It's Alden, Annie."

"Baby Alden?" I asked stupidly. Like there's ever been another one.

"Yes. He's dead."

"Brother Alden?"

"His grandmother Barbara called yesterday."

"Bless Her Heart, Barbara?"

My parents both nodded.

"Holy. Fucking. Shit." I said. Loud. Strong. Incredulous. Then quieter: "BabyAldenBrotherAldenDead."

Gus's house has this cool door knocker, a gnarly wild boar with a nose ring. It was close to midnight when I lifted the bronze ring and let it fall in a series of bangs that started loud and fluttered away to silence. I knew Gus was still there because his van was still there, and after all the strange crying and talking and supposing with my parents, I didn't want to bother them with driving me home. They tried to convince me to stay the night up in my old room, but I lied about having to feed Helen.[84] Gus answered the door and I fell into his arms like a typical, flimsy female. I started crying again. I think he said, "Whoa, there."

He agreed right away to drive me home, didn't even go back in the house to collect his things or tell his dad.[85] In the van I immediately assumed the slumpy window position that I had used last fall after the whole red pen/fork eye-stabbing incident at school. We both said nothing for the first several minutes.

[84] My neighbor had actually just fed her that morning—hopefully using the two pages of instructions I left on how exactly Sweet Precious Love Baby Helen likes her grain to be scattered.

[85] Or Stephen and Gina, who were likely still around.

"Alden is dead, Gus." I told him at a stoplight.

"Baby Alden?"

"Uh-huh."

"*Where Is Brother Alden?* Alden?"

"Yup." After sobbing fits, I always feel like my brain has been rearranged—kind of like after a night of heavy drinking—and the words I use and the way I say things are like some other mixed-up version of me. "Yup"? I never say that.

"What happened?" I could tell Gus was upset. He scooted to the edge of his chair, leaned into the windshield, bit his lower lip.

"He was shot," I said in my second weird voice of the night. The beaten, defeated version of my previous heat-packin' persona. "In Iraq." Then Gus's curiosity broke out of the pack, leaving his sensitivity and his logic limping in the dust. He just fired out all these questions, and from my slumpy post against the window, looking in the side-view mirror at the way my lips moved and made strange shadows, I just answered him. Gave him every little bit I knew.

Every Little Bit I Know[86]

Bless Her Heart Barbara called my parents the day before. BHH Barbara is Alden's father's mother, which we never knew. Apparently it took my father a while to figure out who she was. She had never EVER called before. She must have looked us up in the phonebook. She told my father that Alden had enlisted in the Marines straight out of high school in 1998. He was killed last month during a raid in Fallujah. Bless Her Heart Barbara had thought that my parents should know—that they would be proud.

"A month?" Gus asked. We'd pulled into my driveway. "Why did she wait so long to tell you?"

---

[86] Possible book title.

"I don't know. She probably was busy grieving. Maybe it took her that long to think of us." And though that thought kind of blows my mind—though I'm so fucked up that I would love to think that within five minutes of learning of her grandson's death, Bless Her Heart Barbara would lift her soft pointer finger to her lips and think, *Oh dear, I must tell the Harpers*—I really doubt that's the case. Then I start rambling to Gus.

"You know, this is so messed up. Why do I feel such a significant loss over someone who was kind of insignificant to me? I didn't actually know him. Never fucking met the buck-toothed kid. Technically, logically, I should feel this shitty about every twenty-two-year-old who has died over there. I mean, I've spent the last—I don't know—seven years thinking about this guy and planning some dopey reunion where we become fast friends and suddenly he's like, the maid of honor in my wedding and we go backpacking around Europe together.

"I bet the only reason I feel anything is because I'm feeling bad for myself all over again for the same selfish reasons—for never having a goddamn brother." The engine had been off for several minutes, and it was starting to get cool inside the van. I yanked the hood of my sweatshirt over my head and pulled my hands inside the sleeves.

"Maybe the grief you're feeling isn't for you, but for the full life he didn't have. Maybe your gut is aching for his family and friends who are going to miss him. Because you kind of already know what it's like to miss him . . . even though you didn't know him?" He inflected his voice like a question mark on that last part. Gus reached over and put his hand on my leg. "And obviously you're also kind of freaking out because the volatility of this whole situation is becoming more real. If it can be Alden, it can be David."

And the word hit me like a fucking anvil. David. Ever since Alden's name tumbled out of my father's mouth trailed by that betraying verb "is" and that wicked adjective "dead," I hadn't actually thought about David. Not once. I know it seems weird, especially because of the circumstances of them both being soldiers and them both fighting in the same war and me having a very substantial history of fretting about said war, but I don't know why, I just didn't think about it.

"Yeah, I guess so," I said to Gus. And *then* I felt the weighty urge to talk to David. Whether the weight was emotional need or straight obligation, I felt it. It got heavier and heavier very, very quickly. A suit of armor that stiffened my joints and kind of made me feel like an anonymous robot. I exchanged a brief hug, thank you, goodbye series with Gus and I got out of the van. I let myself in the front door and collapsed at my kitchen table. I folded my hands on top of the woven placemat and sat very, very still. After a few minutes, I adjusted the fringe tassels on both sides of the placemat. Perfectly straight and or-derly. Perfect placemat. Easy life! Then I got up and walked toward the garage.

In the garage, I puttered about the cabinet where I keep gardening equipment and tools. Then I found it. It looked smaller and felt lighter than what I remembered from the one time David and I took it to his buddy's house in Spanaway to pop soda cans off a fallen tree trunk.

I walked around the side yard.

Let myself in the back gate.

Stealth.

Powerful.

Sleek.

Alone.

And then I shot my beautiful chicken.[87]

---

[87] Please turn the page right now.

17

Today I'm calling my book *Almost Perfectly Innocent,* and obviously I did *not* murder Helen. It's just that while I was writing and thinking about Alden being dead and David's chances being just as gloomy, I guess I was craving a sort of drama I could control. Yes, it was a nasty, sick fantasy—especially considering how much I adore Helen—but there was a power in making up that scene that felt kind of good. If I shot Helen, I'd be entirely the one to blame. It's like people who chew their fingernails when they're going through tough times. Michelle— from college—she smiles when people tell her bad news. Someone is saying how their best friend from junior high just tested positive for HIV, and stupid jerkface Michelle is fighting the corners of her mouth from curling upward and baring her pretty teeth.

I don't know what I'm talking about. But I do know this: Grief makes people do weird shit. And this nutso breed of brother-I-had-for-two-months-and-don't-remember-and-never-met-is-dead grief has really got me flirting with absurdity.

How's this for absurd? In the past three days I've shampooed my carpets, rearranged my bookshelves, filed my taxes, experimented with four corn bread recipes,[88] read two books,[89] and laundered all my bedding. I'm pretending it's the normal *spring cleaning* that I do every year, but honestly, it was a lot of putzing around the house waiting for David to call. He's been really busy, and I didn't want to tell him

---

[88] Blue corn, honey swirl, jalapeño, and ricotta corn bread pancakes.

[89] *Fear and Loathing in Las Vegas* (for the first time) and *Remains of the Day* (for the second time).

about Baby Alden as a response to one of his generic, three-line
e-mails.

> Hey Annie,
> I only have a minute to write, but I just wanted to let you know
> that things are going okay. Things have been a bit more
> tumultuous lately and I've been going out on these extra two-day
> missions that are a total bitch. Miss you love you. Yours, D

Things? Things are both okay *and* tumultuous? Since when did David make these kinds of equations? I need to e-mail some of those
blahgers and see how they get by on such meager communication.
These bare bones of vague facts. Wee little snips of status reports.
Logical inconsistencies, for Christ's sake. Back when David was
here, there was so much to discuss and so much time to indulge
frivolous conversations. I would tell him a whole twenty-minute
story about an oral book report I did in seventh grade and how my
bedsheet toga fell off during the presentation. He'd explain to me
why a good cornerback is so important to a high school football
team. We'd argue over which beers to have on tap at the tavern we
fantasized about opening on the waterfront. But now *things are going
okay.* I guess I shouldn't complain. So far he's been luckier than poor
Alden.

   I'm painting my toenails[90] and watching a television program
about modern-day shepherds in France when my cell phone
rings—finally—displaying the telling "012345678."

   "At last!" I answer the phone.

   "Annie?" David says. Unconventional greetings often throw him
off for some reason.

---

   [90] A magenta color officially called "Out on the Town," which I have re-
named "Bleeding Heart."

"Oh David, I'm so glad you called. It's been forever."

"I know. I'm sorry. I've wanted to. You know how it is."[91]

"Yeah," I say.

"Yeah . . . So what's new? How was your spring break? Tell me about camping." And it's weird because I want to tell David all about camping. About Stephen and all the fish we caught and the beautiful Girl Scout fire I made each night. But then it just feels so unbalanced to foist the details of my life onto him when it seems like he is not so into foisting details back my way. And also because I'm holding this load in my arms about Alden.

"Camping was awesome," I say.

"Cool. Catch any big fish?"

"David, Alden died."

"What? Alden?"

"Yeah. My once-upon-a-time brother Alden." And then David gets real quiet. I tell him the whole story, and he stays all shushed up for a long time. Then he says he's sorry—in this tiny, tiny voice—over and over and over and I keep telling him that it's okay and that I'm really just sad for Alden's family and the devastating brevity of his life. And, of course, because I never knew him. David assures me that marines are always doing more dangerous stuff than the army, and he asks a few questions about where Alden was stationed in Iraq, what his MO

---

[91] That's the problem. I don't. I know that he is busy. I know that showers don't happen often and that his sleeping hours are weird and shift all the time. But I don't know any concrete details about how the hours of his workday are truly passed. In my head I have all these visions of him looking at green and black monitors, flipping switches and talking into a headset. I can see him polishing his weapon with a soft rag and sprinting across a patch of sand and flinging himself heroically into the back of a moving jeep. But these aren't images from stories David has told me; they are probably just of a mix of stupid scenes from movies and military recruitment ads I've seen on TV.

was, and of course I don't know much beyond Fallujah and a lucky enemy gunshot. I most definitely don't know. Change seats! Now it's Annie Harper with a dry mouth of paltry details.

"What's weird, David, is that he died over a month ago, and I never noticed him in the Names of the Dead section." I've been puzzling this quite seriously.

"Well, maybe you missed a day?"

"Yeah, maybe. Because I know I'd have stopped at an Alden." Silence. Silence. Silence.

"David, are you okay?"

"Yeah, I'm alright." And then I ask him if anyone in his company has died yet. I can tell this always makes him a little uncomfortable, but they haven't lost a man yet and now I'm superstitious about it. Like if I keep asking, they will all keep not dying. And I know it's odd that I ask because obviously if something happened, he'd tell me. He tells me that no one has died and that one guy I don't know hurt his leg pretty bad in a non-combat-related accident. I say that I'm sorry and that I hope he gets better fast. He's quiet again.

"David?"

"Yeah, babe. I'm sorry. I'm just tired. Worn out. And I'm kind of sad. I just wish I were there with you. I think that since I've been gone, this exact moment is the one moment where more than anything, we really need to hug."

"Seriously," I say.[92]

---

[92] This is one of those things that I'm trying to stop saying. A professor of mine in college told me once that the women of my generation are going to have difficulties transitioning into adult speech patterns. He said that in twenty years there would be a whole lot of lawyers and doctors and teachers and social workers tossing "like" and "no way" into their professional vernacular. And I guess it is a bit embarrassing that I can occasionally drop the "Oh my god" bomb with that ridiculously immature lilt in my voice.

"Well, I hope you feel better about Alden and everything. I can't believe it. I can't believe that he was here too."

"I know."

Silence. Silence. Silence.

"I kind of hate the universe sometimes." String theory is beautiful; war is not.

"Annie, I better get going. I have to work in about a half an hour and I should try and grab some food before I go." Before we hang up I go through my regular *be safe, wear your helmet, never wear earplugs* kind of talk. I say things like *Don't forget to engage in thoughtful inquiry; it's more likely than your brute strength to save your life.* And David is so kind that he doesn't tell me I'm silly and that the U.S. Army has already got strategic thinking down pat.

I've been thinking I might want to print out all the e-mails David has sent me since he's been gone. I will cut super close around the text and pin them up, flush against each other on a bulletin board. Then I can stand before them with three colors of highlighters and study them for subtext and hidden codes. I can count certain words and make a graphical depiction of how his mood has fluctuated throughout this experience. But I don't think I need the graph to know that right now, he's suffering. But I think I do need the graph to find out exactly why. Right now I'm picking up a blanket war sadness. I want him to kindly toss me more details.

The penultimate day of spring break (Easter Eve) I go down to V-Meadows to visit Loretta. Right away she asks to inspect my fingernails for "muck and fish scales." I tell her all about the camping trip: the fires and the quiet nights. She gasps when I describe the freedom of wearing the same socks for three days. And I'm right in the middle of describing Hobo Lake when I start to feel kind of bad about it, wondering how long Loretta has been cooped up in this dismal prison. Will she ever get out? What would her freedom look like? I imagine her hair down, the wind's fingers gently plucking out each of her trusty bobby pins and swirling them to gather in her hand. She clasps her fingers around the pins and does that twirly thing with her arms outstretched; sloughing a year off her age with each exuberant spin. She's in the middle of one of those perfect meadows where they shoot television commercials for fabric softener. She's breathing deep, robust breaths, and the mountain air is filling her feeble lungs with nourishment and life.

But really, as I'm thinking this, Loretta is coughing up a wad of phlegm that she then deposits into a tissue in a way that's so graceful and elegant, I almost think it's a move in an interpretive dance routine and not the viscous product of her gradual decay. I walk over and rub my hand across her shoulders and notice for the first time how petite she is. She's probably a good six inches shorter than me, and her frame feels tinier than those of my students.

"So, what do you want to do today?" My relationship with Loretta has progressed to the point where I don't feel the need to talk all proper Southern belle anymore. Two months ago I'd have said, "How do you wish to pass the afternoon?"

"Well, Annie. Why don't we just relax? Make some iced tea."

"Sounds great," I say. I love how making iced tea is an activity. Making iced tea is enough. We walk down the hall together, slow baby steps to the kitchenette. I pull a box of tea bags from a cabinet, and we talk as Loretta slowly removes the paper wrapping off half a dozen bags.

"So, Miss Harper, how's that big, handsome boyfriend of yours? He behaving himself over there in the front lines?" And I don't correct Loretta when she says "front lines," because I've already tried to explain that David mostly does computer stuff. She just doesn't seem to get it.

"Oh, he's doing okay. Plugging along, I guess." Loretta's shriveled hands struggle to tie the strings of the tea bags together. The way they move reminds me of what it must be like to make a sculpture out of overcooked sausage links. I'm not sure whether or not to intervene and tie the strings myself, so instead, I keep talking. "He's been kind of down lately. He was so upbeat for the first few months. Now I think it's all really wearing on him."

"Poor dear," Loretta says. "I remember when Ron hit that point. I could almost see the sorrow in his handwriting. His script began to sag and slant more. He wrote me the saddest poetry. Some of it was published, you know?"

"Oh yeah? I didn't know Captain Ron Schumacher was a writer?"

"Indeed, he was." She smiles, either with the pride of having had such a sensitive mate or because she's finally succeeding with the strings of the tea bags. Probably a combination of both. The pot of water on the range is starting to bubble around the edges and she places the tea bags into the fury. Patiently watches them sink and steep. "Ron's poetry has been published in numerous literary reviews. Several of the poems are anthologized in collections about the war."

"Oh, wow, Loretta. Do you have copies here? Would you mind if I read some of it?"

"Regrettably, I don't. They're packed up at my daughter's house somewhere. I've been asking her to bring them by. My room has that little bookcase above the desk, you know."

"That's too bad. What did he write about? If you don't mind me asking." Loretta is so interesting. So tough and so interesting.

"Oh, the usual things. Blood. Death. The tragedy of war. The devastation of the human race. That's a title of one of the poems, actually—"The Devastation of the Human Race." She leans against the countertop and folds her arms across her chest. "I was really worried when he sent me that one." And then for some reason we laugh. She starts it. I join. The Devastation of the Human Race! Chuckle. Giggle. Guffaw. Are we laughing at Captain Ron? Are we laughing at devastation? Somehow, it feels really good. I'm comforted by the realization that the wide generational gap between Loretta and me can still accommodate a shared irreverence. An ability to recognize shards of absurdity within blood, death, and the tragedy of war. She has turned the burner off, and we stand there sighing a bit, watching steam collect and condense on the side of the yellow refrigerator. It happens so fast, changing from gas to liquid—sad to goofy—with the simple temperature of the surrounding air.

We finish making the tea and settle down in Loretta's room. I tune the radio to a classical station, and we end up trading stories about sleeping with men. Not "sleeping" the euphemism for sex, but actual sleeping. Loretta slept with Ron three times before their wedding night. She says she was never able to really rest on those three nights. She kept waking up, startled by the weight of his arm across her waist. Jumpy at the smell of someone else being there.

"I'm kind of getting used to sleeping alone now," I tell her. Though Loretta is a bit shocked when I reveal that David practically lived at my place before he left, I can tell that she's not totally judging me by the way she smiles when I describe David's special bathroom treatment.

"Every day, he folded the toilet tissue[93] like that?"

"Every day." I don't tell Loretta that I've kept it there since he left. I know that it's a bit weird of me and perhaps a neurotic breed of sentimentality that she might not understand.

"Quite the gentleman, your boyfriend."

"Quite," I say, and we take dignified sips of our tea.

As I drive home I think about how nice it was to be with Loretta and forget about Dead Alden for a while. I've never told her the whole saga, and it's nice to be a single-issue girl around her. I am a lonely woman with an absent boyfriend. And Loretta can understand and comfort me about it. She's like Helen, but chattier and older.

---

[93] Would Loretta Schumacher ever say "TP"? No way, José.

I'd left my phone in the car, and when I look at it, I have a message from Gus. We haven't spoken since he drove me home the night I found out about Alden. He's wondering what my plans are for Easter and says that if I'm not busy at seven A.M. tomorrow morning, he has a small project he could really use my help with.

I like projects.

I like helping.

I like Gus.

So I call him back.

"Thanks for doing this at such short notice, Annie." Gus is backing out of my driveway, and I notice there are two steaming paper cups in the cup holder. He sees me looking. "Oh yeah, I brought you coffee."

"Thanks," I say, and I pick up the cup closest to me and start to slurp at the plastic lid.

"Yeah, so the guy that usually does this every year had to go in for some emergency kidney stone operation, and the rest of the dudes in my dad's Rotary Club are either too short or have usher duty at their early-bird church services."

"So what is it I have to do again?"

"You'll be my escort. So basically you have to prevent me from stepping on children, hand out eggs to the little squirts . . ."

"I'm really good with little squirts," I say.

"*And* hold my hand as we walk around the park." I laugh and ask Gus where the costume is and if Gina's going to be jealous. He says his dad will meet us there with the gear and that he didn't ask Gina to help because he knows she doesn't like crowds and weird, pseudo-Christian activities.

We get to the park and find Rex's car parked behind the back door to the little public lodge thing that the community uses for craft festivals and summer day camps. He lets us in and we help Gus into the bunny suit. Once Gus has got the body part on, Rex notices that the cottony tail is all lopsided and smashed, probably from spending a year in someone's garage storage space. Rex is bent over to Gus's rear, fluffing the tail back into a round puffball and telling me about how his Rotary Club has sponsored this Easter egg hunt for over fifteen years. Seeing how ridiculous the two of them look at this moment, I think about how Gus and Rex grew up alone. No mom/wife. No sibling/sister. A father and a son. A rabbit keeper and his adorable bunny. They're pretty amazing guys.

Rex stands up and tells me that I look really nice. I thank him and smooth the front of the linen skirt that I had hastily ironed at dawn. I'm wearing open-toed sandals that I guessed would probably wick dew off the park grass and let it settle freshly between my toes.[94] Next we strap the big klutzy bunny mittens over Gus's hands. Rex pulls up a chair so he can lift the mask over Gus's head,[95] but then I tell him to stop. I grab my purse off the nearby table and rummage through it until I find two bobby pins. I turn back to Gus.

"You won't be able to brush your hair back with your bunny hands or flick it out of your eyes by jerking your head with that mask on, so this is totally necessary," I tell him as I brush the front pieces of hair from his forehead and sweep them to the side. I have both bobby pins in my mouth as I say this, so it comes out kind of chewy-sounding and silly. He's smiling. "It will be hard enough to see already," I continue. I slide the first pin across his left temple, and it feels a bit awkward because I can tell that Gus is watching my face and not my hands. As I position the second pin, I notice how soft Gus's hair is and how long it's been since I touched another human with this kind of tenderness. Maybe I played with Michelle's hair when she was here over the holidays, and now and then a student will hug me. David's hair has been that clipped, military buzz since I've known

[94] I was right about this. The sandals did just that.
[95] Gus is super tall. Six-three, I think.

him, so there's something about touching Gus's hair that makes me—embarrassingly, perhaps pathetically—want to stretch my fingers all the way through it.

"Well, you look pretty stupid, but you'll thank me for this later." I step back and realize that with his hair pulled back so taut Gus's eyes really stand out, making him look like a drag queen in some early stage of costuming.

"I will thank you now, even," he says. "Thank you." Rex looks at his watch, places the headpiece over Gus's head, and hurries us along outside. And I guess I'm still reeling in the strange sensations of the hair-petting, so I don't really notice the hordes of children outside until they notice us—or Gus rather—and come running, all five million of them, precisely in our direction.

We get the hang of things fairly quickly. I make sure the space behind Gus's tail stays clear so he can crouch up and down to hug the munchkins and shake their hands. I take his paw and place it on the heads of kids that are too far left and right for him to see with his limited bunny peripheral vision. I hand out plastic eggs filled with candy and stickers, and we accommodate all the mothers who insist on taking pictures. Oddly enough, some of the mothers want me in the picture too. Like the Easter Bunny's attendant is a staple piece of this memory. My pink cardigan does match Gus's fur almost exactly, but each time we assume the pose—Gus's arm across my back, the other hand resting on the shoulder of the child—it feels like some strange, magical family. But I do kind of like it.

When the actual egg hunts[96] start, I lead Gus over to a wooden

---

[96] There's one hunt for ages five through nine where the eggs have actually been hidden in the nooks of the playground, the surrounding trees, and shrubbery. And then there's the four-and-under egg hunt, which is more like an egg-gathering free-for-all where the Rotarians have taped off a rectangular piece of lawn and all the toddlers have to do is stumble around and pick

picnic table so we can sit for a few minutes and regroup before the final Easter Bunny meet-and-greet. I ask him how things are going in there.

"Great," he says. "I just hope my dad dry-cleans this thing before Mr. Richards tries to wear it again next year. I'm sweating profusely."

It is a nice morning. Clear and warm enough so that kids are bumbling around just in sweatshirts or light windbreakers. I'm tired because I stayed up late the night before reading newspapers on the Internet and trying to map out lesson plans for the next few weeks. Gus stretches his arms out across the picnic table and tilts his bunny muzzle up to the sky. I ask if the air circulates much inside there. He says no and that it smells like the coffee he drank for breakfast. I say that it could be worse and that he could be suffering through pork sausage or cottage cheese breath. And then the sun is just so warm, making me feel all relaxed and melty. I wiggle my feet around in the grass to splash some water across my toes, and I scoot in closer to Gus. The fur is soft and cozy against my forearm, like a stuffed animal that's been puked on and washed a hundred times. I close my eyes and lean up against Gus's shoulder. We're both silent, and I cross my feet at the ankles. I exhale a nice long breath and actually doze off.

When I open my eyes, there's a man with a camera about fifteen yards away. I can tell that he's not a dad because it's a real camera with a big lens and film inside. I've lifted my head up, and he's replacing the lens cap and walking over. As he approaches I notice that my Easter basket has slipped out of my hands and that the eggs are splayed across the grass at our feet.

"Sorry if I scared you," the photographer says. Then he reaches into

---

eggs off the ground and put them in their baskets/buckets/plastic shopping bags. Mothers crouch around the sides of the tape peering into the screens of their digital cameras and shouting, "Jeremy, get the blue egg, sweetie. Right there!" It's almost like a sporting event.

his camera bag and hands me a card. "Scott McCormick, *Tacoma News Tribune*."

"Oh," I say, still confused and sleepy. "Okay."

"Hope you don't mind that I snagged a few frames of you two dozing. It was just too adorable. They send one of us out here each year to grab some cheesy shots of the kids for the Local Living section. Can I get your name, miss, and permission to run one of these photos if they turn out nice?" I sit up straight and turn to Gus. I lower my gaze to the bunny mouth, where I can see his eyes. I can tell he's back in character and not going to speak, but his eyes communicate consent.

"Sure," I say. "Why not?" I can hear Gus snickering in his mask as I give my name to Scott McCormick.

Lucky for Miss Harper, it turns out three of her twenty-nine students read the *News Tribune* over their Froot Loops each morning. Or at least their parents do and are sharp enough to recognize their kid's teacher's name. You wouldn't really know it's me from the picture. My head is turned sideways and I'm nuzzled into Gus's bunny armpit, so really only half my face is showing. One arm is draped across my lap, and my other hand is dangling lifelessly above the handle of the dropped, spilling basket. Gus's head is hanging to one side, and an ear is flopping just above my ponytail. With my feet crossed at the ankles and with Gus just looking so big, I am more or less a pastel illustration of a six-year-old you'd find in an old volume of nursery rhymes. I spend the thirty minutes before the warning bell in the teachers' lounge catching up with Carrie about various spring break banalities and other popular gossip topics of boring schoolteachers.[97] When I

---

[97] Changes in state testing. Whose classrooms might move to portable buildings next year. Mrs. Janklow's early retirement. An upcoming assembly about fire safety. The fact that the Coke machine has been out of Diet since before Christmas. It's all very important and interesting.

enter my classroom I see a distinct cluster around Caitlin Robinson's desk. Desk clusters are always a bad sign. It's either some new form of trading cards or mini electronica that I'll have to learn about and enforce bans on. Or else someone got stitches on his hand. Or else someone is really mad at someone else and small alliances are forming. As soon as my presence is noticed, Max Schaffer steps away from the cluster, revealing the perfectly clipped newsprint on Caitlin's desk. He shouts, "Miss Harper, you're famous!"

"I know. Isn't it funny?" I ask lightly, hoping this won't be a big deal and the kids will settle enough for me to get them peacefully sorted into their reading groups. "Did everyone have a nice spring break?" I ask. There's some high-pitched muttering about ski trips and boring older sisters and a movie about aliens that I've heard nothing about. Then that nosy brat Caitlin Robinson pipes up.

"Isn't your boyfriend going to be mad at you because you cheated on him with the Easter Bunny?" Oh, the roar of laughter! Caitlin has just achieved a very high position on the Miss Harper's Class Humor Hall of Fame. She got the language and the tone of her accusation just right, like she spent the entire spring break watching Maury and Jerry Springer. *On today's show: Lovers torn over bizarre infidelities.* I'm sitting in a cushioned chair wearing my pink cardigan, looking all innocent and non-kinky. David is fuming beside me in his fatigues. And Gus Bunny is slouched in his costume in this carefree, confident way, as if to say, "I can't help that I got what she wants." It's really fucking absurd.

"Jeez, Caitlin. No. I was just helping the Easter Bunny at the egg hunt, and we were simply resting there." I can't believe I'm defending myself in front of nine-year-olds.

"Well, my mom said that you two look pretty intimate." *Intimate!* Reason number forty-nine to hate Mrs. Robinson. I take a deep breath that is meant to dissolve my burning desire to wallop Caitlin all the way to the kindergarten wing. The class is still Giggletown, USA, and

I resent the fact that I can feel myself blushing. It's all so very ridiculous.

"The Easter Bunny and I are old friends. And I can assure you that our relationship is purely platonic." Someone asks what platonic means. "It means when you love someone, but it's not romantic. It means you love them just as a friend." The class seems to accept this answer, and I switch gears[98] by asking Garrett Wagner to come adjust the felt weather symbols on the front bulletin board. He moves the sunshine to the side and overlaps a few clouds on each other. "It might rain later," he says.

I say, "Oh, really."

The next day I'm driving Max Schaffer to his violin lesson and he says, "It was your friend Gus, wasn't it?"

"What about Gus?" I ask, trying not to look over at Max while I drive.

"He's the Easter Bunny from the picture." Damn kid is so f-ing perceptive.

"Yep," I say. "It was Gus. And I take it you don't believe in the Easter Bunny, Max."

"Well duh," he says. "I never have. And I know Gus is your best platonic friend." I can't help but smile at how Max inserts the vocab word into his speech.

"Yeah, Max," I say. "I guess he is."

---

[98] At first I hated using this phrase as a teacher. We're always having to "switch gears," and it sounds so cliché and stupid, but there's really no way around it. Switching gears is a fundamental part of instruction.

18

*T*oday I'm calling my book *Shout Across the Ocean*, and I just got off the phone with David. And boy, am I mad at that guy. I feel like someone has lit my ear on fire and implanted a series of ten-pound dumbbells in each of my internal organs. The organs are stretched out—heavy and saggy—and the tips of my fingers are all tingly and sweaty as I type this. And it's not a good kind of tingly.

So two days ago after school, I was goofing off on the computer when I was supposed to be grading social studies tests. I hadn't read the paper that day, so I pulled up the *New York Times* online. I read the headlines, the Science Tuesday section, and then I clicked around to the Names of the Dead. There were two names. One of them was Private Francisco A. Flores, age twenty-four, of Denton, Texas. It took a second for my brain to stir and process the name. I thought: Flores, Flores, Flores, Ray Flores, Polar Bear Flores, *Ray Flores, Saved by a Beanie Baby!* Then I remembered that Ray was the name I made up for David's friend Flores and that David's Flores was in fact from Texas, and could it be the same Flores? I typed and searched and Googled.

Francisco Flores was killed during a convoy inside Baghdad. Their jeep ran over an IED, and though the driver suffered only minor injuries, Flores, the passenger, died on the site. The local paper from Denton showed Mom Flores standing outside a church with a swarm of middle-aged ladies sporting black blouses and fallen faces. I remembered that it was the church ladies who gave Flores the Beanie Babies, and even though Flores is a common name and there could be two hundred

Texan Floreses in the army, I knew.[99] I totally knew that it was David's friend. I guess a Beanie Baby can only save you so many times.

I read that the accident had happened eleven days earlier—as in two days before I talked to David about Alden's death. We'd spoken twice since, and David had mentioned nothing about losing a guy in his company. But I asked, didn't I? I explicitly asked that day on the phone, and David had acted so quiet and somber. Why couldn't he tell me? If the news hadn't been delivered to the family yet, David wouldn't have been able to use the phone at all. So he knew. He'd known. And he hadn't told me. And then I started to feel all weird because my emotions were leaning in the "rage against my boyfriend's dishonesty" direction and not in the "holy shit, a friend of his was killed" or the "poor Flores and his family" directions. That's top-grade selfish, evil[100] Annie Harper for you. But I couldn't help it.

Driving home from school, I tried to level my reactions down to something more reasonable. First: It must be another Flores. David would have told me about his Flores. Second: Maybe he's trying to protect me. Maybe he thinks withholding devastating information will keep my twittering nerves and spastic fits of anxiety from completely consuming me. But can't he see I've actually been kind of fine? I go to work every day. I continue to pay all my bills and cook for myself and keep in touch with my parents and friends and Loretta. I've raised a fucking chicken, for Pete's sake! He can't possibly think I'm too weak for this.

It's the not talking about things that squelches human warmth.

---

[99] I should probably point out here how wrong my instincts were with the chicken fingers thing. But fake-outs happen. Just because our guts occasionally fail doesn't constitute reason enough to completely disregard them.

[100] Change the letters around and you get VILE!!!!

Take Stevens from *Remains of the Day*. He was too busy not talking about how he felt for people and only making comments about the weather and the conditions of table linens that he nearly died in complete loneliness.

David is my boyfriend. He absolutely must share with me.

So today he called and I couldn't keep anything in. After the first usual exchange of pleasantries, I jumped at it. I was already weeping stupid drama tears before I said it.

"So David," I said. "Will you please tell me how your friend Flores is doing?" Silence. Silence. Silence.

"Flores?" His voice wavered, almost cracked on the second syllable.

"Yeah, Flores. Beanie Baby Flores. I haven't heard you talk about him in a while."[101]

Silence. Silence. Silence.

"Oh, Annie. I meant to tell you."

"Don't you know by now that I read everything? I scour every bit of news I can get my eyes on to keep track of how you are and how your coworkers are and what the fuck it is you're doing over there!"

"I don't know, babe. I was upset. I was grieving. You were grieving about Brother Alden. The timing was all off. I was tired. Of course, I was going to tell you eventually." These were all very reasonable excuses now that I think about it. I can't understand the gimongous strain of being a wartime soldier, so I shouldn't expect to understand the effects it has on him, and furthermore, I shouldn't blame him for what those effects were making him do. But I was tired too. Tired of feeling so in the dark about David's life. Here I am, reduced to that lame cliché.

---

[101] How wicked do I sound? Deceptively coaxing someone I love into admitting that his friend was blown into chunks less than two weeks ago. I wish I could explain it. I really wish I could.

"Fine," I said, because I'm really horrible at fighting.

Silence. Silence. Silence.

And then I got this second wind. I harnessed it and used it to jab below the belt. "Anything *else* you're not telling me?"

"No. I don't think so."

"You don't think so?!!" By this point I was pacing back and forth in my living room. I'd grabbed a slipcover from the arm of my couch and I was whipping it around like some sort of floppy nunchucks. "Don't we have some sort of understanding to tell each other everything? I mean, Flores dying doesn't fall under the Vagueness Pact. It was in the fucking newspaper! You could have told me." And then I lowered my voice a bit. "And maybe I could have helped."

The rest of the conversation was me accusing and then backing down and then David alternately apologizing then defending what he did. We took turns making a lot of sense and then making none at all. I cried. And I could hear that he was also kind of crying too. And hearing him cry made me feel so horrible and disgusted with myself. Here I am ripping him a new asshole when his buddy was just killed. I'm supposed to be supportive, but I'm raging. What a fucking mess. We reconciled a little bit, admitting that we are each inching a few degrees closer to crazy. David promised to tell me everything from now on, and I promised not to be such a psychopath. I love you. I love you. We said it. (I'm pretty sure) we meant it. We hung up.

And then I cried more because it kind of feels like I don't know him as much anymore. And because I'm hurt that he didn't want to tell me. That he didn't think I could help. I cried because I can't help. And because I ate a whole pint of chocolate ice cream without taking Lactaid first. And because that makes me such a fucking typical, fucking miserable woman.

And here I am back at the stupid computer working on my stupid whine-a-thon, thinking that writing and typing will help make sense of everything. But it's no fucking tapestry, I'll tell you that. The time is not zipping by along the strings of my loom or the hoop of my embroidery thingo or the clicking needles of my knitting. This whole year is taking forever. David needs to come home. Soon. Soon. Soon. Soooooooooooooooooooon.

19

*T*oday I've given up writing a book, because it's likely that every last reader will hate my guts. Instead, I'm writing a suicide note that will hopefully—if my parents permit—be published in *USA Today* and read out loud by Oprah on a show about the sorts of tumult women go through while their men are at war. Oprah is really good at reading out loud. Just kidding.[102]

The day after The Big Annie and David Verbal Showdown of 2004, I went to see Loretta. I didn't want to tell my mom about the fight or Michelle or Gus or anyone else. It was really just too embarrassing. I sat on the edge of Loretta's bed, and she pulled her rocker up close so she could hold my hands and periodically squeeze them while I told her everything.[103] It took a while to explain the Beanie Baby backstory, but eventually Loretta got it.

"Of course, you feel deceived, Annie. One time Ron refinanced our home without telling me. I nearly beat him to death with our checkbook. It hurts to feel shut out from the person who is supposed to love you the most." Ah, Loretta. Making sense. Making Annie Harper look a little less wicked.

"Yeah. It's hard enough already to ignore the fact that this whole situation is chiseling its way between us, then something like this happens and I completely lose it."

---

[102] Not about Oprah's voice, but about the suicide thing. Counseling? Is it time yet? Does my insurance cover it? Oh, Georgie? Oh W.? Please help!

[103] Everything minus the Alden bits. I don't really know why I'm avoiding that with her.

"You haven't lost it, dear. I've seen women in greater distress. You went to school today. You drove over here. Your hair looks very nice." I laughed a snotty, wet laugh and squeezed Loretta's hands back.

The e-mail I had from David when I got home:

Dear Annie,

Again, I'm sorry about not telling you about Flores. I don't want to talk the issue into the ground, but I want you to know that it had nothing to do with wanting to keep things from you. You know I don't believe in secrets. God, if the ARMY is reading this e-mail, they'll have me for that one. But you know what I mean— keeping secrets from you. SO that being said I just want to make sure I get everything out in the open.

1. I missed a day of work last month because I had the flu. I didn't tell you I had the flu because I knew you'd freak out and it was just a quick one-day thing and I'm totally fine now, but after all this I felt weird about not telling you. And I promise to tell you about all future physical ailments. Even if it's lice or something, though I don't imagine there's much of that going around here.

2. When I was in fourth grade I peed my pants while we watched this filmstrip about volcanoes. It was a really sweet filmstrip. I've never told anyone outside my family and Mr. Costanti's class about it.

3. Now this one might bug you a bit and I totally understand and I want you to know that there's nothing I can do about it but there is this gal in my company, her name is Austin, Jayna Austin, and I guess she has this big crush on me or something. I guess her and like three of the other women in my company started this immature game about who they would choose to sleep with if they knew they were going to get killed the next day. Which is

really stupid because no one here knows what's going to happen
when. It's just gossipy crap. She and I have worked together on
a few projects, but I promise you nothing inappropriate has ever
transpired between us. Austin is totally not my type. I know you
won't really care about this kind of lame-ass Army stuff, but I
wanted to tell you so that you understand that I am dedicated to
telling you EVERYTHING from now on. We're just a bunch of
people who spend A LOT of time together and it's only natural
for us to digress into seventh graders from time to time.

AHhhh. So it feels good to get this out and I promise to tell
you everything all the time. And I know you've been and will
continue to keep doing the same.
Lots of love from the desert,
Big D.

Well, well, well, what have we here? Austin, Jayna. In the real book I will
not write that I think hers sounds like the name of a literary porn star.
In the real book I will not offensively berate our brave soldiers for casual,
who-would-you-rather musings. In the real book I will not Google
"Jayna Austin," "Austin, Jayna," "Jayna Austin David Peterson," "Jayna
Austin Jane Austen," "Jayna Austin sex tape," "Jayna Austin Army
Beauty Queen Winner," or "Jayna Austin stole my boyfriend." In the
real book, I will not imagine David ripping the bodice of another
woman's fatigues to reveal a lacy, olive green bra with a gold bullet ornament hanging from the front clasp. In the real book I will not shed tears
of suspicion over the same boyfriend choosing to use the words "nothing inappropriate has transpired" with me, like he's the HR director at
some mega-corporate company I don't work at. In the real book I will
release one good-natured second of a laugh and silently commend dear
Austin, Jayna, for her excellent taste in handsome soldiers.

No, but really, I haven't decided if this stupid thing even bothers me yet. So far, I don't believe that it truly does. Perhaps I'm a big girl after all. I appreciate David releasing the information to me. I'm sure he felt like such a junior-high acne clown relating the whole ridiculous thing, but he did it. He did it for me. I start to think that maybe I'm not telling David enough. Do I need to come clean about napping on the Easter Bunny? What if my mom sent him the clip from the newspaper? And though his confessions do help a bit, I'm not entirely sure it's assuaged the issue[104] away to nothing.

Yesterday at school, about twenty minutes before dismissal, the office aide brought a note into my class. It said that Charese Atkins was going to be about twenty minutes late picking up Lacey and that I could either wait with Lacey in the classroom or send her to the office where she could sit with the secretaries until Charese arrived. The kids were busy coloring maps for a social studies project, and I scribbled on the back of the note that I could wait with Lacey here. I thanked the fifth-grader office aide and sent her away with my reply.

When the bell rang and the kids scrambled into their jackets and started to plow past me, I simultaneously shouted out a reminder about the night's science homework[105] and managed to make eye contact with Lacey and pull her over.

"Lacey, your mom called. She's going to be a bit late picking you up, so you're going to wait in here with me. Do you want to play computer games or something?"

"Okay," she said, and I guided her to one of the machines.

[104] We're talking about the IN THE DARK/SECRET KEEPER/BORING CORRESPONDENCE ISSUE here.

[105] We're finally learning about the water cycle (the bulletin board's been up for months), and they each must draw an example using real-life things like mud puddles and sunshine or boiling water from macaroni and cheese. They must also memorize how to spell "precipitation."

"So how do you like Tacoma so far, Lacey?" I asked as the computer booted up. It was a weird question to ask a kid, I now realize. Like she's going to say that the bars are kind of crummy and the rush-hour traffic is a bitch.

"I like living with Grandma, but I miss my dad and my friends back in California." It was a very honest, mature answer and I wasn't surprised, really, because Lacey is so bright and articulate. She beeped along in Rainforest Math (a really lame game, I'll admit), and I busied myself tidying the Book Nook and eventually my desk.

When Charese arrived she was wearing a sharp skirt suit, pantyhose, and sunglasses. "Thanks so much for waiting, Miss Harper." She looked down at the front of her dark pinstriped jacket as if it were an explanation. "Job interview. They called me in kind of last minute. Lucky I had this thing ironed, right?" Charese helped Lacey into her jacket and then turned back to me. "You're looking a bit down, Miss Harper. The kids work you over today?" Hanging out with children and an old lady all the time has depleted my abilities to engage in regular adult small talk.

"No, they were fine. I'm just exhausted. You know, personal stuff."

"Oh, so I heard your boyfriend is in the service." It's amazing how well informed this whole community is.

"Yeah. That's right. He's over there." Pause. Pause. Pause. "In Iraq."

"Well, at least you know that over there he's not chasing some other girl's tail. My ex had full beaches of pretty ladies to distract him from me. From us." Her hands made their way to Lacey's shoulders, and I found it weird that she was doing all this daddy bashing in front of her daughter. I said something like *yeah, I guess*, and then Charese went on this huge tirade about how the military breeds infidelity. *You just keep all these men together all the time talking about who bangs what how often, and it's like a giant locker room with guns. And then they take couples away from each other for months on end. You know, the wives can be just as bad. There's this code on base where if a woman whose man is deployed is getting lonely and wants a piece of action, all she has to do is lean a mop upside down outside her back door and that tells all the hungry dudes passing by that she's looking for a little bit of service, if you know what I mean. Horrible, really. Happens all the time. Just the other day I read about this guy who came back from Iraq and found out his wife was pregnant with some other dude's baby, and he shot her, the other guy, and their two kids. His very own two kids. Talk about post-traumatic stress. Right? And then there's all the guys that volunteer for these eight-month deployments in Korea so they can get a break from their fat wives and indulge in poor Russian and Filipina women who get their passports stolen and are forced into prostitution. Hear that all the time.*

As she said all this I just sat there on the edge of my desk, mouth hanging open, eyes darting back and forth to Charese and then Lacey, who started playing with this beaded key chain on her backpack like she'd heard her mother give this same terrible speech a hundred and fifty times.

And I thought I was pessimistic about military life.

I left the school thinking about Charese and how wounded she is. Here I am feeling betrayed because David didn't tell me about Flores's death, a tragedy he was still struggling to swallow, and there's Charese shit-talking her way through a real one. A real-deal-Holyfield betrayal. David barely betrayed me. It might not even count at all. Throw his offense into the BetrayalCalcutron2004 and what does it say? *Cannot compute. Unsubstantiated evidence. Please terminate raging bitch behavior immediately.* What in the world is wrong with you, Annie Harper? He did not betray you. He even gave you an escape clause so you could back out of this game if you somehow felt too threatened or weakened or defeated. Baby baby babyface, Miss Harper. Buck up. Buck the fuck up. Jayna Austin, Hottest Soldier Ever, is ten million times tougher than you.

I stopped by the grocery store on the way home because it was payday and I like to buy myself treats when I'm feeling kind of rich. A nice jar of olives. A fancy slab of cheese. I was walking by the dried fruits when I remembered a ridiculous scene from the camping trip.

We were all sitting around the edge of Hobo Lake eating lunch and talking about how birds feed their young. We were giving Stephen crap because—despite his fancy East Coast education—he didn't know that most birds regurgitate food for their babies. Stephen thought it was both hilarious and disgusting. We were all sharing a bag of dried apricots (except for Gina, who doesn't care for them because the texture reminds her of biting into someone's tongue), and then Gus said, "Do you think that if you eat something dehydrated and regurgitate it back up that the juices from your digestive system will have replaced the original liquids in the same places and rendered the something back into its original texture?"

"Seems like kind of a stretch," Gina had said.

"Yeah. The something would be all masticated," added Stephen, the future dentist.

"Well, there's only one way to find out,"[106] I had said. And so Gus had to try. He took an apricot, chewed it twenty-four times, per Stephen's instructions, and proceeded—I had to turn away several times—to swallow and regurgitate the thing back up. He spun away from us as he urged the final cough out of his body, and we could see him messing with the contents of his hand before turning around to present it.

The color was the same; Gus had effectively prevented any other

---

[106] Gus and I had this canon of expressions in high school that were like silly, pat movie lines that we liked to say because it felt like people didn't say them enough and finding the perfect context to say them was somehow a really beautiful moment. "There's only one way to find out" is one of those lines. Others include: "Mark my words!" "Stranger things have happened," "Wouldn't you like to know?" "It's gonna be a great summer!" and my personal favorite: "It just might be crazy enough to work!"

recently consumed foods from tagging along for the ride north. And the texture of the goop did kind of look like the flesh of a fresh apricot, but the shape was off. While his back was turned, Gus had quickly molded the fruit wad into the shape of a heart. And then he took a step toward Gina and extended his hand in offering, "My lady," he had said in a tone fit for the most dignified, noble prince of the most dignified, noble kingdom ever.

"What?" Gina was appalled. "You want me to eat that? I'm not your baby bird." Stephen and I laughed because Gus wasn't breaking. He was serious. At the time, I didn't think anything less of Gina for not wanting to eat the regurgitated apricot. It was really quite gross. But as I stood there with my shopping cart amongst the raisins and dried peaches and rings of apples—all stiff and brittle, robbed of their natural juices and original textures—I realized what Gus had really done. Gina didn't like the texture of dried apricots. And he took what started as a ridiculous joke—the musings of bored fishermen—and changed the food to suit her. For her. And she didn't even recognize it. None of us did. But now I get it. Had it been me, I like to think that I'd have eaten it. And for a moment in that grocery aisle, I kind of wanted to eat Gus's regurgitated apricot. (ICK!ICK!ICK!, I know.) Not really. Mostly I just wished I could tell him that I now understood how thoughtful the gesture was. It's kind of like his old gum mosaic for that Valentine-hating girl in college. When you care about someone, you want everything to be the best for that person. You go so far as to harness the bits of the universe that he/she finds disagreeable and manipulate them into something that the person can at least tolerate, or, maybe, enjoy. What does it mean that I'm the only one who seems to find Gus's saliva-laced acts of romance admirable? Enviable, even. What kind of weirdo am I?

The kind of weirdo who combats emotional crisis with emotional spending. I bought three flavors of fancy sorbet and got the heck out of that supermarket.

20

*T*oday I'm calling my book *Dreams from the Homeland*, and the cover has an embossed shiny font and a painting of a rolling countryside. The entire book takes place on my back porch as I sit in my rocking chair, sipping whiskey from a chipped mason jar and recounting everything that has happened this year. I've taken the artistic liberty to write Loretta out of Violet Meadows, and she sits next to me correcting my "whos" and "whoms" and slapping my wrist if I start to curse too much.

So I stopped writing again. This time it wasn't because of blahgers. It was because of Private Lynndie England, the Most Disgusting Human Being on the Planet. Well, close at least. Her and her torturing, soulless cohorts of the 372nd Military Police Company at the Abu Ghraib prison. It was a few weeks after Easter when that whole big *60 Minutes II* episode on the scandal ran. I hadn't heard anything of it yet, and I was sitting down to dinner when the program began. I had made stir-fried vegetables with shrimp, and I was very proud of the fact that I hadn't burnt my rice for once. But as the scandal was revealed and discussed, and as those horrifying images kept flashing on my TV screen, I couldn't eat even one broccoli floret. Yeah, I felt sick. But I was totally raging. These are the kinds of things I was yelling out loud in my living room:

Who are these monsters?
What the fuck is wrong with people?
What the fuck is wrong with the U.S. military?
Holy fucking shit!

Humanity is doomed!

I fucking hate her! And him! And him! And him!

And then the rage settled into a profound sadness that made my limbs sink into my sofa as I whispered things like this between heavy, wavering breaths:

No no no no no no no no no.

Those poor, poor men.

What's the matter with the World?

Nothing will ever change.

Nothing will ever get better.

The universe is doomed.

Humanity is doomed.

Everything is doomed.

A few days later Gus had tipped me off about the article that would run in the next week's *New Yorker* and that was already posted online. I printed out a copy once I got to school and turned the first hour of class into surprise silent reading time while I sat at my desk reading and resisting the urge to weep.

And as the days went on and news remained plastered with the details of the accusations, the kinks in chains of commands, and those horrible, horrible images, I slowly became consumed with guilt. Even though David's army people have absolutely nothing to do with those army people, and even though I don't think most of them should even be over there at all, and even though I didn't vote for George W. Bush, my hands were still sweating with guilt. Shame. Shame. Shame. After the Guilt Phase came my Obsession with Lynndie England's Fetus Phase. After hearing of her pregnancy and the child's father being a fellow torturer, I died a thousand deaths for that baby. Would she be allowed to keep it? At what age would it stumble upon the photographs? Can I *please please please* Mister Bush, adopt it and nurture it into a normal, loving child? Will you promise that Mr. and Mrs. Evil will never have a hope of taking it back?

Guilt is a kooky thing, really. While I was guilting it up and feeling like I was a part of some collective consciousness that molded Lynndie England into a ripe little terror, I started to realize something. Maybe I'm projecting my own guilt about my own problems onto these external issues. It's easier to blame the guilt on the horrible photos on the television than it is to properly attribute it to my own real-as-dirt sins. I also think it's easier to tie the guilt to an incident that happened in a flash than it is to identify the guilt as belonging to a set of feelings that have slowly (practically unnoticeably) sneak attacked me over time.

Bam, the pictures on the screen! (Hello, Mr. Guilt! Come right in!)
        OR
        Little by little, Miss Harper has been changing her mind. (Oh hey, Mr. Guilt. How long have you been cowering in the dark corner?)

Here I am, just another dishonest memoirist. This whole project has got to stop. I have so obviously failed at writing/living an honorable story. Dishonorably discharged from my own writing assignment. No medals. No flags. All shame. It's not a memoir to share anymore. I feel guilty for being

TORN

FALLING OUT OF LOVE
WITH A SOLDIER AT WAR

A NOVEL BY

Annie Harper

and also for

Falling / for My Best Friend

A Made-for-Television Movie starring Annie Harper based on the novel by Annie Harper based on the pathetic life of Annie Harper based on the convoluted nature of the brain of Annie Harper. Premieres Friday, May 29, 2004, at 8pm PST. Please check local listings and your own personal tolerance for absurdity, whining, crying, vomit, death, and vapid self-absorption.

So that's that. Good night, moon.

Okay, so I'm going to try to continue writing. It's been another week. Project Wartime Alone Time Memoir-Fem War has been officially abandoned. I can't expect anyone to be interested in a woman whose aspirations to inspire, commiserate, and inform have plummeted into the moral murkiness of run-of-the-mill infidelity pangs. My only audience now is Miss A. Harper. My only hope now is to see what I can possibly save by the act of writing and the reflection it provokes.

What *can* be saved, class?

        a. My relationship with David Peterson
        b. My friendship with Gus Warren
        c. My dirt-stained soul
        d. All of the above

With only a week of school left, I start to get really sappy. This has happened each of the three years I've been teaching and even the semester in college where I student taught for a mere twelve weeks. It stops raining so much in mid-May and I notice the shirtsleeves of my students creeping up and up. Suddenly someone who could barely read out loud is rattling off the last stories in our class reader with a mature adult voice and a storyteller's cadence. About two weeks before the last day, everyone gets their teacher assignments for the next year. There's a bunch of yesssssss-ing from all the lucky ducks who get Mr. Alvarez for fourth grade. He has a class iguana[107] and coaches baseball, which constitutes more cool points than I can ever hope to muster. The rest of the class is stuck with Mrs. Donahue—a sweet lady, though dreadfully conventional and hopelessly boring—and so they bond together in solidarity, relieved that at least they have a few

[107] Its name is el Che.

close friends with whom they can whisper below the radar of her hearing aids.

I start to imagine what kinds of teenagers my students will become. For some, like Max Schaffer, it's easy to envision the upward curve of his academic success. But then I worry. Will he be a hopeless dork? Will raging acne obscure his ability to woo girls with his scientific knowledge and adorable curiosity for life? I can't help but imagine Caitlin Robinson growing chubby and getting pregnant in eleventh grade. Lacey Atkins will star in all the school musicals but take a college scholarship to study physics. In a way I feel like this has been my best class yet. Like they've helped me through these last eight months[108] of loneliness and (gag, gag, gag) self-discovery.[109]

On the last day of school, I hand back the students' final science reports. Toward the end of the year I allow them to go off on their own tangents and write a four-page report (with at least three illustrations, one of them hand-drawn) about whatever they want. An animal. Rockets. Penicillin. Earthquakes. It's a good way to gauge how I've presented the curriculum throughout the year. If everyone writes about rattlesnakes and no one writes about the human body, I know I need to give the digestive system and the chambers of the heart a little more pizzazz the next time I present them to a class.

Max Schaffer wrote a beautiful paper on the mating habits of spiders. At first I was a bit alarmed that *mating* was the topic of a nine-year-old's research, but Max has always been mature for his age. And spiders do woo each other in such fascinating ways! Shaking webs. Emitting fancy hormones. His essay even goes into the several species that eat one another after fornication. Max printed several photo-

---

[108] EIGHT MONTHS!!!

[109] As in I've discovered how to turn a perfectly nifty premise for a feel-good, wholesome memoir into a fucked-up, goofball, tortured confessional. Just you watch.

graphs off the Internet and pasted them on an amazingly intricate hand-drawn web. As I reach his desk to return "Spider Parents" Max tells me that he doesn't need it back.

"I have a copy for myself at home, Miss Harper. I want you to keep that one." If I ever, by the power of my own nature and nurture, rear a child as precious as Max Schaffer, I'll have finally done something worthwhile in this universe. By being his third-grade teacher I already felt this huge sense of accomplishment. I tear a little as I accept the gift.

"Why thank you, Max. It's a wonderful paper. I'm glad to keep a copy for my reference library."

I hand out the large paper grocery sacks that I've been saving since early spring, and I play Billy Joel's *Greatest Hits Volume II* while the kids duck into the bowels of their desks and scoop out a year's worth of clutter and artifacts. Fortunate ones find candy. That eraser that was lost back in January. A Yu-Gi-Oh card they accused someone else of pilfering. Someone makes fun of the music: *I didn't know you were so old, Miss Harper.* I am old, I tell them. And I'm your teacher for three more hours, so shush. I collect the readers and the math books. I ignore the dog-eared copies that are slumping off of their cardboard spines. I pretend not to notice pencil scribblings of robots in margins and blatantly obvious initials scrawled along bindings.

We play a last game of Heads Up Seven Up and I let Jessica Marquez[110] supervise the game—watching for peekers from my desk—while I squeeze into hers and play along. I *love* Heads Up Seven Up. I delight in the girls who are too uncomfortable guessing that a boy has selected them. The boys who thrust their skinny arms out into the aisle, begging for attention, for selection, to take the front stage of the classroom. The squeak of the desks when the heads go down. The

[110] Her budding teacher personality is quite apparent.

soft slap of rubber sneakers trying to make careful, stealthy laps between the rows of buried heads. Oh! And there's occasionally that one
darling kid who's either sleep-deprived or borderline narcoleptic and
doesn't respond to the first "Heads up, seven up" and is left drooling
on his desk until someone really pokes him good.

It's a normal game this last time, though the kids are noticeably
tickled that I'm participating as one of them. I'm selected more than
my fair share of times, and I make a huge show of correctly guessing
that it was Marco Antolini who had twice flicked my thumb. Heads
Up Seven Up is a game where one tries to deceive: to throw off the one
you chose by affecting aloof and unsuspecting postures and expressions. But ultimately, it's a game where if you're accused and you're
guilty, honesty is the only choice. With seven choosers and seven chosen, process of elimination forces direct confessions.

Garrett, you picked me.

Nope.

Danielle?

No.

Marco Antolini?

Yep!

Everyone comes clean in Heads Up Seven Up! No emotional betrayal in this game!

When the time comes to say goodbye, I give a stupid little speech. I
told myself not to make a speech, to just let them breeze away into
summer vacation: basketball camp and that magical ticking sound of
a lawn sprinkler. But like I have mentioned, I am a hardcore sap. I
can't help it.

"I just want you guys to know that you've been a great class and
that I've had such a fun year teaching you and learning from you and
getting to know how wonderful you are. And I hope that you've liked
third grade. I think it's the best grade of all. Look at me, I've found a

way to stay in it year after year. I just played Heads Up Seven Up! Do you know any grown-ups who do that as part of their job?

"The only downside of staying in third grade is that I have to say goodbye to my students each year. And though I'm really sad to say goodbye to you, I'm simultaneously so proud of you and know that you'll all be rock stars in the fourth-grade classroom. And every year after that. Now don't forget your shopping bags. Have a great summer. Come visit me next year. Thanks for being such a stellar class."

And then I sigh. Look at the clock. The class follows my gaze, and we watch the last ten seconds pass together. When the bell rings, I stand by the door, accepting thank yous, hugs, and a few homemade cards. I love the hugs. They're so full of energy and excitement, nothing like the wimpy boyfriend-in-Iraq hugs that I've received so many of. Those pity embraces, damp and flat like a wet ponytail. These hugs—the on-to-fourth-grade hugs—are hugs with potential, hope, and future. Hugs powered by Popsicle sugar and revved by a baseball card clipped to the shiny spoke of a bicycle.

When they're gone, when the last little voices slam inside of minivans and when the last bus[111] zooms away, the quiet is overwhelming.

Silence. Silence. Silence.

I putz around for an hour. Weeping a little. Humming a little. Windexing the surface of each precious desk, hoping that its ex-occupant has a shiny, shiny future.[112] As I'm polishing the second-to-last desk,

---

[111] It's always bus 29 because the driver, Rhonda, always takes a smoke break behind the Dumpster.

[112] And that its next occupant has a basic understanding of arithmetic and can read at grade level!

the static of the intercom interrupts the squeaking and I hear Barfley's serious, football-announcer voice crackle through the speaker above my door.

"Attention educational professionals of Franklin Elementary. This is your principal speaking. A contingent is forming in the teachers' lounge to make its way toward Las Palmas Mexican Restaurant for Taco Tuesday. Buy a margarita, get free tacos!" He pauses for a moment and the formality slips away from his voice. "Come on, everyone. You know you need a drink." Pause. "I mean, a taco."

It's nice to go out with my colleagues. There are several of them whom I rarely see and whom I never would have expected to know the difference between Cuervo and Patron. Las Palmas is greasy and dim, even at four P.M. After a few drinks Carrie flirts with one of the waiters and Mrs. Donahue (I am sooo pleased and surprised she came) asks if the place has a jukebox. It doesn't. Mrs. Petrucci,[113] who teaches kindergarten and is only two years my senior and who should totally be my friend, finds a paper cup of crayons tucked between the napkin holder and the hot sauce on our table. She starts drawing hearts and stars on her paper placemat.

"Christ, Jennifer. Haven't you had enough?" barks Maggie, one of the secretaries, when she notices the cutesy, colorful artwork developing on the table. Jennifer looks up, innocent and flushed in the cheeks.

"I've only had two drinks," she says, and we all laugh. Maggie snags the crayons away from Jennifer and orders her another drink. We end up turning the back room of Las Palmas into an awkward, drunken dance party. Barfley's wife shows up and they grind inappropriately like teenagers and we all make fun of them. I steal Carrie away from her new boyfriend and we have a heated showdown on the

[113] First name: Jennifer.

dartboard. The stakes are high: tequila shots. I end up taking three! All night I keep thinking about how glad I am to be there. As my head lightens I start to ground myself by hugging. By telling the older teachers what great role models they are and by reminding the younger ones that *we need to do this again sometime.* And it's funny because we don't even like each other all that much. No one is super close and no one relies too heavily on anyone else during the school year. Our school is a fairly decent one, so the solidarity amongst the teachers doesn't run that deep. We conduct our own independent universes, occasionally seeking a colleague when a black dry-erase marker runs unexpectedly pale gray. But it's the last day of school. We've shed our broods of children. We've waved them off and set them free, and we're on the brink of three months of quiet. We need a last surge of spirited company. At least I do.

Once I've over-tequilaed myself, I wander into the hallway by the restrooms for a moment of quiet. I get out my phone and scroll through the list of contacts. I stop at Gus. And I want to call him. It's a very base, drunk instinct. I want to call him and ask him to pick me up because I am drunk and because I know he will do it. He will walk me into my house and make sure I have a glass of water or two. Will he remove my loafers and lay me out on the bed? Will he remove the elastic that's holding together my ponytail because he will notice that it is oppressively tight? Will he leave a sleeve of saltines on the bedside table? Will you, Gus? Will you do it for me because I am your best friend ever? Will you do it for me better than David would do it? Will you do it for me better than you would do it for anyone else? My finger is hovering over the send button, and even in my sloppy alcohol brain fuzz I realize that this is the first time since seventh grade that I have ever hesitated to contact Gus Warren. And so I don't do it. Jennifer Petrucci's husband drives the two of us home. And though I'm a crumpled wad of booze-soaked cotton in the backseat—not saying more than a squeaky "thank you" the whole way to my house—I am awful thankful for the Petruccis' company.

And the next day, I'm not entirely alone either. I've got this bulbous-nosed troll of a hangover.

Under my contract as an employee of the Tacoma public schools, I'm obligated to work five days after the last day of school. Those three days are always a weird mix of depressing and liberating. I wear flip-flops and the kinds of sleeveless dresses that Barfley would never deem appropriate for the classroom. I blast loud rock or hip-hop music that is riddled with unabashed profanities. I fill out final report cards and tear down bulletin boards. I take inventory of supplies and pride in the fact that none of my students will be repeating third grade.

With my hangover troll snoozing heavily in the space between my eyes, I rip down the giant mural of the water cycle. The cumulus clouds, fat with cotton balls, the rain drops of silver tin foil, and the river of blue-tinted plastic wrap. I love the water cycle. So efficient and orderly. Growing up in the Pacific Northwest, you get used to the water. A week or so without rain will occasionally make me uneasy. Like something isn't right with the earth. Like there's a glitch somewhere in the rotation. Liquid. Steam. Ice. It's all the same thing. Oh, to be something that can manifest itself in three different ways, but still be essentially, chemically, beautifully the same! As I'm ripping off the blue paper sky, I start to think about what the fuck I'm going to do for the summer. Last summer I worked for a month at a YMCA day camp and spent a lot of time preparing elaborately grilled meals[114] for David. I missed the deadline for the YMCA thing, and as of last week all the spots were filled. Could Teacher Annie gracefully transform into a line

[114] Oysters, pizza, lamb chops.

cook at a homey diner? Could she evaporate into a steamy cocktail waitress? Or should she freeze up in front of her television and wait for that hott hott day in early fall when her boyfriend will be home to re-kindle a love once vibrant and melt her back to normal again?

I'm standing still with a wad of crumpled paper in my hand when I hear a knock at my classroom door. I toss the paper in the trash and walk over to the door. It's Gus!

"Hey. I thought you'd be here."

"Yep. Here. All alone!" I lift my arms to point out the empty space, the lack of braided pigtails and dirty sneakers. "What's going on, Gus?"

"Well." He says this with Excitement, and it's nice to have the big *E* back in my classroom after a day's absence. "I have something for you. I'm really stoked about it. And I have to give it to you right away." Gus is smiling, breathing a little heavy, and reaching for the satchel/man-purse that hangs from his shoulder. He pulls out a book. It's a slim beige paperback with a sepia-toned font on the cover. It looks like a literary magazine from a college campus, printed on an expensive woven paper afforded by a generous university budget, and chock-full of youthful attempts at highbrow literature. My first thought is that Gus has had something published and that he's here to present me with a copy. But then, he's never been one to toot his own horn.

"What it is?" I say moronically as I take it from his hands. And then I read the cover: *Annie Harper's Journal.* What?!! "Whaaaa?" I say, stunned by the look of my name in such a dignified typeface. I momentarily and absurdly assume that Gus has hacked into my computer, found this, my giant tapestry of rambling words, and printed it out and had it bound at the local Kinko's. But the volume is a little too stately for Kinko's. And for another pathetic moment I wonder if Gus has written a journal he wishes were mine and filled all the pages with gushing romantic fantasies about him. What a lunatic I have become. As I open the cover, he starts to explain.

"It's a real published book, Annie. About this woman named Annie Harper who lived in Mississippi during the Civil War. Then I notice the subtitle: *A Southern Mother's Legacy.* "I just got it in the mail yesterday, so I haven't read much, but it's her account of home life during the Civil War. A historian stumbled upon her handwritten journals and turned them into this book. Isn't it incredible?" I don't know if Gus means that the book itself is independently incredible or that it's incredible because I am also Annie Harper and I am also a woman on the home front and I am also trying to write about it.[115] I decide he must mean the latter. In a way.

"But *I'm* Annie Harper." My voice is meek and quiet, and suddenly I feel like a fraud. Like she's already done it, but with larger risks and more sophisticated prose. With a sharper understanding of the political situation and with a courage that's comprised of more than goofy humor and self-pity. AND WITHOUT ALLOWING HER RELATIONSHIP TO DECOMPOSE. Before I even read it, I know that I am the weaker, stupider, more annoying, more boring Annie Harper. I flip past the title page, the acknowledgments. I don't even stop at the stuffy photographs of Annie Harper the First posed in her starched high collars and boned bodices. I skip right to the first page of the introduction, and stuck in the middle of the editor's commentary is a snippet of Annie Harper's prose.

I am not thinking of giving you any historical account of battles or following the varied fortunes of war. . . . I only aim to give you an insight into the home life which you can never find in any history of the times—.

She's done it. It's like she's wrote my fucking thesis statement for me back in 1876. By goddamn mother-loving candlelight! It takes just

[115] But I've never told Gus that I'm writing about it.

moments of scanning the editor's introduction and the first few pages of the text to ascertain that Annie Harper wrote this journal for her daughter. For the sake of posterity. It occurs to me that this is a concept that my generation might be neglecting. Perhaps it relates to the whole lack-of-artifacts problem. What will our electronic era leave behind? Big, fat nothing. Especially when we only care about being recognized now. Off I went, trying to document, not for the educational purposes of others, but for the benefit of myself. Give me kudos for my bravery and charm. Don't let me bother giving guidance to my descendants. Let me be hapless in my commentary. No worries if the things I say grow to shame my future children and cause them to legally divorce me in their early teens. No problem! I do not mind! I realize I've been silent and stunned for a few long moments, and I look up at Gus, who hasn't moved.

"How did you find this?" I turn to the copyright page and see that the book was published in 1983 by the Flower Mound Writing[116] Company in Denton, Texas.[117] There was a second printing.

"The Internet," Gus says.

"The Internet?" I say, like I'm the old Annie Harper and have never seen a typewriter.

"Yeah, you know. The World Wide Web." Gus looks a little nervous.

"You Googled me?" I don't mean it to sound so harsh and accusatory.

"Yeah. So what. I Google stuff." I let the awkwardness settle for a moment, and then I hug him. I feel his fingers clasp momentarily be-

---

[116] ISBN: 0-910655-01-4, edited with Introduction and Notes by Jeannie Marie Deen.

[117] Eerie coincidence: You may remember that Francisco/Ray Flores was from Denton, Texas. Was! Oh, the bitter sadness of the past tense!

hind my back and I get one nice breath of fabric softener and something vaguely breadlike.

"Thank you so *so* much, Gus. This is amazing. An artifact. A treasure. You are a treasure finder." We let go.

"You're very welcome. I knew you'd like it. And I thought maybe it could help you some."

"I'm getting by," I say. Silence. Silence. Silence. "Hey, it's summer. I made it to summer." Our smiles widen simultaneously because we both know it's coming. I've lobbed Gus an easy one and he's winding up, ready to blast it out of the park. His voice is robust and so happy when he says it:

"It's gonna be a great summer!"

21

*F*or obvious reasons, today I'm calling my book *Annie Harper's Journal*, and I've just discovered that copyright rules don't apply to titles. Just the actual text. So I can use it. Flower Mound Writing Company will have to print thousands more copies because after everyone reads my book they'll naturally want to read her book too. And I don't have to worry about being all good anymore. If I move forward with the idea that this writing is a mere log, a raw, uncut journal (rather than a neatly wrapped, Chicken Soup for the Wartime Soul memoir), then who will blame me when my heart emerges a little black and tattered? I can tell the truth and hopefully not be loathed for it. Who knows? Maybe Annie Harper the First will be just as much a sicko. And people will love to read the two texts together. Serious Literature people will write academic papers about the similarities between the Annie Harpers. What my book says about her, and hers about me. Some great-great-great-granddaughter of Annie Harper the First will probably contact me and we'll be interviewed together on *The View*.

After Gus left my classroom,[118] I sat down in the Book Nook with *Annie Harper's Journal*. I had this rush of hope similar to when I found the soldiers' wives' blogs. I thought: Here it is. An artifact. This must be helpful, authentic, and sincere, because someone thought it was worthwhile to print a thousand copies and sell them for $7.95 apiece. I read the first ten pages or so, where Annie described the political state of Mississippi before the war and how her grandfather

---

[118] It's barely mid-June, but he has to start preparing for the Fourth of July beer season by making tons of vinyl signs.

raised her to be more literate than the average Southern girl. Other Annie Harper had a writing style that was confident, proper, and direct. She saved heavy emotional lines—*When the polls closed November 4th, 1860, Liberty covered her face with her mantle and fled from her unhappy children, to return no more for sixteen years*—for when she really wanted to drive her point home. But after those first ten pages, I got bored. I wanted to hear Annie Harper talk about Annie Harper. Emancipation, Secession, Whigs, all very important Civil War things, but hey, Mrs. Harper: You guessed wrong. We *can* find all that in the "history of the times." I want to know how bad she misses her husband. I want to know what she's cooking for dinner. Oh wait, what her slave is cooking for dinner. I hate Annie Harper.

I've resolved to set *Annie Harper's Journal* aside for a few weeks. I need some time to recoup from the flurry of the end of the school year, to get my ducks in a row for summer, and to lasso my heart so I can sink my hands into its most ridiculous nooks and crannies and pull out a reasonable prognosis regarding sweet, sweet David Peterson. I want to give *Annie Harper's Journal* a good, serious study. I want to come back to Gus for a critical discussion about all the interesting ideas and observations that I will certainly glean from the text. I don't want him to think I tossed the gift away; I just want to give my name twin the serious read she deserves. More on Annie Harper the First to come. I promise.

Interesting Thing:

On the way home from my last day (the real, no-students last day) at Franklin Elementary, I stopped at the farmers' market[119] to pick up

---

[119] This market has a goat cheese vendor who I made friends with last year. She's this old hippie named Doris, and she's always trying to convince me to start my own goat business. She said that there's so much

some of the season's first strawberries and some fresh greens for dinner. The farmers' market is in the parking lot of a shopping complex
that includes a Goodwill, an all-you-can-eat Chinese buffet, and a sex
store. But the location manages to be a good fit for the market and
draws a varied mass of customers: couples who stumble upon the market after picking up a few S&M toys; hip, alternative high school kids
who just purchased second-hand Levis; and those who come by every
week on purpose. And since it's a farmers' market—loaded with organic things earthy and leafy—I wasn't surprised at all when I ran
into Gina. She was examining a bundle of scallions, peering into their
tubey roots like they were actually alien tentacles about to communicate some brilliant message about the future of humanity. I walked
over to say hello. I hadn't seen Gina since the camping trip, so I
thought it would be nice to catch up.

"Oh hey, Annie," she said. It wasn't as enthusiastic as her usual *let
me tell you about the great nonprofit I work for* voice. "I didn't know you
shop at this market."

"Yeah. My school's just down the street. I come here a lot. Doris's
goat cheese is amaz—oh right, vegan. Sorry. But yeah, I come here.
How are you?"

"Pretty well. I've been kind of down about Gus and all, but it's
fine." What? My first thought was that since I last saw him two days
before, Gus had suffered some major accident. Fallen off a ladder.
Crashed his delivery van into the side of the bowling alley. Why
hadn't someone told me? Someone would tell me. My next thought
was that he'd decided to move to Tibet or something and had just told
Gina. But Gus would also tell me right away if he were moving to

---

cheap land just east of Puyallup that's perfect for them to graze. And if I
sell my goats' milk to her company, I should be able to support myself off
of a mere seventy-five goats. And I'd only have to spend five to six hours a
day milking!

Tibet. He'd at least tell me he was thinking about it. Gina read my silence as confusion. "He told you we broke up, didn't he?"

"No. He didn't tell me." And then I tried to think of all the right things to say, but I've never been good at condolences. I wasn't about to tell Gina how flawed Gus was or that she'd get over him in no time. I really didn't know much about the intensity of their relationship. And secretly inside I was thrilled by this news. Nothing against Gina, nothing at all, a lovely woman she is. In another version of this universe, perhaps she and I are bosom friends. My tongue swept around the inside of my mouth searching for an appropriate word to unite us as women, to offer her comfort, and to wholly conceal an elation derived from a situation that had brought her such lousy sorrow. So brilliantly I said, "That's too bad. Have you tried these beet greens?" And incredibly, Gina responded well.

"Yes, I love beet greens."

"Me too."

Silence. Silence. Silence.

"You're lucky, Annie. You know that, right?"

"Because I work so close to this market?"

"No. Because you have a terrific best friend." And then Gina gave me this look of extreme envy. She picked up a tomato and raised it to her nose. Took a breath. Here it seemed like Gus had broken up with her and she's calling him terrific. Such maturity blows my mind. But there was a heavy sadness too. Like she believed that now, since she was Gus's ex-girlfriend, she would never be great friends with him like I was. Her Gus phase—her access to his bizarre imagination, incredibly thoughtful memory, and Max Schaffer–esque curiosity—had abruptly ended. The whole thing has made me consider that perhaps my longings for my own Gus romance are likely as advantageous as they are ridiculous. Her fallen eyes and forced smiles have convinced me that the risk of losing him is sooooo not worth it.

Gina and I exchanged a few more pleasantries. She told me about the band she's joining, and I told her about my plans to visit Boston next month to see my friend from college, Michelle, and that I'll probably see Stephen (our camping buddy) too. As we said goodbye near the green cartons of fresh strawberries, I saw her glancing at a young couple that wouldn't let go of each other's hands while trying to point out which carton of berries had the best stems for chocolate dipping. And though I don't even know if chocolate is vegan, I could definitely tell that Gina was sad. I was too.

I'm still puzzling why Gus didn't tell me about Gina. Maybe he'd just broken up with her before he gave me the book and didn't want to pull attention away from the moment of me diving into Annie Harper's time capsule. That's so like him. I can't decide if I should call him—everyone needs to discuss a breakup—or if I should just wait until he tells me. And whoa now, here I am assuming that Gus broke up with Gina. She didn't say. But the heaviness in her eyes made it seem that way. The way she called him terrific and me lucky. She didn't seem horribly conflicted.

I just got off the phone with David. It was the super lame kind of talking that everybody does, but that nobody ever includes in books or movies because it's too fucking dull. Unless the people are naked. (We were not naked.) Or unless the people are dangling from a rooftop by a shredded rope and trying to calm themselves by regular chitchat. (We were not dangling from a shredded rope.) Or unless the talking is really just in the place of some other more important conversation that one or more of the people just can't get herself to have or even admit to needing to have.[120]

---

[120] BINGO!

David: So how was the last day of school?

Annie: Oh, it was nice. Kind of sad. I'll miss them, of course.

D: But you're free now.

A: That's right. Free for the summer.

D: Wish I was[121] free.

A: No kidding. Home stretch, though, right?

D: That's right.

A: Just a few more months.

D: Just a few more months.

Silence. Silence. Silence.

D: How are your parents?

A: They're good. Yours?

D: Good. Excited for me to come home.

A: Of course they are.

And maybe it's because he's always so tired and I'm always so tired + conflicted + guilt-stricken + confused, but I swear this has been the oomph level of our last four telephone conversations. It's like we should just record them and play them to each other when we pick up the phone. Mundane-a-thon 2004! Summer Mopefest Live! Don't touch that dial! No wait, go ahead. Then come back in three minutes and you'll hear the same damn thing. Here this is supposed to be a rich, vivid (however difficult) experience for us—especially him—and we're talking about how our mothers are doing. (!!!???!?!?) Isn't my mother supposedly telling David how she's doing? He never asks about my students anymore. In years past, he could tell who my favorites were before I could. Because I'd be sharing anecdotes about the cutest ones and whining to him about the yay-hoos and spitting off my life's details like I absolutely had to tell him. Like I'm this wet, heavy Washington cloud that needs to get the rain out at least once a

---

[121] "Were" is actually the proper conjugation.

week. And I knew more about his life. Who in his company was getting promotions and who was failing their PT tests. He hasn't told me about a pregnant army wife all year![122]

I've been thinking about this a lot, and so I'm going to try to map out a theory. Here goes:

A. Relationships require sharing because sharing and knowing things about one another makes humans feel close.
B. Sharing requires time to communicate.
C. David and I have little time to communicate.
D. I am a teacher, and therefore, sharing is even more important for me, as it stands for harmony and community.
E. If there is a lack of sharing, the intensity of emotion between two people dwindles. Without concrete anecdotes to elicit sympathy, mutual joy, and admiration, the couple must rely on past experiences to sustain a feeling of closeness.
F. The past is boring. I know it already.
G. I want to know what David is doing now.
H. I want David to care about what I am doing now.[123]
I. The gestation period of an elephant is twenty-two months.
J. If humans were elephants, one of David's buddies' wives could be completing her first trimester.
K. Annie Harper the Second is one loony organism.

But maybe it's not the strains of the situation that have brought us down. Maybe it's the strains of the situation that have revealed a larger hole in what I thought was a sturdy and interesting relationship? If our closeness has always been grounded in plain banter and plain closeness, what kind of relationship is that? Besides one another, what

---

[122] Wait. No one is getting pregnant while the sperm's away. Duh.
[123] How come he never asks about Helen?

shared interests do we even have? Beer? Snuggling? Badminton? Do I owe the W.A.R. and the George W. for tossing me into this lame situation that has ended up revealing something true? Has the tragedy of others saved me from a long life of yawned *So how is your mother?* I'm taking this issue to Loretta.

"Loretta, David and I are growing apart." I whinnied it out like a teenager complaining about his parents' objection to buying him a drum set. Like I was blinded by my confusion, unable to extract any reason for why the obstacle even exists. I wanted an easy answer from Loretta. A quick, simple fix. I wanted to rail on the surface of a tight, loud snare.

"Oh honey, of course you feel that way." We were sipping lemonade made from lemons I brought and a dozen packets of Sweet'N Low. Loretta said she's too old to worry about the health risks of artificial sweeteners. ("I'm already sterile, and my bones are petrified peanut brittle.")

"It's not like you've been able to talk to him like you always have. That's the hardest part."

"Not talking?"

"Yes. Being physically away from someone you love is easy. If you can speak all the time and keep abreast of each other's goings ons, you'll be fine. You don't need to be beside someone to have an intimate relationship. But if the communication isn't regular—if you're not writing and he's not writing every single day and with specific information and feelings—then naturally, you'll have drifted."

"Every day? Did you and Ron write every day?"

"Of course. Why don't you try it?" Loretta said this like she was suggesting a new brand of laundry detergent that is oh-so-conveniently on sale. So simple, child. Do a few loads of whites!

"Well, David can't get to the Internet every day, and I'm just now done with school."

"Man knows how to hold a pen, doesn't he?"

"Yeah."

"And you know how to hold a pen?"

"I certainly do."

"Then maybe you two just need to try a little harder these last few months. Go buy yourself a book of stamps, Annie Harper. Write your heart out to this man, if you love him." Loretta is probably right. It's not time to give up yet. Tough times don't always constitute grounds for surrender. Maybe I do still love David. Maybe it's just my dormant hormones mischievously poking me with goofy shit about Gus. How has Lonesome George held out for so long!? Annie Harper the First wouldn't give up now. No sir-ee. I considered telling Loretta about the note David left me about the Laws of My Heart—just so she knows that I've got an escape clause. But I decided to keep it in and march onward into the frothy blur of a faded relationship. I'm hoping for clear, practical sunshine once I make it through. I've resolved to visit the post office on Monday and to tell David all about mine and Loretta's shared theory and to try my best to feel like I'm in a relationship that's more than checking the newspaper to make sure the other party hasn't died. WAHOOOOOOOOOOOO!!!!!

Okay, since I'm trying to be more honest with this writing tapestry, let's just go with a modest "wahoo."

22

*T*oday I'm calling my book *On the Tailbone of the Luck Monster.*

I had spent a pleasant afternoon at Spanaway Lake. It's a small lake in one of the less savory neighborhoods of South Tacoma. It's surrounded by a modest park with bike paths and picnic tables where local teenagers eat Taco Bell food and make out. It's one of my favorite of Gus's teasing points that he used to play live-action, role-playing Dungeons & Dragons there in junior high. I brought a book and the latest issues of the *Economist* and *Us Weekly.* Though I didn't start reading the former periodical until I had breezed completely through the latter, I still felt like I accomplished much in the form of adult reading. I'd brought a tuna sandwich, two bananas, and a roll of those minty Girl Scout cookies that I'd frozen in the spring.[124]

In the late afternoon, the park gets swallowed in shadows. If you try not to think about all the sex offenders who pick up victims there and about the rumored two-headed fish that circle the brown lake, then the dusky hours can have a fairly magical feel. Surrounded by

---

[124] If you thought the Girl Scouts were a dying breed, you're wrong. There were five (5!!) of them in Miss Harper's 2003–2004 class. And I ridiculously purchased four boxes of cookies from each scout. That's twenty boxes at four dollars apiece. An easy and absurd math problem. Luckily, I prevented a summer of serious cookie gorging by foisting three boxes onto my parents, one onto Loretta (for diabetic lows), two onto David, and two onto Gus. How many does Miss Harper have left, boys and girls? Still, a lot.

massive evergreens (sometimes up to the shore, with roots draping into the water), everything at Spanaway Lake feels soft and covered. As I was reaching down to inspect what was either an agate or a worn chunk of a brown beer bottle, I spotted a mother duck and her brood of ducklings dipping into the water. There were eight of them. I know this because I followed them stealthily along the little path that borders the lake's edge as they careened in and out of nooks of cattails and skunkweed. There was one duckling that kept lollygagging behind and two little ass kissers that were determined to follow their mother right flush behind her waving webbed feet. They were faster than I expected. I was walking at a fair clip to keep up with them, and at moments when I thought I'd lost them, my heart would sink. I'd say something like *No no, baby ducky family. Wait for Annie.*

And I don't need George W. Bush to lay down the cash for a therapist just so she can tell me this: You have issues being alone. I'd been with David nearly 24/7 since our senior year of college. When he wasn't around, my students were. In the summers there were more students. Friends. And when he takes off, what do I do? I acquire an unconventional pet, foster a friendship with a ninety-three-year-old woman who is basically a captive audience, and go klutzily stumbling into love with my best friend, who just happens to be around all the time.[125] I *was* my relationship before half of it left for a far-off desert. And now Alden's dead, things with David are going stale, and I'm chasing ducklings around dirty lakes, enthralled by their darling togetherness. I realized this as I galloped up a little hill to hopefully meet the ducks on the other side. And then I stopped. I saw them. The

[125] Honestly, because he was away in Dominica, Gus and I hadn't spent much time together since summers during college. Very little overlap with my David phase too. But we did always keep in touch. He sent me funny postcards about his island antics and this piggy bank he made from a coconut shell.

mother had turned squarely, pointing her butt feathers (and then eight tiny sets of butt feathers) directly, perhaps purposefully, at me. They swam to the middle of the lake. I returned to my car and ate a few more cookies. Drove home.

It was nearly dark, and my arms were loaded with a few groceries and my stuff from the park. I entered the house through the front door. Dropped my purse on the sofa and stumbled into the kitchen. I unloaded the box of cereal and two cans of SpaghettiOs into the pantry. I took a zucchini squash from the fridge and began to slice it with this knife my mother bought me for my birthday last year. I love slicing with this knife. It makes beautiful whisking noises as it slides through the gnarliest potatoes and carrots as if they were mere room-temp sticks of butter. After tough days at school, I'd come home and cut and slice and dice the stress away. (There are many bags of chopped onions in my freezer.) After I finished cutting the zucchini, I remembered Helen. *I wonder what Helen's up to,* I mused, reaching for the switch to ignite the patio light.

And then I saw the feathers. White and speckled about the lawn like someone had dropped a box of packing peanuts and left its contents to spread in the wind. *Helen,* I thought, *why are you molting so! This is just the sort of thing Edward Harrington warned me about.* But then as my eyes roved to the further corners of the yard, the potted plants on the little cement patio, the patch of dirt before the entrance to Helen's sunroom, I realized that the feathers—the soft, shiny plumes and quills and bits of down—were *everywhere.* And in quantities that could only mean two things:
1) Someone had filmed a pillow fight scene for a teen movie in my backyard.
Or
2) Helen was completely naked.
   I busted through the back door and onto the patio, breathing

heavy, the chopping knife gripped firmly in my hand. "Helen," I shouted. "Helen! Come out!"

Silence. Silence. Silence.

My eyes adjusted to the glare of the porch light and started to pan across the fence line. It's not a nice fence. If you were imagining a clean, white wooden fence up until now, I'm sorry I must shatter that pleasant image. My yard—like many a South Tacoma yard—has a waist-high, chain-link fence. The poles that punctuate the grid every few meters are shiny and capped by those little round dome things that make them look somehow safer and less industrial. In the far left corner of the yard, I spotted a darkness where there didn't used to be one. The corner was just past the reach of the porch light, and as I walked out to it, feathers sticking to the heels of my flip-flops, my insides darkened too. With anxiety. With sadness. With dread.

It was a hole! Some monster had dug a hole under my fence, shimmied its way through, *and,* evidenced by the contrasting spray of bright feathers trailing through the tunnel, made away with my precious Helen!

I returned to the house and placed the knife in the sink. I took the cutting board of zucchini coins and let them cascade gracefully into the trash can. I turned off the water I was boiling for pasta and opened the door of my refrigerator. I selected a bottle of Stella from another untouched six-pack left behind from the pre-David-in-Iraq days. I tore through the contents of three drawers before I found the bottle opener, ripped off the lid, and took a long, cold, tough-girl drink. And then I called Gus.

By the time he arrived, I'd started my second beer. I offered him one and he took it.

"So where do you think she is?" Gus asked after his first swig.

"Bird Heaven," I said dejectedly. "Where even penguins can fly." I jumped up to sit on the kitchen table where I was tall enough to see out the window. By this point, the breeze had blown most of Helen's feathers to the east side of the yard, and they clung to the links of the fence, dancing around like mini flags or ribbons. Part of me wanted to grab a ziplock bag from the cabinet and run outside. I could collect a small bundle and stuff my last bits of Helen along with sprigs of lavender into a little sachet bag to keep in my sock drawer. Or I could take the feathers and glue them to the rim of a hat. I could tie flies for fishing. I could stash the quills in that little box with my baby teeth.

"There's a chance she could still be alive." Gus didn't say this with enough confidence to make it annoying. It was just a token stab of hope. That line you say when there's really no good line at all.

"No, Gus. She's dead. Someone's dog heard her fussing about, smelled her juicy flesh, and then barged in and snatched her. I just hope I don't find her mutilated corpse down by my mailbox." And I should point out that I wasn't crying. Yes, I did call him to come over. I needed someone, but I wasn't *hysterical*. I wanted to tell Gus how foolish I felt for thinking I could keep a suburban chicken alive. I wanted to tell him that I felt inadequate and that it was my fault for not reinforcing the fence or for not making a coop door that was too small for the average prowling canine.

"It's warm in here," Gus said. "Do you want to take the beers out back and sit? Maybe Helen will be lured home by the sweet sound of your voice?"

"Very funny," I said as I moved toward the door.

Outside I unfolded the two vinyl lawn chairs and lit one of those citronella candles in the terracotta pots. My mother gave me a set of them when I first started renting this house last year. *You'll love having a patio, Annie. It's what summer nights are for.* Had my mother imagined I'd use the candle to light a vigil for my dead and gone pet chicken, perhaps she'd have purchased tea lights in foggy glass votives. I wished we had a tiki torch. Those were definitely more Helen's style.

"So what are you doing this weekend?" Gus asked once our chairs had stopped squeaking and our beverages were making frequent journeys to and from our lips.

"I don't know. I've been kind of lousy at making plans lately."

"Yeah."

"What are you doing? Do you have to work?"

"No. I don't know. I broke up with Gina." Gus said this in a very dude way that's atypical for him. Like he was trying to mix the perfect voice cocktail of testosterone and nonchalance.

"I know," I said. If I were a smoker, this would have been the moment where I took a long, slow drag.

"What?"

"Gina told me. We ran into each other at the farmers' market."

"How'd she seem?" I know Gus must have liked Gina fairly well to have dated her for over six months, so his concern seemed authentic—more than just curiosity.

"She's sad. But not so heartbroken that she can't enjoy beet greens. I think she'll survive. Why'd you do it?" Annie Harper's cocktail: two parts teasing, two parts no-bullshit, several twists of curiosity, just a splash of nonchalance.

"I was tired of her. Isn't that usually the reason? I mean, unless one person does something particularly evil to the other person, most relationships end at the pasty hands of boredom."

"Pasty hands of boredom?" I laughed.

"What? You've never seen them?" Gus lifted his drink and paused for a moment. "It's kind of like you've been watching television and you're sleepy. The couch, it feels good, and the sounds of the TV are nice and soothing. You're not particularly riveted by the program, and you let your consciousness fade in and out. You're comfortable enough that you entertain the idea of riding out the whole night on the sofa. With the mutterings of infomercials and throw pillows with semiabrasive, stained upholstery. But you don't mind it. You're so tired, you *keep not leaving.* In the back of your head—where you're still kind of awake and capable of reason—you know you should get up and go to the bedroom. But there's something that's keeping you there. It just seems good enough. You can't fathom that the bed is really any more comfortable. But then somehow—amazingly—you do it. You stand up. You walk to the bed and it's true. It's unarguably better. Your legs stretch out all the way, and the pillow cases are smooth and cold and wonderful."

"And what does this have to do with you and Gina?" I crossed my ankles and turned my head away while I asked it.

"Gina was a fine girlfriend. Thoughtful, kind, definitely smart, but at the end of the day, I never fully felt it. Felt rested. There was that crick in my neck. I was sleeping on the sofa. And now I'm free, sprawling out in my clean, quiet bed. I was so tired when I first got back from Dominica. Gina was the first couch I fell into. And she turned out to be kind of boring to me. Pleasant-boring, but still boring."

"Yeah."

"Ya, mahn. I should have done it months ago. Before I saw that Juiceman juicer guy so many times."

"It does seem like a great appliance."

"Gina just wasn't right for me."

It was the most words Gus had spoken to me about a relationship since the failed chewing-gum mosaic. And even that was kind of superficial. Whether he fell in love or got any good action down in Dominica is a mystery to me. And granted, we'd each had a few beers and were still all thrown off and flustered by Helen's absence, but it felt nice for him to spill a few things to me—weird and metaphorical and absent of Annie-Love confessions as they were. We finished the six-pack and I cautiously told Gus that I sleep on my sofa at least two nights a week and that I kind of know what he means. I was really glad he was there. Just as I started thinking that I should probably *do something*—stroll around the neighborhood shouting Helen's name, search her coop with a flashlight for evidence, call the police[126]—a couple appeared from around the side of the house. They were young and sweaty. The man was wearing a backwards baseball cap and the woman wore cutoff jeans. Both had hooded sweatshirts. They must have let themselves in through the side gate. I jumped a bit when I saw them. The man spoke first.

"Hi. Sorry to interrupt. I'm Pete. This is Jenn. We just moved in down the street this morning." We all traded hellos, names, and firm handshakes chilled by the night air. It was a very normal exchange. Like midnight neighbor gatherings were commonplace in these parts. Then there was an awkward silence where I stared at Pete and Jenn's pockets bulging with random moving items. I could see an outline of packaging tape in the kangaroo pouch of Jenn's hoodie. She had several rubber bands around her wrist. A little flashlight head peeked out of Pete's pants.

"Annie. We're really sorry. Our dog, Roger, he escaped from our yard, and he came back a few hours ago with . . ." Jenn was twisting her fingers, the concern in her eyes leaping out and bouncing around the yard. It was like she didn't care if the movers broke her wedding china or if their new house had no running water because she was obviously upset about something else.

". . . with what we think is your chicken." She turned to Pete. He took over.

"He's never done anything like this before. We were so confused to see him with a chicken in this neighborhood. But then we asked the Madsens next door what they thought, and they told us about you and that it was probably your chicken and oh, we really feel so awful. I know this isn't a great way to start things off in a new town, but . . ."

"No." I took a step toward them. I felt like they were two of my

126 ?????????? ? ? ?

students who had just spilled dirty paint water all over the floor. Not an act of recklessness or a sign that they weren't paying attention, but a pure, simple accident. "It's okay," I said. "It's not your fault. Dogs are dogs. He couldn't help it."

"Your coop is really terrific." Jenn sniffed and wiped her nose on her sleeve, which instantly made me like her. "I feel so bad. We feel so bad."

"We're sorry to come over so late, but we didn't want you to be up all night worried." Pete looked at Jenn, then at me again.

"It's okay. It's really okay."

"Annie's tough." Gus stepped forward and put a hand on my shoulder. "And Helen had a really great life here."

"Helen is such a nice name," Jenn said and smiled a bit. I started hoping we would all become friends. I imagined backyard barbecues where Roger (amazingly, I didn't hate him!) would pant at my feet and we'd all laugh about the strange circumstances of our first meeting. Gus and I would be holding hands and Jenn would be carrying a tray of handcrafted beef patties over to her aproned husband.

Our conversation shifted to the normal pleasantries of new acquaintances. Pete and Jenn had moved from Olympia because of a new bank job Pete just landed at Wells Fargo. Jenn was five months pregnant.[127] Before they left, Pete—much to Jenn's embarrassment—handed me an envelope.

"I know there's nothing we can do to replace Helen, but someone gave us this as a wedding gift last year and we've never signed up. Jenn says regifting is tacky, but I wanted to do something." I opened the envelope to find a gift certificate to the Chesalon Wine and Cheese of the Month Club. There was a number to call when you were ready to start receiving your first of six monthly pairings.

---

[127] She hid it well with the sweatshirt and the packaging tape. When she told us about the baby, I said "Cool!" So dorky.

"This is great," I said. "You didn't have to. But thanks. I'll use it. I'll enjoy it."

"I don't care much for cheese, and Pete's really more of a beer guy." Jenn had relaxed now that the gift was well received. We all said good-byes, Jenn rambled off several more apologies, and Pete whispered something into Gus's ear right before they turned and evaporated into the darkness of the side yard.

Gus and I returned to our chairs, and I flipped the gift certificate around in my hands.

"Wow," I said.

"No kidding," Gus said.

"What did Pete tell you when he left?"

"He said that he'd taken Helen's—um—remains and placed them in a cedar cigar box. And if you don't want to bury it or anything, he said you can just throw it away." I knew that this was the type of kind-ness that melted Gus's heart then nearly bubbled it out of his chest. He was grinning so hard, but trying to fight it back like he was worried I'd find his smile inappropriate. I laughed.

"That's incredible," I said, giving him the green light to let his cheeks flex freely. "I bet it's the cigar box from his wedding night." And then Gus jumped up from his chair.

"Hold on a second," he said and bolted toward Helen's coop. He bent down to the handle that pulled the drawer-floor-egg-retriever out from the bottom of the house. He looked at me. "Annie, do you mind?" I shook my head. Gus pulled out the drawer slowly. He placed his hands on his knees and leaned his face in close to the shavings—a dangerous proximity to an understandably rank blend of smells. And then I heard him sigh. Not a defeated sigh, but a quick, relieved, al-most surprised sigh. He returned to the patio and squatted before me, his face serene, almost blank.

"Miss Harper," he said with his hands pressed together in a gentle bowl, cradling the smooth brightness of Helen's final gift to me.

"Her last egg," I whispered, not taking my eyes off it. It was perfectly shaped and glowing. Like Helen had gathered all the sunlight of the day and condensed it into this ultimate creation. I looked up at Gus, who was smiling now: half sad, half happy for me. "How should I cook it?" I asked. We both crunched our faces up for a minute, silently going through egg preparation methods, analyzing them for levels of tastiness, beauty, and respect. I couldn't decide.

"Wait," Gus said. "Don't. Don't cook it. Let me take it home, and I'll bring it back for you tomorrow."

"Why?" I was too tired, too semidrunk, and too brain-dead to even wonder what Gus had in mind.

"Just trust me, Annie." And I did. I thanked Gus for coming over, and he thanked me for letting him help. We picked up the beer bottles and I noted how the clanking sound would normally cause Helen to skitter around in her coop. Before he left, Gus asked me if I'd read much of *Annie Harper's Journal* yet. I told him that I had not, but I would do so soon. He seemed rather anxious about it. Then he went home.

I couldn't sleep for a while. I kept thinking about how not sad I was about Helen. When I thought about her brutal, violent murder, my stomach turned and my chest tightened, but when I thought about her being dead—being gone forever—I didn't actually feel too bad. Sure, I loved her. And I know that she helped me tremendously over these last few months. It was like Helen was her own kind of war victim. A veteran who served with honor, loyalty, and pluck. But she was a *chicken*. I almost feel ridiculous writing this. Maybe it's glaringly obvious, but my sadness for her loss is nothing like what I feel over the loss of Flores—of Brother Alden. If anything, her death reminds me of the travesty that is theirs. And I didn't even know Flores and Alden! I have no real excuse to be sad about anything! David, the Flores family, BHH Barbara, Alden's adoption-balking mother, and anyone else whose loved ones actually die in actual unlucky ticks of the universe, now they have the right to shed buckets of tears. I wonder how David is doing with it. I wonder why I don't know.[128]

I spent the next day over at my parents' house helping my mother in the garden. We both wore large-brimmed hats, and we chatted during the commercial breaks of *This American Life* on NPR. Both of my parents were very sweet about Helen's death. My mother hugged me and said things like *Oh, sweetie. And you've already been through so much.* And! It didn't bother me. So my mother and I share a similar penchant for melodrama. She says out loud all the same things I kind of think inside.

"Don't think for a second, Annie, that this is your fault. Accidents happen. Helen had a good life." Awww, my sweet mother. If she only knew of my other failures. I should really talk to her more. As if there aren't enough slimy layers of guilt in my life, spending the day with my dear parents reminded me of how little I've used their proffered support over the last year. Not that I don't value the relationship I've fostered with Loretta, but why did I open up to her when I had them? They are also smart. They are so openly loving. I guess my intentions with Violet Meadows were originally rooted in escapism. I thought being with Loretta would take me away from my own life, but then I went and turned it into another wing of the Annie-centric Universe. Jeez Louise.

My dad offered to come over and help me tear down the coop if I wanted. I told him I wasn't sure yet and that maybe I'd get a new chicken in due course. My parents didn't note the absurdity of the whole thing. They thought that Pete and Jenn seemed great and were so glad Gus was there to support me. We grilled a lovely piece of salmon. Ate it at the kitchen table with the windows open, the omega-3 pumping through our bodies, lubing up our innards, and moistening

---

[128] I forgot to get stamps.

our eyes while we talked for a bit about Alden and what kind of kid he might have been. For once it was nice to be around my parents while emotionally troubled. They somehow made it easy to pretend that I'm actually fine. And they were so good at supporting and loving me in my fineness that I almost believed that the fineness was real. It's easy to be the old me around them. The one who was a devout wartime girlfriend. The one who believed she loved David Peterson loads and loads and loads and loads.

When I got home there was a small box on the welcome mat of the front door. From the driveway, I thought it was Helen's cigar-box coffin, but I soon realized it was cardboard and far too cubelike. I took the box inside and set it on the kitchen table. It was unmarked, and the flaps were taped down with clear tape. I ran a knife across the tape and the flaps popped open. The box was stuffed to the brim with popcorn—white and unbuttered.[129] I ate a few pieces and carefully brushed the top layer aside, digging into the box gently with my fingers. My thumb brushed against a thin plastic cord and I grabbed it. Pulled it up.

It was so magnificent, I gasped. Painted blue with daisies and irises blooming up from the base. On the top of the egg was a golden sun with orange rays swirling down the slopes of the sides. Two of the rays wove together and bonded in an elegant cursive scrawl. *Helen,* it said. Not too big to distract from the aesthetic of the design, but not small enough to go easily unnoticed. The surface was shiny, smooth, and sturdy: obviously the product of a careful shellac job. There was a tiny hole on the bottom and two others on the top where the cord was attached. I imagined Gus's gangly hands, smashed together in still concentration, gripping the tiny eye of a needle. I could see his full lips tenderly pressed to the shell, his cheek muscles tense, his lungs lightly

---

[129] Helen really loved her corn.

blowing the yolk and the white into a small glass bowl. Affixed to the top of the cord was a mini plastic suction cup. It confused me for a moment, but then I understood. I stood up, dangling Helen's last egg between my thumb and forefinger. I carried it to the window by the sink and cautiously pressed the suction cup to the glass. I felt my cheeks pinch into a wide, healthy smile before dropping abruptly. And then I cried.

And cried.

And cried.

And cried.

23

*T*oday I'm calling my book *What I Did on My Boyfriend Vacation*, and it's a five-paragraph essay handwritten on wide rule. There are three spelling mistakes and one unfortunate incident of subject-verb disagreement. Go ahead. Fail me. See if I care.[130]

David calls two days after Helen dies, and I tell him the whole story. When I'm done, this is the first question he asks/thing he says: *What kind of dog was it?* I don't know! I shout this at him.

"Aren't you supposed to say you're sorry for my loss first? Aren't you supposed to be comforting me? My pet was just murdered, David." I'm genuinely annoyed.

"Sorry, babe. I was just curious. You didn't seem too upset when you told me. I mean, it's just a chicken. It's not like some animal with high brain power and the capacity to love." And I want to say *What do you know about chickens?* or *Don't tell me about the capacity to love.* I want to say *Gus understands Helen* or *Gus feels bad; he made me a magical, beautiful commemorative fucking ornament about how bad he feels bad.* But I don't say any of those things.

"David. I didn't mean to pick a fight. It just doesn't seem like you're sad about it."

"Annie. I'm *not* sad about it. You think with everything I'm going through and everything I'm seeing here, that I'd be *sad* about one

---

[130] ABORT MISSION EVERYTHING (see how easily this is done, George?). Memoir is out. Raw, uncut journal is out. Writing to produce a product is out. New goal: Write myself back to sanity.

slaughtered chicken? Thousands of chickens are killed every day. It's a *chicken!* I'm sorry. I'm just not sad." Oh, how he has a very good point! But I can't help it; it bothers me.

"But Helen was *my* chicken," I say in my small, whiny child voice. I almost add *and so you should be sad for me.* But I don't say that either. I tell David I know I'm being ridiculous. It's just that it was stressful for me, and that just because my stress is drastically different from his stress, it doesn't mean I'm not entitled to have it. However trivial it may be. And then I say something about how I don't really know what he's going through and therefore, I don't know how absurd my whining is by contrast. He acknowledges the validity of my points and starts telling me how one of his buddies just got the first season of *Da Ali G Show* on DVD and that they've been watching it every night and that it's sooo funny. Yawn.

I'm holding Loretta's hand when I tell her about Helen. I don't tell her about the feathers being everywhere because I don't want her to think Helen died after a miserable struggle. It's not the kind of thing you emphasize when discussing death with the ancient.

"Oh, Annie. I'm so sorry, dear."

"It's okay. I'm fine. Helen was a great chicken. She brought me a lot of joy and taught me so much about being the best me.[131] And I definitely owe you for it. She *was* your idea." Loretta lets go of my hand, flips both of her wrists at me, and settles them in her lap.

"Stuff-a-nonsense," she says. "I owe *you* for putting you both[132] through this."

"Loretta, you're crazy. It's nobody's fault but that silly dog's. And maybe mine for not having a more secure yard."

"Why is everyone always calling me crazy?" Loretta squacks, and

[131] Cheesefest 2004, but I do mean it.
[132] By "both" I think she means me and Helen.

we both laugh a bit. Later when she's sitting in her rocker and I'm on the bed—both of us playing video poker on mute[133]—we talk about Flores for a while and how it's such a different type of loss.

"It's like how jars of salsa come in different levels of spiciness, but essentially it's just varied degrees of the same flavor," I say. "Once I tasted the zing and the sharp punch of Flores's death,[134] the loss of Helen was rather mild. Sad, but gently so." And then I stare out the window for several long moments and think about how much I sound like Gus. *The unmistakable flavor of grief. The pasty hands of boredom.* "Hey Loretta," I say when I snap out of it. "There's something I want to show you." I tell her the story about how after Pete and Jenn left, Gus found Loretta's final egg. And then I reach into my purse for the small Tupperware container and carefully lift out the ornament for Loretta's inspection. And approval. She smiles, obviously, because it's so damn pretty. Her eyes narrow and she hands it back to me gingerly.[135] Our fingertips touch for a moment in the exchange. Loretta looks at me: two parts seriousness, three parts knowing, two parts happy.

"I see now, Annie." She folds her hands in her lap. "What the dickens are you going to do?"

A few days later Gus calls me and asks if I want to come over and watch a movie at his apartment. It's the kind of thing we did all the time in high school, summers and spring breaks during college. But it's been a while—years since circumstance has allowed our friendship to pick up

[133] We're actually quite good at this now. It's not as distracting as you'd think.

[134] I am feeling really bad that I haven't told Loretta anything about Alden. But is it really that big of a deal? Of course, I'm thinking about him as we talk about spicy death salsa. Oh my.

[135] I am only using this word because it's Loretta. No one except people like Loretta can do things gingerly.

its old ways and habits. We have our own homes now, and so it feels different. It's a weeknight, and I have no plans other than to maybe tweeze my eyebrows and read something, so I agree to come. Casual old Gus. Dorky old Annie. I ask if he wants me to bring anything. He says no.

On the way over I wonder what he wants to watch. I hope it's not a *Godfather* marathon or some documentary about an obscure musician I don't know. Gus lets me into his tiny apartment, and I immediately plop on a beanbag chair.[136] I have already thanked him on the phone for the spectacular transformation he performed on Helen's egg, but something is urging me to do so again in person. But with a hug. Just as I'm thinking about it, Gus says "So have you decided about getting a new chicken yet?" He's in the kitchen behind me, and I can hear him riffling through a drawer of utensils.

"Oh, no. As much as I'd love to pay Edward Harrington another visit, I don't think I'm ready yet. And since I'm going to Boston soon anyway, I don't want to burden someone with feeding her—Helen II, you know, the new chicken."

"I guess that makes sense. I'm making guacamole. Do you mind peeling some garlic while I chop?" I spring up from the chair and I notice that it's a more difficult leap to make with seven more years on my body.

"Oh, yeah. No problem. Sorry I didn't offer to help. I just saw the beanbag and got sucked into it. It reminded me of your dad's basement and all the stupid time we spent in there doing stupid things. All the time I spent sprawled on it whining to you about Brother Alden." Gus looks up from the jalapeño he's chopping. He's very serious.

"That's not stupid, Annie. I'm sure I can think of seventeen stupider things you talked about from that chair," he teases me. His smile threatens to recount fourteen stupid Annie Harper teen ideas.

---

[136] Gus doesn't have many possessions. This blue flannel beanbag used to occupy the basement of his father's home.

"Let's not go into it." I grab the head of garlic from a basket on the counter, rip off two cloves, and start to peel. My nails are short, so it's rather difficult to make the first little tear. It reminds me of the membrane around one of Helen's hard-boiled eggs.

"There's lemonade if you want some." Gus tilts his head toward the fridge and catches me staring into the bowl of mashed avocado, tomato, and onion. I hand him the two shiny, clean cloves and grab two glasses down from the cabinet. "I made it just before you got here, so it won't be chilled. You'll need ice."

"Hmm. Lemonade. So, what? Did you break down and buy the Juiceman juicer one night?"

"No. I used this." Gus pulls an old-fashioned crystal juicer from the sink. Pulp and seeds still stick to its angular edges, rendering it imperfect, but still beautiful. "It was my mother's."[137]

"Wow. Never seen that one. It's lovely." I take the lemonade out of the fridge and swirl the pitcher a few times to mix the pulp and sugar that has settled on the bottom. In the freezer I find a single ice cube tray amongst several frozen lake trout from our fishing trip. There are four remaining cubes, and I divide them between our glasses. I reach for the faucet, pull the lever to the far right, and start to refill the tray.

"Wait," Gus says, and he sets down the salt he was shaking over the guac and swings the sink fixture over to the left side. "Hot water freezes faster." And he doesn't say it this condescending, stupid-Annie way. He says it like it's this astonishing, beautiful secret. And the look in his face (the lift in his eyebrows and the slowly curling smile)

---

[137] Gus has a lot of things that *were* his mother's. Since she left when he was just a few months old—and I guess in some sort of fury—she didn't take much. Gus has always liked to use her things though. "It's nice that she has given me more than just a life," he often says, which I've always thought was a very mature take on it.

confirms that it is. And that he's going to tell me about it. It's the look I know I should make with every lesson I teach my students. It's the look Max Schaffer gave when he handed me his gorgeous essay about spider sex. It's the look that says: *Here is the universe. Isn't it wonderful?*

"Yeah, it's called the Mpemba effect, and people have been trying to prove it for centuries. It's hard to wrap your mind around, right? Water needs to chill before it can freeze—won't that take more time? But, no. Experiments have shown that hot water, not all the time, but most of the time, freezes faster than cold water under certain conditions." Gus dips the tip of his pinkie finger into the guacamole and tastes it. "Needs more lime. Anyway, even Aristotle pointed this out at one point. But people kept on not believing it until this schoolkid in Tanzania—I forget his first name, but his last name was Mpemba— just wouldn't back down. He was a part-time ice cream vendor, and he made the observations about freezing while making ice cream. No one believed him. A teacher told him he must have confused the results. Eventually, he did a study with another teacher and they got it published in the sixties. So he's not really the discoverer, but the *rediscoverer.* I wish I knew more about thermodynamics and exactly why it works, but I know that it's one of many—something like sixty-eight—anomalies of water. The layperson always thinks that water is this simple, predictable substance because it's so abundant. But it's not. It's much more complicated. Surface tension. Boiling point. Water breaks a ton of rules. I mean, you know how they're always saying that if a planet has water, then there's a chance for life? I think it has something to do with all the anomalies. Like life itself is an anomaly of the physical world. That's the problem with being a philosophy major. Everything real I know is a mile wide and an inch deep. I need to read more. I think this is done. Taste." Gus dips his pinkie into the bowl again, holds it out to me like a challenging, stern, tough-love teacher. I lean in slowly without moving my feet, close my eyes, and remove the sample in a single, firm swipe.

"It's perfect," I say. "And that was very nice."

"What?"

"The story. About Mpemba. And the ice cream."

"Oh, right. Thank you."

"Thank *you* for sharing."

I have a hard time concentrating throughout the first several scenes of the movie[138] because I'm remembering a time when David told me the same thing about making ice. We were at my apartment and I was filling the tray and he was standing behind me, big and strong and shadowy. He said, "Use warm water, hon," and then bent down to peer into the fridge. And that's all he said. And then I didn't say anything. I just did it. Both of us, unquestioning, uncurious, unable to stop thinking about the bland burgers we were grilling and the status of our cheddar cheese supply.

Comfortable.

Accepting.

Tepid.

But then I get into the movie more. It's alternately disturbing and beautiful. Marco, the boyfriend of the bullfighter, is lodged in this weird place between grieving and hoping. How do you act both sad and optimistic? Though a war is by no means a coma, I can kind of relate to Marco. My heart sinks for him. And when he befriends the bizarre nurse, Benigno, as both a distraction and out of genuine human interest, it makes perfect sense to me.

You're hurt, lonely, and confused?

Okay. Do something else.

There's this scene where the nurse tells the motionless ballerina

---

[138] It's a Spanish film called *Hable con ella* (*Talk to Her*) about a comatose female bullfighter, her boyfriend, and this fucked-up nurse who is obsessed with another comatose woman: a beautiful ballerina.

about this silent film he's just seen. The viewer sees the film under Benigno's narration. It's about a scientist whose experiments have run amok and his entire body is physically shrinking at an alarming pace. His wife is mega distraught and the final scenes—before he dissolves into nothing—show him as wee little inch-long man, climbing into his inevitable death. Into her vagina! And it's hard to think of the man as small and the rubber vagina as normal-sized. Even with the frame flashing to the woman's normal face and back to the tiny scientist, sobbing before her rubber labia, he just doesn't seem small. The plastic vagina just seems big. And that's about where I fall asleep. It's not that I'm disliking the movie; I'm simply tired. Blame it on the guacamole resting slack and cozy in my gut. Or the lack of afternoon coffee. Or maybe on the fact that I'm just comfortable dozing between Gus and rubber vaginas.

I wake up to Gus squeezing my calf over my jeans, and I notice that I've nuzzled my feet under his thigh. "Annie," he whispers. "I'm sorry you fell asleep. It was a really powerful ending."

"Yeah, me too. I didn't mean to. What happened? Did either of the women wake up from their comas?" Gus takes his hand off my leg and I shiver a bit, realizing I'm cold. He reaches to grab a blanket draped along the back of the couch and then clutches it to his chest.

"I can give you this blanket and we can play the ending again. *Or,* I can give you this blanket and we can not play the ending again. *Or,* I can not give you the blanket and we can play the ending. *Or,* we can do none of the above." I rub my eyes to moisten my contact lenses, and when I'm done I look straight at Gus's eyes, which are not crusty or sleepy or annoyed by my narcolepsy.

"Yes to blanket," I say, and I thrust a fist into the air. "And yes to replaying the ending!"

Gus tosses the flannel throw over me like it's a picnic blanket and I'm a shady patch of grass. He tucks the blanket's edge under my toes and I try to will his hands into touching my feet for longer. Extended tender hand/foot contact. Does that count as infidelity? Surely David has other soldiers—maybe even Jayna Austin—rub down his tired hooves? Do their hands not linger? But Gus's hands shy away and he asks, "What do you last remember?"

"The rubber vagina!"

"Rubber vagina, here we come!"

As I drive home, I feel very peaceful. Maybe it was the mini nap or the salty/sweet combo of the guac and lemonade. I've fallen asleep midway through at least eighty-nine movies in the company of at least fourteen different friends and family members. When the credits roll and my companions rustle about or nudge me or change the channel to barking late-night talk shows, I usually emerge from my drooling pose and receive some playful chastisement for konking out and missing this kissy part or that car exploding. Some people get offended— *how could you pass out with that beautiful scenery?* Others are more aloof—*well, it's your loss, Annie.* But no one has ever offered to rewatch the end with me. Right then. Maybe everyone thinks I'll just fall back asleep again and that a second chance would be totally futile. But to Gus it seemed like perfect logic. And to me it seemed like perfect logic. And ultimately, it was perfectly successful. I saw the end. I enjoyed it. It was great to be given that chance.

24

*T*oday I'm calling my book *Between a War and a Window*, and by window I mean those tiny round airplane windows where the glass is so thick you can't even see your reflection. And I mean the window of the Dairy DeLite that Gus paints for every holiday. And I mean the window above my kitchen sink where I used to stare fondly at Helen. And I mean the windows of my classroom where we taped up a million snowflakes this past winter, back when I was full of love and hope and certainty.

I just got back from a week in Boston! It was mostly marvelous. I felt like a criminal out on bail—a temporary delay before a punishment I deserve. I didn't have to think about David so much, and I didn't have to feel bad for thinking about Gus from time to time. Michelle has this adorable Cambridge apartment in an area called Davis Square, which isn't much of a square, but more of an intersection: a really great intersection with ice cream shops on three of the four corners.

The first few days Michelle had to work, so I mostly traipsed around the city alone. My first morning, I walked the entire Freedom Trail, which is this painted red line (or sometimes section of red bricks) that zigzags around all the historical parts of Boston. The towering, gold-topped statehouse, that church where Paul Revere hung the lanterns, the site (it's basically a median of an intersection) of the famous Boston Massacre. Though I'd been to Europe before, this trip was my first to the American East, and thus, the oldness of everything was rather overwhelming. Not simply because things are old, but because they're still smoothly functioning. Slanty buildings that house the offices of hotshot lawyers. Ancient gravestones that still stand and that are carefully mowed around centuries after their occupants are laid to rest. There's this big meeting house—Faneuil Hall—from the 1700s that's now a sleek, colorful food court selling overpriced corndogs and beers. Had the revolutionaries been told their sanctuary of ideas and community would transform into a bustling strip of fast-food joints and crappy bars, they'd have guffawed their funny wigs off.

Michelle had recommended that I explore the North End—Boston's old Italian neighborhood—and stop somewhere for cannoli. Much of the Freedom Trail weaves in and out of the small, marinara-scented streets, so I folded up my maps and veered off the red line to wander.[139] I found a quiet café on a street that angled invitingly off one of the North End's main drags. A college-aged kid with a tight-fitting New England Patriots T-shirt was seated behind the counter reading a book. His face was clear but had a raw redness to it that suggested a previous battle with acne and the recent application of some hard-core medicated ointment. I draped my windbreaker over a stool and plopped down. The kid stood up to lean on the espresso machine and take my order. It was one of those mega old espresso machines—thick ceramic and dense chrome—that could probably support the combined weight of the entire Patriots' defensive line. I ordered a latte and a cannoli. After I said it, I stressed out for a second about whether or not

---

[139] For some reason, while walking the Freedom Trail, I couldn't shake this preoccupation with literally walking right on it. Like a kid who mustn't step on a crack for fear of severely injuring his mother, my gaze was constantly being pulled down to my sneakers, striving for careful heel-toe placement on the narrow stripe. Narrow = about eight inches in most parts.

I should have said "cannolo" or some other singular construction. But when the kid started to grind the espresso and steam the milk, the noises drowning out my insecurities, I started not to mind. This is my vacation, I thought. No one knows me. No one (save Michelle and Stephen, obviously) gives a flying fuck that I am here. I'm just another dope with a misfolded map and a neon fanny pack.[140]

"Here you are," said the kid as he placed the latte before my folded hands on the counter. I know I went to college in Seattle and am therefore supposed to be difficult to impress when it comes to coffee, but this kid was genuinely talented. In pouring the frothy milk over the espresso, he'd created a connected chain of three perfect hearts. Immediately, I blushed. Which I know was totally stupid because he was nineteen and I was wearing an ugly T-shirt from my intramural college volleyball team. I guessed he probably made latte hearts for all the crusty old men who were sitting at the tables along the windows. I was mentally trying to squeeze the blood from my cheeks when he returned with the *cannolo*.

"Thanks a lot," I said when he gently slid the ceramic plate next to the latte. "This latte is beautiful," I added because I didn't want him to think I was all love-struck and speechless because of the hearts and the heat in my face. I also wanted to be polite and honest.

"Why, thanks. It only took ten years to perfect my technique." He smiled and started scrubbing the milk residue off the hulk espresso machine's dainty steam wand.

"Ten years?" I flashed him the dubious look I give my students when I think they're bending the truth during show-and-tell. Your cat had *seventeen* kittens, Marco? Come on.

"Ten years." He dragged out both syllables. Then he folded the damp rag and draped it over his shoulder. "My grandparents own the

---

[140] Only if I actually had a fanny pack. I am kind of the type.

place. Put me to work when I was ten. My name's Tyler. Nice to meet you." He wiped his hand on his apron and extended it across the counter.

"Oh. Nice to meet you too. I'm Annie." His hand was sturdy and rough, simultaneously belying his age and proving his work history.

"You visiting Boston or are you from here?"

"Visiting." I took a drink of my latte, careful to check my upper lip for excess foam before I spoke again. "I'm from Washington. I'm visiting a friend from school."

"DC?"

"What? No. Washington, the state." Then Tyler[141] made some comment about the rain and the Seattle Mariners while I snuck in my first bite of el cannolo. It was rich and sweet, and the texture of the smooth ricotta and the crunchy pastry shell made my teeth hesitate to bite down all the way. Like there was something either very sharp or very precious inside that I should avoid. I was thinking about whether or not I had Lactaid in my purse when I realized that Tyler was asking me a question. He was asking what school I attended in Washington. He used the words "do you go to," which means he thought I was still a student and perhaps even a student of a traditional age.[142] Maybe his age. I did say I was visiting a *friend from school* and not *an old friend from college*, and I was wearing a T-shirt, and I am always carded at Tacoma bars and occasionally at rated-R movies. I nearly launched into a *No, no. I'm almost twenty-five. I* teach *school. Ha. Ha. Ha.* But

---

[141] I was really expecting his name to be Marco or Luigi or Frankie. Tyler? It just didn't fit.

[142] I know. I know. There are many twenty-five-year-olds pursuing undergraduate degrees, but I always feel so much older. Maybe because I like gardening and wearing bathrobes around the house. Also: College just feels so long ago.

then I didn't. Tyler, despite the waxy red skin, was oddly attractive. His football T-shirt didn't quite pin him as a jock, and his narrow black jeans could have meant anything from stage crew to hipster. He wasn't an obvious type. He was wiry, but muscular. Dark, but not overly hairy. A pleasant bundle of dichotomies. Not who you'd pick from a lineup as someone who can pull a mean shot of espresso.

"Oh. I go to the University of Washington," I told him. How big of a lie is a gracefully shifted verb tense? *Go. Went.* Just a little slippery time travel. Let Tyler meet the Annie Harper of 1998. All fun. No boyfriend. No horrific cesspool of mental infidelities. Intramural volleyball fiend. Able to stomach more than one illegally acquired, artificially fruit-flavored alcoholic malt beverage! Isn't lying about who you are a fundamental element of vacationing?

"Cool. I go to UMass Boston. History major. What do you study?"

"Education." I'm surprised how easy it is to skip a few years back in my Answers to Typical Questions Asked by Strangers repertoire.

"Right on. What do you want to teach?"

"Elementary school. Ideally, third grade." It was a breeze being the old me. Refreshing and light and full of hope. I was ready for anything Tyler could throw out. I wasn't worrying about my boyfriend's chances to die one moment, then plotting ways to break up with him the next. I was years before that, draped in a blanket of optimistic innocence.

Tyler continued to encourage pleasant small talk and asked what I had planned for my visit. I told him about the various outings Michelle had in mind for the week. While our chat took a break so Tyler could attend to other customers, I noticed his book pressed open on the back counter. He had finished making change for a small old woman and caught me squinting to read the title of the book.

"You want to see it?" Tyler seemed flattered that I was curious about his reading selections. He tossed me the paperback. *Dark Tide: The Great Boston Molasses Flood of 1919.*

"Awesome," I said without even trying to sound nineteen. "I've never heard about this. A molasses flood!?" I started scanning the description on the back of the book as Tyler picked up a broom.

"Well, you're not the only one. Most Bostonians haven't even heard about it. There used to be a bunch of rum distilleries around this neighborhood, and one morning a giant tank of boiling molasses exploded over two million gallons into the streets."

"Holy hot sugar," I said.

"Yeah, it was a nightmare. Twenty-one people died. And a few horses. Loads of buildings were destroyed, and it took years to clean up. The author tries to investigate whether it was a true accident or if a group of anarchists set if off on purpose. It's a sweet book." Tyler had stopped sweeping and bounced the broom between his hands excitedly as he spoke.

"Ha, ha. Sweet book." I dorkily laughed at his unintended pun and was quite charmed that he didn't notice it.

"Yeah. My grandfather says that down on Commercial Street on a hot day, you can still smell the molasses seeping up from the cobblestones."

"Wow. That's too beautiful. But sad." Another customer came in for coffee, and I started reading the book's introduction. January 15, 1919. I stopped for a minute, hung up on the date. The ratification of the Eighteenth Amendment! Prohibition! I disregarded that Tyler was talking to someone else and shouted across the counter. "Oh my God, this happened on the last day before prohibition? What irony!" Tyler chuckled at my enthusiasm.

"Sweet irony," he said. I read for a few more minutes and realized I should probably head back to my careful Freedom Trail tiptoe. I scooted the book across the counter and thanked Tyler for the conversation and fine Italian refreshments. He scooted the book back.

"Keep it," he said. "I've actually already read it."

"No. It's okay. You don't—"

"Annie. Take it. You're going to be a great teacher."

Walking away from the café, I felt quite warm about my encounter with Tyler the barista. He thinks I'll be a great teacher. I think I am a pretty good teacher. Maybe I haven't made the best decisions (1. staying with David for so long although he makes me boring, 2. avoiding my parents this year when we could have been growing closer) in my twenty-five years, but there are a few things I did right. I chose the right trade. I was a smart, focused nineteen-year-old. I knew what I wanted exactly and I got it. Oh, what I wouldn't give right now for a bit of that certainty.

Several minutes later, as I was crossing this scary bridge over to the Bunker Hill Memorial, I made plans for the molasses book. Read it. Take some notes about points I'd like to remember. Give it to Gus. That night I told Michelle about Tyler and the molasses flood. I told her about giving the book to Gus and how much he'd love it.

"What about David? Why not send it to David?" Her tone took me by surprise. Like she was challenging me to tell her everything. Like she already had her suspicions, even though I'd been so careful not to reveal the pathetic, evil-fueled agony my heart was dragging me through. And even though the real reason is that I know Gus appreciates molasses floods more than David appreciates molasses floods and it actually has nothing to do with the fact that I'm losing one and perversely hoping to gain the other, I told Michelle that passing the book to David would be futile.

"He'll be back so soon." I stared at my feet. "The mail takes forever."

The next day I called Stephen. We'd been e-mailing before my trip. He only had one morning class that day, and we'd made a playdate to picnic at this cemetery in a neighborhood called Jamaica Plain. He had told me that it's not like a West Coast cemetery, but more like a park and that it would be a nice respite from the crowds in downtown Boston. He met me by Michelle's apartment in Cambridge and we took two trains and a bus to the cemetery.

And Stephen was right. The place was gorgeous and nearly empty on a Wednesday afternoon. The terrain was hilly, and healthy, towering trees flourished along the walkways and at the crests of small hills. I thought that it was probably a very wonderful place to be a tree. Sucking nutrient-rich soil from the remains of the dead, resting a comforting bough or shadow on the shoulder of a lonely widow. These trees are not for lumber or to provide habitats for raccoon families; these are trees to console. As we first walked around in search of a perfect picnic spot, I was quiet and the cemetery was empty. Reading gravestones and the small signs that indicated the names of the alleyways between rows of plots. They're all named after flowers and plants. Hydrangea Way or Willow Row. Quickly, it became apparent why the cemetery was so devoid of carnation-toting mourners. The tombstones—many of them elaborate marble statues and concrete mini mausoleums—were mega, super old. Wealthy merchant families from the early 1800s, local politicians from the Civil War era, and inventors and investors of serious fortunes. And for a moment it made me sad to think of the deceased and the fact that anyone who knew them closely was also deceased (likely buried just paces away) and that these bodies were just lying there, alone, with their identifying stone tags and the slight possibility that some historically minded passerby might recognize a name.

"I wonder where Brother Alden is buried." I said this out loud without a preamble and after minutes of complete silence.[143]

---

[143] Though we are not yet great friends, Stephen's and my experience of fishing together created the ability to share long, comfortable silences early on in our friendship.

"You could probably find out." I looked over at Stephen, surprised that he understood the context of my sudden musing. I quickly understood that Gus must have filled him in about the whole crazy story. It made me happy to know that Gus was speaking of me to Stephen.

"Yeah, I guess I could. I wasn't allowed to search for Alden when he was alive, but what damage could I do to him know?" I imagined myself sprinting to his grave in some sunny California beach burial ground. There is no grass. It's a sand graveyard. When I find his place, I collapse on it, wiggling my body deep into the warm sand. Closer to him. *Oh, Alden,* I say, and then I grab a seashell off the sand and start to make edits to his tombstone's inscription. Where it says BELOVED SON AND FRIEND I scrape just below in ragged, straight lines: AND BROTHER.

While I was thinking all this, Stephen pointed out a nice patch of grass between two trees where we should plant ourselves for lunch. As we walked toward it, I continued thinking about the absurd sand graveyard. How deep the tombstones must be planted and how many decades of erosion it would take to wash the bodies to sea.

Stephen had brought cheese, crackers, salami, gingersnaps, and grapes. I had brought pickles, hummus, carrots, Cheetos, bananas, and iced tea. We made this elaborate spread of the foods and then decided that the Cheetos didn't quite match the rest of the items in tone. We placed the open bag inside my backpack so the commercial logo and shiny nutrition label didn't distract from our buffet of natural offerings. Stephen talked about dental school and told funny stories about him and Gus from college. I talked about teaching, and Stephen laughed and consoled at the appropriate times when I told him the story of Helen's death. Once we'd consumed almost the entire spread, we talked about Alden a bit too.

"Do you think he knew about the time he spent with your family?" Stephen asked. I had always assumed that he hadn't. Who would tell their child that sort of thing? *Hey, I gave you away for a while, but then I decided you weren't so awful, so I finagled you back. That's cool, right?* But the way Stephen said it made it seem kind of possible. Maybe Bless Her Heart Barbara had told Alden the truth. Maybe he was estranged from his mother by age sixteen and was handed his entire file from a social worker.

"I don't know, Stephen, but I like to think that if he knew, he'd have looked for us. I mean, not expecting to join the family or anything, but to say hello. To say *Look, I turned out okay. Thanks for feeding me and snuggling me those first three months.*" And after I said those words I got really sad again for my parents. I'm always thinking about the Alden thing as it applies to me. Annie playing Chutes and Ladders alone. Annie watching Care Bears with nine different stuffed animals in her lap. Annie being a shy, awkward preteen because she has no sibling with whom she can socialize. Here I've been mourning something I never had while my parents were totally crushed by the loss of something real and precious. A child they loved and fed and snuggled. A child that was as much theirs as I was. Maybe the emptiness I felt over Alden's being gone wasn't all for me but comprised partially of actual empathy for my parents? Not just a simple A. Harper Pity Party. Was that possible? Is Miss Harper capable of such semicomplex, not-entirely-selfish emotions? Alden is their story, not mine. I am just a supporting character in a family drama. I'm the child actor who still has time to go to normal school because her role in the movie is that small. My parents went through something huge that I will never fully understand. Everything I've gone through has been fake and romanticized. Jesus Christ. I realized I was cussing silently in my head in a cemetery with a friend who I was supposed to be talking to. And so I piped up.

"I guess we'll never know," I said to Stephen. And then my phone rang. 012345678. David. "David," I said out loud and made some awkward motion to Stephen that signaled I needed to take the call and step away for a few minutes. After I picked up the phone and started the usual "howareyous" with David, I wandered down to the bank of the cemetery's glassy pond. I was telling David about my first days in Boston, and I sat in this wooden chair under a tree. The chair was carved out of a girthy log—an oblique angle sliced and sanded to form a surprisingly comfortable recline. Our conversation was pleasant but unremarkable. David seemed in okay spirits, and he cited his proximity to completing the deployment several times. He asked if I had received the birthday package he sent me yet,[144] and I told him I had not. He teased me a bit for being on a picnic with another man and I told him he'd been picnicking with other men for months so it was fair. And then a giant stone fell from the sky and pinned me to the ground by my chest. It was a true scientific miracle since the stone was made of a previously undiscovered element called Guiltesium Infintesibitchide. The mass of Guiltesium Infintesibitchide in grams/mol is 983, which if you give a fuck about chemistry at all you'll understand is a wicked dense material. Luckily, I walked away from the scene with only minor bruising.

When I returned to our picnic spot, we packed the scraps back into our bags and Stephen led me toward the grave of e. e. cummings. He had asked "Do you want to see the grave of e. e. cummings?"

And I had said "Okay!" with a lot of enthusiasm because I was on vacation and it was sunny and I was up for anything that might distract me from the horrible thought I was thinking at that moment.[145]

---

[144] My birthday is tomorrow. Wahoo—twenty-five.

[145] Well, that's good that I talked to David because now I probably won't

Stephen said nothing to prepare me for the sight of the famous modernist's grave. Since the cemetery hosted many a beautiful and extravagant monument, I was expecting e. e.'s to be the same, but with some quirky twist. A sentence fragment embodied in an oddly cut stone.

"Almost there," Stephen said, and we scrambled up a little hillside to a shady line of graves along the trees. "Ta-da," he said and stopped. I swung my head to each side, expecting something big and eye level. Stephen pointed down, directly to our feet.

EDWARD ESTLIN CUMMINGS
1894–1962

And then I laughed and laughed and laughed. It was a very inappropriate thing to do in a graveyard—the noise turning the heads of foraging squirrels and bouncing off the marble facades of somber memorials—but the full name and the all-caps lettering struck me as hilarious. When my bellowing faded into an exhausted sigh, I looked right at Stephen, whose arms were folded over his chest, his posture slouched back, head tilted in amusement.

"Funny," he said flatly. "When I took Gus here in college, he had the exact same reaction."

Stephen and I took the same bus back downtown and then parted ways. He had to meet a prospective Harvard dental student for drinks, and I was headed back to Michelle's to clean up for dinner. Maybe it was being around all the corpses or thinking about Alden or talking to David in his war zone, but I had this really sick fantasy on the sub-

---

need to talk to him until the end of the trip and I don't have to worry about keeping a close eye on my cell phone and I can just enjoy myself.

way ride to Cambridge. There was a middle-aged man sitting next to
me on the train. I only looked at his face right before I sat, but there
was something very tense about it. A tightness in his jaw. A severity in
his eyes. He was wearing a Red Sox hat and a frown so profound that
I figured the team must have lost some important game that afternoon. And for several minutes I really wanted to turn and look at him.
To check and see if the frown was accompanying him through every
lurch and turn of the subway car. But I didn't. Instead, and I really
don't know why, I imagined he was a terrorist. It was my first terrorist
fantasy: wholly uncomfortable and completely transporting.

The scene. Terrorist silently pulls a gun from his jacket and positions it against my temple. *Hey,* he shouts. *Everybody, listen up.* People
put down their magazines and math textbooks. Conversations halt.
The snoozers lift their heads and force their wimpy eyes in our direction. *If anyone comes near me before I'm done talking, I shoot this girl. I
have a bomb in this bag that I can detonate simply by pressing this button
at my hip. I am going to blow up this entire subway car, killing myself, all
of you, and this young lady right here. It is my destiny to die today. Just
moments from now. However, if one of you will give me permission, if one
of you can say the words "Sir, please kill the girl," I will shoot her, I will
shoot myself, and the rest of you sinners will be spared. If no one speaks up,
the bomb blows and we all die together. Any of you. It could be your decision. You could be a hero. That is, if you have the courage to watch this
pretty lady's brains splatter across this window. And then my brains. Just
say the words and the future is yours. When I finish this sentence, you will
have thirty seconds to decide.* And suddenly everyone in the car is looking at me, judging me, wondering what sort of sins I've committed
and what sort of companion I will make as we all hold hands and walk
toward the gates of heaven. I see a woman with a small child scan my
fingers for a wedding ring. I can almost see her thinking that it's
worth sparing her child if I have none of my own. A professorial-looking

type across from me is twisting his fingers, trying to deduce some logical way out of this story-problem disaster. In the fantasy, Tyler from the café is in the car. He's standing, white-knuckle grip to a pole, staring at me, shaking his head, and mouthing the word "sorry." But the time is ticking away and no one is saying anything. The man beside me is still, silent. Hand on the gun: steady. Other hand on the belt: steady. Counting silently. What number is he at? Twenty-one? Nine?

And though I don't want to die, I don't, I don't, I don't, I am restless and anxious and so full of some pungent elixir that is the combination of every possible emotion ever. It's like mixing all the fountain sodas together at a pizza parlor. Strong. Overwhelming. Indescribable. The people on the train keep turning their faces to each other, searching eyeballs for approval. *Are we worth it? Am I worth it? Are you worth it?* All these people with families and babies and bigger hearts and more life insurance than me. And no one is saying anything. Why can't they? Don't they get it? One is less than fifty. *It won't be your fault!* I want to scream. *No one will blame you. No one will blame you. Say it. Say it. Say it.* But that's the thing. Humans (ME) inherently don't want to hurt each other (DAVID), but the universe is such that we end up doing it anyway (I THINK I LOVE GUS MORE). I am so close to the bomber my upper arm makes a seal against his rib cage and I feel his lungs swell significantly, purposefully, because he knows it's his final breath. I make my most pleading look at the professor, Tyler, the mother, David, Gus, Caitlin Fucking Robinson. Somebody say it!

"Sir, please kill the girl." The voice is calm and kind of sweet. Quiet to almost a whisper. A very intentional volume because its speaker wants both to be heard by the killer and then not heard by the rest of the crowd. I have just a few moments, the time it takes for the gunman to release his final measured shot of carbon dioxide into the air before his scattered remains take over in chaotic decomposition.

And in that last moment, I get it. I see that I've found the loophole. I recognize the voice. It's mine.

Totally fucked up. Right? Luckily, the somber man beside me was not a deal-making terrorist, so I got off safely at my stop and started walking to Michelle's house. I tried to put my finger on where such an elaborate, violent fantasy came from. What were the origins of this desire to paint myself as the valiant martyr? The only way I could emerge from my present situation as the martyr is to tough out my relationship until David returns and it becomes clear whether or not there is something worth preserving. And really, that's the wimpiest form of martyrdom I've ever heard. What do I lose? I tolerate another two months of scratchy phone calls and blasé, irritable e-mail chains. Big whoop! But the terrorist fantasy has left me feeling something urgent. The man made it crystal fucking clear. Someone has to lose. Someone must be the bad guy.

The rest of the trip was fairly lovely. There was some bar hopping with Michelle's friends in honor of my twenty-fifth birthday. A cozy night in, where we baked brownies and watched girly movies. Michelle braided my hair while I rattled off a few of my concerns over mine and David's dehydrated relationship. I came so close to telling her that somewhere between a chewed-up apricot and a plaster hand turkey I had fallen in love with my childhood buddy. Michelle is smart and articulate and clever (and perhaps more perceptive than she lets on), but this was the sum of her advice: "Just wait, Annie. I guess you just have to wait." So much for the terrorist's urgency.

I had a morning flight back to Seattle. The coffee I drank at the airport was pumping robust surges of energy through my limbs, and I was disappointed to waste such a buzz by sitting down and strapping into the airplane. I had the middle seat. Before the plane took off, I pulled a spiral notebook from my bag to take some notes about the week,[146] and after writing for several minutes I discovered some papers tucked into the back of the notebook. It was Max Schaffer's essay on spiders. I had thrown it in there on the last day of school with the plan to read it over again at my leisure when I wasn't rushed by the stack of twenty-eight other papers to grade. So I read it again there on the plane. It delighted me so much that I was all smiles and giggles when I ordered my ginger ale from the flight attendant. When I finished, turning back to my notebook and sticking to the Annie Harper the Second trajectory seemed dull and stifling. I remembered *Dark Tide: The Great Boston Molasses Flood of 1919*, which I was already halfway through, but I had foolishly checked it inside my luggage. I considered striking up a conversation with the people next to me,[147] but since we'd been in the air for about fifteen minutes already, it felt as though the window of opportunity had passed. And so I did something I hadn't done since the fifth grade. (It came fairly easily since I'm such an evil, lying memoirist.) I wrote a short story. Extra credit for me!!!

Back in the Seattle airport I had about twenty minutes before my parents arrived to pick me up. I was rather pleased with the effects of my morning coffee, so I swung into a line at a Starbucks kiosk and bought more: a refueling to help me through the vacation roundup that my parents would surely require. As I was stirring my milk in with the little wooden stick, watching the swirls and thinking fancifully of Tyler and his silly hearts, I heard a familiar voice. "Okay, I love you. Bye." And then the snap of a flip phone. It was Charese Atkins.

[146] I actually wrote down the entire subway terrorist fantasy before we even took off.

[147] A teenager reading *Rolling Stone* and a middle-aged woman with chin hairs.

"Oh, hey, Charese." She was adding packs of Equal to her latte two at a time.

"Miss Harper." She seemed a bit rushed but still genuinely glad to see me. "Headed out for vacation?"

"No. I'm just back from Boston. Visiting friends. And you?"

"For better or for worse, I'm headed back down to San Diego." She gave me a look that said *I can't believe I'm doing this, but if you think I'm crazy, it's okay because I also think I'm rather crazy.* I resolved to work on my version of that look when I get home. It's probably quite handy.

"To see your ex?" I asked tentatively.

"That's right. He's being deployed in a few weeks and he said he really wanted to see me before he left. Missed me. Loved me. All that crap. And so, fuck, I'm going down."

"Wow. Intense." I took a dribbly sip of my coffee.

"No kidding. At first, I wasn't going to budge. I thought I was so done with him. But he's Lacey's daddy and he was my husband and he's going into something so lousy that maybe he kind of deserves to be cut some slack. He could die over there without ever getting to see us again."

"So Lacey's coming too?"

"Yeah. My mom's bringing her down in a few days. Rick and I thought it was best for us to reconcile a few things before we bring her on the scene. He's dying to see her."

"I can't blame him. Lacey's a great kid."

"Thanks." And then Charese looked at her watch and cursed the time. We said good-bye and she rushed off to her flight. I wheeled my stuff outside to where the cars loop around and around until the picker-uppers spot the arrivers and they pull over to hug until the airport workers hurry them along. I sat on my suitcase and thought about what Charese had said about cutting Lacey's father some slack because of what he was about to go through. *Have I been cutting*

David enough slack? I thought. Was I too harsh about the Flores thing? The Helen thing? The boring thing? The thing thing thing thing?[148]

Then my parents came. I was glad to see them. I talked about the molasses flood nearly the whole ride home.

[148] What kind of girl breaks up with a man in a war zone? I mean, I know that women have been doing the Dear John thing since the beginning of wars, but how do they muster up the ovaries to break someone's heart while he's so horribly busy doing horrible things? This is why I should have taken up with the Knitters. Surely they know someone who's gracefully done it. If two people aren't right for one another, why should a war be a reason to keep them together? What if David dies tomorrow in a moment where I don't actually love him like he thinks I do? And earlier that afternoon he had a chance to have steamy, rich, passionate, danger war sex with Jayna Hotstuff Austin. And he didn't do it because he loves me and because he believes I love him. And in that case he would be dying in a blanket of delusion. TO DIE INSIDE A LIE. That's what I should call the heavy-metal symphony I should compose about my life. What's worse: To continue under disingenuous auspices? Or to kick someone who is already down? But then, there is also the escape clause note. He wrote it. I didn't write it. It was all his idea. His words. A permission slip. A coupon. A coupon he left on a pillow. On purpose. He gave it to me. I swear.

25

*T*oday I've chosen to represent my feelings and experiences in a series of humorous, light-hearted short stories. I've titled the collection *That's What Humans Do*, and the following story was cowritten by myself, Annie Harper, age twenty-five, and Max Schaffer, age nine.

A Romance in Eight Legs

ONE

The female desert spider is difficult to impress. When a male spider comes looking for action—looking to spread his genes like biology tells him he has to—he must be very, very careful. Approaching the female's web, he uses his front legs to shake her perfectly crafted masterpiece with certain socially appropriate vibrations. Vibrations that tell her he's not food. Vibrations that tell her he's deeply interested. Vibrations that tell her what orifice he's shooting for.

In a series of arm-flapping, booty-shaking, abdomen-twisting movements, the male does his best to show the female that his are some genes worth passing on. Nature's proven choreography. All the hip spiders break it down like this. These pedipalps, baby, are loaded with some sperm your precious eggs are aching for. Oh, yeah.

And that's how scientists thought it went. For a very long time. Now they know that there's a little more to it. Good moves won't get you everything. Before it all starts, before the eight-legged seduction ensues, the male releases a pheromone. A scent that tells his potential mate he's ready. Ready to perform. I'm not food, sweetie, I'm the father of your children! She receives this smell, and if she's willing—willing to humor his chivalrous romantic boogie—she sends a scent back. He dances. She watches. Game on.

TWO

"God, Ivy, you are so difficult to impress. Look at that guy's shoes. They match his shirt perfectly. And he just picked up that girl's purse—that's so sweet. And he's drinking Stella. You love Stella. Go talk to him."

"No. I don't want to talk to him." Ivy smoothes her hair behind her ears. Takes a drink of her rum and Coke, letting the ice hit her teeth and chill them for almost long enough to hurt.

"He's been totally checking you out all night. I'm surprised he hasn't asked you to dance. Bought you a drink or something." Ivy's best friend, Carly, is a queen of social mores.

"Whatever. I doubt he's a good dancer," Ivy says, giving his shoes a more careful inspection. They are nice. A few minutes later, returning from the ladies' room, they find him dancing. With his guy friends. Ivy almost wants to laugh at his arm-flapping, booty-shaking, abdomen-twisting movements, but she doesn't. She never thought 50 Cent could inspire such an odd, gangly, but nonetheless spirited routine. He catches her watching him and he winks. She usually hates winks. Thinks that only octogenarians can effectively pull them off. But there's something about it. Maybe the way it lasted such a brief, fleeting moment? The way he didn't stop moving to acknowledge her? The way his hair almost covered his eye so that he could have been twitching—not winking at all? Call it some weird glitch in her biology, but it worked. He danced. She watched. Game on.

On their first date, they do that typical stroll-through-the-park thing. She's eating an apple and they're talking about bad teenage

jobs they once had. She's almost done with the fruit, just nib-
bling around the seeds and the stem. "You're not one of those
weird people who eats the whole thing, are you?" he says, and she
pauses. Lets the hand holding the core drop to her side.

"You mean those people who eat the core and the seeds and
everything?"

"Yeah, those." He smiles. It's almost challenging. She raises
her arm, an eyebrow, stares straight into his eyes, and attacks
half of the remaining core. Seriously chomps it. She struggles to
chew the bitter, fibrous innards, and he laughs momentarily. For
about thirty seconds they walk in silence as Ivy tediously masticates the apple's remains. After a final, triumphant swallow and a
deft tongue maneuver to clean her teeth of any stringy remnants,
she smiles.

"Yes," she says. "I am one of those weird people."

"Fantastic," he says, and he kisses her.

Three weeks and four dates later and it's Valentine's Day.
Adam gets Ivy a wok. Ivy gets Adam convertible mitten gloves.
They both seem pleased that their gifts are of comparable mone-
tary value and sentimentality. Things are going well.

"So, you really like him?" Carly is always rummaging through
her purse for something. Pulling out tampons when she needs a
pen. Loose change when she wants keys.

"Yeah. I like him. We get along really well. He's nice." Ivy
shrugs her lips.

"Don't say nice, Ivy. Everyone is nice. That's such a lousy de-
scriptor. How's the sex?"

"Christ, Carly. The sex is fine. He's very considerate. Eager to
please. No back hair."

"Well, that's good." Carly opens and closes another lipstick
tube and tosses it back in the pit.

"Yeah, I guess so. And he smells nice." Ivy means it. He smells fabulous.

"Shut up with the *nice* already."

"Fine. He smells fabulous."

THREE

The male European nursery web spider provides before he penetrates. In order to approach a female for mating, he must present her with a gift. This reverse dowry comes in the form of a meal. Something large, something tasty, something the omni-hungry female will not be able to refuse.

A larger gift shows the female that this male's got skills. Skills she'd want her spiderlings to inherit. Skills that bring home the bacon. Or housefly. Or aphid. After a successful hunt, the male wraps the fresh insect in layers of his own silk. These layers of gossamer ribbons make the gift seem larger. Harder to unwrap. Longer to eat. Buying him time. And as the female unpacks and devours her nuptial gift—he goes for it. She masticates. They copulate. All at the same time.

FOUR

"Oh sweet, Adam. This is the most fantastic sofa ever." Ivy collapses on the brushed leather, sprawling out every limb. Just because she can.

"Well, the most fantastic deal ever was signed this week, so I figured it was time to splurge." He lifts one of Ivy's legs and slides under it.

"And I got something else too." Ivy's head unburrows from between folds of taupe as Adam digs a package out from behind one of the sofa's eight or nine pillows. It's a shiny white box. Wrapped in layers of gossamer ribbons. At the sight of the box, Ivy tenses her glute muscles and the sofa gives beneath her. Not jewelry. Not jewelry, she thinks. He places the gift in her hands, and it takes a minute for Ivy to unravel its wrappings. She stares for a moment at the gift in her palms, letting the weight of its light contents sink in.

"The Royal Ballet of London."

"Yep."

"These are, like, the best seats ever."

"Yep."

"Oh my God, Adam. Thank you."

"You didn't even know they were coming to Boston, did you?" Ivy's eyes snag on the block-letter date printed on the two snuggling tickets.

"This is three months from now."

Adam tells Ivy that now she has plenty of time to buy a new dress or something. She hugs him then wiggles her head back into the crack in the sofa. She sighs. They snuggle. All at the same time.

FIVE

Successful mating of the funnel-web spider relies on old-fashioned anesthetics. The female's typically reluctant, often feisty, maybe even relentlessly chaste demeanor makes getting laid a tricky matter. The male uses a pheromone, a chemical he releases within close proximity of his chosen mate to sedate her. This fast-acting drug renders her totally out of it. Just as it renders him totally safe for uninterrupted, unobjected intercourse. But he must be speedy, for this comatose state can last minutes. Can last hours. Can last indefinitely.

SIX

"Here's your drink, babe. This place is fucking packed."

"Thanks. Well, at least we have a table." Ivy stirs the rum and Coke with its straw before taking a sip. Her lips curl and her nose twists. "Ish, this tastes kind of gross, what did you get me?"

"Bacardi and Diet."

"Oh. Well, okay."

"Do you want to order food?"

"Whatever, I don't really care. You can order for me, Adam." And he does.

Sometimes she lets him do that. Often she lets him pick the movie. "I don't care, Adam. Just not too many guns and cars blowing up." In bed one night, Adam strokes Ivy's hair so nicely. So tenderly. In a way that makes her head tingle and her eyes narrow so much that she doesn't even mind that he's simultaneously watching an hour-long special edition of *COPS*. Her "Books to Read" list doesn't shorten. And it doesn't grow, either. Ivy spends so much time with Adam that she drops out of yoga and calls her parents less. They drink lots of wine. And sometimes, Ivy doesn't even bother to read the label.

Carly asks Ivy one day why she stopped looking for a new job.

"Dude, Ivy, what happened to getting a new job?"

"I don't know, I just kind of forgot. Work goes so much faster now that I can IM Adam all day."

"That's sick."

"You're sick." They're at a nail salon and Carly is examining a bright orange bottle of polish. "I can't believe you're looking at that color."

"Orange is really big right now, Ivy. You're so totally out of it."

"Shit. Maybe I am." Ivy thinks that maybe she is. Maybe Adam has sucked the life out of her with his nice car and his brazen good looks. And as the tiny woman trims the cuticles of

Ivy's small feet, she contemplates trimming Adam out of her life. The pedicurist applies a muted pink paint to her nails, and Ivy thinks about napping in Adam's plush sofa. With her toes under the drier, she decides to keep her mate for the time being. She's not super happy. But she's fine. This relationship can last. For now, indefinitely.

SEVEN

The female St. Andrew's Cross spider takes fornication to a whole new level. Into the next world even. Once the male's pedipalps have slid back and forth and back and forth enough times into her reproductive openings for her to assume a sufficient amount of sperm has been deposited—she fucking kills him. Right then. Right in the middle of it all. Fertilization as a prelude to homicide. In some cases, the female will even begin to eat the male while his sex organs are still in motion. Going in for the kill. With a whole new meaning.

EIGHT

"So you're going to do it?"

"Yep."

"You're going in for the kill?"

"Don't be sick, Carly. You act like it's something fun. I hate breaking up with people."

"But you have to. Before you melt into watching the WB on Saturdays while the two of you flip through linen catalogs." Ivy can picture Carly nodding while she speaks on the other side of the phone.

"Yeah. You're right. It's just that he's so nice. He's so damn nice. He just so nicely made me dull. Nicely dragged me into his sticky web of banality."

"Whoa now, 'sticky web of banality.' That is my girl. Ivy, you're almost back. Go get him."

This wasn't supposed to happen, she thinks. Eight limbs tangled in silky sheets. His penis sliding back and forth and back and forth enough times for Ivy to nearly get there. She's having such a good time, really. On her back, left leg hooked on his right shoulder, with each pulse she entertains different phrasing in her head, and it feels awesome. *Adam, it's just that I. We're so different and you. You know, it's only because.* She contemplates actually doing it. Right then. Right in the middle of it all.

The bed smells fabulous. Vibrations. Abdomens twisting. She gives him the gift of a wet tongue to a dry ear. He rolls her on top to buy them both some time. His midmorning, hint-of-toothpaste breath almost lulls her into forgetting her visit's initial intentions. And as it all reaches the top, Ivy remembers that it's not a climax, it's a prelude. She must stop. She has to. Going in for the kill, she relaxes her upper body on his chest and stretches her arms to the headboard.

"David?" she says. And before he can answer, Annie is pulling herself up to her elbows. Her right hand, that had just momentarily reached the crack between the headboard and the mattress, catches something on its way up. The thin-threaded white of a delicate female weapon. Annie rubs the fabric between her fingers; the first time it's touched her skin.

"Annie, I can explain." She sits up. Looks closer at the intricate pattern of the garment's silky weave. "It's not what you think, babe." She dismounts the bed deftly. Pulls on her sweatpants, her sweatshirt, letting her head pause inside the cotton for long enough to almost make her dizzy.

"It was only this one time, I promise."

Emerging from the worn gray fabric, Annie's eyes are blank. Her posture calm. Her lips sealed. And as she tosses the panties back onto the bed, she actually hears David say he's sorry.

"I'm sorry."

And inside her mouth, her tongue moves slowly, thoughtfully, left to right across the sharp ridge of her upper teeth, tracing the weapons she didn't use.

THE END[149]

Ctrl S[150]

---

[149] Consider taking out the word penis.

[150] Why am I waiting and hoping for David to seriously wound me so I can have a way out of this? That is fucked up, Miss Harper. I've got to bare my fangs and accept my role as the wounder. At least this time.

26

*T*oday I'm calling my book *Red, White, and Brutally Honest.*

"David, it'sjustthatIdon'tfeelasclosetoyouanymore. Becausewealwaystalkaboutthesamethingsandyouneverseemexcitedtotalktomeand Ineverseemexcitedtotalktoyouandwhat'sthepointofdoinganythingifitdoesn'tmakeyoufeelgood." I say this so fast that I'm certain that half the words were eaten by the lag time between our phones.

"But not doing it would make me feel worse. I know it sucks, babe. And I know I haven't been myself, but we've almost made it. I'll be back so soon, and things will be just how they were."

And I want to ask him if he really thinks that. But instead I just say that he's probably right. I tell him that we should e-mail more. I think that would help, I say. He tells me to e-mail him that night, but whoa now, horsies, here I am typing about him and not e-mailing him. And I'm probably going to continue not e-mailing him for the rest of the evening. I am probably going to sit on my patio and drink my first delivery from the Chesalon Wine and Cheese of the Month Club[151] and try to throw rocks between the holes of my fence.[152] Yes, I think I will do just that, thank you. Yes, please uncork the wine for

---

[151] This month's pairing: A South African sauvignon blanc and a chunk of Ossau-Iraty (oh-soh ee-RAH-tee), a semisoft sheep's milk cheese from the French Pyrenees. A cool, crisp wine meets the toasty, nutty cheese in a somewhat jarring, but ultimately satisfying juxtaposition.

[152] I used to do this all the time before Helen moved in. It spooked her. It's nice to do it again, though. I have different point levels for getting through different holes on the fence. The siblingless are great at making up one-person games.

me. No, I don't mind if I have no crackers and have to pair the fancy cheese with stale tortilla chips and lick it off my fingers. Who do you think I am?

Before I go, I must include something from an e-mail Max Schaffer just sent me:

Okay. I already knew that art and graphic design were not Max's stronger skills, but this is just weird. Perhaps hootenanny is a play on my first name? It makes a little more sense in his e-mail, where he explains he's working on his mouse skills so his parents will buy him this computer program about cartography. Ha!

I'm back at the computer. I am high-drama back.

Scene: Eleven P.M. the next day. The sun is long gone, but its brutal heat has lingered—affixed itself to doorknobs, the creases of shower curtains, the spaces in the tops of potato chip bags. The heat is fogging up the protective plastic that covers photos in albums. It has snuck into the crisper drawer of Annie Harper's fridge and is working its

way up a stalk of celery, wilting, changing, ruining, and astounding
everything with its ability to permeate.

Enter Annie Harper, sweaty as a chili dog. She pulls one, two, three
paper towels off a roll in the kitchen even though she knows it's a ri-
diculous waste of precious wood pulp. She's that hot. She wipes her
brow, her neck, each of her hands, and settles down to her laptop at
the table. She writes:

So this morning I wake up and make coffee with my French press. I
cook an omelet with icky, hormoney, supermarket eggs. The day starts
out hott. I put on a bikini to lay out in the yard on my plastic recliner
lounger thing and finally read *Annie Harper's Motherfucking Journal.* I
make it through page thirty, where Old Annie is discussing how and
when the slaves left after emancipation. And though she's all elegant
with her writing style and her lack of sentence fragments and dangling
prepositions, she actually complains about the slaves taking off. She
says that the more favored slaves with the best lives were the first to
vamoose. She then rails on them for it. Like you wouldn't leave too,
fat, ugly Annie Harper? She even uses the word "urchins." And I
know it's tough to wrap my mind around and I'm supposed to be
thinking *Annie Harper the First was educated to think slavery was okay;*
that doesn't mean she's an entirely horrible person, but I can't help it. She
pisses me off. I hate her fucking guts. Why was Gus so anxious for me
to read this dumb book? So yeah, maybe I have fallen out of love with
my boyfriend and into love with another dude while said boyfriend is
stuck fighting a war because he got free college. But Annie Harper the
First had slaves. You tell me who's more evil. And with this frustration, I toss the book onto the grass and close my eyes for a few minutes. I think about her cooks and stable hands heading up a jubilant
trail northward. *Fuck you, Annie Harper,* I think. Which is probably
not what her newly freed slaves thought. It was probably something

stronger, bigger, and more emotionally sophisticated than I could ever imagine. And then I fall asleep.

When I wake up, my skin is all moist and stuck to the plastic bands of the lounger. I peel myself off to turn over, I take a sip of my water, and I notice a slip of paper that fell out of the book when I tossed it on the lawn. I bend down to pick it up. It's one of those pink "While You Were Out" slips that has spots to write the time and date, the caller, and the message. It's blank on the front. I turn it over.

> *Dear Annie,*
> *We need to talk about Brother Alden.*
> *Please call me when you find this.*
> *Yours,*
> *Gus*

Wha wha what? What does Gus know about Brother Alden? Why is he planting notes and patiently waiting for me to find them when he obviously has things to tell me? We *need* to talk. But not urgently? I'm utterly perplexed. I leave the book, the lounger, the water glass all exactly as they are, and I march inside to my cell phone.

"Gus?" I say with a tone that encompasses both stress and inquiry.

"Hey, Annie," he sounds as normal and casual and happy as always. I hear a spraying, splashing sound in the background.

"I found the note in *Annie Harper's Journal.*" The water noise stops.

"What are you doing right now?"

"Nothing."

"Can you meet me at Hansen's Furniture on Pacific Avenue in ten minutes?"

"Yeah. Sure."

I throw a ratty sundress over my swimsuit and put a headband over my greasy hair. I beat him there. I sit on a curb outside the store and

wait. I'm so busy puzzling what in tarnation Gus has to tell me about
Brother Alden that I don't puzzle why he has asked to meet me here. At
a furniture store. His van pulls up and I notice that one side is clean and
shiny. The other has drying suds slumping down to the tires. A swirled
layer of dirt that was deprived of a rinse job because of my call.

"Hi," I say.

"Hi," Gus says. "Let's go inside." He opens the door for me. He's
wearing a tight gray T-shirt that he's had since high school. The sleeves
are frayed, and the fabric on the shoulders has thinned to the point
where it's almost translucent. It clings to his ribs in a way that makes me
want to brush my fingers down their ridges and order him an entire
pepperoni pizza. I follow him to the far side of the store, where a pretend
living room is set up. There's a leather sofa and two upholstered chairs
circling an oak coffee table. He tells me to take a seat and not to put my
feet up. We both choose the sofa, and the leather is cool and firm.

"So," I say.

"So," Gus says. He leans forward, puts his hands on his knees, and
twists his shoulders to face me. Then he leans back again. He bends
one knee up to rest on the couch and turns to face me more squarely.
I can see him being mindful not to touch the leather with his dirty
sneaker. I swallow.

"Annie. What I'm going to tell you is really, really weird. It's part
of the universe's twists and turns that we will never ever understand."
And while he's blabbing, I'm still trying to imagine what it could be.
Did he find out that Alden knew about the Harpers all along and was
planning a trip to visit us when he returned from Iraq? Did he discover that Alden was a secret member of al Qaeda? But then it's hard
to keep imagining because I've never seen Gus look this intense before. I watch a drop of sweat slide from behind his ear and soak into
the collar of his shirt. He can't keep his hands still. If it's about *my*
nonbrother, then why is *he* freaking out?

"What is it?" I finally say.

"Annie," he looks me straight in the eye and places both of his hands on my bare thigh. He grips. He loosens it. "Brother Alden." Pause. Pause. Pause. "He's my brother too." I don't say anything because I don't know enough at this point to comment. My only thought is that Gus is making one of his metaphors and he's going to say that he feels like he lost a brother also because we both talked about Alden so much back in high school. I'm silent and so he continues. "After you found out that Alden died, I started searching around on the Internet. Because I've always been curious about him. And it was easy because he was a young soldier from California and his name was Alden and he died in Iraq. So I found him. And there were pictures of his family at the service crying and one of his mother tossing this bouquet of flowers on his casket. And there was something about her that looked really familiar. The caption said her name is Julia Crandall. And of course I don't remember my mom since she disappeared when I was so young, but there's these few pictures that my dad has that he didn't know I knew about.

"So I printed out the picture from the newspaper, took it to my dad's place, and found the old photos he keeps in this tackle box in his closet. And Annie, it's her. I didn't believe it at first because fuck, what are the odds? And the photos my dad has are over twenty-five years old. But I was so overwhelmed that I had to tell him and show him. I had to know. He said my mother's name is Juliette Crandall, which of course, I knew the Juliette part, but he never told me her last name. Probably because he was scared I'd go looking for her and because he knew she was too much of a flake to bother changing it. And it isn't much of a name change if you ask me. If you're going to ditch your kid and his father and run away and never come back, at least you'd change your last name. Right?" Gus is leaning so close to me that I could lean in and kiss him. But I can't move. I can only watch the sweat drip and his lips move fast faster fastest. I'm scared that if I change my position at all, if I adjust the halter of my bikini, which is kind of pulling my

hair, I'll render myself completely incapable of listening and compre-
hending any of the craziness he's spewing onto me.

"And my dad confirmed it. He took one look at the picture from
Alden's funeral and said 'Jesus Christ, son of God, it's her.'" Then it all
starts to settle with me.

"Wait. Wait. Wait," I say. I stand up and spin around a few times
like a cat looking for the perfect place to lie in the sun. I yank my bikini bottoms out of my ass and plop down a little closer to Gus than
before. "So you're saying[153] that when you were a toddler, your mother
up and left you and Rex. And then she met someone else and got pregnant again. And before she had this other baby she decided to give it
away. And my parents decided to take it. And they did. And then
Julia/Juliette decided she should take the baby back. And she did. And
she moved them to California, where she raised him and convinced
him that signing up for a war was a swell idea. And so he did it. And
then he died. And now we're here."

Silence. Silence. Silence. Gus nods.

I sigh. Not just a breath sigh, but the kind that engages the vocal
chords and uses the diaphragm with the earnest hope to expel and be
done with some emotion or hard, fucked-up fact. Then I lean forward
and melt into Gus's arms. The strangest, sweatiest, quasi-incestuous
embrace ever to occur on a sofa that nobody owns. I realize why he
chose this location for this moment; it's neutral territory. I whisper
into his ear, and my bottom lip momentarily flicks against his earlobe
(not on purpose, I promise): "I hate her."

We leave Hansen's Furniture and take Gus's van to a bar called the
Shamrock that has both air-conditioning and a friendly Great Dane

---

[153] This is really how people talk in these mega intense situations. I always thought it was a movie thing where the revelation is reiterated just for
the sake of audience comprehension.

that wanders around resting its fat head in the laps of patrons. I've never been there, but even without these two selling points, whatever Gus wants to do is fine. In the course of several hours Gus and I suppose and speculate and ponder our brains out. If Juliette was no longer in love with Rex, how could she leave Gus behind? Did she take Alden back because she was guilt-stricken about abandoning yet another child? Will she come looking for Gus now? Should Gus contact her first? What would Bless Her Heart Barbara do? Is Bless Her Heart Barbara Gus's grandma? I've never seen Gus cry before, and I hold one of his hands as he tears. He's had many weeks to process this and he's still crying. His mother chose not to know him. And then she replaced him. What a jerk. The waitress brings us another round of Sierra Nevadas.

"Gus, why did you wait so long to tell me? Why did you put the note in *Annie Harper's Journal*?" I take the ketchup bottle from our table and start sliding it back and forth between my hands.

"I guess I needed time to think things out. And I found out about the book as a result of all my Internet sleuth work, and so it just seemed right to give it time before I told you." He rubs both his hands through his hair and they linger while they hold all the hair back, tightening the skin on his forehead and clearly revealing the red in his eyes.

"So Alden was more yours than mine," I say, and I smile weakly. "You realize this makes our teen movie about looking for him so much more interesting." Gus chuckles and picks up his beer. His forearms look so tense and troubled. He takes a sip.

"I guess so," he says. "But at the same time, he's still an absence to both of us. And we were still nothing to him."

27

Today my memoirs are being expressed as a multimedia art installation in a dark alleyway. There are LCD monitors and tapestries and a speaker that says my name forward and backward over and over again. Annie Harper. Reprah Einna. Annie Harper. Reprah Einna. There is red paint splattered across chicken wire. And there's a silent video of me that's a close-up of my face painted white. Except my lips are a shocking, bright red. I'm mouthing the words *No fucking way, no fucking way, no fucking way* over and over again. The installation is called *The Charisma of Coincidence.*

The day after I found out about Our Brother Alden, I went to go tell Loretta. I figured telling Loretta would be good practice for telling my parents. I wanted to be their perfect, perfectly articulate child when I revealed it to them. And I felt like there was so much emotion plugging my ears and smudging my glasses[154] that I just had to get some of it out. Gus and I had decided that after everyone knows, and if my parents and his dad and the two of us all want to get together and talk about everything,[155] we can have a barbecue sometime next week.

When I arrived at Violet Meadows and checked in with Jean, she told me that Loretta was with the doctor and that I couldn't see her for

---

[154] Not true. It was actually sweat on the glasses, I believe.

[155] But what is there really to say? My parents still have one child. Gus still has no mother. Alden is still dead. Nothing is different except for this connection that we know exists, and we now can get drunk and bask in the eerie shadow of its reality.

twenty minutes. My stomach instantly spun, and I leaned over onto Jean's desk, resting my fingertips on the surface like two angry spiders.

"Is she okay?" I stuck my neck out and noticed that my movement had set all the bobblehead kitty cats on her computer into a steady, nodding fury. As if they were telling me not to fret. *Loretta, meow, just fine, meow.*

"She's fine. Just a routine checkup. She's old, Annie. She sees a doctor once a month."

"Oh," I said. "Good." And then I plopped into the chair across from Jean's desk even though I wasn't invited. Even though I could tell she was annoyed. "Hey, Jean?" I said. She spun her chair around and it squeaked kind of like a mewing cat and I wondered if she liked the sound. "Does anyone, you know, like family, ever come to visit Loretta?" Jean thought for a moment.

"Yeah. There's a niece that comes by every few months."

"Oh. And how long has her husband been dead?" Jean rolled her eyes and yanked open a metal filing cabinet. Rifled through for Loretta's file. She opened it up across the desk. I leaned forward to peek.

"Ron Schumacher died in 1995." Jean turned back to her computer, and I kept reading upside down. I was looking at this rubric of Loretta's basic facts.

"Shouldn't it say Captain Ron Schumacher?" I asked.

"Why?"

"Because her husband was a World War II veteran," I said.

"No, he wasn't."

"Yes, he was."

"No. He wasn't."

"Was too."

"Was not."

"Was too." It felt like we could go on forever. Or at least until the end of recess. "He was in the navy, and they lived in Kansas, and then they moved to Washington when he got back. She has letters. He wrote poems about it." See? See, stupid, flabby Jean!

"Loretta Schumacher has lived in Tacoma her entire life. Her husband lived in Tacoma his entire life. He was injured at a very young age in a logging accident and walked with a cane until he got sick and died. I know. I've talked to the niece. She doesn't come often, but she pays on time and she's very friendly when she's here. I don't know what kind of yarns Loretta has spun for you, Annie, but her husband was *not* a soldier and she definitely did *not* live in Kansas."

"But what about her children? I know they come to visit. Ronnie? Opal? Diana, the rodeo queen?" Jean folded her arms across her chest and lowered her chin.

"She doesn't have any children, Annie." And I stammered off a series of "buts" and "she saids," and Jean just shook her head and raised her eyebrows, and with that gesture she nearly managed to destroy everything I thought was real and beautiful about Violet Meadows. Her look said that my believing Loretta's alternate life was more ridiculous than Loretta having invented it in the first place. And because I was so shocked and so confused and so crowded by Jean and her depressing, death-broker office, I made this frustrated grunting noise and said, "Whatever, Jean."[156] And then I stood up and left. I padded into the rec room and took a seat on a sofa next to a man named Henry who was watching *Jeopardy!* It was a very old episode on the Game Show Network. Alex's hair was dark and his face smooth. And even though I was sitting next to a shriveled man with a respirator, seeing the youthful exuberance of the trivia master made me feel ancient.

"What is salmonella?" Henry said and raised a finger toward the ceiling. How could Loretta make all that up? I thought. All the details and the anecdotes. The serious empathy and understanding she delivered to me while we drank tea and giggled about sex. Why would she

---

[156] Brillantly mature, Miss Harper!

lie to me? Or is she confused about the actual facts of her own life? Undiagnosed Alzheimer's, perhaps? I couldn't tell if I felt betrayed or if I was still incredulous, but I didn't have much time to think about it. Henry was saying "What is Montpelier?" when Jean poked her head out of her office and told me that the doctor was gone and that I could go in. If you still want to, she added.

I told Henry to have a nice afternoon and walked slowly[157] down the hall toward Loretta's room. I stood at the doorway for many long moments, my fist suspended in the air, poised to knock, to enter, to waltz into a comfortable, chocolate-pudding-flavored lie. What do I do? Do I call Loretta on her bullshit? She's ninety-three; how can she still have bullshit? Do I just keep playing along? The last thing I want is for Loretta to feel like she's disappointed me. Maybe Jean was wrong. Maybe Loretta has been dispensing the sweet truth all along. And then my arm fell. I was thinking so hard that my fist just dropped and bumped along the wooden door weakly on its way down, like a poorly skipped stone barely lifting off a lake's surface. An unintentional, exhausted knock. I heard Loretta shuffling over to the door.

"Good afternoon, Annie!" She swooped her arm to present the gray room, and I walked in. Took my spot on the bed as I usually do. And as I plopped down on the quilt and she assumed her regular position in the rocking chair, I noticed the similarities to a patient/counselor situation. I was coming by, confused and muddled, for my weekly visit. Loretta was chipper, welcoming, open-minded. I lounged comfortably, primed to open my mouth and spill my nasty, turbulent guts to her. She sat upright: the voice of reason, clear as a bell.

"So, how are you?" she said.

"Pretty good," I said. "Did your doctor's visit go alright?"

"Indeed it did. I think he's a little frustrated with my snail's pace of

[157] I pretty much do everything slowly in Violet Meadows. Nobody likes a show-off.

deterioration. I'm very healthy for my age, you know." Then we both laughed.

"Yeah, Loretta, your youthful vigor is pretty damn impressive."

"So, are things still rocky with David? Are you writing him more like we discussed?"[158] Loretta said this like she was skeptical that I'd done anything to revitalize my relationship. But also in a way which revealed that she didn't blame me if I hadn't. I kicked my flip-flops off and folded my legs (criss-cross-applesauce style) up onto the bed.

"Not really," I said. "Well. There was Helen dying, then I was in Boston, and not. Oh, Loretta." I just couldn't get myself to start my story when my brain was still murky with confusion over the validity of hers. Then I looked at her for a long moment. I followed the lines around her eyes as they bent toward the blotchy redness on her cheeks. The wrinkles on her forehead and the ones around her mouth. How did they get there? Were the initial creases from worrying about Ron while he steered submarines off the coast of Normandy? Or were they from the years of grimacing while she helped him up the stairs to the local bank, his bum leg weighing down the marriage? And just when my wondering was about to plunge into a deeper series of imagined scenarios, all the wrinkles reversed. Each line—dozens of sine and cosine graphs—reciprocated and pulled up, and I looked up to her eyes and they were dancing and smiling in a way that transcended all war fronts and Kansas post offices and nursing homes in South Tacoma.

"Annie? Am I losing you? What were you going to tell me?" She waved a hand in front of my face, a gesture I imagined the V-Meadows staff used to check the status of their more fragile and life-wavering residents.

---

[158] *"Like we discussed!!!!"* Mr. Bush, please pay Loretta Schumacher two hundred bucks an hour for all the time she's spent with me, all the guidance she's provided me, and for all the word vomit of mine she's kindly mopped up. Yours, AH.

"Yes. Sorry. I'm here." I asked Loretta if she wanted to hear a really weird, but true, story. I spouted off a lengthy disclaimer about the oddness of it all and an apology about how I hadn't told her anything about what had led up to it. And even though in the course of a few minutes Loretta's past had transformed from a clearly depicted, sweeping love story to a bundle of vagueness and uncertainty, for some reason, I didn't care. Maybe it's because I'm wildly selfish, but I like to think it's because I still *know* Loretta. Maybe she is a delusional story weaver, but I'm fairly certain that doesn't matter. I know that she likes lemon in her hot tea but not in her cold tea and songs with extended trumpet solos. I know that she listens and shares and comforts and compliments. And that she's been such an enormous friend to me. While I was explaining all the Alden backstory—how my parents had him, then didn't have him, and how I found out as a teen—I was thinking about how wise Loretta is. Maybe she's had several conversation partners while at Violet Meadows. Maybe she knows that changing her story so it relates to someone else's story will help that person cope with the more abrasive edges of our universe. At ninety-three, perhaps she's right sick of her true past. Why not concoct a new one to help a crazy young fool who probably needs it?

And I know that even though she might be a liar, Loretta is still a compassionate, feeling creature. It takes more than storytelling to constitute true phoniness. Loretta's fake past feels more authentic to me than Annie Harper the First's real one. She wept when I told her that Alden was killed just months ago. She lifted her hands to cover the drop of her jaw when I told her that Alden was Gus's half-brother.

"Isn't it nuts?" I said.

"Bonkers," she said.

"And this is my *real life*."

"Your *real life*."

· · · · · ·

I gave Loretta a big hug when I left. She told me to call her if there was anything, *anything*, I needed to talk about. "Annie," she said as I moved toward the door. "I've been here for a long time, and there are many people who, because of age or disease or whatnot, have become very, very confused. And the confusion is often frightening. Not knowing what you feel or what you think or how things really are. But the confused ones—I honestly think they're better off than the droolers. The ones whose minds have numbed and slowed and who don't even notice when a stranger is wiping off their behinds. That blind acceptance is far worse. At least when you're confused, Annie, at least you know that your brain is doing *something*."

Q: How wrong is a lie when it serves to lessen someone else's pain?
A:

Subject: with my deepest regrets
Date: Wednesday, July 14, 2004
From: missharpercandoit@yahoo.com
To: david.peterson13@us.army.mil

Dear David,

This is probably the worst e-mail you'll ever get from me. This is actually my fourth draft of it and I've come to the conclusion that it will always be the ugliest piece of writing that I will ever produce. And though I would prefer to tell you in person, or at least on the phone, that's obviously impossible. You haven't called in a few days. I just need to get this out.

Last week Gus and I went to the circus. He got free tickets from a coworker and I agreed to go because a) I'd never been to a circus and b) I'm not really doing much of anything these days. In many

ways, the circus met my expectations. There were many
beautifully sculpted women in sparkly lycra outfits and scores of
adorable children with their grandfathers. But the circus was not
in a tent. It was in the Tacoma Dome. So that was disappointing.
Naturally, I was really excited for the animals. Despite knowing
that circuses are definitely not the optimal lifestyle for an elephant
or a tiger, I was still anxious with the knowledge that I would soon
see a real elephant and a real tiger in the flesh. We would be
sharing molecules of air and maybe I would hear them roar.

But when the ringmaster (he was satisfyingly portly) announced
the arrival of the show's three prize pachyderms, and as the
spotlight panned toward the entrance of the concrete tunnel
where the elephants were posed to emerge, my heart fucking
sank. There was the first elephant, thick and gray and draped in
blue silk and pink ribbons. And there was the concrete archway,
thick and gray and draping the elephant in complete human
wrongness. They just didn't match. A bad fit that seems like a
good idea and still delights thousands of people. But elephants
do not belong in The Tacoma Dome. It's a place for RV shows
and monster trucks and Garth Brooks concerts. Not elephants.

Gus could tell that I was upset about something and so he
bought me some cotton candy. He said, "I know you think you
don't want it, but as soon as you taste it you'll realize that it's the
only thing you've ever truly wanted." And he gave the vendor the
money. And the vendor gave him the cotton candy. And then
Gus gave it to me. And then I gave it a long, long look. And then I
looked up at Gus. I leaned in and I gave him the biggest, richest
kiss I'd kissed in a very long time. I know this is probably horribly
upsetting for me to tell you in such detail, but this is the truth,
David. And because I've completely betrayed you I feel like I owe
you at least the favor of fully disclosed, brutal honesty. It was a

very nice kiss. But I must clarify that while in it, I did not have some profound realization. I didn't think *this is the only thing that I've ever truly wanted.* Now that would be a lie. Instead I thought *this is what I want now.*

After the circus, Gus came over to my place for a drink. Later that night after he left, I was brushing my teeth when I noticed the toilet paper had been messed up. You know, the way you used to fold it. In an act of sentimentality, I had left it untouched since your last night here. But Gus had thoughtlessly messed it up to blow his nose. I found the crumpled bit full of his snot in the trash can. I feel wretched about this. I have totally wronged you.

But because kissing Gus is what I want now, I obviously can't be your girlfriend any longer. I am so so sorry. Please know that our relationship has always been wonderful and that I think you are one of the kindest, sweetest, charmingest people in the universe. I am so enormously proud of you and everything you've done and how you've handled it so well. I apparently have not.

Perhaps I should say, "I hope we can be friends going forward."
Perhaps I should say, "I never meant to hurt you like this."
Perhaps I should say, "You will always have a very special place in my heart."
Perhaps I should say, "It's not you; it's me."

It's me. It's me. It's me.

Take care of yourself, David. You are almost done.

Love,

Annie Harper

| SEND | SAVE | CANCEL |

28

*T*oday I'm calling my book *Miss Harper Can Do It* after my e-mail address. And by "do it" I mean, I can break your heart in revolting, terrible ways. Ways that are so evil that when you will tell your future girlfriends about them over shared ice cream sundaes, the girlfriends will be so sick and disgusted by my evilness, they won't eat another bite of the ice cream. Then she'll put her hand tenderly on your wrist and you can have the rest of the sundae all to yourself. Even the cherry. If you even like those. Remember this.

So tonight I watched a particularly satisfying segment on the local news. It was a story about a program at Purdy, the local women's prison, where long-term inmates train dogs for the blind. Since a prisoner has heaps of free time, she can devote nearly all of it to raising and training a puppy. Helping an eager Labrador become the useful citizen she never was. Most of the inmates in the program were convicted of nonviolent crimes: theft, fraud, and larceny. Embarrassing acts of desperation. And though I was feeling so thoroughly terrible for being such a deceiver myself, the story cheered me up slightly. I started to think about second chances, rehabilitation, and soft, wet puppy tongues. I started to think that a jumpsuit, a leash, and a confident command voice were all that stood between me and clear, spotless happiness. The women seemed so pleased with themselves. They smiled politely during their interviews. The inmates spoke about how hard it is to give up the dogs when it's time, but how grateful they are to be doing this job. The segment was still going when my phone rang. It was David. I picked up.

"So what are you up to tonight, babe?" His voice was more playful than usual.

"Not much. Watching a show about lady prisons." And then I asked how he was doing and he asked how I was doing. We were both something like "fine" or "fairly well," and so I guess it was nice to have an even-keeled, reasonably positive status report on both sides. And as he rattled off some story about someone getting promoted, I wondered what the conversation would have been like if I had actually sent that fucked-up e-mail about the cotton candy kiss.[159] Would he be shouting *What the hell is wrong with you, Annie?* or *You disgusting, loathsome bitch!* or *How could you do this to me when I'm over here?* And though I kind of wanted to hear those things from David—I wanted him to be so disgusted with me that the idea of ever being my boyfriend again would become instantaneously and irrevocably appalling—I knew deep down in the gaping pit of my ugly heart that his nonugly heart would never ever ever lash out like that. But if he could say them and he could think of me as this huge nasty-ass sinner, then maybe he wouldn't be so wounded. Much easier to get over an evil subhuman beast than it is a troubled but mostly kind soul whose needs you couldn't fulfill. Right? But instead of verbally reminding me of all the varieties of filth that I really, truly am, David told me about how one of his sisters, Shannon, just got engaged. He had recently spoken to her on the phone and heard how incredibly excited she was about marrying her longtime boyfriend, Bruno.

"Yeah, Annie, it was so interesting. Shannon said to me, 'Sometimes when I'm alone and I think of Bruno and how we'll be sharing everything forever, the thought brings me so much joy that my body literally tingles with love.'"

"Literally tingles, huh?" I said, pronouncing each syllable in literally with an exaggerated staccato.

"And Annie, to hear Shannon talk like this, I realized something that I've probably kind of known for a while now."

"That Bruno is a really cool guy?" I asked.

[159] I've never even been to a circus.

"No." And he paused. "That you're not tingling anymore."

"Me? What? What do you mean? *Literally* tingling?"

"You've lost it, Annie. You *don't* tingle." And he said it strong and fast: a true accusation. I am shocked. David was supposed to be distracted by guns and raids and car bombs. His mind was supposed to be completely engrossed in the horrible war game his career has tossed him into. He wasn't supposed to be noticing my fading interest in our relationship. He wasn't supposed to notice the gradual drain in my enthusiasm and the way I looked for lame excuses to be angry with him.[160] And he isn't supposed to use gross baby words like "tingle" to call me out on my well-guarded apathy. It seems ridiculous now, as I write this, but I always assumed that the war has been numbing his romantic sensors. It seems ridiculous now that I actually believed I could go on faking it until his feet were back planted safely on U.S. land. I have been so so so unfair.

And as he waited for my reply, my defense, my confession, I still wanted to deny it. I still wanted to smother him in sweet lies and tender compliments and faux heartfelt apologies. But then I remembered the laws-of-your-heart permission slip he gave me last summer. (And then I remembered Gus.) Maybe I was mistaken in thinking David didn't actually want me to take the offer seriously—it was a hastily scribbled note that followed a note about doughnuts. We've never even talked about it. But here he is, very well aware of my lack of tingling: my desire to escape. Not that I believe in that sort of physiological reaction to love, but I get it.

---

[160] Unreasonable knitting-group-joining pressure. Proposed lying about third-grader haikus. Lack of Loretta enthusiasm. Big-time chicken skepticism. Lack of Helen death empathy. Flores death secret keeping and other vastly less serious secret keeping about Jayna Austin, First Captain of Sexiness. And probably fifty more ridiculous little things I can't remember now. What a troublemaker I've been. Sheesh.

"David," I said. "I'm sorry."

Silence. Silence. Silence.

"You want to break up with me, don't you?" *Don't you? Don't you? Don't you?*

"I think so." Annie Harper, BIG FAT WUSS.

"You *think* so?" He doesn't say it in a mean way. He says it like he's wet and cold and his words are partially muffled by rain. And then I say *I'm sorry* about fifty times in a row. And then he says *I knew it* about fifty times in a row. We never get to the long, articulate discussion about the effects of the W.A.R. on our romantic connection—on how it sneakily revealed that said connection wasn't as substantial as we originally believed. I never told him that I had fallen in love with someone else. He did not accuse me of it. As far as breakups go, it wasn't heated or bittersweet or an eloquent breed of sad. It was just plain old, mundane, stuttering-fool sad. It was the breakup that 3,457,938,724 couples have already had. And after we hung up and I sat at the foot of my bed and cried into my shirtsleeves for several minutes, I realized something horribly revolting (but at this point, unsurprising) about myself.

I wanted the circus breakup instead.

I spent the rest of the evening composing a laundry list of people I needed to tell about my monumental failure. In no particular order, I needed to get in touch with:

> Loretta Schumacher
> Joyce and Greg Harper (soon-to-be-shamed
>   parents of Annie Harper)
> Annie Harper I (via ouija board)
> Helen Harper (via chicken ouija board)
> Michelle Carter
> Charese Atkins

The Stitch 'n' Bitch Knitting Wives Who
Are Not Mean or Losers
Gus????!!?!?!

¿Gus?

29

*T*oday I'm calling my pathetic use of electronic space *Confession-Booth Graffiti Artist,* and I've been hibernating in my house for almost a week. I bought a portable AC unit, and I've been sitting in front of it basking in the way I can waste resources and waste time and waste my life away. David has not attempted to contact me. I have made only two ventures into the outside world of Happy Meals and Happy Hours and Happy Reminders of nonevil humans. The first time I went to my parents' house unannounced. They were hanging a painting of a country cottage inside the downstairs bathroom, and my mom was saying "Now more to the left, Greg" when I surprised them by peeking my head through the door. They smiled instantly because they love unexpected visits. But it only took a quick second for them both to notice that I was distraught. Before there was a breath of space for them to ask, I spat it out.

"David and I broke up." My dad, who was straddling the toilet and holding the painting against the wall, quickly maneuvered out of his stance and set the painting down inside the tub. My mother did not chastise him about the moisture in the tub potentially damaging the frame. Instead she said something like *Oh, Annie* and hugged me. And this time, I really *really* wanted it. This was the hug she was trying to give me back when David left. At the time, it meant nothing. It was a hug of ceremony and hope. And hope, in my opinion, isn't very well represented by an embrace. Hope is a fist thrust into the air. A stack of preaddressed, stamped envelopes. A knitting circle or an upbeat blog. I guess flag-waving was the thing to do after all. The day David left and my mom had me over for quiche, the hugging wasn't quite right. Nothing bad had happened, no one had suffered, no one had died, L.O.V.E. was still robust and still intact. But now, with loss behind us, and failure stuck to the heels of my shoes—a glaring white and obvious toilet paper train—the hug was *so* in order. This hug (her strong arms around my shoulders and my father's heavy hand resting in the middle of my tired, evil back), this hug was fucking loaded.

We settled into the living room, and I told them honestly and frankly about the demise of the David Peterson/Annie Harper union. And somehow, they didn't hate me for it. They said things like *You did the right thing* and *No use in keeping up a charade* and *War does strange things to people.* I was scared my mother would accuse me of making a mistake, that she would ask me how sure I was and if I'd thought it out for long. But no, they totally got it. I considered throwing in the whole secret-love-for-Gus thing, but I abstained. For some reason I thought they'd find it foolish and immature. That admitting I was in love with Gus would discredit the valid reasons I had for ending things with David. And my parents really knew Gus as my best friend. Would they find the desire to involve myself romantically with him completely absurd? Would they think I'd lost all sensibility? And plus, it was an embarrassing thing to admit to them. It was like telling them who I wanted to ask me to "couples skate" at the roller rink in seventh grade. It made me feel so young.

The three of us drank coffee, and after a few cups the caffeine was surging and urging me into a boldness I couldn't repress.

"So," I said. "Do you think I've ruined my life?" My mom scoffed and set her cup down on a coaster. My dad verbalized the scoff with an awesome, paternal authority that was just the thing I wanted to hear.

"God no, Annie. You are so young!"

. . . . . .

After two days of solitude and dry armpits, I went to visit Loretta. On the way over I realized that I had finally gone to my parents first. When something real[161] actually happened, I sought them right away and with little hesitation. Thank goodness for this nonstained chamber of my heart.

"So I'm a big failure, Loretta. David and I broke up. He knew I wanted to do it. He said so. And then it was done. It's over. I totally suck at everything."

"My my my, Annie." Loretta shuffled over to my side and joined me on her bed. "You do not totally suck at everything. Maybe you did become a lousy girlfriend to that young man, but you've been a wonderful friend to me." She placed a hand on my thigh. "That's all I care about."

"Phew," I said and smiled. "You've been a wonderful friend too." We exchanged knowing looks. The shared grin of the world's two greatest deceivers. If we'd have been holding martini glasses or champagne flutes or teacups, we'd have clinked them together at this moment. But instead Loretta took my hand and we smiled for several more moments. And though her hand was a very different texture than mine—older and rougher—the temperature of our palms was exactly the same.

Again, I wanted to talk about Gus. I wanted to get all sixth grade and ask Loretta *So, do you think he likes me? I mean like like likes me? Do you think he'll ask me to couples skate with him? Do you think he's ready to move on after Gina? Do you think I'm permanently stuck in the "just friends" category? Did you see how dreamy his new haircut is?* GAG.

[161] Not a chicken dying or a chicken-finger-fakeout death or the revelation of a shared past that didn't matter because Alden (a stranger) is dead. No. SOMETHING THAT WAS ACTUALLY AFFECTING ME.

Please kill me. Loretta and I are close, but not close enough for me to put her through this quite yet. One thing at a time, Miss Harper. One thing. One thing.

So those are the only people I've told. Back to the AC unit. Do you think I can chill my cheeks into a dignified, ice-queen blue?

30 [162]

*M*y mother, Loretta, and Gus have each called several times to express their concern over my homebody-ness. I tell them I'm fine and that I'm just taking some alone time to reflect and read and relax. I haven't spilled the beans about David to Gus because I simply feel weird about it. It's not that I'm afraid I'll launch into some loose-lipped love confessional. I've become quite skilled at keeping that in. My fear is of him judging me. The last thing I want in this universe and every single alternate universe is for Gus to think I am a bad person. For Gus to see what mess I've dragged David through and how capable I am of delivering blows below the belt. Additionally, because I've been secretly in love with Gus for much of this year, I've been withholding discussions about my relationship with David. He probably has no idea that things were going so miserably. Is he going to be angry with me for not confiding in him, my supposed best platonic friend? I am such a hopeless ruiner. Ruining everything. I could ruin already ruined ancient ruins, I'm so ruintastic.

I am flipping through an L.L.Bean catalog[163] when Gus calls me again. I've made far too many excuses not to see him, and he's had enough of it. He says he's coming over, he's bringing food, and we're going to grill it, eat it, and relax. No mention of long, serious discussions about my recent hermit tendencies, so I don't argue. Instead, I hang up. I take a shower, braid my wet hair into a single French braid,

---

[162] Title of this chapter purposefully withheld. ☺

[163] I could probably ruin one of those indestructible, waterproof, Gore-Tex jackets with just a drop of my toxic saliva.

and get out the portable vacuum. I pull the cushions out from the sofa, and there are enough crumbs inside to keep a flock of pigeons happy for an entire morning. As I vacuum, I try to tell myself that it's not Gus coming over that's making me feel better. My back loosens and my eyes seem to open wider. I tell myself it's the crumbs. The way they zoom straight into the vacuum and disappear forever. Good-bye mess! Good-bye millions of specks of emotional gobbledygook! So long! When I turn the vacuum off, I hear the doorbell.

"Hi Annie," he says.

"Hi," I say, and he plows through me to the kitchen.

I pour us each a glass of white wine[164] while Gus forages through my assortment of vinegars and spices. He mixes a marinade in a clear glass bowl. He's chopping up chunks of a sirloin tip steak when he says, "So what's going on, Annie?"

"Stuff," I say. "Things."

"Oh," he says. "Do you want to talk about it? It's not about Our Brother Alden, is it?" He drops a handful of the meat chunks into the marinade, and I watch the fatty edges of them stick to the clear sides of the bowl. He starts rinsing a red bell pepper.

"No. Well. Yeah. Well. Not really," I say. "I don't want to talk about it now at least. I mean, probably. Eventually. Yeah. I will want to. I'm just kind of in this place where I need to figure out what I really want and what I really feel and what I should really expect from the universe." I take a drink of my wine, hoping I don't sound too cryptic or psychotic or boring. Gus turns around from the counter to look at me. I say: "I didn't articulate that very well. Sorry."

"No, I get it," he says. He guts the red pepper and begins to chop it into squares.

---

[164] A Riesling. Month two of the Chesalon club. I already ate the fancy blue cheese. The remnants of it are now preparing to further their aging process in the controlled environment of my vacuum bag.

"What's on the menu?" I ask.

"Shish kebabs."

"Great. I have metal skewers." I stand up and yank open a drawer, pull out the bundle of sharp sticks. Gus turns around and they're at chest level, like I'm about to stab him in the heart with my collection of tiny daggers. I imagine a cartoon image of the human heart, blood squirting playfully from ten new orifices.

"Yikes," he says, and we both pick up our heads and look at each other's eyes and laugh exactly two snorting chuckles. I return to my chair and my wine and Gus continues to chop and clean and prep in silence. I watch the whole time, trying not to stare at his back for too long at once. In case he turns around. The onion takes its turn. A zucchini. Cherry tomatoes. Finally, he pulls a plastic sack of loose white mushrooms from his shopping bag. He holds it in his hands and stares at it for a long time. He dumps the mushrooms in the colander and gives them a gentle rinse with the spray gun. (I think of telling him that it's better for the mushrooms to wipe them clean with a wet cloth.) He takes a dish towel from the oven rack, folds it into fourths, turns, and places it on the kitchen table in front of me. He takes the colander of mushrooms and places it on top of the towel.

"You want me to destem these?" I reach my hand out to snag the biggest mushroom off the top of the pile. He grabs my hand to stop it.

"No. Not yet." Gus sits down across from me and folds his hands on the table. He exhales. Stands up to retrieve his wine glass from the counter. He sits again and takes a huge, loud gulp. I watch his Adam's apple dip down his neck and bob back up. I bite my lip.

Silence. Silence. Silence.

"Annie," he finally says. "This might not be the best time for this, but there's something I need to explain." I don't say anything. I start flexing my butt muscles on my chair and I nod. Gus continues. "Well. Um. Gosh. I don't. Maybe. Never mind. Annie?"

"Uh-huh," I say, and I snake my feet around the legs of my chair.

"Okay. I remember this one time when you and I cooked pizza in my dad's kitchen. It was the summer right after we graduated college. Right before I left for the Peace Corps. You were cleaning mushrooms, I was rambling on about something stupid like I do, and you told me to shut up. You said you wanted to hear the sound of the mushroom stem being pulled from the cap. That it was such a great sound."

"I do love that sound." My hands are resting in my lap like an obedient child at a dinnertime lecture.

"But you said it wasn't nearly as wonderful as the sound of a mushroom being harvested. Then you mentioned this episode of *Mister Rogers* you once saw where he goes to a mushroom farm and picks them himself. You said that the gentle plucking/popping noise of the mushroom being pulled from the soil was probably your favorite sound of all time."

"It was amazing. I'll always remember it. They never show that episode." I'm whispery and serious.

Gus takes a big breath.

"And ever since, every single time I eat a mushroom or clean a mushroom or see one growing in a lawn, I think of you, Annie. And I think of that sound. And how much you love it." Gus wiggles his chair closer to the table, pulls along the collar of his T-shirt, and looks me straight in the eyes. "And how much I fucking love you." He lifts his arms to his head and throws them down. "Crap. I shouldn't have said fucking. I meant, *I love you.*"

And before I can even think or process or respond (or smile!), he's standing up and moving toward his shopping bag on the counter. In a very serious voice he asks, "Do you have a VCR?" I nod, still silent. He pulls a VHS cassette from the bag and extends his other hand to me. I take it and stand up. He leads me soundlessly to the living room and I sit on the coffee table. Gus crouches and slides the tape into the machine. He fusses with the buttons. "Nearly every weekday since I got back from Dominica, I've turned on PBS at eight A.M. to check the show. And you're right; they almost never show the episode. But last week they did show it. And I got it. And it's yours to watch and hear and listen to whenever you want forever." He turns to me and beams with pride and truth and affection. He fast-forwards to the scene and comes to sit beside me on the coffee table.

Mister Rogers is wearing a hard hat with a headlamp.

"Oh my God," I say. My voice is low, awed. "I totally forgot that the mushroom farm is underground." Gus takes my right hand between both of his.

"Yes! It's an old mining cave! There are tons of farms like this in rural Pennsylvania!" He is so excited. I am so excited. Mister Rogers is so excited. He's talking to the main farmer about the ideal temperature conditions for mushroom growing. I slide my other arm behind Gus's back, and Mister Rogers is telling the viewer that some kinds of mushrooms are poisonous and one should never eat mushrooms found in the wild. And then it happens. We both stop breathing and watch the kind, sweet man push up the sleeves of his red cardigan and gently tug the mushrooms one by one from a waist-high trough of dirt. The sound is clear and lovely and just how I remember it. I realize that perhaps the acoustics of the cave contribute to the exquisite tones of Mister Rogers's mushroom harvest. He says that it doesn't feel like picking any other vegetable. He says it's such an "interesting sensation." And he articulates each syllable in "interesting" in a way that has the power to curb the speech impediments of every child on earth. It is so so so beautiful. I love love love it. I love Gus. I'm taking quick, shallow breaths when the program switches back to Mr. Rogers's home. I feel a tear swell in the corner of my left eye and I turn to face him. "Thank you so much." I lift my hands to his cheeks and pull my face to him and we kiss. And it's a million times better than the ridiculous cotton candy kiss I'd imagined. There are no sad elephants or evil lies in this kiss. It is only pure and genuine and ours. Our arms bump and reposition; the legs of the coffee table wobble slightly. Minutes later I am still kissing Gus, but more comfortably so on the sofa. He is stopping every few moments to open his eyes and smile at me. Mister Rogers is singing now. *Now I'll be back / when the day is new.* I don't have to look to know that he's already changed his shoes and is buttoning the three buttons of his single-breasted sports jacket. *And I'll have more ideas for you / and you'll have things you'll want to talk about.* And it's like Gus and I are both saying it and promising it to each other. I'll be here. Back tomorrow and the next day and the next day. I'll bring questions and ideas and discoveries.

I will too.

31

*T*oday I'm calling my book *Arachne vs. Penelope: Live on Pay-Per-View!*
It's early September now. A good month and change since Gus found
the mushroom episode and since I owned up to what I really wanted.
I just spent about an hour researching on the Internet. I was trying to
figure out what this stupid weaving Greek lady was actually doing. It
really seemed important to know the real truth about her. So I plugged
terms like "greek woman weaving husband mythology" into Google,
and it was actually quite easy to find her. But before I did, I was distracted by the story of Arachne from Ovid's *Metamorphosis*.

Arachne was this superstar weaver who claimed to be better than
Athena, the patroness of weaving. Athena heard of this, disguised herself as an old lady, and coaxed Arachne into admitting she wanted to
take on the goddess in a full-out weaving smackdown. So of course this
was arranged. Athena made something marvelous. And Arachne also
made something marvelous, but it was an amazingly detailed depiction of all these infidelities the gods had committed against mortals.
Athena was enraged at the blatant disrespect and destroyed Arachne's
tapestry and her precious loom in a mega display of power. Arachne
then realized how horrible it was of her to express such ego and create
such an offensive piece of art. She became so overwhelmed with guilt
that she eventually hung herself. But then Athena took pity on her and
loosened the noose by turning it into a spiderweb and transfiguring
Arachne into a spider. This is more of a rivalry story and not the one of
romantic loyalty that I was looking for. But as soon as I'm done typing
this, I'm totally e-mailing Max Schaffer about it. That is, of course, if
he doesn't already know.

But now for Penelope. I'm kind of embarrassed that I didn't figure it out or remember on my own. Yeah, I've never actually read the *Odyssey*, but I feel like it should be implanted in my literary subconscious from hanging out with English majors in college and from playing a fair amount of Trivial Pursuit with my family. Penelope is the wife of Odysseus. He goes off to the Trojan War and doesn't come back for twenty (20!!!!) years. While he's gone Penelope devises a bunch of clever plots to ward off eager suitors who suppose that Odysseus is never coming back. Even a few of the gods meddle and try to lure Penelope into shacking up with someone else. In one of her more ingenious methods of man deterrence, she announces that she will be weaving a burial shroud for her father-in-law, and as soon as she finishes it, she will choose a suitor. She weaves every day, but at night she sneakily unweaves much of the day's work. So she never has to finish. And it works! She remains faithful, and sure enough, eventually, old O. comes hobbling back from the war. She's leery that it's actually him, and they have some adorable battle of wits before she believes him and they lovingly reunite.

After I discovered Penelope's story, everything started to make much more sense. David left for a war and I started weaving. Except I wasn't weaving, I was writing this motherfucking, self-indulgent, wannabe-stunning memoir confessional. But unlike Penelope, I just kept going and going and going. Never looking back to erase and keep my focus on how great things were before David left. I just couldn't stand still. And without him here, it became obvious that the textile holding us together was one crafted during our relative youth. Not exactly shoddy, but perhaps ill-fitting and definitely not all-weather. So I kept weaving my ugly word web and thinking and changing in his absence. And I've probably failed in Penelope's eyes because I let myself be wooed by someone else. I was unfaithful and impatient and definitely not her. But I like to think I discovered more about myself and launched into a relationship that is laced with more shared curiosities, fervor, and thoughtful inquiry. Blah blah blah. This is a different war, Penelope. And what was my Trojan horse full of? Third graders? Beanie Babies? Ice cubes? Shiny caps of white mushrooms?

So school starts tomorrow. I've picked out my outfit for the first day and laid it carefully across the chair in my bedroom. I have a mere twenty-six kids this year: an even thirteen/thirteen boy/girl split. David is returning in one week.

Later tonight, hours after sunset and once the temperature has dropped a good fifteen degrees, Gus and I will wash his "Fun in the Sun" paintings off the windows of the Dairy DeLite. When we're done, we will stand quietly—holding hands and drippy squeegees—staring through the clean-ass glass into the dark Tacoma night. I want to say that before we start on the next seasonal cartoonscape, we will first paint a glorious masterpiece. A bold, confident song will play on the restaurant's loudspeakers, and we will dance and flick our brushes and run each other's fingers across the windows with smooth, cool paint. But there are broken shopping carts rolling and feral cats pooping in the parking lot outside. Our universe is not quite fanciful enough for that magnificent love dance. Instead, when we are done staring, and the last drops of moisture on the glass have evaporated, we will start to paint the pumpkins again. Yes, it's a little early for Halloween decor, but the owner of the Dairy DeLite said that it was Gus's best mural last year and that he'd like to have it up for longer this time.

Gus will do most of the work: painting outlines and giving me detailed instructions on how to fill them in. Big strokes here. Small, dotted strokes here. Like this. Great. Perfect. You're perfect. And though it will be just a regular night of regular painting, I will know that it is the end or the beginning of something. A tiny tick on the timeline of Annie Harpers. And therefore, in my sappiness, I will be unable to resist the temptation to foist significance onto the scene.

See those two ghosts: That's Flores and that's Brother Alden. There's Loretta, an ancient witch in a wooden chair. This small wizard with the raised wand is Max Schaffer. Gus, here you are—a jack-o-lantern with a gaping smile and missing teeth. And David, poor David, he's this scarecrow. See the post jammed up his back and through his heart? He'll get down soon; I'm fairly certain of it. And here I am—a witch, naturally. Can we make my grin a little less devious? Can we make my eyes a little more open?

Epilogueish Thing

December 18, 2004

Dear Kind Reader,

When I started writing, I planned to rewrite. To prettily arrange all my anecdotes and ideas and feelings. To cut and add and present my life as a touching, engaging narrative rather than a mushed-together, steaming pile of moldy Play-Doh. I was going to spend months with my red pen and my red, red heart. Bah! I am so over that. But, should I wish to show this to anyone (publishers, shrinks, George W. Bush, Loretta Schumacher), there are certain things that might be helpful to know. And I think it will be helpful to me (emotionally/spiritually/ridiculously/ psychotically) to get a few more things out on the page.

So I present . . . THE APPENDICES!! (Annie Harper the First's journal had appendices, so I can too.)

   I. Miss Harper's 2003–2004 Third Grade Class List
  II. Physical Descriptions of Humans in This Story and Other Facts of Potential Interest
 III. Known (and Interesting!) Anomalies of Water (Gus wrote this one. ☺)
 IV. Stupid Things I Considered Calling My Memoirs
  V. Cool Facts About Chickens

Please do note that these were all composed in relative haste. Gus and I are leaving tomorrow to spend the holidays back in Dominica. The town where he used to live suffered some rather substantial damage from Hurricane Ivan. We're going to help clean up some of the mess and help one of Gus's farmer friends put some crops in the ground. Wahoo agriculture! (Edward Harrington, look at me now!) After the miserable election results last month, we really just wanted to do something helpful.

So we are.

With all my love!

Annie Harper

Antolini, Marco: A yay-hoo indeed, but actually quite bright and never mean-spirited.

Atkins, Lacey: Second favorite.

Bouvert, Alexandra: Mega shy. Perfect attendance! (She got a special award at the end of the year for this.)

Carlton, Jasmine: Really into drawing, not as much into everything else. Her ADD was diagnosed in February after I recommended her to the school counselor. And though I'm still a little squirmish about medicating children, Jasmine's academic improvement post-February was astounding.

Carter, Diondre: Will charm lots of girls in high school.

Davidson, Lenny: Mediocre student. Laughed at my jokes more than others. I was sad to see after winter break that his parents had clipped off his beautiful rattail.

Espinoza, Thomas: The better behaved of the Thomases. Started the year chubby but ended it trim. I attribute the weight loss to a growth spurt and his huge interest in Dance Dance Revolution.

Ghate, Somya: Moved here from India when she was five. Well adapted and bright. Doesn't like math so much.

Gutierrez, Joey: Wiggles his legs nonstop under his desk. Drives me nuts! But I can take it because while he's wiggling he's also a very attentive listener.

Johnstone, Blake: Has immaculate penmanship. Sharpens his pencil many times daily.

Jones, Maria: Jessica Marquez's BFF.

Lin, Gracie: Very aware of endangered species. Tried to start a club to raise money for Siberian tigers.

Marquez, Jessica: Loves weddings.

Martinez-Carbajo, Alex: Big baseball fan. Once ate twenty-four chicken nuggets from the cafeteria!

Matthews, Damian: Responsible for starting the Yu-Gi-Oh nightmare of late September. Made up for it by being very enthusiastic about Math Olympics.

McDonnell, Lizzie: Spunky and confident. Major kudos for befriending Lacey Atkins when she was so new.

Morris, Ben: Whines about nearly everything. Very loud.

Peterson, Thomas: Not related to Lieutenant David Peterson. Though they do both have buzzed hair.

Rivington, Jordan: Female. Really good at singsongy patty-cake games, and more importantly, never self-conscious about still playing them as a third grader.

Robinson, Caitlin: Despite Denise being a bit of a witch, Caitlin is mostly a very sweet kid. She's very generous with the Avon sample–sized lotions and lip balms from her mother's business.

Ryles, Janelle: Probably the only person at Franklin Elementary who actually owns a horse. Admirably, she never boasted about it.

Schaffer, Max: Favorite!

Small, Danielle: I had to have a talk with Danielle back in March because she kept braiding friendship bracelets under her desk during class. After I caught her doing it for the third time and made her stay in for lunch recess, later that afternoon when she left I found a green and pink bracelet on my desk.

Taylor, David: The kid who wears sweatpants every day except for special occasions.

VanOudenardren, Spencer: Poor Spencer. His parents are über–health nuts and send him to school with gluten-free bread and eggplant polenta. But he does have the shiniest, prettiest hair and beautiful, glowing skin.

Wagner, Garrett: Despite being a fainter, Garrett has mad four-square skills. Never talks out of turn.

Wells, Katie: Has the kind of type A personality that will make her either head cheerleader or head of the forensics team in high school. But at age nine, it's impossible to tell which way she'll fall.

Williams, Hannah: Frequently looking at her reflection in the window. The only person who jumped on Gracie Lin's save-the-tigers bandwagon.

Wright, Stephen: An excellent artist. Has six older siblings, but never looks awkward or sloppy in his hand-me-downs.

Appendix II
Physical Descriptions of Humans in This Story
and Other Facts of Potential Interest

In looking over several scenes, I realize that the physical characteristics of some people were very poorly described. I know them. I know what they look like. But I wasn't all too conscientious about actually telling and showing what they look like in my writing. People are into that.

Atkins, Charese: Tall. Very nice legs. A general aura of glamour evident by the frequent usage of designer handbags.
Atkins, Lacey: Round-faced, but in the way that will disappear with puberty and reveal stunning cheekbones just like her mother's.
Barkley, Gene (Barfley): Obviously at odds with his pattern baldness. Muscular legs are often hidden. Sagging gut is not. Prone to wearing beige sweaters with flecks of different-colored wool in the weave.
Carter, Michelle: Blonder in the summer. Looks hott hott hott in scrubs.
Chang, Stephen: Half Chinese. Half Irish. Excellent posture. Very clean teeth.
Harper, Annie: Wears glasses two to three days a week. Fit and smallish. Long, dark hair that spends very little time on her shoulders. Extremely badass.
Harper, Rebecca: Soft, dexterous hands. A fine quilter, hugger, and cook.
Harper, Greg: Looks healthier than his cholesterol level suggests.
Harrington, Edward: The sweet kind of man you'd see eating strips

of bacon in a TV commercial for a local pancake restaurant. A face that says "safety."

Mezzo, Hillary: Never without a French manicure.

Montoya, Alden: Dark eyes and long limbs. Brave, honorable, perfect.

Peterson, David: That classically attractive man you may have seen on an army recruiting ad. Could be a bouncer at a tame nightclub or a model for athletic gear.

Rayburn, Jean: Her eyes are a very becoming pale blue. More of a kindred spirit than her sour expression indicates.

Robinson, Caitlin: Always well groomed. No stains on any of her clothes. Owns many beautiful hair clips.

Robinson, Denise: Constantly repositioning her legs to hide her varicose veins. Ha. Ha. Ha!

Schaffer, Max: Wears trendy plastic-rimmed glasses. Does not tuck in his shirts. Never lets his mouth gape open.

Schumacher, Loretta: Practically perfect in every way.

Small, Carrie: Really huge breasts! Lucky she teaches first and not eighth grade.

Warren, Gus: Dreamy. Smiles and sweats a lot.

Q: **Did Stephen already know that Alden was Gus's brother when you came to Boston?**

A: Yes! That bully secret keeper!

Q: **How do you get kicked out of the army for having US$500,000?**

A: Still not entirely sure. Perhaps if you're too rich, the army doesn't think you'll be able to take orders well. But Elvis still did it. Right?

Q: **Has Julia/Juliette tried to contact Gus yet?**

A: No. Never.

Q: **Did Gus know that you and David had broken up when he came over with his mushrooms and his open heart?**

A: Yes. I have since learned that my dear mother told him. That woman is far more perceptive than she lets on.

Q: How is Loretta's health?

A: She caught a nasty flu in October, went to the hospital for three wretched days, but pulled through triumphantly.

Appendix III
*Known (and Interesting!) Anomalies of Water**

1. Water has an unusually high viscosity. Viscosity means how easy it is for molecules to wiggle around relative to each other. It depends on the strength of the bonds holding the molecule together. This is called cohesiveness. Water is so cohesive because of its serious 3-D structure of hydrogen bonding. Think of a 3-D puzzle versus a 2-D one. The first is going to be much more complicated to deconstruct. This also accounts for water's nasty surface tension. Think of how much it hurts to belly flop off a high dive.

2. Water shrinks as it melts, but as temperatures continue to decrease, it then expands as it freezes. Most substances behave in the opposite manner, shrinking as they freeze, because the individual molecules are stuck in fixed positions while the substance is solid, and when they're liquid they require more space to move around. I like to remember this one by thinking of how when humans are really cold they bundle up. Expanding in size as we freeze. Those New England winters at Yale were brutal.

3. Water has an outrageously high heat of vaporization. The highest of any liquid. Even at 100 degrees Celsius, there are still tons of hydrogen bonds in water that need to break for it to reach the gas phase. Watched or not, pots take wicked long to boil.

4. Pressure reduces the melting point of ice. Adding pressure to a liquid usually promotes freezing—and thus a higher melting point—but water works the opposite way.

* This appendix was brought to you by Gus Warren, the letter H, the number 2, and the letter O.

5. Water has the highest thermal conductivity of any liquid. That means energy can run through it with considerable ease. So in a lightning storm it's probably better to stand in a swimming pool of rubbing alcohol than a swimming pool full of water. If you have that option.

6. The Mpemba effect! (Annie said I didn't have to explain this one because she already has me doing so somewhere in this book she won't yet let me read.)

Appendix IV
Stupid Things I Considered Calling My Memoirs

1. *Wartime Alone Time: When Abstinence Fights for Freedom*
2. *Spoon the Air*
3. *Grace in His Absence*
4. *Dear John*
5. *Don't You Call Me a Hero*
6. *Nine Times Forever Equals Way Too Long*
7. *Time Out for Karma*
8. *Without an Artifact*
9. *Almost Too Ripe for Squeezing*
10. *So Very Alone*
11. *Pins and Fucking Needles*
12. *While Fleeing the Coop of Terror*
13. *Inside the Yolk of the Sun*
14. *Reactivating the Fumes*
15. *101 Ways to Go Nuts While Your Lover Is at War*
16. *Caution: This Book Has a Surprise Middle Part*
17. *Almost Perfectly Innocent*
18. *Shout Across the Ocean*
19. *Untitled Suicide Note*
20. *Dreams from the Homeland*
21. *Annie Harper's Journal*
22. *On the Tailbone of the Luck Monster*
23. *What I Did on My Boyfriend Vacation*
24. *Between a War and a Window*
25. *That's What Humans Do*
26. *Red, White, and Brutally Honest*

27. *The Charisma of Coincidence*
28. *Miss Harper Can Do It*
29. *Confession-Booth Graffiti Artist*
30. *(no title given for suspense purposes)*
31. *Arachne vs. Penelope: Live on Pay-Per-View!*

Appendix V
Cool Facts About Chickens

1. Chickens were domesticated over eight thousand years ago!
2. An egg-laying chicken will lay about one egg per day for five to six days and then take a few days off to rest.
3. You have to take the eggs away as they're laid or else the chicken will stop and start brooding after she's collected six or seven. This little group is called a clutch. I wonder if there's a relation to the style of handbag of the same name.
4. A chicken cackles to check where all the other chickens are. And they cackle back to say, "I'm here!" That's why Helen was rather quiet with her vocals. She figured out pretty fast that she was the only hen around.
5. The word for "fear of chickens" is "alektorophobia." Can you even imagine? What kind of ninnies are scared of chickens?
6. Since chickens don't have teeth, they mash up their food with grit, which they keep in their gizzard. They put food down there to chew it up before they send it along to their stomachs. I had to buy grit and sprinkle it around Helen's coop because there wasn't the right kind of gravel in my yard for her to find it naturally.
7. 2005 will be the Year of the Cock!
8. Chickens have just one orifice for pooping, peeing, and laying eggs. Though this sounds mega gross, it's really quite efficient. The poop and pee (which is not like our pee, but globby and mucky) come out one tube and the eggs come out another. And both tubes meet at the same opening. However, there is this nifty flap of skin that moves over and sticks out when the egg comes out so that the egg never touches any part of the chicken's body where the poop

was. This is also the same hole they use for S.E.X. Except I kind of deprived poor Helen of that. We were chaste together!

9. A chicken's heart beats 280–315 times a minute. I felt like at times over this past year mine has too.

10. It takes over four pounds of chicken food to make one dozen eggs. So ultimately, my egg-eating phase was not too economical.

11. A hen usually lives for about five to seven years, but under the right conditions they can live up to twenty. Rest in peace, sweet Helen Harrington-Harper.

Acknowledgments

Many sincere and serious thanks to:

First there was Seth, who afforded me a generous glimpse into his life with the U.S. Army. Thank you for tolerating all my questions back when they were rooted in plain old curiosity and affection.

Sally Wofford-Girand, my incredible agent, for helping a no-cred, no-experience nobody shine up her manuscript into something to be proud of. You understood Annie Harper from the get-go and knew where to send her. And of course, Melissa Sarver, for all your work along the way and for plucking me out of the slush.

Kendra Harpster, my editor, who had so many brilliant ideas for the manuscript and who has really managed to push me into sounding smarter and more interesting than I actually am. Thanks to you and everyone at Viking who has worked so hard at getting this book out and making it look way snazzier than Annie Harper could have ever imagined.

Brian Hurley, Carolyn Morrisroe, and Robert Repino for being the smartest, most helpful friends. I swear I'd never get anything done without you three as heroes and advisers.

David Seal for wisely egging me on back in the day.

Maja Nikolic and Elena Santogade, simply the best role models, cheerleaders, counselors, and secret keepers a girl could have.

My sister, Emily Berentson, for having the biggest heart and the dirtiest fingernails and with them inspiring me to work with children.

My brother, Mike Berentson and his wife, Renata. I'm sorry for stealing a bit of your life and sloppily braiding it into this book. You've been so brave in your relationship and so helpful with this project. Mike, I'm tremendously proud of the way you excelled in your military career and the choices you made to fit love into your life.

And then there are a handful of women who've endured so much of my whining, musing, unreturned phone calls, and general obnoxious claptrap over the course of my entire life. Abbey Raish, Stephanie Linnell, Carly Meznarich, Kelsey Loftness, Tina Collom, Ashley Wells, and Abigail Quesinberry, I owe you big time forever.

Sam Trott, I'm sorry I told you the complete contents of this book in a graceless, out-of-order, overcaffeinated fashion before I ever let you read any of it. Please know that I only got the actual writing done because circumstances had you away from me for far longer than I would have liked.

And finally, Mom and Dad, thank you for always permitting my silliness and for your unconditional pride and encouragement.